"MAYBE YOU ARE AFRAID, SEÑORA...AFRAID OF BEING A WOMAN."

Rosemary's breath caught, and Lario continued softly, "I would do nothing that you did not want...for then I would find no pleasure."

Pleasure. The word taunted her. Did such a word exist in the realm of a woman's sexuality? Rosemary shuddered at her forbidden thoughts. I must try to sleep, she told herself.

But the steady, strong beat of Lario's heart against her cheek, the enveloping warmth, the masculine smell of him assaulted her senses. She felt lightheaded, yet she knew she could not ignore the sensations of pleasure that prickled her skin. As the seconds raced by, she could not suppress the yearning, burning her like a branding iron. She was painfully aware of Lario as a man in every nerve of her body.

Lario's fingers came up to cup her chin. "You are curious?" In the dimness, lights danced mockingly in his ____ ____ d Rosemary nodd___

D0956560

Fawcett Popular Library Books
by Parris Afton Bonds:

☐ THE FLASH OF THE FIREFLY   04497 $2.25

☐ LOVE TIDE   04521 $1.95

☐ SAVAGE ENCHANTMENT   04332 $2.25

☐ SWEET GOLDEN SUN   04226 $1.95

Buy them at your local bookstore or use this handy coupon for ordering.

COLUMBIA BOOK SERVICE (a CBS Publications Co.)
32275 Mally Road, P.O. Box FB, Madison Heights, MI 48071

Please send me the books I have checked above. Orders for less than 5 books must
include 75¢ for the first book and 25¢ for each additional book to cover postage
and handling. Orders for 5 books or more postage is FREE. Send check or money
order only.

Cost $_____	Name _____
Sales tax*_____	Address _____
Postage_____	City _____
Total $_____	State_____ Zip _____

*The government requires us to collect sales tax in all states except AK, DE,
MT, NH and OR.

This offer expires 1 March 82   8999

DUST DEVIL

by

Parris Afton Bonds

FAWCETT POPULAR LIBRARY • NEW YORK

DUST DEVIL

Published by Fawcett Popular Library, a unit of CBS Publications, the Consumer Publishing Division of CBS Inc.

Copyright © 1981 by Parris Afton Bonds

All Rights Reserved

ISBN: 0-445-04667-8

Printed in the United States of America

First Fawcett Popular Library printing: August 1981

10 9 8 7 6 5 4 3 2 1

**FOR WILMA AND RITA
WHO MADE THIS POSSIBLE**

AND

**KATE AND KAREN
EDITORS WHO HAD FAITH**

Special thanks to Senator and Mrs. Bill Lee who opened their home to me; to Muriel Johnson who shared the story of her hunted years in the Philippines with me; to Sam Fritcher; Deborah Adyt, David Alcoze and to my brother Jack Wilkes, whose technical advice aided me greatly;

and to the real Sin-they

It was long ago—perhaps 25,000 years ago. The hide-clad young man fingered the edge of his stone-tipped throwing spear as he looked out over the valley from his vantage point in the Sandia Mountains. To the north, he could see a plateau cut by streams into mesas. He wondered if game might be plentiful in those canyons. Perhaps he would go and see...

On one of the quiet mesas of the Pajarito Plateau, above the silent canyons with their remains of ancient cities, an atomic scientist looks out from his laboratory in Los Alamos and sees in the distance the Sandia Mountains. For a moment, he wonders about that daring man who first settled in New Mexico...

Tourism and Travel Division
New Mexico Commerce and Industry

From the desert I come to thee,
   On a stallion shod with fire;
And the winds are left behind
   In the speed of my desire.
Under thy window I stand,
   And the midnight hears my cry:
I love thee, I love but thee,
   With a love that shall not die
      Till the sun grows cold,
      And the stars are old,
      And the leaves of the Judgment
      Book unfold.

Bayard Taylor
"Bedouin Song"

Part One

1

The black eyes betrayed none of the cynicism the man felt as his keen gaze swept over the flood of dignitaries and the state's most powerful businessmen who gathered along with the press and the more curious citizens of Santa Fe to honor him as he took the oath of office.

He saw in some of the faces both the envy of his position...and the distaste for what he was. And he permitted a hard smile to briefly curl his long lips.

His glance fell on the brittle old woman who, confined in the wheelchair, occupied the center front row of those assembled to hear his Inaugural Address. Her back was ramrod straight; her turquoise eyes—clear as the New Mexico skies—were alert in the seamed face. Her lips parted slightly, as if acknowledging the triumph in his smile.

The man's dark head canted almost imperceptibly, then his gaze brushed beyond her, searching the sea of faces for that one particular face. But nowhere did he see her laughing eyes. Always those laughing eyes...

"Ladies and gentlemen...fellow New Mexicans," he began. His voice came clearly, deep and powerful, with the same assurance that bespoke his every movement. Each person there felt the electric quality that flowed under the man's cold reserve, and sensed, too, that fierceness and passion for danger the man had inherited from his ancestors.

"I gratefully accept the trust and responsibility the people of our state have given me on this first day of 1946. It is a time for more than one first, for more than one celebration. Within the past year the world has witnessed the cataclysmic explosion of the first atomic bomb—here in the Jornado del Muerto of New Mexico.

"Within the past year the most influential woman in our state celebrated her centennial birthday." He paused and introduced the venerable woman seated in the wheelchair, and she nodded her head curtly in response to the thunderous applause.

There existed another celebration, another first that the new governor could mention, but in that moment of victory he would not flaunt it before those present.

Only the old woman in the first row knew to what extent

the man's victory reached. And as he spoke to the assembly of the future that awaited the Enchanted Land of New Mexico, the old woman's mind looked not to the future but wandered in the past...reviewing in the record of her memory what she had done over eighty-six years to bring about this day of victory...and what she had done in loving.

2

May 10, 1857
Meerut, India

A small child's shrill cry sliced through the night. It was a cry that chilled through to the bone in spite of the evening's sultriness.

At the first cry the twelve-year-old girl sprang up from the hiding place in the carriage house, but one hand of the children's amah clamped over her mouth, pulling her back into the shadows. And so the girl had to watch in agonizing horror as the Indian troops spilled out of the bungalow into the torch-lit courtyard...and as her parents were hauled in front of one vine-covered wall and executed, their bodies crumpling before the bright spurt of gunfire like puppets whose strings have been cut.

And she had to watch as her two-year-old brother's doll-like body was tossed from the sharp point of one Indian soldier's lance to another, though the child was killed immediately after the first thrust and spared further pain.

Not so for the young girl. She carried the pain of the Sepoy Rebellion inside her like a parasitic worm. It lived and writhed and ate. It would take a journey that would span half the globe and the range of her emotions to bring about her catharsis.

3

June 3, 1860
Territory of New Mexico

> *It is in this magnificent land, my dear Rosemary, along the banks of the Pecos, whose fresh water flows as sweetly as Erin's Shannon, that you shall rule my domain with myself. Imagine here among the people of*

*color, the Indians and Spanish, our sons shall establish
a glorious dynasty greater than the Stuarts or Tudors
ever dreamed!*

Rosemary Gallagher had cause to recall Stephen's letter
more than once during her journey to Santa Fe. From the
Overland Stage's window her critical eye swept first over the
endless stretch of shoulder-high grass that rolled across the
Llano Estacado like waves on the ocean, then later over the
barren expanse of alkaline desert...not a house nor a single
tree, not even a small hill to interrupt the level horizon; not
a sound to break the overpowering silence.

She had grown up on a continent bursting at the seams
with people. Now she began to entertain private doubts about
whether she would be able to love this raw, untamed land
and its lonely wilderness. During the crossing on the Cunard
from Ireland to Galveston, a sister of the St. Cecilia Order
had told Rosemary of her experience in the missions of the
Southwest—and how the oppression could drive a woman,
isolated by her race and sex, to the verge of madness.

Had not Stephen hinted she would be one of the few white
women in the Territory? In his letters he had mentioned the
washerwoman at Fort Marcy and Hilda Goldman, his partner's wife in his Santa Fe Trading Post. And there was the
Governor's wife and daughter. But there lived not one white
woman on the five million three hundred acres which com-
prised the DeVega Land Grant, known as Cambria since
Stephen Rhodes acquired it—in the year of Rosemary's birth,
1845.

For the tenth time Rosemary reached for the lace handkerchief in her sleeve cuff and wiped at the dust that caked
her face and the back of her neck. Canvas covers were dropped
over the stage's window now to keep out the dust, but the
heat and the smell of the three unwashed passengers were
even worse. Still, life in India had inured her to some hard-
ships, which obviously was not the case with one of the passengers, a stocky, well-to-do Chihuahuan merchant.

At every chance he complained of the miserable food of
hard biscuits and dried beef, which were eaten quickly at
intermittent way stations, and the lice in the bed ticking at
night.

Rosemary bore these discomforts with determined patience. But what seemed almost unbearable to her was the
unending proximity with the third passenger, the Indian,
Lario...the contact of their shoulders when the stage hit a
rock or his hand at her elbow when she descended from the

10

high step of the Concord coach. When their gazes chanced to cross, it was as if he were able to look past her eyes into her mind, to read there both her fear and her contempt for him.

Stephen had written that once she reached San Antonio, the last outpost before the West began, he would send his trusted foreman to escort her to Santa Fe. But Rosemary had never expected an Indian.

It had been three years since she had even let herself think about Indians. But the three years had not dimmed the memory of the Sepoy Rebellion. Only in the last five months, since Rosemary had accepted Stephen Rhodes's letter proposing marriage, had she permitted herself to speculate on life with him in the Indian country of the New Mexico Territory.

Perhaps she had been foolhardy and impetuous. But after living in the household of her aunt and uncle for two years, she knew that despite their love she could not have remained another month in their home any more than she could have accepted the suitors who besieged her uncle for her hand before she could even celebrate her fifteenth birthday. But she was a young woman grown, a woman who wanted her own home now.

Tall and gangling, with large eyes that made her thin, angular face seem vulnerable, Rosemary had been a wall-flower in comparison with other young ladies her age—until it became known that an ample dowry would likely be provided by her uncle. She was not deceived by the sudden interest shown by the available men of Waterford, Ireland, only derisive.

No, not for her the oily smooth words of love from some suitor who within the first year of marriage would court his mistresses with the same impassioned speech. A man with great imagination and the audacity to reach for his goals attracted Rosemary much more.

It had been Stephen's letters to her uncle, his business partner in a sheep venture, that had first caught her own imagination. The power behind the words, even the bold scrawl of the handwriting, indicated here was an enterprising man—not a dandyish fop of Queen Victoria's parlors—who had envisioned an empire and had claimed it while the land was still a part of Mexico.

And so she had begun the correspondence with Stephen that had ended with his marriage proposal; for there in the New Mexico Territory, where women were scarce, Stephen wanted a fit mate, an Anglo woman. "A companion I can share everything with," he had written.

Though not a word of love had been written in all of his

correspondence, it mattered not to Rosemary. For in exchange he offered her a home. For the first time in all her life of moving about with her father's East India Company and then living with her relatives after her family's death, she would have what she desired most in the world.

A permanent home of her own.

A home—good Lord, Stephen was offering her a kingdom! And though her aunt, fearful of the girl's gentle nature, advised Rosemary to give more thought to what the perils of life would be in that primitive territory, Rosemary had not hesitated. Never again would she be homeless.

But at what price, she wondered, as she looked across at the swarthy Navajo with whom she shared the coach. His sharp gaze fastened on her as if he had seen her sudden shudder of repulsion. Uncomfortable, she shifted under his unwavering stare and would have sworn she saw an amusement lurking in the masked eyes.

He might not resemble the hideous, leprous Indians who begged along India's dirty streets, but he was no less loathsome to her. Still, he was not quite the wild savage her uncle had depicted upon his return from his business trip to Santa Fe—the painted face and long straggly hair.

The Indian before her wore his dark hair tied at the nape of his neck in a knot, or *chongo,* with a red flannel bandana about his forehead. And instead of only a breechcloth, he was clad in a double-breasted, nut-brown linsey shirt, fringed buckskin trousers, and a silver concho belt that accentuated the narrow hips and flat stomach.

There was a rawhide leanness about him, a hard masculinity stamped into the powerful cast of his features that made her uneasy in his presence. She recalled the first time she had met him, outside the Menger Hotel in San Antonio five days earlier. She had known that old stifling feeling of terror that attacked her at the sight of an Indian but had fought it off as she asked stiffly, "Are you the foreman for the Cambria Ranch?"

She was tall for a woman, but he was still much taller—tall even for a Navajo, so that she had to tilt her head to look into a pair of eyes as black as a raven's wings. She had seen in their depths the dawning of skeptical recognition.

He had reached into his shirt pocket and produced a tintype, holding it out to her. "Yes, I am Lario Santiago, the *caporal* of the Cambria," he said in softly accented English. "And you are the Señorita Gallagher?" The faintest smile of mockery had touched the full lips, softening the hawklike nose and the high slash of the cheekbones.

12

Rosemary had grimaced. "Aye, that I am!" She did not need to look at the picture she had sent Stephen to see the wide mouth, the large unblinking eyes, the heavy hair severely bound in a small knot at the back of her head. How fortunate, she thought, that the sepia tintype had no color as an oil portrait did. The riotous red hair and eyes that were neither green nor blue might have made even a determined man like Stephen Rhodes change his mind about marriage.

At fifteen, having transversed the Asian continent from Karachi to Singapore, she had already acquired more maturity than someone twice her age. However, she could not yet perceive, as had her aunt and others likewise observant, the striking beauty, waiting like a budding rose to unfold—nor the passion that would be the rose's thorn.

4

At Fort Fillmore, where Rosemary and Lario transferred to the Santa Fe Mail Stage, they were joined by a white-bearded Methodist circuit rider and a cavalry officer of the First United States Dragoons who was under orders to proceed to Fort Union, just north of Cambria.

Carefully keeping his curved saber out of the way of her full skirts, the lieutenant took the seat next to the minister. Lario he ignored, as Lario did him. But the girl the soldier could not keep his eyes from, although she was certainly not what he would call appealing, with the odd-colored eyes and the too-wide mouth. Yet there was something about her—perhaps it was the generous lower lip that promised a sensuality of which she was still unaware. Or perhaps he was intrigued by the tiny pox pit which a quirk of nature had placed above her left cheekbone like some beauty mark. Hell, the soldier thought, he'd been too long in that womanless country.

Rosemary's reserve thawed upon learning that Grant Raffin knew of the Cambria Ranch. "Hasn't everyone heard of Cambria Castle?" he asked with a beguiling smile. "In the six months I've been stationed out here Cambria's all I've heard about. It's Latin for Wales, isn't it?"

So, Rosemary thought, not everyone in the Territory was illiterate, as her uncle had led her to believe. She had been told that not one woman in a thousand, if there were that many in the Territory, even knew how to write her own name. "Aye, it is. Stephen is Welsh. But he has refused to tell me anything about Cambria. He writes that he wants to surprise me, but I can tell he's very proud of the ranch." She leaned forward, her great eyes shining with excitement. "What's it like?"

Grant removed his plumed hat which was looped on the right side and displayed yellow-brown hair lighter than his mustache and side whiskers. With the back of his sleeve he brushed away the perspiration that had formed beneath the hat's headband, saying, "Stephen Rhodes should be proud. Cambria's like a territory unto itself, with its own towns and missions and stores. But the Castle—I've never seen it, only heard talk about it."

Disappointed, Rosemary sat back. Even her dreams now were of Cambria. It never occurred to her to ask Lario, nor did her fiancé's *caporal* volunteer the information. Instead he trained his keen eyes on the rugged terrain outside. The few times their gazes caught she found herself fidgeting, although she told herself there was no reason for it. He extended a natural courtesy to her at the prescribed times, while the remainder of the time he seemed to totally disregard her, finding more to interest him in the limitless stretch of sand dunes and lava beds.

While the minister slept, his whiskers flying with each snoring breath, Grant answered Rosemary's questions about his home in Washington, D.C., and regaled her with the milder scandals of its political society.

"My father, who was a judge, was such a rake my mother wouldn't hear of me going into politics," Grant concluded with a depreciative smile. "So I wound up at Virginia Military Institute."

"And you plan to make a career of it?" Rosemary prompted.

As best he could in the cramped coach, Grant stretched out long legs clad in shiny half-boots. "Not if I can help it. The military will never make you rich."

"Oh?" Rosemary appraised the handsome soldier, marking him with maybe twenty-five years. It would be so easy, she thought, to succumb to his charm, to fall in love with him. But his type, she told herself, was often here one day, gone the next. Yet Stephen, his kind would be as permanent as the rocky mountains in the distance. "Is wealth what you want most from life?"

Grant's distinctly etched brows arched. "Isn't that what you want, Miss Gallagher?" Before she could reply, he

14

laughed, saying, "I know I don't want a military career. I suppose politics is in my blood. And out here there's the opportunity to make a name in politics."

At four that afternoon the burly driver and his bewhiskered shotgun messenger halted to dine and graze the horses at Robledo, the last way station before the Jornada del Muerto, the Journey of Death. That evening the stage would leave the fertile green valley of the Rio Grande River and begin the long stretch of nearly one hundred and fifty miles across the desert.

The evening was wondrously clear, and in the soft atmosphere of New Mexico's southern latitude the stars shone with great brilliancy. Moonlight traced the Sierra Caballo's serrated peaks and outlined the tall soap-weeds that grew upon the Jornada. A profound hush lay on the desert so that the only noise to be heard was the clatter of the horses' hooves and the rumbling sound of the wheels upon the hard alkaline road.

Sometime after dawn a rest was permitted, and the horses were watered. Rosemary stretched her legs, walking over the deadly glitter of the gypsum bed that was snow white but bone dry.

"Better keep close to the coach," Grant cautioned as he caught up with her. Beneath his mustache he flashed an irresistible smile. "You wouldn't want to lose your hair to Indians." One gloved hand came up to touch a wayward tendril. "I'll bet your hair is lovely hanging loose," he said in a husky voice.

Rosemary's gaze went past Grant's face to Lario, who had climbed on the stage's roof to scan the land. His dark gaze rested on her. Did he think she was flirting with Grant Raffin? No doubt he'd go straight to Stephen and report everything she did. She tossed her head, and for a brief moment the calm blue-green eyes danced with mischievous flirtation. "Ah now, Lieutenant Raffin, only Stephen will be knowing that."

Grant's eyes, as dark blue as his dress uniform, narrowed, uncertain of what they had seen. Had the quiet, slender girl a spirit he had not detected? She had, of course, crossed an ocean and half a continent on her own. He wondered if Stephen Rhodes realized the value of his mail-order bride.

And this Stephen Rhodes, here was a man it might do well to know.

The stage resumed its journey, but a tension seemed to hang in the coach's air as heavy as the morning mist over the desert floor. Even Grant seemed preoccupied. He caught

Rosemary watching as he checked his Navy Colt, spinning the chamber. He nodded toward Lario, saying, "It seems your guardian expects us to see Apaches before the day is out."

The vinegarish minister paled at the mention of Apaches. Tugging nervously at his long beard, his glance slid to Lario. "And what's to prevent his kind from turning on us?" he asked with a jerk of his head toward the Indian.

Lario's stony gaze flickered over the three passengers, not missing the repulsion mixed with fright on the young woman's countenance. "Right now there are only the Apache out there for you to worry about," he said in carefully measured words. "And they are the Navajo's sworn enemy."

Rosemary's own nerves grew more taut as the minutes passed. At about noon the excited shouts of the driver ripped through the coach's silence, and the next moment Rosemary spotted Indians bobbing up and down, in sight and out again, as they rode single file over the sand hills two miles distant.

At the same time the stage's speed increased, careening around the road's curve. Lario threw open the door and, gripping his Sharp's carbine, hauled himself to the stage's roof. The minister jumped back from the window as if he had seen the Angel of Death. "Do something, Lieutenant!" he choked.

Grant leveled his Colt out the stage's window. "I can't do a damn thing—pardon me, ma'am—until they get within range, Reverend. Now why don't you try praying?"

Then, to Grant's astonishment, Rosemary grabbed at his pistol, crying, "No!"

"What in tarnation do you think you're doing!" he yelled as he wrestled with her for the pistol. "Watch it, it'll go off!"

Rosemary stopped struggling but did not relinquish the gun. Her lower lip quivered. "I hate the Indian more than you could ever know—but I hate killing worse. Maybe they don't mean any harm, maybe it won't be necessary to shoot."

Grant's dark-blue eyes rolled up in despair, and he eased the pistol from Rosemary's grasp. "And maybe they will, then what will—"

At that moment shots interrupted whatever Grant was about to say, and the messenger shouted down, "Hold your fire!"

Grant edged his head out the window and drew it in quickly again, this time smiling. "A caravan of Mexican freighters are coming this way. It looks as though they've scared off our visitors."

From the stage's far side legs appeared, and Lario slipped agilely through the door's window. He slid into the seat opposite Rosemary and a few minutes later closed his eyes, as if prepared to sleep despite the previous excitement and the raucous shouts of the caravan's bullwhackers and mule-skinners that now passed by.

As the stage drew nearer to Santa Fe, it passed more and more traffic—mule trains, ox carts, covered wagons, and near-naked Indians leading burros almost hidden under heavy loads. At last, late that afternoon, gauzy clouds lifted their fogbank to reveal the carnelian Sangre de Cristo mountains whose foothills curved like two arms about the Villa de Santa Fe de San Francisco, and Rosemary felt the thrill of anticipation course through her.

From the distance the adobe buildings with their flat roofs looked like little mud boxes. Upon closer inspection the town appeared no better. "This godforsaken village is the capital of the Territory?" the reverend muttered to no one in particular.

Rosemary's gaze took in the drab, squat adobe houses that, along with an occasional cornfield, haphazardly lined the irregular pattern of dusty streets and found the city no worse than the squalor of Delhi. Indeed, the surrounding landscape possessed a savage beauty that appealed to her Oriental-developed values.

Peeping out of the doorways were many women whose faces were besmeared with crimson clay, giving them the appearance of wearing masks. In response to the startled look on Rosemary's face, Grant's lips widened in suppressed amusement. "It's the juice of the alegria plant," he explained. "The women protect their skin from the sun this way."

The lathered horses eventually plodded to a halt in the plaza before the only hotel in Santa Fe, the Exchange Hotel, more commonly known as La Fonda. A two-story adobe building with a covered walkway running its length, it took up an entire block. Beneath this *portales* a crowd had gathered to greet the mail coach's arrival.

Anxiously, Rosemary searched the throng of people. She saw soldiers on leave from Ft. Marcy, vaqueros in leather chaps, a few grubby prospectors down out of the Cerrillos Hills, and here and there a well-dressed civilian in frock coat and top hat. A wry smile touched her lips when she realized she had no idea of what Stephen looked like.

"Rhodes has hair the color of the sunset—much like yours," Lario said.

Rosemary turned from the window to see the Indian's sulphur black eyes crinkle with humor, and for a moment she wondered if the Navajo could read her mind as easily as he

17

read the puma tracks he had pointed out near a bone-dry creek where the stage had halted with a warped wheel.

"Rosemary!"

She whirled around as the coach's door was swung open. The crowd parted now for a man of medium height but with massive shoulders. His curly hair was brick red, matching the short, well-trimmed beard and walrus mustache. It was a forceful face, with full lips and narrow nose. But it was the eyes, darker than the coal of Wales, that held Rosemary. She saw there the pride and strength of will.

Stephen lifted her from the coach. Before everyone his head lowered over her face, and her eyes closed as his lips claimed hers. It was her first kiss, and Rosemary trembled as his mouth seemed to devour her. Her head swam with this first taste of passion, and her knees buckled.

At last he released her. "We'd best be wed tomorrow," he laughed breathlessly. "I'll have no man accuse our first-born of a doubtful birthright."

Rosemary was as tall as Stephen, and their gazes locked as they read in each other's eyes the deep conviction that this marriage was preordained. At that moment Rosemary could envision their children's children and their children riding over the miles of the Cambria Ranch they would one day inherit from Stephen and herself. As Stephen had written, they would create a glorious dynasty.

Then what was it in Lario's velvety black eyes that burned in her brain so?

5

If Rosemary could ignore the macabre string of Indian ears that festooned one wall of the Palace of the Governors, the party following the wedding in the Palacio's chapel was comparable to any royal ball she had ever read about.

The Palacio was the oldest public building in the United States, antedating both the Jamestown and Plymouth settlements, and it showed its age. Many of its offices were separated by cotton curtains hung from heavy beams blackened and stained with age, and a few of the floors were still nothing but packed dirt. In some of the rooms bleached muslin had been tacked to the beams to prevent the dirt roof from sifting through the burlaped ceiling, and figured calico was nailed halfway up the walls to keep the whitewash from coming off on the clothes.

The largest room of the Palacio, the council-chamber, was packed that afternoon with people, almost all men, enjoying the opportunity to celebrate anything. At one end of the room a refreshment table had been set up with a large glass bowl of grape brandy from Bernillo on one side and two heavy crocks of the fiery Taos Lightning on the other.

At the opposite end of the room on a raised platform ornamented with red muslin drapery a five-piece military band played romantic waltzes and the lively songs, "Oh, Susanna" and "My Nelly Was a Lady."

Stephen was a good dancer, holding Rosemary at just the proper distance as he led her about the room to the music of the banjos, clarinets, and harp, but too often he was interrupted by men hungry for the sight and touch of a white woman. And Stephen good-naturedly yielded, especially to Lieutenant Raffin when Rosemary explained that the officer had been prepared to defend the stage against an Indian attack.

""Tis glad I am that you were able to come today," she told Grant as he took her in her arms for a waltz.

"Do you think I'd miss seeing the most beautiful belle in Santa Fe?" he teased.

Even in the exquisite wedding gown of ivory lace and rose satin, Rosemary knew she could not be called beautiful. She turned her head away, saying, "Your flattery is wasted here, Lieutenant."

"Grant," he corrected.

A giant of a mountain man, a trapper with hair plastered down with bear grease, interrupted, begging a dance, and Grant saved Rosemary's feet from another trampling, saying, "We were just going for a cup of brandy."

But even then the two were detained. "There you are, Lieutenant Raffin!" the governor's daughter said. She tapped her fan saucily on Grant's sleeve, even while her cornflower blue eyes coolly surveyed the tall, thin woman with him. Relief that the newcomer was at once plain of face and married flickered across Libby's vapidly pretty features before she said, "Don't you know all the women are dying to meet Mr. Rhodes's fiancée?"

Grant bowed gallantly. "I surrender to the charm of another citizen of the South. Kentucky, isn't it?"

"Why, sir, you do have a memory." She flashed the officer another confident smile and spread her hoops in a curtsey.

19

"Now you simply must tell all the women about the latest fashions," she informed Rosemary as she led her away.

All what women, Rosemary wondered. There was Libby's mother, the sad-looking Clara Caden. And the birdlike Hilda Goldman. But other than those two, there was only a scattering of Mexican matrons who had either married the few well-to-do Mexican land-grant recipients or the growing number of American men who were coming to claim the opportunities offered in Santa Fe. The Mexican women merely smiled behind lazily swishing fans, and Rosemary felt helpless about conversing with them. In India the tutor had taught her Italian and French but no Spanish.

However, Clara, who sorely missed the comforts of civilization, barraged Rosemary with questions. Did the women in Ireland wear hoop skirts also? Had she ever been presented to the Queen? What about the hound's-leg sleeve and the fichu—were they out of style now?

For a few moments Clara's pale, lackluster face radiated with enthusiasm, and Rosemary wondered if this was in store for her also—the slow withering of the mind and body in an alien land.

At last Stephen rescued Rosemary, telling her it was time to leave for Cambria. In one of the Palacio's small offices, protected only by a curtain, she quickly changed into a navy blue gabardine traveling suit. When she joined Stephen outside, the two of them were pelted with rice as they departed in a buckboard wagon packed with wedding gifts and provisions needed for the three-day trip to Cambria.

Following the Old Santa Fe Trail, they reached Glorieta Pass late that afternoon, and when Rosemary looked over her shoulder she could see the three mountain ranges that encapsulated Santa Fe against time's progress—the Sandia and Manzana to the south, the Jémez Range to the west, and the Sangre de Cristo.

In many places the mountains crowded close to the wheel-rutted trail, and in other places the wagon rolled perilously near yawning gorges. When it was almost too dark to see the trail, Stephen halted the buckboard in an alpine meadow dotted with tall aspen and fir and laced by a narrow stream that rose up out of the Truchas Mountains and rushed toward the Pecos River.

He lifted her from the wagon and led her across the damp grass out onto a rocky spur from which could be seen a wide valley, already in deepening shadows, and the vague spread of purple plain beyond. Three thousand feet below, the land spread at their feet like a huge relief map. He held her before

20

him, her back against his chest. "Cambria," he said, making the name sound like an incantation. "As far as you can see— and still further."

"Oh, Stephen, I don't want to stop here! I've waited this long, can't we spend our first night on Cambria soil?"

"'Tis too dangerous to travel any further tonight. This is Apache country now."

"Will there be trouble from the Apaches?"

"Lately 'tis been the Utes and Arapaho who have been raiding the smaller ranchos, stealing horses mostly—sometimes a Mexican child to sell as a slave to the tribes. But Lario is up ahead, scouting. We shouldn't run into trouble. Besides, Indians dinna like to move around at night."

"Do these Indians...do they ever attack Cambria?" Rosemary held her breath, afraid even in the safety of Stephen's arms.

"Not since last spring." Unaware of her latent fear, he led her back toward the wagon. "Lario made a gift of twin lambs to Perro Amarillo—Yellow Dog. He's chief of the Cibola Apache band, the most warring of the tribes in this area. So far, his band has bypassed our three ranches."

"Three?"

Stephen laughed. "I be forgetting you don't know anything about Cambria. So large it is that we have three smaller ranches—camps they be called—so the *vaqueros* and shepherds don't have to make the long trip back to the main ranch every evening. The Wild Cat Camp runs our few cattle, and we've the Alta Piñon for our winter grazing in the Cuervo Mountains, but the largest, Cimarron Draw, is sharecropped out for sheep by Lario's band."

"He's a chief?"

Stephen shrugged and began to remove the canvas that covered the mound of provisions in the wagon. "He could be, I guess. But the Navajo live in family communities, and unless warring, dinna be looking to any one man as their chief."

While Stephen began to build a fire, Rosemary broke out the supply of beans and smoked meat. Never had she smelled the distinctively sweet odor of burning piñon, and as the coffee perked, she sat with her arms about her knees against the evening's sudden chill, for it was colder there in the mountains. Stephen came and placed a blanket around her, his hands lingering at her shoulders.

Over dinner they made small talk to bridge the gap of their little knowledge of each other. "When I was eight," Stephen told Rosemary, "I began working in the coal mines,

21

and as I passed the lighted homes where the gentry entertained, I promised meself I would one day be me own man."

He looked down into his coffee cup with a cynical smile. "I learned to ape their mannerisms and studied to improve me speech, so that when I did succeed no man could question me right."

"Is that when you decided to come to the United States?" Rosemary asked gently.

"Yes... when I finally had enough money to escape those black holes." He looked up at Rosemary then, and she saw the haunted look in his eyes. "I was twenty-two when I made me way to America, where one heard titles and aristocracy did not make the man. But in New York wealth did—and I had none. So I came west on the Santa Fe Trail to trade."

"And made your wealth," she supplied.

"Aye, but 'tis more than that—'tis the excitement, the challenge. I dinna know if I can explain it to you, but it be sort of like a card game, like whist or monte. Me freighting company I started out with, the Santa Fe Trading Post, then Cambria... they be markers along the way. Indications of me success."

"Then 'tis the game you enjoy—not its reward."

"Exactly!" he said, pleased that her female mind had grasped so easily what he himself could merely hint at.

"Nevertheless," she pressed, "a poorly timed bluff could cost you more than your markers."

"You've played cards before," he accused and found himself somewhat pleased at the scandalous idea.

Rosemary shook her head. "Mah-Jongg. I learned to play it in India. 'Tis a simple game played with bamboo tiles, but the scoring system is complicated. A marker like Cambria would not be overlooked in Mah-Jongg."

Stephen tossed out the dregs of his coffee cup. "I've risked me life many times over the years for every *vara* of that land grant. 'Tis something I dinna take lightly. Just as a wife I dinna take lightly."

Embarrassed by Stephen's intensity, Rosemary concentrated on her dinner, but too soon it was finished and Stephen was banking the dancing flames. The fire's light illuminated the vigor and power in his face, which the beard could not hide. Rosemary found it difficult to believe that Stephen was more than twenty-five years older than she. He seemed closer to thirty than forty.

As Stephen made the bedroll, his freckled hands moving as deftly as a cardsharp's, Rosemary trembled with the knowledge of what was to come. Asian girls were taught

22

early in life the duties of pleasing a man. *But so soon!* cried out something inside Rosemary. Not two years before she had had her first menses, discovered with a mixture of guilt and pleasure the sudden burgeoning of her breasts.

Stephen turned toward her. His black eyes met hers across the flickering embers, and she thought how those eyes smoldered just as hotly as the fire's coals. "Rosemary."

There could be no further delay. Payment for Cambria was due. Rosemary raised her arms in a genuine gesture of warm welcome.

The Navajo sat astride the chestnut stallion, his knees hooked under the lariat tied loosely about the animal's barrel. The small ears of the Arab horse pricked forward as they picked up the sound of what the Navajo had been watching for the past quarter of an hour.

From the view of the bare sandstone butte, Lario followed the progress of the lone wagon across the lush gamma grass that carpeted the Pecos Valley below. The man in the wagon represented the end to the way of life of the Indian's people, the *Dine'é*. The others—the small ranchers, the prospectors, even the soldiers, most of whom would return to their families in the States when their time was up—represented no permanent threat.

But it was Rhodes, and his hunger for power, that would bring about the end to the Navajo and their Athabascan brothers. Yet the *Dine'é* could not see that, Lario reflected, and a line of bitterness stretched flat his lips. Slowly the *Dine'é* were being emasculated...reduced to eating Rhodes's gifts of beef and mutton and begging whiskey.

"A man with nothing to do is no man at all," the Mormon missionary had once told him. But in his zeal to educate the dirty, ragged Indian boy the missionary had neglected phrases like Manifest Destiny. Yet it had not taken the boy long to recognize the slow erosion of his people and their land, to realize that the Thing That Steals the Land, the surveyor's compass, was as fatal as the fiery blast of the Long Arm.

At one time Lario had believed that the white man's knowledge he had acquired could help his people. Now he was no longer so sure. The Athabascans had been raised on hardship and danger. "The best light cavalry there is," Kit Carson often said. "They can shoot from the back of a galloping horse like Tartars." Indeed, the Athabascans were descendents of the Tartars.

Now the *Dine'é* were reeling under the blows of the ever-encroaching civilization, and Lario wondered if there was a way to save The People, if there was an answer to the dilemma. His brain burned with the continually nagging question. He felt so inadequate.

It would be so easy, he had often thought, to take his short buffalo bow or his skinning knife and end Rhodes's life. But it would not stop the influx of men just as greedy. No, better to have patience. Let the Anglos fight among themselves for the power. Then...

And the woman in the wagon? His eyes narrowed, seeing again the hair the shade of the fall leaves. Burnt red, like a ceremonial campfire sometimes, sometimes pale orange when the sun's light fell just so. He heard again her Anglo's stiff tongue trying to pronounce *acequia,* the Spanish word for ditch, and a faint smile touched his lips. He thought of the fine bones of her face, whose expression was at times scornful and at other times wary, and he thought of the slender body and the lithe way she moved it.

Rhodes could not see that in a few years the woman's angularities would smooth into flowing lines, like the life-giving streams. The woman would not ease into the dimpled fat of the Mexican women who had enjoyed too many siestas, or into the stocky solidarity of the Indian women who had known only coarse work and exposure to the harsh winters and fiery summers.

And why did this Rosemary Gallagher not see that she was being used, as Rhodes used everyone? But then she was still young—what, fifteen or sixteen to his own thirty-one summers?

Impatience finally overtook Lario, and his knees pressed against his horse's sides. There was not space in his thoughts for a woman. Especially an Anglo.

6

Rosemary knew now. And wondered that so much had been made of the wedding night. Within that first month she had grown accustomed to Stephen's nightly visits. They were punctual and precise. Even to his leave-taking immediately afterward. And his lovemaking was neither as abhorrent as the gossipy matrons of Waterford, Ireland, had made it out to be nor as romantic as the Brontë sisters had depicted it in their books.

What did surprise Rosemary was how easily she slipped back into the feudal way of life she had known in the Orient. Cambria operated on much the same scale, with Stephen the lord of his fief. And like in the Orient, there were servants, mostly Mexican and Indian children, who performed the most menial tasks, from brushing out Rosemary's unruly waist-length hair each night to emptying the chamber pots each morning.

Rosemary had fallen in love with Cambria that first day she passed onto its land...the steep escarpments, purple peaks, and low rolling valleys that suddenly gave way to red deserts. Cambria was vibrant colors and varied landscape.

But it was the Castle with its heavy earthen walls stenciled by pink hollyhock and wild, golden roses de castilla, and its spiraling turrets, dormer windows, and the wide balustraded verandas that would bind her heart to Cambria.

She had first seen the house, which, with its seventy-three rooms, was indeed large enough to be called a castle, when Stephen had brought the wagon around a jutting wall of rock and halted there on the pine-crested bluff. Set under the Pecos escarpment, the Castle topped a low knoll at the center of the horseshoe bend of the Pecos River. Clustering about it were the corrals, stables, and other outbuildings for the employees. At the knoll's bottom reposed Cambria's village—several structures, mostly of adobe, that bordered a road paralleling the river's bend.

Anyone seeing the Castle was at once impressed by the magnificence of the man-made creation in a land dominated by the magnificence of nature. Cambria's Castle ruled over everything around it. And about it there was an aura of warmth and security that Rosemary had never known.

"Twenty years ago I started with a one-room log cabin," Stephen said proudly. "I've tried to make it as much like a European chateau as possible."

The interior was equally impressive with calico-papered walls, massive tables topped with white marble, and Brussels carpets—all brought in by wagon over the Santa Fe Trail. Crimson velvet draperies veiled mica windowpanes. "I plan to have glass panes brought in on the next wagons out of Independence," Stephen told Rosemary as he led her through the enormous house. "As you can see, it takes a leprechaun's pot of gold to keep Cambria operating, and there still be much to do."

An elegant staircase of polished mahogany dominated the

main room. Rosemary's fingers trailed along the smooth, cool balustrade, touching its curves...just as her fingers lovingly touched everything they came in contact with. It was her house. To the rear of the house was the large kitchen which on some nights served enough food for sixty guests, though five to ten was more the usual number each night.

Also to the rear of the house was a set of rooms expressly for the men. But within the first month Rosemary violated the taboo and marched past Stephen's bedroom suite and into the great office. Both Rosemary and Stephen faced each other, stunned—Stephen, that she had entered the male sanctuary, and Rosemary, by her surroundings. The huge room was adorned with stuffed birds, elk and deer heads, several bear rugs, and a white buffalo rug. In one corner stood a round, green, baize-covered table reserved for Stephen's nightly card games.

Somewhat dazed, Rosemary took a seat opposite the massive desk on the camelback horsehide-upholstered sofa. Calmly she folded her hands in her lap while Stephen puffed agitatedly on a dundeen pipe. "Well?" he asked at last.

"Stephen, I've tried to occupy myself with the running of the Castle. But with its wealth of servants..." She shrugged. There was not enough to fill her days. Nor was knitting and needlepoint in the sitting room off her bedroom enough to fill her evenings. She sorely missed, more than she had supposed, the company of other women.

Stephen tapped the pipe's clay bowl against the palm of his hand. "And?"

"The children here—both the girls and boys should be educated. I'd like to set up a schoolroom in the adobe chapel. I know the outer walls are crumbling to dust, but the chapel itself is still serviceable."

To her surprise Stephen agreed. "Just as long as the schooling doesn't interfere with the children's jobs." Then he leaned forward, and a reluctant smile formed beneath the dark red mustache. "I couldn't be happier with me choice of women. It's a wife I wanted who would be bringing the touches of civilization to Cambria." And it was true, he thought. He had not expected much, and though she was a homely thing, all eyes, she quite fulfilled what he sought for a wife—a gentle, well-bred, and intelligent young Anglo woman.

Armed with books that had been shipped months before with her trunks of clothes, Rosemary began visiting the village, talking with the Mexican women as they baked bread in their outdoor beehive ovens or washed clothing in cauldrons of boiling lyesoap. In poorly accented Spanish mixed with Italian and an intermittent Hindustani phrase, Rosemary cajoled the mothers to let their children attend the school held each afternoon during the siesta.

Consuela, the Castle's old cook, began to volunteer gossip—the names of the ill, the newborns, the homes where death had recently struck, and Rosemary would tuck sticks of peppermint candy or a gift for a newborn in her basket along with her books.

After the school hour Rosemary always made a point of visiting with old Miguel, who ran the one store in the village. His grandson, the six-year-old Pedro, was in her class, and she tried to teach the child and his grandfather how to play Mah-Jongg but had to settle for dominoes.

Inevitably, she ran into Lario. She had left the store, after losing a game of dominoes to Miguel, and had meant to inspect the livery stable at the rear of the store. She did not recognize until it was too late the bare-chested man working over the forge's fiery heat. The copper skin gleamed with a sheen of perspiration, and despite the deceptive leanness, the corded muscles in his arms and shoulders rippled with each movement. At one wrist was a leather band for protection from the slap of the bowstring and about his upper left arm was a band of handworked silver.

The ringing of his hammer against the anvil had masked her approach. Her heart thudding, she carefully began to edge her way back outside. But, as if warned by some sixth sense, Lario looked around. "You wanted something, Señora?"

It was a polite enough question, but something about the way he emphasized the title irritated Rosemary, momentarily drowning out her fear of him. "I—I was looking for a suitable riding horse." How inane! Rosemary wanted to bite her tongue.

Lario's heavy-lidded gaze took in her gray cotton shirtwaist dress, and she flushed. "For later, of course."

"Of course," he said and went back to hammering on the white metal.

Forgetting her fear, Rosemary moved nearer to better view the exquisite piece of craftsmanship. "How beautiful!" she marveled, admiring the intricate design of silver and turquoise. The work of the silver band was strong and true and untouched by foreign influence.

A brief smile of pleasure passed over his face. "A gift for the Señora," he said. He held the bracelet out to her, his deep-set eyes watching her inquiringly.

"No! No, thank you," Rosemary gasped, trying to keep her returning paranoia under control, but Lario's detached gaze seemed as hot to her as the flame leaping from the forge. She murmured something polite—what she did not know—and stumbled from the stable. Outside, she leaned weakly against the stable's weathered frame and drew in deep, labored breaths. In her ears her blood pounded in tempo with that of Lario's hammer at the forge.

"I heard you've been playing dominoes with old Miguel," Stephen said that evening as he led her into dinner.

Rosemary cast a curious glance at her husband but only said, "Aye, I've been thinking about turning the store into a trading post."

Stephen's bushy red brows jerked upward. "A trading post? What's wrong with the store?"

"'Tis fine for tobacco and coffee and ammunition," she said and hurried on to tell him about the project that had been in the back of her mind for some time. "But what about things like hairpins and materials...and books?"

Stephen halted before the dining room's double doors and took her hands. "I understand what you be saying. But these people have no money. To be sure, Miguel knows how to appraise what the people do bring in for trade, but 'tis nothing he knows about keeping a ledger, about debits and credits."

Rosemary held her ground. "But I do."

Stephen sighed. "Come to me office tomorrow morning."

Victorious, Rosemary was exceedingly charming that evening to the array of trappers and traders and casual travelers who happened to traverse the kingdom, and they were enchanted by their first sight in a long time of a white woman.

Though Stephen still frowned on Rosemary's interest in the business that took place in the forbidden office in the rear of the Castle, she learned little by little, through the keeping of the trading post's ledger, about other facets of the Cambria empire. "These be things that you wouldn't understand," he would explain when she asked.

She was persistent. "That little man that was here yesterday—why doesn't he go directly to the forts to sell his sheep? Why come to you?"

"Because," he reluctantly told her, "our Santa Fe Trading Post enjoys a near monopoly in supplying the government with beef and mutton and flour for our military posts."

"But that's unfair!"

Stephen laughed out loud and gathered her to him. "Where be your loyalty, wife?"

But the next morning he took pains to explain things more fully. "The ranchers in the lower Pecos Valley depend upon

28

me to buy their sheep and cattle since they dinna have the knowledge or men available to get them to Las Cruces and Demming. In turn I see to it their ranches are protected from the Indians and cattle rustlers that be drifting up from Texas."

Rosemary watched as Stephen patted the tousled dark curls of the servant girl, Isabel, when she returned the filled coffee cup to him and felt a moment's pride that he was so good with the children employed at the Castle. He would make a good father, she reflected, and wondered if she was yet with child.

Stephen tossed down the coffee and rose. "By the way, Shackelford—the banker you met at our wedding—he'll be coming for a few days' stay. You might be wanting to give him a room on the lower floor. He has lumbago, I understand."

Rosemary opened her mouth, and Stephen laid his blunt finger across her lips. Brought up in the old world where women were relegated to the house, he felt both appalled and impressed by Rosemary's inquisitive nature. Though almost sixteen now, she seemed years older. But he knew he had made the right decision in taking her for a wife—a decision he had postponed far too long.

"Before you be asking me why again," he said, "I'll tell you this time—only because you look so fetching this morning with your hair down."

Rosemary smiled, glad now that she had stopped wearing her nightcap, for it was simply too hot some nights.

"Shackelford wants to discuss filling the vacancy created when Jesus Moreno died—he was the county's last probate judge."

Rosemary's fingers flew to her lips. "Wasn't the poor man at our dinner table several weeks ago?"

"The same. Unfortunately, it seems he took eight or nine dollars from a cowpuncher in a game of monte, and the cowpuncher dinna like it."

"Nine dollars hardly seems justification for murdering a man, Stephen!"

"Exactly, as I've been trying to tell you, me dear—you don't understand the West. I much prefer to see you in our bedroom instead of me office."

Though Stephen might complain of her interest in Cambria's business affairs, Rosemary was determined he would find no reason for complaint in her bed.

On the nights that Stephen did not host a card game she would spend longer than necessary at her bath. Then she would slip into the four-poster with its velvet hangings and await his arrival. Some nights, especially Saturdays, she could hear from the village below the gay fiddle music of the *bailes*—the dances held in the store's large room. And she would wish she were at the *baile*, any place but there waiting for Stephen.

Rosemary truly liked and admired her husband and chastised herself time after time for such disloyal thoughts. So when he came to her, clad in a robe that did not conceal that he was in the prime of life, she was most compliant as he instructed her, "Lift your legs, like so," or "Slower now."

Later, after he had left, she would wonder why she should be so dissatisfied, so tense during his visits. He treated her with great courtesy and even affection. He was a husband to be proud of. He had given her a home worthy of a princess.

It was merely the normal letdown after months of anticipation. Bridal blues the matrons called it.

Of all people, Rosemary told herself, she should be the last to succumb to romantic illusions. Still . . .

7

Though Rosemary's fluency in Spanish increased so that she did not miss conversing in her native tongue as much, she nevertheless yearned for female companionship. In the Castle there was only old Consuela and the staff of boys and girls, of which there seemed to be a constant turnover. And in the village the people held her in such a deep respect that it was impossible to converse with them as an equal. At her approach the men removed their hats and the women humbly dropped their gazes.

So the arrival of Doña Margarita Sanchez y Chavez marked a vast improvement in Rosemary's life. Rita, as Rosemary came to call the woman three years older than she, was the wife of the much older Jiraldo Sanchez y Chavez, a slablike Spanish hidalgo whose grandfather had been awarded a community land grant by Spain's king. Not quite a hundred and thirty miles to the northeast, the Sanchez land grant was much smaller than Cambria.

As *patrón,* Don Jiraldo could control by influence and manipulation the vote of his people, and lately both he and Stephen had developed an intense interest in the Territory's growing political awareness and especially in the power wielded by the Republican Party. Therefore, once or twice a month, Don Jiraldo and Rita made the journey to Cambria, staying over several nights at the Castle.

And while Don Jiraldo and Stephen retired to Stephen's offices to gamble and discuss the problems of nesters and the evils of cattle, Rita entertained Rosemary with gossip of the Territory. New Mexico's population was so small that any happening of importance was flashed from mouth to mouth as quickly as any message over telegraph wires.

"Ahh, Rosita," Rita said one evening when they were alone in the sitting room that Rosemary had converted to her office. "Always about others I have talked. This time it is about myself I wish to share."

The petite woman ceased rocking and leaned forward, her small hands clasped before her lips. "Tonight at *cena* I wish you to rejoice with us. For five years now I have been childless. Finally I am to bear Jiraldo a child, *gracias a Dios!*"

Rosemary stifled her envy and hugged her friend with felicitation. In the four months of marriage Stephen had without fail questioned Rosemary about her menses.

"Have you had your flux?" he would ask her as he cleansed himself of his lovemaking before taking his leave.

And as shocking and painful as Stephen's bluntness was, Rosemary found it even more painful to admit she was not with child. A child was what Stephen wanted most, the only thing he lacked. The only thing she could give him.

The Christmas season arrived, bringing with it the cold winds whistling down out of the blue mountains to the northwest. It also brought roomfuls of guests, most of them from Santa Fe to stay through the Novena, the series of nine daily masses lasting from the sixteenth of December through Christmas. Stephen was preoccupied with the male guests, discussing politics more than ever, and Rosemary, with Rita's aid, coped with the last-minute preparations.

Although mutton and an occasional beef were the main staple in New Mexican households, Stephen suggested that Rosemary have roasted venison served Christmas Eve. "Father Felipe shall be here from Las Vegas to say the Novena," he told her, "and he has a liking for the venison's wild taste. Talk to Lario about supplying us with two or three deer."

Rosemary was tempted to send one of the little boys to deliver Stephen's request. But annoyed by her irrational fear of Indians, and especially of Lario it seemed, Rosemary instead sent the Indian a message that she wished to see him in her office. As she waited for him, she wished that Rita were with her rather than taking a siesta. Perhaps, she hoped, Lario would be away at one of the three ranches.

It was Lario who actually took care of the day-to-day details of running Cambria...from seeing that corral fences were mended to handling the curly-haired gunslingers, instructing them which ranges they would ride in protection...from the rough job of breaking in newly captured mustangs to the delicate, painstaking work of silversmithing.

He was something of an enigma to Rosemary—a fairly well-educated man by frontier standards yet still superstitious enough, she learned, to wear as an amulet the sacred turquoise stone which was set in his silver bracelet. He was soft-spoken with measured movements that equaled the grace of a woman. Yet she had once watched from her office window as he mastered a particularly vicious mustang in one of the corrals encircled by Lario's wranglers.

There came the jingle of spur's rowels on the stairs, and Rosemary felt the too-familiar tightening in her stomach. She dipped her pen in the secretary's inkwell and calmly forced her mind to the ledger's list of names—their purchases and what they traded in return. One plow, her mind read...for a pack of beaver pelts. Pair of boots...three Apache scalps.

"Señora?"

Rosemary jumped in spite of herself. The pen dropped from her fingers and rolled off onto the floor. "Aye, Lario," she replied sharply, angry at her clumsiness. "I need—would it be..." Her voice was muffled as she leaned to pick up the pen.

His dark hand met her pale one. Rosemary froze. Her gaze lifted to meet the deep-set eagle eyes. For the first time she noticed how deeply black they were, without any other color to tint them—blacker even than Stephen's which had the slight shade of coal-dust gray to lend them color. One could drown in their inky depths, she thought.

Suddenly her office seemed terribly small. It was agonizing to draw a breath, and she felt lightheaded.

At that moment Lario handed her the pen and rose. Not a trace of emotion showed in the eyes that were crinkled with weather lines—the only lines in the otherwise smoothly planed brown face. "You needed something, Señora?"

Anxious to be free of his overpowering presence, Rosemary's request tumbled out. "There will be many guests for Christmas dinner, Lario. Would it be possible for you to slay two deer—for Consuela to roast?"

"I will have *venado* for you by morning, Señora." He turned to go but at the door stepped aside for Rita, saying, *"Buenos días."*

She flashed coquettish eyes up at him, and when he had left, she rolled her eyes and said, "This Lario, he is a very handsome man—even I take notice and compare him with my husband who has the body of a wet noodle!"

Rosemary laughed at the woman's refreshing candor, and the tension eased from her.

Rita, who was now large with advancing pregnancy, threw up her hands, saying, "I give up—I cannot rest with that Gila monster down the hall screeching for something every other minute!"

Rosemary knew the "monster" Rita referred to was Hilda Goldman. As the wife of Stephen's partner, she had expected the best guest rooms in the Castle, but Rosemary had given them to Governor Caden and Clara and Libby. As it was, the Goldmans occupied rooms several doors down from Don Jiraldo—and this, Rosemary discovered, was a social error; for the German woman, who was in her late forties and childless, was fiercely jealous of Rita's vivacious personality and let Rosemary know she would not associate with the Sanchez y Chavez couple, even if they were of aristocratic Spanish blood.

As the others waited for the couple to appear downstairs for the Novena Hilda declared to Libby, who sat languidly fanning herself, "The Mexicans are only a little better than the Indians!"

Father Felipe's tonsured head broke out in perspiration, and Governor Caden tugged at his white goatee to cover his embarrassment. Hilda's husband, a pink little man, grew beet red and slammed his brandy glass down, sloshing the liquor. *"Dumkopt!* It's depending on Sanchez ve are to pull the votes from hiz—" He broke off, seeing Stephen's frown.

"Pardon us, Father," Stephen said. "Politics should never be mixed with religion."

The fact that Stephen even bothered to observe religious traditions amazed Rosemary, for he had written her, *"Heaven and hell dinna exist for me. Whether I fail or succeed, me dear, will not depend on relics or rosaries!"*

Yet he had agreed to a Catholic wedding, and Rosemary could only feel a deep sense of gratitude toward him. He had been good to her in all ways, and it was with much pleasure that she looked forward to the end of the Christmas Eve dinner. Then all the occupants of the Castle, the guests as well as the servants and their families, would assemble at the adobe chapel for the traditional distribution of gifts to the large number of Indian and Mexican families who worked for Stephen Rhodes, *el patrón*.

Afterward she and Stephen would be alone, and she could give him her gift.

When the dark onion soup, fruit compote, and baked squash had been consumed along with the roast venison and stewed mutton, the guests braved the cold weather to descend to the village. Soft snowflakes drifted down on them to enhance the magic of Christmas Eve.

Farolitos, small bonfires of dry, pitchy wood, outlined the drive, which was swept smooth daily, and lit the way to the chapel. There was laughter and singing, for Stephen's excellent cherry brandy had done more than warm the blood and ease the digestion.

Behind Father Felipe, Rosemary, and Stephen, Rita could be heard singing a merry carol with Governor Caden and several other guests. Libby, with no available men to court her, walked with her mother and Hilda. All three looked as grim as funeral attendants. Louis and Jiraldo, who was hobbling along with the aid of his cane, brought up the procession's rear.

The people who could not crowd inside the packed chapel stood deferentially aside for Stephen and Rosemary to pass by. In the chapel's small room everyone stood shoulder to shoulder, wating in gay anticipation for the arrival of the good padre and *El Patrón* and *su esposa.*

Rosemary's cheeks were flushed from the cold and excitement, and she welcomed the warmth of the press of people who were dressed in their best clothes. Beneath a white velvet cape Rosemary wore her best—a taffeta gown of apple green, the basque of which was almost too small for her now.

Stephen moved onto the altar's dais and wished everyone a merry Christmas in Spanish, telling them that as a gift from the Castle each family was to receive a calf and lamb. After the applause and cheering had subsided, he pulled Rosemary to his side. From his brocaded waistcoat pocket he produced an object wrapped in white paper.

"For *La Patrona,*" he said. "Open it."

"Oh!" Rosemary breathed, when she saw the exquisite piece of jewelry. The soft lines of silver encompassed four perfect turquoise stones.

"I wanted to have a sidesaddle made for you," Stephen said, "but Lario suggested you might be preferring the bracelet."

"Thank you, Stephen," Rosemary said, but her gaze slid past him to Lario, who stood in the room's far corner.

34

"You mentioned having a gift for me?" Stephen prompted after she shyly kissed him on the cheek and the crowd once again erupted in cheers.

"Aye," she said hesitantly. "But not now. Not before—" Her gaze flickered to the multitude of faces—Miguel, Consuela, Pedro, all the villagers she was coming to know.

"But now be the perfect time," Stephen said. "It emphasizes the solidarity of Cambria and its traditions."

Trapped, Rosemary's glance switched from Stephen to the expectant faces around them. "I—we—are to have a child early next summer."

8

As Rosemary went about her daily duties, she often marveled that Stephen could be so certain she carried a son. She hoped the child would bring them even closer, that she would come to better understand the man she married. But although Stephen was overjoyed about the coming child and almost overly solicitous about her health, checking to see that she ate properly and felt well, Rosemary saw no more of him than before.

In fact, less; for he came no more to her bed at night.

And Rosemary winced guiltily when she realized she was relieved. Then, of course, as her flat stomach gradually rounded, she was glad Stephen did not see her misshapen ugliness.

"You must get more exercise, Rosemary," he said one morning at breakfast. "You look pale."

Rosemary set down her cup of chocolate. She sorely missed English tea and thought she would never acquire a taste for the bitter coffee. "The weather has been so cold lately."

"I'll have Lario hitch up the buckboard and take you for a ride. A little sun will do you good."

"I'd really rather not," she protested. "There's so much to—"

"Nonsense!" Stephen said, rising. "We've plenty of help here. Our first concern be the baby's health. Besides, spring has come to the prairie. You'll enjoy the ride."

Instantly the newest serving girl, Magdalena, appeared with Stephen's hat. "It's sorry I am you will be missing the constitutional convention, dear. But I should return from

Santa Fe as soon as we've a delegate elected—within a fortnight I should say." He kissed Rosemary on the cheek and took his hat from Magdalena, tweaking the cherubic ten-year-old on the chin.

Desolately Rosemary looked after Stephen's back. She desperately wanted to go with him. It had been so long, since Christmas, that she had talked with anyone other than to exchange a few pleasantries with the villagers who, because of their devotion to her, were terribly shy in her presence.

By now Rita would have had her baby, and Rosemary could only hope that Stephen would bring her back some word about the Sanchez household. Rosemary sighed and rose from her untouched food. She would have to consign herself to spending the next few days knitting clothing for the baby, due now in less than three months.

She stationed herself in the rocking chair before her office window. To her it was the most beautiful view from the Castle. The window faced the southwest, taking in the village below with the undulating emerald prairie that stretched out beyond the Pecos's bend. To the far west, below the horny backbone of the mountains, the firs and spruces were putting on their blue-green coats.

But it was the ugly cottonwood tree at the edge of the Castle's knoll that always snapped up Rosemary's attention. Other than the shrubby tamarisks and poplars that marked the Pecos's course it was the only tree for mile upon mile. Old and twisted, its main trunk burnt by lightning, it was nevertheless magnificent. Its budding branches could offer shade to a hundred people or more. There was something about its strength that attracted Rosemary so that in the previous summer's hotter days she often had sought out its shade to read.

It was nearly midafternoon, when the spring sunshine flooded her office, that a girl came to tell Rosemary that Lario waited outside with the buckboard to take her for a ride. Twice she dropped a stitch while trying to decide whether to go. Lario was only following orders, but she knew, big as she was, she would feel more awkward than ever with him. Finally she jammed her needles away. She had to get outside.

Despite the cool temperature, the sunshine felt warm, and Rosemary stood on the veranda steps and tilted her face up to receive the sun's full radiance.

Lario watched from the wagon. Filled as Rosemary was with new life, he thought she looked like what Changing Woman, the Navajo Goddess of Life, must look. Annoyed at his wandering thoughts, he asked more harshly than he intended, "Where should you like to go, Señora?"

Rosemary frowned at Lario, refusing to quail. She jerked her woolen shawl about her. "Where is there to go?" Her gaze swept the horizon. As far as the eye could see, mountains and prairie and desert hemmed in her narrow world. "Somewhere," she muttered. "Anywhere!"

Lario's hand cupped her elbow as he helped her into the wagon, and her breath caught as if she had been pricked by a needle. His eyes scanned her face, searching for the habitual look of dislike she wore when she was around him. He guessed she was one of those who held the Indian in contempt, but that look was not there this time—only what he thought to be fear.

Rosemary pulled her shawl tighter about her to shield her greatly rounded stomach and forced a cold smile. "I must be out of breath."

"An hour southwest is a pueblo—where my family lives," Lario said, flicking the reins. "Would you like to visit it?"

That was the last thing she wanted to do. But wasn't that what one was supposed to do when thrown by a horse—get back on again? "That will be fine," she replied primly, her chin held high, her back stiff.

She sensed that Lario could not help but be aware of her fear, which in her mind weakened her position from the outset and challenged her authority as mistress of Cambria, so her next comment was tinged with spite. "I had no idea there were Indian villages on Stephen's land."

A faint smile touched his lips, and she demanded, "What is so amusing?"

"My people—the *Dine'é*—would call this their land, Señora."

"But Stephen told me the land grant originally belonged to the DeVega family."

"The Spanish and Mexican governments have been very free about giving away what is not theirs to give."

"Oh?" Rosemary's brows arched. "I suppose the land belongs to your people by right of first possession?"

Lario's countenance was poker straight. "I think that is how the Anglo law could call it."

Rosemary stole a glance at the Navajo and saw the finely carved lips flatten in a straight line, and she hurried to fill the awkward silence. "Then Stephen bought the land from the DeVegas?"

Lario looked at the woman beside him for the first time since they left the Castle. "That is what your husband has told you?"

"We have not talked about it that much," she said defensively.

Lario changed the subject. "I see you wear the bracelet."

Unconsciously Rosemary's fingers slipped up to touch the silver band at her wrist. "'Tis a lovely piece of work."

"My grandfather works in the silver, and he taught me. You will meet him today. And my mother and sister. My brothers are higher up in the greener pastures watching our sheep."

The buckboard followed the green-gold thread of cottonwood trees that traced the river's course southward toward Texas and Old Mexico, until the green-gold along the banks shaded off into olive and silver and the cottonwoods shrank to juniper, rabbit brush, and wild pumpkin on a floor of bleached sand.

Then, striking westward, it left the life-giving Pecos River for the high desert, an ever-changing land of shifting sand dunes where there was nothing. No sign of habitation or life. Suddenly it seemed they were rimmed in by the foothills of the Pedernales Mountains. Here and there the candlebush waved its flaming tapers and cholla cactus glowed silver with new growth. Rabbits scurried under the chaparral from the wagon's approach, and prairie dogs crossed their arms as if they were praying. To the far north a spring shower blew across the sky like a torn curtain.

Immediately before Rosemary on a rocky mesa was a pueblo of not more than half a dozen hogans which looked like part of the rock. They were dome-shaped structures made of saplings plastered with sand-baked clay. In a corn field two young women were hoeing. They wore long full calico skirts that covered the top of their knee-high laced moccasins and full velveteen shirts outside their skirts with brightly colored woven belts.

At the approach of the buckboard the two women stopped and looked up. The taller one dropped her hoe and ran toward the wagon. "Lario!"

"My sister, Toysei," Lario said.

The second girl followed shyly at a distance. The two young women halted now and guardedly moved closer as their doe-eyed gazes took in the woman with skin as creamy pale as the white flowering Spanish bayonet and hair the color of autumn's aspen leaves—neither red nor brown but somewhere in between.

"Adala, a neighbor," Lario said, introducing the second young woman. "Es Señora Rhodes," he told the girl as he climbed out of the wagon.

38

Adala greeted Rosemary with the two-toned Navajo, *"Ahalani,"* but Lario's sister stiffened and spat something else in Navajo. Rosemary could not understand Lario's reply but knew it to be a command. The young woman stalked off toward the hogan.

He took her arm, and again the weakness swept through her. Pregnancy nerves, she told herself. "Come inside," Lario said. "My mother will have cool water for you."

Rosemary's heels dug in, and she held back as visions of a torch-lit night in Meerut, India, zigzagged through her mind like a bolt of lightning. Lario turned to face her. "You are afraid. Why?"

What to tell him—that another race of people massacred her family and she was therefore afraid of all dark-skinned people? How silly it sounded. A tight smile curved her lips. "Only a little—one hears about how savage the Indian is."

"And you think we shall scalp you?" Lario's laugh was short. "A Navajo mother tells her children if they are not good the white man will steal them in the night and sell them for slaves."

Rosemary's long lashes dropped to hide the shame in her eyes; for the children in her own house were slaves, though the New Mexicans called it by a euphemism—debt peonage. It came under the statutory law dignified with the title of "Law regulating contracts between masters and servants." But what it was actually was that parents driven into a "state of slavery" because they could not support themselves had the right to bind their children out as peons, thus becoming slaves for life.

Lario turned away, and she followed him through a spacious yard enclosed with a palisade of mesquite stakes. Nearby stood a clumsy Mexican cart with disklike solid wooden wheels. Inside the hogan the walls were smoothly whitewashed. A rug of gray jerga lay on the packed earth floor.

As Rosemary's eyes focused, she saw in one corner a woman weaving on an upright loom. The woman, Lario's mother—War Blanket—nodded solemnly at the introduction he made in the Navajo tongue. She was an older version of Toysei, only the hair braided about the willow hoops at her ears was gray rather than a lustrous black.

Only then did Rosemary perceive the old man sitting on the floor. To her he looked terribly old. His skin was a leather layer of wrinkles, his eyes hooded; yet there was an agelessness about him. Maspha did not acknowledge her presence but quickly destroyed the painting he had created with the different colored layers of powdered rock on dirt.

"It is a curing ceremony for someone my grandfather knows is ill," Lario said. "But no outsider may watch."

The old man looked up then, and Rosemary was struck by the intensity of his gaze. He said something, and Lario frowned. "What is it?" Rosemary asked.

Lario glanced at his grandfather, then at her. "He has been expecting me to bring you, he says. He claims he has seen you in his sandpaintings." He shrugged, saying, "Would you like to wait here while I give the horses water? I will not be gone long."

He turned to Toysei. "The Señora is thirsty."

Rosemary did not want to be left alone. While Toysei grudgingly poured water from the *olla*, Rosemary forced herself to be calm and looked about the room, seeing the fox pelts and strings of waxy red peppers on the walls. There was a firepit in the hogan's center, and near the walls richly colored blankets were folded in piles for sleeping. From the well-smoked *vigas*, or roof poles, hung a cradle of deerskin by thongs, and Rosemary crossed to it. Inside the cradle lay a tiny form with thick black hair and eyes and a pink face.

"How precious!" Rosemary murmured, taking the clay cup Toysei held out to her. The maternal instinct in Rosemary was stirred, and her free hand went to her stomach. Not long to wait, she thought. "The baby—is it yours?"

Toysei nodded, and Rosemary noted the young woman's guard seemed to relax as she gazed at her baby. "It is a boy child," Toysei replied, spacing her words with difficulty. "Lucero."

"Your husband—?" Rosemary asked unthinkingly.

"Dead," Toysei said flatly. "The White Death."

Rosemary shuddered. She had come to learn that tuberculosis ran rampant among the Indian tribes. "Where did you learn English?" she asked, moving away from the sensitive subject.

"Lario taught me. My mother and brothers cannot speak the English. Some Spanish, though."

It occurred to Rosemary that perhaps she could teach English to those who wished to learn, in exchange for Navajo, though she was certain she would never master the language that was based on intonation rather than prescribed grammar. Perhaps she could even eventually overcome her aversion to the Indian people.

"If you would like, Toysei, Lario could bring you and your

brothers to the Castle sometimes, and we could practice English and Navajo together."

Toysei's flat face closed over. "I do not like it there."

"Oh? Then you've been there before?"

"*Si*. Once as a child. After your husband, Señor Esteban, took the land, I do not go."

Rosemary looked to the mother, who smiled, nodding her head, and continued her weaving. The rhythmic thump of the warp against the loom was the only sound in the room, for the grandfather, with his eyes closed in his drooping head, appeared to be sleeping now. "What do you mean, 'he took the land'?"

The baby starting fussing, and Toysei lifted it from its cradle. The back of his head, like that of a lot of Navajo babies, was flattened from the cradleboard. "My words are like the air," Toysei said, turning away. "They are nothing."

"Please explain for me. I want to know."

The baby began to howl now, and Toysei pulled aside her blouse and gave him her nipple. "The land—it belonged before *su esposo,* your husband, to the *familia* DeVega. The son of Señor DeVega, he liked the games of chance played at the *casa* of Doña Tules Barcelo. Many times he lost to Señor Esteban. Much money over a long time. Then he lost the land to Señor Esteban and...he hangs himself from the lights of candles."

"Oh, no!" Rosemary breathed.

As if glad to horrify the woman, Toysei continued, "And his father, Don Emiliano, tells Señor Esteban he will fight with *pistoles*. And Don Emiliano is killed." Toysei shrugged her shoulders. "He was a very old man."

"Toysei!" It was Lario. A scowl narrowed his eyes.

9

Silence strained the ride back to the Castle. When it became unbearable, Rosemary said, "Your sister has exaggerated, has she not? And even if Stephen did acquire the DeVega land grant by gambling, it's happened before."

Lario looked at her, and, though he said nothing, she read the accusation in his gaze. "But it was Don Emiliano who challenged Stephen!" she cried out.

"Maybe," Lario replied, using the English word most often

spoken by the cryptic Indians, and switched his gaze back to the land that was crisscrossed with a maze of tracks made by Navajo wagons.

Mentally Rosemary defended Stephen. She knew beyond all doubt she would protect Cambria had she won it, even if it meant killing for what belonged to her. Still, she meant to ask Stephen more about the DeVega episode when he returned.

But a week before Stephen was due back, while she went over the household account, pains began to sear her back, then wrapped about her sides to invade her womb. The pen dropped from her fingers and spattered ink on the neatly penned columns. She took a deep breath to ease the pain, but its intensity grew as did her ragged breathing. "Magdalena!"

Rosemary called out once more, and the girl was at her door. "Señora! ¿Qué pasa?"

Rosemary doubled over. "El bebé. Help—¡ayúdame!"

The girl fled and returned immediately with Consuela. The old cook lumbered across the room as rapidly as her thick legs would carry her. She took one look at Rosemary and shouted over her shoulder, "¡Vaya por Lario!"

Rosemary was next aware of Lario's dark gaze, of being lifted, supported against the wide expanse of his chest, as he carried her to her bedroom. She moaned in spite of herself, and he whispered in Navajo, "Enui"—it is all right.

But it was not. No one had told Rosemary about child birthing, yet she knew she was in labor far too soon by her calculations. Almost three months too soon. Above her, beyond the haze of pain, she heard Consuela's voice whispering in Spanish, "She is too narrow to carry."

"Stephen..." Rosemary managed to get out. She was failing him.

She opened her eyes to see Lario's grim face. His swarthy hand smoothed back the hair that clung to the perspiration dotting her temples. "I will go for him, Señora."

"No!" Rosemary grasped at his hand, holding it tightly as another pain cut through her abdomen. She had witnessed Stephen's wrath. She did not want him with her now, not now. "Go away—everyone," she said weakly after the pain had ebbed.

Lario cast a sharp glance at Consuela, and the old woman nodded her graying head.

For the next seven hours Rosemary was aware of very little but the scissorlike pains. Occasionally the mist cleared, and she knew that Consuela was with her, bathing her forehead and murmuring gentle words of comfort. And as the pain took hold, never leaving her at the end and as her body sought to rid itself of its six-months' burden, Rosemary knew it was Consuela's big-boned strength which held her arms pinioned, who urged her between gapped teeth, *"Empuje—* push!"

At last Rosemary knew immediate and great relief as she felt the solid mass force itself out. The pain was over! "I want to see my baby," she gasped.

The silence told her everything. She forced her eyes to focus. Consuela's black cotton dress was blood-splattered. In the woman's hands was a tiny, lifeless, blue-gray form.

"No!" Rosemary cried out.

When next she awoke, bright sunlight fell on Magdalena who sat near the bed in the rocking chair. "What time is it?" she asked in a whisper.

"It is eight in the morning, Señora. You are better, no?"

She had slept the whole night through. "The baby. What was it?"

Magdalena hesitated. She fidgeted with one of her braids, her eyes downcast. "A son, Señora," she said softly.

Rosemary closed her eyes against the tears, and the girl said, "Lario is burying your son now."

At once Rosemary tried to sit up, but Magdalena said, "No, you must rest, Señora!"

"I want to be there. 'Tis my son. I must be there!"

Magdalena paused, then said, "I will get Lario."

By the time Rosemary struggled to get into the chenille robe at the foot of her bed, Magdalena was at the door with Lario towering behind her. "Señora?" he asked.

Rosemary pulled the gown closed around her neck, conscious of Lario's Indian eyes that never missed anything. "Take me to my son's grave."

A mother's keening over her dead child Lario understood. As he bent over Rosemary, she saw in his solemn face sympathy, but it did not bother her as did the pity she saw in the face of the servants. Pulling a blanket from the bed, he enfolded Rosemary in it as if she were a child like Magdalena and scooped her up against him. "You will be all right?" he asked as he carried her from the house and placed her on the seat of the buckboard.

Rosemary nodded, and he said, "The heat—it was necessary we bury the baby now."

For a moment she forgot that Lario was an Indian, the hated enemy. She placed a hand on his arm. "Thank you," she said simply.

43

The half-closed eyes searched her face, searching there for what he had heard in her voice.

At that moment Rosemary hated anyone seeing her, knowing that under the sunlight she must look haggard, but she reasoned that by now she had no looks to lose, and so met his scrutiny unflinchingly.

Lario drove the wagon to the edge of the knoll. Beneath the gigantic, twisted cottonwood was a small mound of freshly turned earth. "I thought you would like him here," he said solemnly.

Rosemary went rigid. Then she stumbled from the wagon and fell on her knees in the dirt. *Child of her flesh!* Deep breaths expelled from her body as she steeled herself against the tears that threatened. She had failed Stephen. Her body had failed the child. And she had failed Cambria.

She thought of the wooden cradle waiting in her bedroom. And the pile of baby clothes she had sewn and knitted. And her shoulders heaved with unspent tears.

Some minutes later she was aware of Lario lifting her, cradling her in his arms as he put her in the wagon and took her back to the Castle. Only later, as she sat alone in her darkened study looking out at the shadowed turn of earth beneath the great tree, did she wonder how Lario was aware that the cottonwood, like Cambria, was a special source of strength and peace and security for her.

Stephen kissed Rosemary's forehead, and his mustache and beard tickled her skin. "I should have insisted you get more rest, dear. Are you all right now?"

"I'm fine, Stephen. Really." Rosemary glanced through the sweep of her lashes to see how he took the loss of the baby. The tone of his words was noncommittal. She stretched out a hand, grabbing his as he turned away. "There will be other children, Stephen."

His eyes looked as empty as abandoned mines, and her heart went out to him. "Rita delivered a daughter last week," he said. "Inez Rosamaría Victoria Sanchez y Chavez."

So, Rita had named the child for her. A burden doubly difficult to bear at the moment, Rosemary reflected despondently. "How did everything go in Santa Fe?"

The black eyes seemed to gleam with life again. "Excellent, Rosemary. When Caden's term expires, he's agreed to be our delegate to Congress. And you remember that old nester down on the Wild Cat Camp—while I was at the Governor's Palace I was able to buy off the auction block his fifty head of cattle and the cabin—a ramshackle place it is."

44

Rosemary had never seen the old man but had heard often enough Stephen's damnation of the nester and the Homestead Act which threatened Cambria's land-grant rights. "Why were they on the auction block? Why didn't he sell his holdings outright?"

"His credit was overextended. And no one seemed to want to buy his holdings—so he was forced to auction."

Rosemary bit her lip. "I see."

Stephen rose to leave but halted at her bedroom door as he remembered something else. "You be recalling that young chap you traveled with on the Mail Stage?"

Rosemary nodded. "Lieutenant Raffin?"

"Aye. He's courting Caden's daughter. Louis and I were thinking—it might do well to keep the young chap in mind for a place in the party."

"You mean the Santa Fe Ring?" Stephen's brows rose in surprise, and she said, "I've heard the Ring mentioned when you and the others discuss politics."

Stephen crossed back to her bedside. His hand caught her chin gently and tilted it upward. "I dinna give you enough credit. You are unlike other women. When you are well again, Rosemary..."

Her eyes met his in acknowledgement. She owed him a son.

And as if he knew the exact day her flux had run its course, he came to her, shutting the bedroom door quietly behind him. Rosemary had not been sleeping. The intense summer heat combined with her vague unrest prevented sleep. At the sound of the door opening and closing, her lids snapped open. Stephen leaned over her and pulled the yellow eyelet coverlet from her now-slim body. "Rosemary." It was a whisper.

Obediently Rosemary raised her arms to admit her husband into her bed. Inwardly she stifled the resistance which ate at her as Stephen's hands worked impatiently at the ties of her flannel gown. His hands cupped her rounded breasts, squeezing them while his mouth devoured hers. But mercifully the foreplay lasted only seconds. Stephen maneuvered Rosemary's legs into the most conducive position for conceiving, and she knew she need endure only minutes more before Stephen would empty himself.

An invasion! her mind screamed. *A wife's duty,* she reminded herself. How many more nights—fourteen, fifteen—before she would know if she had conceived?

The following week Rita and Jiraldo visited, bringing with them their daughter, a beautiful infant, weighing already fifteen pounds at two months. Once the two women were closeted in Rosemary's office, Rosemary burst out, "Rita, do you—do you mind having to—" she twisted her hands together and paced the floor before Rita who sat contentedly in the rocker nursing her daughter.

Without someone to share her intimate thoughts with, Rosemary often felt she would dry up and whither there on that limitless prairie like the uprooted sagebrush. But now these thoughts seemed outrageous. At last she whirled on her friend. "Does it bother you having relations with Jiraldo?"

"So that's it, Rosita." Rita's broad smile turned to gentle laughter. "No, because my dear husband's body is most of the time like a wet noodle in more ways than one!"

"Oh, Rita!" Rosemary's laughter joined that of her friend's. They talked like conspirators, laughing one moment, bemoaning the fate of womankind the next.

"Have you heard, Rosita—Clara Caden, she has left her husband?"

"I knew she wasn't happy here, but..." Rosemary's voice trailed off. She could not conceive of leaving Cambria.

"*¡Si!* She went back to the United States. They say her family is of the blackblood."

Rosemary laughed. "Blueblood, you mean. Did Libby go with her mother? Stephen tells me Grant Raffin is courting her."

"That is so. And, *ay di mi,* gossip whispers that he is a very handsome man!" Then, "Your husband, Rosita, he is not a bad-looking man. But you do not enjoy his—"

Rosemary nodded, and Rita said, "At least not every night, eh?"

"Never," Rosemary admitted miserably. It was not the first time she had thought she was perhaps abnormal. "Sometimes I wonder if I truly have the instincts of a female. I feel more like a—" her hand slapped her desk—"as neuter as this block of wood, Rita!"

"*Mi amiga, mi hermana,* for you are more like a sister than a friend—what you need is to take yourself *un amado*...a lover."

Rosemary's eyes grew wide. "You have done this, Rita?"

The velvet brown eyes gleamed mischievously. "It will do wonders for your—what do you call it—female instincts."

"I could not do it."

Rita's eyes narrowed, and Rosemary hurried on. "'Tis not that I be judging you, 'tis just the manner in which I was raised, Rita. 'Tis beyond my wildest—"

"*¡Mierda!*" the older woman cursed. "Don't tell me the idea

46

has never crossed your mind, Rosemary Rhodes. Not with that Navajo *caporal* about you!"

10

Captain Grant Raffin raised his wineglass in a toast. Its ruby contents glistened in the prism lights of the chandeliers. "To the heir of Cambria," he said, inclining his head in Rosemary's direction at the table's far end. "And to the Union's glorious victory over the Confederacy."

"I concur with both," Stephen replied with a grand gesture of his own wineglass. "And to the New Year of 1862."

Only Rosemary could tell that Stephen had imbibed more than his usual. But then, she thought, he had a right to do so. Hopefully, within a week or so, his longed-for son would be born. Her hand slipped to her greatly extended stomach. This time the months of waiting had slipped by with few problems, only the discomfort which accompanied her size...waddling like a duck, no riding allowed, no sleeping on her stomach.

But confined as she was, she had been able to accomplish much more. Her ledgers were up to date, the store, with Miguel's help, doing a booming business in trading, and a small school-house, already under construction. Best though— through a letter from her uncle—she was able to persuade Stephen to breed out the churro sheep and introduce the Rambouillet, a breed of the Spanish Merino which her uncle claimed could thrive where there was little food.

Everything Rosemary did at that time seemed to work for the best, like Midas's touch. She almost wished she could stay pregnant forever. Not only did her cheeks glow with the bloom of pregnancy and her eyes and hair shine, but, to her great relief, she was once more reprieved from Stephen's nightly visits.

"The var vill never touch uz," Louis Goldman declared, and Rosemary returned her attention to the dinner. Louis swallowed another spoonful of the cherry compote, saying, "Ve got too many forts—Stanton, Marcy, Union, Craig—and now thiz Fort Sumner. The yellow Confederates vould not dare invade the Territory!"

"You had best hope not, Señor Goldman," Jiraldo said.

"If your Union troops are forced to retreat, your Trading Post will lose its contract with the government, will it not?"

Rosemary could see the trouble brewing between the Mexican and the German. "But if it comes to that, gentlemen," she interposed smoothly, "surely we will all suffer. Our sheep, our cattle, even our homes may be requisitioned—"

"And your Mexican land grants will be vorthless," Louis charged. "Vorthless as the yellowed paper they are printed on!"

"Gentlemen! Gentlemen!" Stephen interrupted and, when he had their attention, went on evenly, "Your bickering is spoiling our dinner party." His gaze moved to rest on Governor Caden's face. "Besides, I'm sure that when the governor becomes our representative in Washington, he will be seeing to it that the deeds to our land grants be properly filed and recognized. We want every possibility covered, aye, Caden?"

The elderly man tugged at his white goatee, cornered. "I shall do all I can, Stephen, to see that your interests are protected."

He would be only too happy to comply, Rosemary thought tartly, not at all sorry for the man that his wife had left him. In going over the old, musty accounts she had come across the governor's I.O.U. to Stephen in the amount of five thousand dollars. No wonder Stephen wanted the man in Washington instead of the Governor's Palace. How much more could be accomplished through the direct channels to the White House!

Rosemary had never been able to like Caden. He had the gray, oily look of soft cheese, she thought, and his daughter's baby-doll face was irritatingly stupid. Rosemary's glance slid down the length of the table to watch as Libby fluttered golden lashes at Grant, who seemed to be listening intently to what the young woman was saying.

In a way, Rosemary thought, Grant was much like Stephen. An opportunist. Already Grant seemed to have inveigled his way into the Santa Fe Ring, or the *Casa*, as Rita discreetly called it. She had heard that Grant had arrested the cowboy who had killed the Mexican probate judge...but somehow the cowboy had conveniently escaped from the fort's jail some months later. Now Grant had the appointment as captain at Fort Sumner, which was under construction on the southern edge of Cambria territory.

Grant caught her gaze on him, and his lips formed a smile that excluded everyone but her. However, his words were for the guests in general. "There will be no need to worry about confiscation of your property," he promised in a firm voice. "You have my word that not one Rebel foot shall cross into our Territory."

"Bravo!" Rita said, and her eyes flashed flirtatiously across the rim of her wineglass. She knew nothing and cared nothing for politics and the foolish war going on in the United States. But the captain, now...he was a very handsome man.

"We shall certainly rest easier, Captain Raffin," Libby said, dabbing at her small, bowlike mouth with the fine linen napkin to cover her flush.

Grant flashed each lady a reassuring smile, charming them; yet Rosemary was curious as to what Stephen thought about Grant, if he had underestimated Grant as she first had. But apparently not, or he would not have asked her to issue the officer an invitation to the New Year's dinner.

Next year, when she was no longer large with child, Stephen had promised her there would be more parties, more people, not just the intimate dinner with friends. The night before he had surprised her, coming to her bedroom just to talk with her. They had discussed small things—the feasibility of a windmill, the possibility of telegraph wires—and lightly debated the idea of improving on their cattle herds, which Stephen was against; Rosemary hoped to persuade him that cattle and sheep could feed together on the same ranges, that the sheep could eat the finer grass the cattle missed. "Mark my words, Stephen Rhodes, cattle will one day be more important in the Territory than sheep!"

Stephen, who by nature Rosemary had learned, was reserved and undemonstrative, had pulled her into his arms and laid his hand on her greatly rounded belly. "You are beautiful as you are now...carrying our son."

Rosemary had blushed in pleasure, and she blushed now with the memory of the intimate moment as her gaze sought Stephen's. He nodded discreetly. She understood. It was time for the women to withdraw.

The talk would now be centered entirely on the War Between the States. And with all tempers near the breaking point due to the uncertainty of the people's allegiance in the Territory, the table would be no place for the women.

"Rita," Rosemary said, "do you think Inez is awake yet? The women would like to see the baby."

Rosemary knew the last thing Hilda wanted to see was the Mexican baby, and she felt a small measure of guilt at the perverse satisfaction she received in baiting Louis's wife.

Although Hilda's lips folded together, Rita took the cue. "*Sí*, Rosita, it is time for her feeding."

As if a silent signal had been issued, Magdalena appeared with a tray of brandy glasses and a decanter, and the men began to draw out their cigars. The women made their way toward the double doors of the drawing room. But Rosemary heard Jiraldo demand, "And what of *los indios,* Captain Raffin? Not three weeks ago a band of Navajos raided *mi campo del sur.* Thirty head of sheep they stole! What will you do about them?"

"I have special plans for the Navajo and Apache, gentlemen," Grant replied with a calm assurance. "Even now in Washington, negotiations—"

But Magdalena closed the drawing-room doors, and Rosemary did not hear the rest, part of which would have the greatest of effects on her future.

Rita stayed with Rosemary until the child was born, five days later. It was an easy birth, and Stephen was jubilant. The child was a son, James Gallagher Rhodes.

"Your husband, Rosita, he is very good to you, is he not?" Rita asked as she watched Rosemary suckle the infant at her breast.

True, a jubilant Stephen had presented her that morning with earrings of pure gold nuggets taken from the mines at Rincon. And while the baby was given the name of Stephen's father, Stephen did suggest bestowing the middle name of Gallagher on their son; but Rosemary suspected that was an astute gesture made in tribute to his partnership with her uncle rather than out of deference to herself.

"I shall miss you, Rita," Rosemary said, avoiding answering her friend's question.

And she meant it, for Rita's vivacity kept Rosemary's loneliness at bay, stilled the emptiness that gnawed within her— an emptiness that could not be assuaged by Stephen's gifts or his intense attentions when he was not occupied by his political affairs, for he could be overwhelmingly charming when he chose to do so.

And as she thought about Stephen, it dawned on her that he would soon be directing his more intimate attentions toward her; for a healthy man like Stephen could not go long without sexual release. And Rosemary sensed Stephen was the type of man who would want a long line of children to glorify his existence and his name.

But on this point she erred. For Stephen did not deign to visit her bed as she had expected.

One morning, when Jamie was almost seven months, she

teasingly questioned Stephen about brothers and sisters for Jamie.

Stephen paused in sipping the thick, black coffee. "I have me son," he answered and went back to reading his weekly *New Mexican* newspaper.

And have his son he did, for Stephen spent every free moment with the child, pitching him in the air and roughhousing with him until Rosemary's breath caught in fright for the baby. She sensed that Stephen planned to monopolize his son; that he would exclude her from his son as much as she was excluded from his office.

She told herself she should be happy that Stephen cared so much for his son. And did she not have what she wanted—a healthy son, a husband, and a home...Cambria? In the space of less than two years she had come a long way from the penniless waif she had been.

Rosemary would repeat these blessings to herself at night, like counting sheep, to bring the escape that sleep offered. But some nights even sleep was denied her, for Jamie would wake screaming, and she would hurry to him.

Jamie awoke continually one August night, which was so hot even the thick sandstone walls could not keep out the heat. Rather than relinquish the maternal role to one of the servant girls, Rosemary herself went to the baby's side each time he awakened. For a few moments she held the small, precious form, feeling his soft breath in the hollow of her neck. "'Tis all right, my pet," she whispered as he whimpered in his sleep. She laid him back in the crib, wiping the damp auburn curls from his forehead and fanning him until he quieted.

Instead of returning to her adjoining bedroom, she padded to the kitchen on bare feet in search of the fresh water preserved in the large adobe *jarra*. From beyond the kitchen in the direction of Stephen's forbidden offices came the staccato bursts of sobs. Rosemary set aside the dipper, straining to listen for the soft recurring sound that was almost ear-piercing in the silence of the vast house.

She thought she caught the crying again and felt her way through the darkened hallway to the sound's source, Stephen's office. Light seeped from beneath one doorway. When her light knock brought no response, Rosemary opened the door.

Shock washed over her like ice-cold water. The sputtering candlelight in the wall sconce flickered on the horsehair sofa opposite the desk. The sofa's two occupants, their nude bodies

51

pale in the room's dimness, turned to stare—revealing Stephen's enraged face and Magdalena's tear-stained one.

The little girl huddled against one end of the sofa, her head hanging abjectly. Stephen sprang up. "What the bloody—"

Rosemary took a step backward from the man who snarled like a rabid dog. "You bitch—what be you sneaking about me place?" He took a step toward her, and she whirled and ran. Behind her she heard him groping for his pants, swearing vile words, the meaning of which she had not the slightest idea.

Her hands clapped over her ears to shut out the shouted curses even as her bare feet sped across the Castle's hardwood floors out onto the veranda, and down the pebbled drive. The stones ground into her feet. Somewhere behind her she heard voices. A lantern flashed in the darkness.

Driven by animal instincts, Rosemary left the wide road that wound down toward the village and struck out in the darkness across a sparsely vegetated slope. Moments later she stumbled over a greasewood bush and went sprawling in the gritty sand. She sat up, gasping. Her knee burned where she had scraped it, and her flannel gown was ripped up one side.

Then Rosemary began to become sick to her stomach. The sight of the child, naked and crying...and Stephen—dear God, her husband, what kind of man was he? She had heard whispered words about people such as he—perverted—but her own husband? And the poor child...and how many other children?

Rosemary retched, feeling as if the dry heaving of her stomach would tear her insides out. When at last there was no further churning, she crawled weakly to her knees, then her feet. Behind her every window in the Castle was alight.

Run! Run! a voice within her screamed. And once again instinct directed her steps down the slope toward the more sluggardly swing of the Pecos, where its sandbars afforded a crossing.

The rest of the night she kept her feet moving through sheer volition. One foot in front of the other. With no sleep she moved blindly across the terrain, only vaguely aware of the sharp rocks of the lava beds that bruised her feet or the juniper-covered hills that crowded in on her. Thirst ruled her tormented mind and nagged her parched throat—a thirst that blotted out everything as the torturous sun began its climb in the bright cobalt sky.

Sometime that day, when the sun seemed like a red-hot

coal pulsating just above her head, she sank to her knees. In the distance what looked like a tornado of sand, a dust devil, danced on the rim of a red mesa. *A dust storm may come,* her brain recorded numbly. *My footprints will be blotted out.* Then thickets of withered, dead-looking cactus and patches of wild pumpkin rose up to meet her as she sagged forward with the final thought—one of relief—*I will not be found.*

But she was.

11

Rosemary awoke to find black heavy-lidded eyes that regarded her inquiringly. "You are all right?" Lario asked.

She nodded. Tentatively she raised up from the blanket and rested on one elbow, her long hair spilling over one shoulder like red wine. White-plastered walls of a one-room adobe hogan encircled her. "Where am I?" It came out like a croak.

"In my home, Señora. The pueblo of my people. I brought you here this evening—out of the sandstorm."

The dust devil—it was the last thing she remembered. Rosemary's hand went to her head, only to feel the grit encrusted on her skin and scalp. "My husband—" she began, not knowing exactly how to phrase her thoughts.

"He does not know you are here." The long eyes were shuttered, revealing nothing of Lario's thoughts. He rose from where he crouched over her and said, "You are hungry. Soon we will eat. Rest."

Relief flooded Rosemary that Lario did not seem to expect an explanation from her. Indeed, it seemed he expected nothing, and she was only too willing to lay there as he moved about the room—slowly, leisurely, but with purpose.

From the firepit in the room's center drifted the mouth-watering odor of roasting mutton. The blazing piñon logs painted red shadows on the plain white walls. Above the fireplace were indented shelves where blue candles burned in their tin holders. Her gaze strayed upward to fasten on the cinnamon-colored shafts of pine which held up the low ceiling. These *vigas* carried with them the memory of forests—Irish forests—and Rosemary shut her eyes. Ireland. She should have stayed there. She had been foolishly willful to come to a strange country, to a strange man, and hope to make a home.

Stephen with Magdalena. My God, the girl was only ten! No wonder so many children came and went in the Castle, both boys and girls. Rosemary recalled the strange look she had often caught in the children's eyes. She had thought it merely the aloof attitude of Mexican and Indian children...but it had been the haunted look of fear and confusion. Why had she been so blind to what was going on in her own home?

Rosemary opened her eyes to find Lario standing above her, watching. "You knew?" she asked.

He hunkered down and spread another blanket over her. "It gets cold at night this high up."

"You knew!" she accused this time.

"Should I have told you, Señora—that your husband likes children?"

"Why—why do they stay?"

Lario shrugged. "Hunger. Shelter. Their parents owe money. There are many reasons."

He rose before she could ask more and went to kneel at the fire. When he returned to squat before her, he had a bowl in his hands. Wordlessly he spoon-fed her as if she were a child. The mutton was delicious. When she finished the last bite, he stood up. "I will stay the night in my mother's lodge," he said as he crossed to the *jarra* and filled a gourd with water. "You will be safe here."

"You aren't going to take me back?"

He knelt at her side and offered her the gourd, saying, "That is for you to decide, Señora."

Over the gourd's rim her eyes challenged him. "And if I don't want to go back—what will you tell my husband?"

Lario smiled. "That the Señora could not be found."

Just where would she go, she wondered after Lario had left the hogan. She could return to Ireland. Stephen's gift, her golden earrings, would buy her passage back there. She could never return to her aunt's dominion, but perhaps she could support herself as a tutor or governess.

But what about Jamie? Rosemary knew she could not give him up...and she knew Stephen would never let her leave with the baby. But did she really want to leave? She had come to love the land. The wildness of it. Cambria! Its exotic beauty. Its dangerous nature. She sensed Ireland would be boring after life in the New Mexico Territory.

And yet she could never let Stephen touch her again. The very sight of those freckled hands would repulse her now. To even be in the same room with him would be revolting to her. But to look forward to a life that stretched on in emptiness....

Rosemary could find no answer. She tossed beneath the blankets throughout the night. There was the rattle of the wind like sleet upon the dead leaves of the tree-branch roof to keep her company, to echo her confused thoughts.

When morning came, Toysei was at the hogan's door with a bowl of cornmush for Rosemary's breakfast. Behind Toysei Adala hung back like a shy doe. The girl had delicate brown skin with soft, brown, long-lashed eyes. "Lario is in the mountains with his brothers," Toysei said without preamble. "He will return tonight." Then the two young women were gone.

The dust storm grew worse that day, yet a surge of restlessness agitated Rosemary into escaping the hogan where she was plagued by thoughts of Lario. The sight of his possessions—an anvil to one side of the doorway, his bedroll on the other, the leather vest on the wall peg—distracted her from the decision she must make.

Muffled in the Indian blanket which she kept drawn up over her mouth and nose, Rosemary left the hogan to walk under the aged, wind-distorted cottonwoods. She followed the wagon-rutted path that led downward to the plateau rather than upward where she might encounter Lario or his brothers.

The air, shimmering with the turbid pink light of the storm, was a moving tapestry of sand. The longer Rosemary walked, the greater blew the sand and wind. She lifted her face to its blast, as if the sand would cleanse away the shame and horror of the day before.

Eventually the storm's intensity grew so great that it was impossible for Rosemary to see where she walked. The thought that any moment she might wander from the trail and plunge into some gashed canyon snapped her out of her cataleptic state. She halted and, like a bat without the aid of sight, tried to sense something solid near her to protect her from the wind's blast—a boulder, a gully, a ridge.

The sand stung her face and clogged the air so that breathing was an effort. Panic pricked her. She whirled about, uncertain now of which direction she had come. It was nigh impossible to stand erect. When the wind whipped the blanket from her, she crouched and shielded her nearly nude body from the sand's onslaught. "Lario!" She could barely hear her own voice above the roar of the wind. "Lario!"

Suddenly she was engulfed in blackness and lifted, to be thrown roughly across something hard that knocked the breath from her. Stunned, some seconds passed before she realized she was wrapped once more in a scratchy blanket and slung across the saddle of a mule or horse. She struggled and a hand swatted her behind. *"Dulce!"*

Rosemary recognized Lario's soft, low voice and stiffened indignantly.

At last the animal came to a halt, and she felt herself lifted again and deposited on the hard ground. She fought her way out of the blanket to see the rocky ledge that protruded above her and on both sides, forming a shallow cave. Not two yards away Lario tied his chestnut stallion to a growth of juniper that hedged the sheer walls. He turned to her. Impatience crowded in upon his normally uninflected voice.

"You are a fool!" he said, and Rosemary knew he was not only talking about her folly in leaving the hogan. She had willfully closed her eyes to the truth about the kind of man Stephen was. But pride kept her from acknowledging to Lario that greed for the house, the land—for Cambria—had brought her to this. "How did you find me?" she asked, averting her eyes from his angry, penetrating glare.

In the small rock-walled enclosure Lario sat, next to her but not touching, his ankles crossed. "Adala told me what direction you had taken. My horse kept me on the path."

For a while the two of them, isolated as if they were in a ship's cabin on the ocean with the great waves crashing about it, listened to the wind's shriek. But Lario's dispassionate silence began to unnerve Rosemary, whose emotions already had been strained to raveled threads.

She hugged her knees, silently telling herself she was skittish merely because she did not like the man with her. It was only natural she should feel that way about him after losing her family to Indian revolutionists. What mattered the continent...an Indian was an Indian. True, Lario was cleaner than most Indians she had come in contact with and perhaps better educated; but nevertheless, he thought like an Indian—and that was enough to make her abhor his presence.

Yet the silence became so intense that it seemed louder than the wind that raged outside, and Rosemary, forced now to acknowledge the other's presence, blurted out the first thing that came into her head. "The pretty girl with your sister—Adala—are you two to marry?"

"It is so arranged by our parents."

Rosemary recognized that whatever questions she asked of Lario, she would learn little from his answers and would have to be content with what he wished her to know. Suddenly

56

it came to her that he probably disliked her as much as she did him; that he, incredible as it seemed to her, possibly felt she was beneath his disdain. And at that, she smiled, relaxing her emotional defense ever so slightly.

"How long will it last—the sandstorm?" she asked.

If Lario were surprised by the almost pleasant, conversational tone of her voice, he gave no indication. "By morning it should blow itself out." He rolled to his stomach, stretching out as far as the confining space would allow, and rested his forehead on his arms. His shirtsleeve muffled his voice. "You will need to rest. We will leave early for Cambria."

"What makes you think I have decided to return?"

"Because you are a practical woman, Señora—or else you would not have come so far for a man you did not know."

"You mean because love was not involved? Then are you not also a practical person?" she challenged. "Marrying because your parents made an arrangement—instead of marrying for love?"

His dark gaze swung up to hers, its arrow thrust pinning her where she sat. "And what makes you think I am not?"

"Well, I thought—" Rosemary tore her gaze from his and fixed her eyes on the red-pink bleakness without. "I'm sorry— I did not mean to become personal."

"Why, Señora? Are you afraid of becoming too personal with the lowly Indian?" he derided. "Give the animals a few scraps, and you've done your good deed!"

He remembered the few times he had watched her descend from the Castle, a basket of fruit or knitted clothing on her arm. He had watched the way she moved—tall, slender, graceful as the catamount—and as wary and aloof. And he had hated her for it—for her impersonal charity.

"That's not true!"

Lario shrugged, and Rosemary knew he did not accept her answer. When he laid his forehead on his crossed arms to sleep, she was caught short at the sense of rejection she felt.

As the night approached and grew colder, Rosemary huddled within Lario's blanket, shivering. She knew he must be as cold or colder. Yet she hesitated in awakening him.

Had fear and conditioning made her truly the hard and impersonal woman he had described? Had it prejudiced her?

Softly she crawled to him and stretched out beside his long frame, spreading the blanket over both of them. But the cold of the rock beneath continued to seep through her tattered gown to chill her.

Then Lario startled her by turning over and drawing her into the warm cocoon of his arms. At her resistance he said,

"I will not hurt you, Señora." Then, "I wondered when the cold would overcome your fear."

Rosemary heard the amusement in his voice. "I am *not* afraid," she began but broke off her angry flow of words. "Aye, you're right, Lario," she said more slowly. In the night's darkness, where his all-knowing eyes were hidden from her, her admission was made easier. "I am afraid, and I don't know why...because you have been nothing but courteous."

His voice was muffled in her hair. "Maybe you are afraid, Señora...of being a woman."

Rosemary's breath caught, and Lario continued softly, "I would do nothing that you did not want...for then I would find no pleasure."

Pleasure. The word taunted her. Did such a word exist in the realm of the woman's sexuality? Even the word "sexuality" was taboo in a woman's vocabulary, and Rosemary shuddered at her forbidden thoughts. I must try to sleep, she told herself.

But the steady, strong beat of Lario's heart against her cheek, the enveloping warmth that acted as a narcotic, the masculine smell of leather and woodsmoke—these assaulted her senses. Her breath quickened. Her stomach knotted as if she had been running. She felt lightheaded, yet she knew she could not ignore the pleasurable sensations that prickled her skin.

Shame at her desire washed over her, and she was glad that Lario could not see the furious blush that made her uncomfortably warm. Still, as the seconds raced by, she could not suppress the yearning that waxed ever stronger, burning into her groin like a branding iron. She was painfully aware of Lario as a man in every separate nerve of her body. Her body rigidified, stiff as an icicle and as brittle, so that she thought she would surely shatter if he touched her.

Lario's fingers came up to cup her chin and tilt it upward, and she quivered violently at his touch. Her heart beat heavily, like a canary's throat. "You are curious?" In the dimness lights danced mockingly in his eyes.

Feeling as shy as the virgin she had once been, Rosemary nodded. She did not know what to expect, whether he would kiss her first or take her immediately, purging her of this terrible urgency that gripped her.

But he did neither. He pulled her close to him, so that the two of them molded, and pressed her head into the hollow of his neck. Slowly, gently, his free hand caressed the smooth indentation of her backbone. The blanket fell away. He whispered something against her ear that was not Spanish, and

58

Rosemary trembled at the implied sensuousness. His warm, sure hands stroked her shoulders, her arms, even the palms of her hands as if every particle of her were as precious as the white man's gold. And slowly she felt the bow-string tautness ease from her.

The wind howled about them, drowning out everything but the desire that crescendoed between them. Then Lario pulled away from Rosemary, and she at once felt bereft. "If you want to change your mind, do it now." His voice was husky, almost angry.

How could she think, she wondered feverishly, when he was so close to her? Lario's presence completely consumed her. His beautiful long-lashed eyes, the harsh planes of his face, the gentle-firm lips, and the wondrously hard, lean body. Once more she could only nod in response.

One hand came up to touch her breast, brushing it as lightly as a feather; the other explored her curves and hollows through the thick yellow gown. When his fingers began to loose its buttons and hooks, Rosemary shivered with the dread of past experience. "Lario," she whispered and knew she was stalling, "kiss me...please."

Lario stiffened. The touching of the lips, the invasion of the mouth, was a custom of the Anglo. His last year at the Mormon missionary's school, the year he was fourteen, the daughter of a wealthy hidalgo had initiated him into the rites of manhood. He had been both frightened and excited, as was the Anglo woman who lay beneath him now, but most of all he had been revulsed by the Spanish girl's lizardlike tongue, had known the cloying sense of strangulation. He asked himself what he was doing with this haughty Anglo woman. What he was about to begin could only invite trouble. Not only was she not of the *Dine'é,* she belonged to Rhodes, his enemy.

And yet he wanted her, had wanted her from that first meeting on the boardwalk in San Antonio, when the sun had emblazoned her hair, and the catlike, turquoise eyes had flashed at him with both contempt and fear. He had known other women, both of the *Dine'é* and the Spanish, and yet there was a magic, a Nightmagic, about this slender woman that could not be denied nor explained. And it was not solely because she was different, because she was white.

He only knew he wanted her.

Later he would purify himself, cleanse himself of her, in the sweatlodge. But now...

Gently his mouth came down over hers, touching her lips like butterfly wings, then possessing them as his tongue

59

searched her mouth, giving and receiving. To her dismay, Rosemary realized she was returning his kiss. Slowly her arms went up to encircle Lario's neck. He kissed her hair and eyelids, the smallpox mark on her cheek, and the pulse that beat in the hollow of her throat.

Then he eased her arms from around his neck, even as he continued to kiss her, and she felt the nightgown, the last wall of her defense slip from her. His lips touched her nipples, his tongue teasing them to peaks, and Rosemary shook under the gentleness of his passion and the deliberation of his love-making. When his fingers slipped down to caress the silken skin of her inner thighs, she tensed.

"No, *carina*," he said softly.

Suddenly she was tired of waiting. "Lario..."she moaned. And she felt the hardness of him as he moved up over her body. Instinctively she fitted her movements to the slow measured cadence of his.

They moved together—inexorably—toward a point that seemed to span a lifetime, and as the unbearable pleasure surged through her she wanted it to last forever and clutched at Lario as orgasmic tremors wracked her body and too quickly receded.

12

Lario leaned from the saddle to draw the young woman up before him. He saw the compressed lips that only that morning had willingly offered him their warmth. Was she once again reverting to the grand lady of Cambria?

Mentally he shrugged. It was no more than he had expected. He had played the part of the stag for her. And yet he had to admit she had surprised him through the duration of the one night. There had been no false reserve that he had encountered among some of the women of the *Dine'é*, nor the dignified façade that had masked the wantonness of the Spanish women who, he surmised, had been intrigued by his race.

No, the young woman had behaved differently. Something in him had responded to her spirit. She had reached beyond the needs of his body—and it disturbed him. He was angry that he should feel anything for the Anglo woman...and angry that he should feel the old hurt at the white man's disdain.

Enui—it was well she was returning, as he had known she would. He had seen the light in her eye at the mention of her son. And he had sensed in her the need for her home—for the land, as if she drew her strength from it even as he did.

When she pulled away at contact with him, he said harshly, "You can tell your husband the dust storm delayed our return."

Rosemary sat rigidly astride the horse, keeping her eyes on the horizon before her. The wind had fallen at sunrise, and the air had cleared to a crystal sharpness. "So much sky," she murmured, then as if coming back to the present, turned her head so that she could see Lario's smoky black eyes. "Don't be judging me," she said, her voice as harsh as his. "You know only what you see and hear—and that is not enough!"

Their anger was their defense. "I know what kind of woman barters her body for a house."

"And what kind of man tries to be something he's not?" she snapped. "No man at all!"

Rosemary could feel the anger rising off Lario like heat off a curling iron, and she was half afraid he might kill her then and half hopeful he would. She saw no way out of the whirlpooling dilemma.

She knew she should be weighted down with shame. She had sinned in adultery. Yet the people of that primitive, virginal land could condone that, she knew. For life in the Territory was lived on increments of dangerous seconds, plateaus of higher, sustained emotions where nothing was more important than surviving the next moment . . . and everything was important—from the overpowering fragrance of the pink verbena strewn like a huge rug over the desert in spring to the solace offered by another human. As long as that solace was not sought with an Indian. For that was admitting the Indian as a person with feeling . . . and that was forbidden.

And to love Lario was forbidden. Not just by her own race, but even by himself. His beautiful lips that fascinated her so had offered no words of love, only a temporary haven from the world to which she had to return.

Rosemary steeled herself to face Stephen. Sitting on the stallion before Lario, she rode down the street of Cambria's village, her chin held high. Tentative smiles mixed with curious stares greeted her. When Lario halted his Arab before

61

the veranda steps, she slipped down off the horse and went into the house without a last look or parting word.

She went directly to Stephen's office, not even stopping to wash up or repair her gown, which revealed one long leg and the curve of one breast. Stephen looked up when she entered and slowly raised the whiskey glass to his lips to give himself time to digest the sight of the woman who stood so rebelliously before him. The proud tilt of her chin, the tumbled hair, the blazing eyes. He opened his mouth to speak, and she said, "Don't make excuses to me, Stephen. I am not interested."

He'd be damned if he'd let her make him feel guilty, and he forgot whatever flash of beauty he had seen exposed in that one moment. "Not making any excuses, my dear." He rose and came around his desk to stand before her. Now he saw only a dirty and tired woman. His breath was foul with the whiskey as he sneered into her face. "Understand me now, Rosemary. 'Tis marrying you I did for one reason only—to breed! You're a prize ewe or heifer I be ordering for breeding—to produce a line of pure Anglo blood to rule Cambria. Nothing more!"

Rosemary turned away and went to stand at the window that looked out on the gristmill Stephen was having built. But she saw nothing. She longed only to flee, to clap her hands over her ears and escape the cutting words. Just as she had longed to cry out *No!* to every mile that had brought her closer to Cambria...to turn to Lario and beg him let her stay with him in his pueblo. But fear and pride and so many other things forbade her. It was not she whom Lario wanted. And Rosemary saw again the lovely dark eyes of Adala.

No, her home was there at Cambria. It was the only home she had, and she would not relinquish it. No more than she could relinquish her son. Her words were brisk when she turned back to Stephen. "With Jamie you have your dynasty. I only request—nay, demand—two things. Leave me alone...and leave the children alone. There will be no more children as servants in the Castle!"

The whiskey glass shattered against the wood-paneled wall only a fraction from her head. "You dare dictate terms to me!" he roared.

"I dare and I do!" Rosemary advanced on Stephen with clenched fists. "Because, for one, you will want no tales that Stephen Rhodes's wife forsook him to besmirch our son's inheritance."

Stephen's blunt hands came up to grab Rosemary about her neck. "I could easily silence any tales—"

"About your perverted cavorting?" She laughed and shoved his hands from her. "Like all tyrants, Stephen, you are a man of great imagination. And like all tyrants you tend to overlook the small things—but 'tis those small things that can collapse an empire. I keep your accounts, Stephen. Remember?"

It had taken Rosemary only a few months of going through the books to derive a clear picture of Stephen's finances. In effect he had a mortgage on everything in Cambria. By simply demanding payment of the debts on his books he could take every ranch and waterhole and every head of stock within two hundred miles. But there was not enough cash market for anything. And any concerted effort on his creditors, namely her uncle and a few others, could force Stephen to sell his holdings, drive him out of his kingdom, Cambria.

"My uncle, Stephen, is an astute man. My untimely death might precipitate his financial backing to be withdrawn. If he were able to persuade the rest of your creditors to follow suit..." She let her words trail off, hoping Stephen would accept her bluff.

She could only count on the fact that Stephen, though he could never love Cambria as she did, wanted it just as greatly. For him Cambria was a symbol of the power and wealth he had coveted as a child of the mines.

Stephen's jaws clenched, and his eyes blazed, but his words were deadly calm. "I be wanting a loving wife and mother for Cambria—at least as far as the outside world is concerned. If ever it appears otherwise, then you be worthless to me."

Rosemary understood all too well. "Then we are in agreement."

Over the next few weeks Rosemary tried to ignore whatever thoughts she had of Lario. She would not let herself admit to shame or guilt. Yet whenever she happened to see him, a hot flush would rush to her skin. She remembered too vividly the warm touch of copper skin beneath her fingers, the corded hardness of his hips and thighs, and the dark eyes that made love to her as passionately as did his gentle, knowing hands.

Those few times she did see him—when he came to the Castle on business or she passed him on her daily visits to the now-completed one-room schoolhouse—his eyes gazed at her in a strictly impersonal manner, as if the two of them had never come together in an intimate act of nature.

Once, when she had stopped by the store to return the ledgers, she gathered her courage and asked Miguel what he knew of Lario. The old man paused in shelving the adzes she

63

had ordered. He squinted his rheumy eyes and scratched at his thatch of white hair. "That one, Lario, I remember more than the others. He is of the Tahtchini Navajos. When the DeVegas had the land—I was younger then, Señora, and more patient—the *niños* used to come here for candy sticks. All but Lario. He would stand and watch, but when I held out a stick for him—that one would stubbornly shake his head. But I could see the hunger for the *dulce* in those black eyes of his."

"Where is Lario's father?"

Miguel made the sign of the cross. "One day when Lario was maybe four, he was in the fields with his father when *los Rurales Mexicanos*—lawless Mexican soldiers they were— tried to take him to sell in Saltillo. When the father attempted to stop them, they killed him, but that Lario escaped through the tall grass."

The old man shrugged. "After that, I do not know, Señora. Some say a Man of God took Lario with him to a place called Ramah. When Lario Santiago returned, he was the man you see now."

Miguel's grandson scampered into the store, ending the conversation between the two adults with his raucous, whistling imitation of a cottonwood dove. Rosemary tousled Pedro's thick hair and thanked Miguel before leaving.

She felt she knew little more about Lario than before.

13

Rosemary now hired all the house servants, mostly men and women from the village and Pedro along with a few other Mexican boys. Stephen never acknowledged her existence unless they entertained, which was now not as often, as he spent more and more time in Santa Fe forging his political ties.

He was, however, always polite and unfailingly courteous to her, whether they had as a guest only one old codgery prospector who chanced upon the Castle in his wanderings, or fifteen tired, rough, trail riders.

For the Mexican celebrations of All Saints' and All Souls' Days of the thirty-first of October and the first of November, Stephen did suggest a small dinner party. Grant came in unexpectedly from Fort Sumner that afternoon, and Rosemary persuaded him to stay for dinner. But the way he looked at her when she greeted him, the way his eyes followed her, made her uneasy. It was as if he were aware that she had had more than one man, as if the scarlet letter were indeed etched on her forehead.

She left him with Stephen and Jiraldo, relieved to escape his watchful gaze, and joined Rita to sit on the veranda swing and watch the two children play, for though November was already upon them, the days were unusually warm and lovely.

"I think Inez will make a good mother," Rosemary said, sipping at her fruit punch as her gaze rested on Rita's two-year-old who tried to help Jamie stand.

But Jamie, almost a year now, wanted to crawl. Shouting "Ma—Ma," he fell to his pudgy knees and began crawling toward Rosemary. She was glad Stephen was closeted with Jiraldo and Grant in his office. Too many times she had seen Stephen's dark frown when Jamie refused to walk.

"He's not yet a year!" she pointed out at these times. "Don't rush him!"

"Jiraldo and Rita's daughter walked at ten months," Stephen would counter.

"But girls mature earlier than boys, Stephen. Do not be so demanding with Jamie."

"I'll not raise a weakling. I had the roughest life possible, and 'tis a better man it made of me."

The first time Stephen had brought this up, Rosemary had turned away, incredulous that Stephen should so deem himself. After that it was all she could do to keep from sneering when their argument reached that point.

Still, she wondered if she was being too protective of her only child. Jamie was such a darling baby, soft and round, with auburn hair and hazel eyes that took in everything with such a solemn expression. It was impossible not to want to cuddle the child.

"Inez adores Jamie," Rita was saying. "Forever she pesters me to bring her to see him." The woman stopped as her daughter toddled to her and offered the little girl a sip from her glass. Beneath a cap of blue-black ringlets peered the softest brown eyes. She had inherited her father's tall, spare frame—a promise she would not run to corpulence as most Mexican women did in later years. With her gentle but awkward movements she reminded Rosemary of a fawn.

"Your daughter is so lovely," Rosemary said. "I envy you."

"And how I envy you, *mi amiga.*"

"Me?"

"*Sí,* your own beauty. You are so—willowy, I think it was Libby said once."

A rueful smile curved Rosemary's lips. "I think she meant skinny."

"And now more than ever you have *chispa,* you sparkle. Your cheeks—"

"Are lovelier than wild roses," a voice behind the two women supplied.

Rosemary turned about in her swing to see Grant standing at the door. In his blue military uniform he always looked so handsome that she found it difficult not to be swept off her feet by his continued flattery and charm—until she looked into the eyes. Blue rock.

"Why don't you join us for some sangria, Grant?" she said. Grant took a seat in one of the leather-tooled chairs, and Rosemary clapped her hands, bringing a Mexican man of forty to take her order in Spanish. He returned with a *jarra* of the native beverage and a clean glass on a silver tray, and Rosemary wondered if the tray was one of those fashioned by Lario in his spare time.

"Business brings you here?" she asked of Grant as she poured the sangria and handed him the glass.

"I had hoped to start an affair with you two lovely ladies."

Rita's hand cut through the air in a gesture of impatience. "Bah! Business and politics—they are the only two things you men know!"

Grant laughed with Rita and Rosemary, but later, when Rita went to pull a wandering Inez from her precarious perch on the hitching rail, he looked at Rosemary over the rim of his glass and said, "You've grown more beautiful."

Beautiful. Lovely. These were words Rosemary had never thought to associate with herself. And for once she believed Grant was not plying her with his customary flattery.

"One would think you're in love," he said.

Rosemary looked at him quickly before averting her eyes. "You must excuse me, Grant, but I need to check the mill. I promised Consuela I'd bring flour—"

"I'll go along with you," Grant offered easily. "I'm tired of sitting and need the exercise."

"Well—"

"Go on, Rosita," Rita said with an impish smile. "I'll watch Jamie."

Rosemary wrinkled her nose at Rita and stiffly walked around toward the rear of the Castle with an amused Grant at her side. She had no sooner stepped inside the mill's dark,

66

ool doorway when Grant caught her by the shoulders and urned her toward him. "Grant," she protested, half laughing, 'what are you doing?"

He grinned. "Be still—you know Rita approves of us."

"Don't be silly!" She could not believe he was serious. They tood in the open doorway where anyone who happened to glance in that direction would see them.

Grant's smile left his face. "I'm not being silly. You and are alike, Rosemary. We're determined and practical, and vhen we want something we don't stop until we have it."

Rosemary pressed her hands against his chest, feeling the blue wool rough against her fingertips. "Well, 'tis you who s not being very practical now! This is ridiculous!"

"That's what I'm trying to say. I'm practical about everything—but you." He pulled her to him and kissed her thoroughly, and she was not even aware of his mustache abrading her skin as her senses were rendered numb in the suffocation f his kiss.

At last she pulled away...only to look past him and see ario leading his horse to one of the corrals. His dark eyes ooked at her as if she were slime on stagnant water, and he continued on past the mill.

She wanted to pick up her hoop skirts and run after him, but she said calmly, "I told you that you were being silly, Grant." He chuckled and released her, and she moved toward he bin of flour, feeling the ache that ground against her tomach like the mill's giant roller against the grain. "Now vhy are you here?"

"To get your approval of my marriage to Libby next month."

"You have my best wishes, of course. But I don't believe is my approval that brought you here today."

Grant frowned and jammed his hands into his pockets. You're right. We've trouble. A troop of Rebels—Texas Volunteers—has taken the Mesilla Valley at Valverde. And vord has come another troop is marching toward Glorieta Pass."

Rosemary spun around, dropping the flour ladle. "Cambria—is it in danger?"

Grant noted that she had said "it," not "we." Stephen had chosen well. Sometime, if he could ever catch her alone long enough, he would like to sort out the truth to their marriage. Rumor had it she was an heiress, while some said she was a penniless member of Irish royalty.

Then there had sifted to him the gossip that summer of er sudden appearance in the village, in a torn gown and

67

wrapped in a blanket and sitting before Lario on the Indian's horse. There were speculations for that also...that she had gone walking and lost her way in a dust storm...and then there were those who said she had become angry with *el patrón*, and he could not stand to lose her and had sent Lario to bring her back. The latter sounded more accurate to Grant, for Rosemary had only to enter the room and one could see the enormous respect Stephen paid his wife. Still, there was something Grant could not quite put his finger on....

"Possibly Cambria stands in danger," he told her. "But with the Confederacy threatening to cut off the gold shipments out of New Mexico, Colorado, and California, our War Department will be beefing up the western forts. General Canby has sent for reinforcements from Colorado for Fort Union and Fort Marcy."

It was Stephen who informed Rosemary a week later how much graver the threat to Cambria had become. The Confederate forces under a Major Pyron had taken Santa Fe and were now encamped at the mouth of Apache Canyon. The congress had been forced to move their territorial capital to the Exchange Hotel in Las Vegas.

Rosemary halted in spooning the mashed apple between Jamie's rosebud lips. "Can Canby hold the Rebels?" she asked breathlessly.

"The Rebs be like the ants, Rosemary." Stephen bit off the end of a cigar and spit it into the cuspidor. "They do not stop. They just keep coming."

Jamie began to squall, and Rosemary fed him the remaining spoonfuls of fruit, but her attention was now centered wholly on Stephen. "Cambria?" she asked.

On this point, the safety of the land, she and Stephen were united. That and Jamie's welfare, although the two of them held different viewpoints as to what constituted their son's best interest.

Stephen blew a cloud of smoke, then smiled. "The Confederacy is one ant I'll crush beneath my boot. I'm taking Lario and some of his men north to Glorieta Pass. The B troops from Fort Stanton and Raffin's troops are going also. Raffin wants to be in on this as much as I do. 'Tis a CO's post he'll be assured after this bloody war is over."

Scrappers. That was what the Irish called men like Stephen and Grant. They loved a challenge, a good fight. Too bad, and Rosemary braked her thoughts. Dear God, was it wrong to want someone as malignant as Stephen to die? But who was she to judge? She, an adulteress.

"But I don't like leaving Cambria unprotected," Stephen was saying. "Perhaps I should leave Lario in charge."

"No!" Lario's presence was equally tormenting but in a different way. For the sight of him never failed to remind her that only he could slake the passion in her that his presence ignited. And this shameful knowledge made her hate both herself and Lario.

Rosemary caught Stephen's stare of surprise and hastily wiped Jamie's food-covered mouth, masking her vehemence. With his enormous ego and pride in his pure Anglo blood, Stephen would probably never conceive of the idea that she could give herself to an Indian. Nevertheless, he was a shrewd man.

"You'll need all the help you can get," she said with feigned concern. "You've told me yourself that Lario knows this country better than anyone. Cambria will be all right. Just make certain the Rebels do not get this far."

Rosemary played the dutiful wife and stood on the veranda to wave good-bye as her husband rode away with Lario and almost a hundred of Cambria's men. But it was Lario who held her gaze. Even at a distance, she could separate him from the rest of the men. The red bandana about his head, the carbine sheathed at his saddle holster, the easy way he sat on the Arab horse.

With Stephen and Lario went all her tension. She could relax her guard. Her shameful secret was safe, she thought.

14

A column of smoke penciled the western sky, and Rosemary frowned. It was hardly likely to be a forest fire. It was too far up in the mountains, above the timberline. But the cabin Stephen had leased to the old prospector was in that vicinity. Her lips tightened. The Rebels—or the Apaches?

She turned her gaze to the southwest. A dark line on the horizon loomed larger with each passing minute. Stephen had ridden out five days earlier, but she doubted the band of riders that she could not yet distinguish would be coming from that direction. She spun and went inside. From the gun cabinet in Stephen's trophy room she took the Springfield. She had no idea how to use it. But whoever was riding toward the Castle did not know that.

"Mrs. Rhodes!" a voice called out from the veranda. It belonged to Cody Strahan, a boy of no more than seventeen years who had drifted up from near the Texas border when Sibley and his Rebels had burned out his ranch.

Partly out of pity, partly out of need with all the men gone who were capable of toting a rifle, Rosemary had hired the kid. Cody was mostly legs, the long limber kind that looked like they would buckle at the knees like a jack-in-the-box when he walked. He seemed a pleasant, polite young man until one looked into the eyes...there was something that said he no longer belonged to a civilized world.

Still, Rosemary sensed he was a cool and trustworthy young man, the only one she could depend on at the moment; though he was just a boy; almost her age she reminded herself. But she felt eons older.

Rosemary shut the door of the gun cabinet, grabbed up a heavy woolen rebozo, and hurried back out onto the veranda. The house servants trailed out onto the veranda behind her.

The peach fuzz on Cody's face glistened with perspiration despite the brisk winter wind. "Indians," he whispered as the horsemen in blankets and buckskins rode into the suddenly vacant village below. "'Pears to be Apaches, ma'am."

"Es Perro Amarillo," Consuela grunted. "Yellow Dog."

"So soon?" Rosemary asked. Just that summer Stephen had told her that Lario had given the chief four ewes and a ram from the best of the Rambouillet herd, which, she thought bitterly, the chief's band had no doubt eaten.

She passed the Springfield to Cody. "Wait here." As she descended the veranda steps the wind whipped her skirts about her. She stopped at the edge of the well-trimmed grounds while the bulky figure on horseback rode out ahead of the other Apaches.

"Cuidado, Señora," Consuela called from the veranda. "Do not trust him. *¡Es un selvaje!"*

It was the first time Rosemary had seen Perro Amarillo, or Yellow Dog, as the white man called him, and he did look like a savage, dressed as he was in a dirty blanket and a black silk top hat. When he was within yards of her he halted. Sitting before him on the mustang was a small child, a boy of perhaps three.

Yellow Dog's face wore a dull, bestial expression. "Your man—where is he?"

Behind her Rosemary heard the crunch of boots as Cody came to her side. "He will be back soon," she answered. Would they attack the Castle? There were nearly twenty of them, armed with tasseled lances and sinew-backed bows. But Rosemary was reassured by the presence of Yellow Dog's son. Surely they would not attack with the boy there. "What is it you wish?"

"Guns. Knives. It is cold. We must kill more buffalo."

"I have only the guns for our people, Yellow Dog." She forced her voice to remain calm, to speak slowly. "But we have sacks of flour in the gristmill I would like to give your people."

Yellow Dog shook his head, and his braids flopped on his shoulders. "No."

Rosemary inclined her head toward Cody's, whispering something, and he turned on his heel and disappeared inside the Castle.

"You have *tiswin* for *Yellow Dog?*"

"No, I have no *tiswin.*" The last thing she needed was for the band to become drunk on corn whiskey. "But I do have this for you, Yellow Dog," and she took the white buffalo rug Cody returned with and walked forward with it stretched out over her arms for all the Apaches to see its beauty.

Her hair tingled at the nape of her neck as she drew close to Yellow Dog and his men. They could kill her easily. The terrible vision of her brother's tiny body being tossed from lance to lance flashed before her eyes, and she felt the old fear crash over her like a tidal wave. Still, she moved until she stood next to the mustang, close enough to see the face of the chief's son, and she shuddered. It was as opaque and unreadable as his father's. The stone-brown eyes looked right through her. She passed the rug up to Yellow Dog. "As a gift of our friendship."

The Indian's dirt-grooved hands held the snow-white rug for a long moment. Then he nodded. He reined his pony in sharply and turned away with the band falling in behind him.

Rosemary let out a sigh of relief. But when she reached the veranda, she found she was trembling, her legs weak. She leaned her forehead against the veranda's cedar post for support. The rough bark scratched her head. Now perspiration dotted her upper lip, and the chill wind turned the droplets to frost.

"Señora," Consuela said, "it is better that you lay down, no?"

"Here, let me give you a hand, ma'am," Cody said.

Rosemary shook her head. "No, I'll be all right. Keep an

eye on Yellow Dog." However, she accepted Consuela's stout arm and let the old woman lead her indoors out of the cold.

"I'll be fine," Rosemary murmured again as she went to stand before the fire that roared in the marbled fireplace. She stretched out her hands to clutch the mantel. "Just give me a few moments. Yellow Dog frightened me more than I realized."

Consuela looked at the slim body and taut face with its angular contours and frowned. "It is not Yellow Dog, Señora, that makes you so."

Rosemary turned from the fire's warm blaze when she heard the certainty in Consuela's voice. "What?" she asked, puzzled.

"You no can tell, Señora? You are *embarazada*."

Rosemary took a step backward. "'Tis impossible! I couldn't be pregnant! I haven't..."

Why had she not been aware of her body's changes? She had been pregnant before. Twice. Enough to realize this time. But before, she had been eagerly awaiting the indications that she was with child, and this time...

Her gaze went back to Consuela's face. And she knew that Consuela was also aware of the truth.

Sweet Jesus, Stephen would tolerate a lot for the sake of Cambria. But not a child that was not his.

Stephen leaned his head against the back of the chair and closed his eyes. Rosemary and Consuela exchanged looks. The cook nodded her head once in affirmation before trudging into the kitchen.

"I'm worn out," Stephen mumbled. "Three days it took us, but we drove those bloody bastards out of Santa Fe and all the way back down Mesilla Valley."

"And Grant?" Rosemary asked softly. "Is he all right?" She wore an off-the-shoulder dress of midnight blue satin and had her hair dressed in ringlets rather than the usual chignon. What lay before her was a distasteful, repugnant act. But it had to be done. She would not be driven from Cambria. She would not give up her home.

Stephen opened his eyes and raised the glass to his lips, swilling the whiskey quickly. "Grant carried the day at Peralta. It will earn him his major's rank for certain."

Rosemary wanted to ask about Lario for she had not seen him ride into the village with the other men, but she was afraid of arousing Stephen's suspicion. He saved her from her agony, saying, "Lario was no less daring. Several times he took chances the troopers would not. As if he did not care for

72

his safety." The last came out on Stephen's tongue with a slur, and he set the liquor from him.

Rosemary felt ill with the realization that Lario could have been killed. She wondered if he was now in the village below with some flashing, dark-eyed maiden or had returned to his pueblo and Adala. By an effort of will she forced herself to rise and walk around the table to stand behind Stephen. She put her hands on his shoulders. "Come to bed, Stephen. You're tired."

Stephen squinted up at Rosemary and shook his head, trying to shake away the alcohol's fumes that clouded his mind. The animal instincts that had enabled him to survive the coal mines as a child rose in him like the hair on a dog's neck. But the sexual urge overcame all intuitive caution. Why not take her? he thought through the haze of his drunken stupor. She wasn't so bad looking—if one was drunk enough. And he laughed aloud.

"Come'n Rosie," he said and grabbed her about the waist for support to pull himself up out of the chair. Funny, he thought, how liquor could get to you when you were dead tired. He did not know when he had been this drunk.

Rosemary shut her eyes and forced her rigid limbs to relax as Stephen fumbled at the buttons of his pants. She heard his erratic footsteps as he stumbled in the dark looking for her bed and felt the give of the feather mattress when his hands searched for her body. "Here," she whispered, for once instructing him.

"Ridin' you not so bad, Rosie." His breath quickened, and he increased the tempo of his movements so that within moments he fell limply across her, panting. "Not so bad," he mumbled. "Not so bad."

When Stephen's staccato snorts of sleep reached through to Rosemary's self-induced trance, she cautiously slid from beneath the heavy weight of Stephen's right side. His sour breath assailed her, and she turned her face away and closed her eyes...only to find the black eyes of another face painted on the canvas of her mind.

Grant stood much too close, the passion of his face exposed to anyone who looked for it. Rosemary cast a surreptitious glance at Libby, but the young wife, ballooning in the first months of her own pregnancy, seemed not to notice. She sat on one of the benches that lined Fort Sumner's mess hall, which was now cleared of its long tables, and talked desultorily with the wife of Lieutenant Colonel Kit Carson, Josepha of the rich Jaramillo family.

"You're not listening to what I'm saying, Rosemary," Grant whispered at her ear.

"What?" she asked distractedly. Her foot tapped with the fiddler's rapid rendition of the "Pigeon Wing." She longed to join the reel in progress, but the idea of a pregnant woman dancing was scandalous. She did not know why she even bothered to make the full day's trip for the fort's valentine party; and yet that was not entirely true.

During the day's journey she had been able to catch glimpses of Lario when he returned to the buckboard to discuss with Stephen the terrain ahead or the next halt for water and rest. Hungrily her eyes devoured his lean frame and caressed the sinewy muscles of his shoulders. If Lario had not made the journey at Colonel Carson's request, she doubted if she would have gone.

"I said," Grant repeated with some exasperation, "that if I did not know better, I would accuse you of having a lover."

Rosemary's gaze flew upward to Grant's handsome face. Was he only joking? "I do," she said lightly. "My husband. We're expecting a child also, Grant." Indelicate to tell a man of such a condition but necessary at this point, Rosemary told herself. "In four months."

Three months to be more exact, she thought. Thank goodness she was tall and carried the baby low. She was still small, though the tightly laced stays were cutting into her ribs.

Grant covered his surprise, saying, "That explains the sparkle in your eyes. You're positively radiant."

Rosemary wanted to change the dangerous subject. "That little man who just walked outside with Lario and Stephen— is he the famous Kit Carson?"

A smile twitched Grant's mustache at her obvious ploy. "The same. With the withdrawal of the Union troops back to the battlefronts in the East, the Indian attacks have increased, and Carson's been ordered by General James Carleton to take the New Mexico Volunteers and put a halt to these attacks."

Rosemary shivered, remembering the old prospector that Lario had brought in the week after Yellow Dog's visit. The old man dangled over the back of Lario's Arab, his mangled head already covered with maggots.

"Come along," Grant said, his hand taking her arm possessively. "I'll introduce you."

The three men stood in the center of the fort's parade grounds. Stephen was pointing out the new barracks, the hospital, and the ice house. "I have been explaining to Colonel

74

Carson," Stephen said when Grant and Rosemary joined them, "that the fort will make an excellent reservation post. I've arranged with the Secretary of the Interior to lease our land that surrounds the fort to the government."

So Stephen was turning another penny, Rosemary thought sourly. She looked at Lario who hunkered on one knee, calmly smoking. The cigarette's flare lit his inscrutable face. "What reservation are you talking about?" she asked, making a half-hearted attempt to be sociable.

"You must realize, Mrs. Rhodes," Kit Carson said, and she found it odd that this fearless man had such a high-pitched voice, "that the War Department's withdrawal of troops from the Territory is, from the Apache and Navajo point of view, a victory. They reason that the white soldiers have given up and retreated to their own country. No white man will be safe until every Apache and Navajo Indian is patrolled on the reservation. Captain Raffin here will be in charge of the reservation, ma'am."

Rosemary looked around her, recalling the barren, flat land that stretched outside the fort and finding it difficult to believe the government wanted people to live there. Her gaze halted on Grant. Another feather for his cap, she thought, but the mention of Lario's name drew her eyes back to his dark face. She wished she could read his thoughts or that he would say something, but he only waited patiently as Kit Carson continued.

"I've been hoping to persuade Lario Santiago to convince his Navajo people there are advantages to living here on the Bosque Redondo Reservation. Raffin has here a clinic, and the fort'll soon have a doctor. The Bureau of Indian Affairs is having built a trader's post just outside the fort to distribute to the Indians beef and flour, and they will be taught to farm."

Kit squatted down now to face Lario. The old scout's keen eyes in the seamed face glowed intently. "Your people must understand that warfare will solve nothing."

Lario's voice was soft but firm. *"Naat'aani,"* he said, using the Navajo form of address for headman, "my people, the *Dine'é,* and the Apache, they are not farmers, *Naat'aani.* They are shepherds and herdsmen. They would not like being tied down like a hobbled horse. They would die. But I will talk with the Navajo *Naat'aani*—Manuelito."

"Tell your chiefs also," Grant said, the dislike he had for Lario showing in his eyes, "that if they do not come peacefully, every man, woman, and child found off the reservation will be shot. All your pueblos' food supplies will be destroyed—as will your race. These are orders from General Carleton."

75

Lario rose. His black eyes rested only a fraction of a second on Rosemary before his burning gaze went to meet that of Grant's. "Maybe much blood will flow before you are finished."

"I hope you can help to avoid that," Kit said.

In the moonlight the scout's silvery hair was as light as Lario's was dark. But the blue eyes of the scout and the black eyes of the Indian were both filled with unfathomable sadness.

15

Rosemary looked down at the fuzzy red head of hair that nuzzled at her breast, tugging so hard that the nipple hurt with the flow of milk. A great love for the child coursed through her. The baby was a tenacious thing, weighing less than five pounds at birth, but squalling mad, refusing to give up its birthright in its fight to survive.

Rosemary had immediately named her daughter Stephanie lest there be any doubt as to the infant's paternity. The child had her bright red hair, but her eyes were as black as Stephen's. Their almond shape, slightly tilted at the corners, gave an indication of her true heritage only to the most suspect observer.

"She *is* beautiful, isn't she?" Rosemary murmured, and Consuela, who had served once more as midwife, nodded in agreement. In her devotion to *la patrona,* her mistress, her wise eyes never betrayed what they both knew.

According to everyone's calculations, except for those of the two women, the baby came three weeks early. Stephen, therefore, was still in Santa Fe. Had he been at Cambria at the time of Stephanie's birth, Rosemary doubted he would have shown any marked interest. He had his son.

And Lario? Was he aware that another child had been born in the Castle? Probably not, she thought. And most certainly he did not know it was his child. For should he learn the truth she had no misgivings that, as fond of children as the Navajo were, Lario would never permit her to keep the child in Stephen's household.

But on that point she need not worry, for Lario was still in the western part of the New Mexican Territory, which had been severely reduced in size now that a portion of it had been made into the Territory of Arizona. Whether Lario was succeeding at his peace mission was debatable. According to *The Las Vegas Gazette,* a Navajo chieftain, Barboncito, was credited with the robbery of several stages and the destruction at Raton of the "iron street," as the superstitious Navajo called the railroad line.

Stephen was furious; for her husband, always the entrepreneur, had invested heavily in the Atchison, Topeka and Santa Fe Railroad which, if completed, would create a new aristocracy from the wealth it would engender.

At Stephanie's birth Stephen had been in Santa Fe trying to negotiate with representatives from Washington to buy portions of the checkerboard plots of land on either side of the railroad that were to be sold once the War Between the States ended, as everyone felt it would surely end soon. That month, April of 1863, marked the war's second anniversary.

When Stephanie was not quite three months old, Rita traveled to see the child, cheering Rosemary with the latest gossip. "I am sure Esteban will tell you when he returns from Santa Fe," she said after Consuela left the room, "but it is said that Congress has again refused to grant our Territory stateship."

Rosemary laughed. "Statehood, you mean."

"*Sí.* Because we have slaves it is said." Rita tapped her foot angrily. "The peons—how would they live, what would they eat, if we did not take care of them?"

The question of the debt peonage seemed a vicious cycle to Rosemary, who as a child had three servants at her disposal, yet she was not quite certain what better arrangement could be found.

"I thought you did not like to discuss politics, Rita," she said in an effort to turn the subject in another direction.

"I was getting to that." Rita put a fingertip to her pink lips as if trying to recall, but the ends of her mouth curved upward in spite of her mock seriousness. "Ahh, *sí!* Now I recall. With a month still to go before the baby comes Libby Raffin has put on much weight. And Grant has sent her back to Santa Fe to have the care of a good doctor."

Rosemary had heard nothing from Fort Sumner since her visit there in February, but she had supposed that Grant was occupied trying to keep the rebelling Navajo and Apache in check. She tickled Stephanie under the chin to wake her and get her to finish nursing. "Your eyes are too bright, Rita. That is not all, is it?"

Rita chuckled. "It is said that when Grant comes to visit her, he also visits his mistress—none other than Doña Lura

Armadeo! Imagine, she must have at least forty-five or fifty years, Rosita!"

The notorious Lura! She was reputed to have been the mistress of the first Territorial governor. She was noted as a gambler and kept a large gaming house. Rosemary could only envy the woman who defied society's opinion to live her life the way she wanted.

Jamie came toddling through the office doorway as fast as his little legs would carry him with Inez chasing behind. "Mama!" he cried. "Mama!" He came to a halt before Rosemary. His lips quivered when he saw she held the small thing again. His mother was his refuge, and his spot was threatened.

Rosemary looked down at the large eyes whose lashes were spiked with tears and understood at once. She loved her firstborn dearly and wondered if she would ever feel as close to her daughter as she did to him. She handed Stephanie over to Rita, who tried to quiet the baby's enraged cries at being taken from its source of nourishment.

"Come here, pet," Rosemary said and stretched out her arms to engulf the little boy who threw himself in her lap. "Shall we go for a picnic today?"

Jamie enjoyed this most of all, but the delightful trips into the foothills to search for pretty bright stones after lunch were no longer taken. Not only did Cambria's inhabitants have Indian attacks to fear, but reports reached them that, increasingly, Mexican bandidos from south of the border and the lawless Comancheros were also taking advantage of the soldiers' absence from the forts.

"We'll picnic beneath the shady cottonwood, and you can throw rocks in the river and watch them splash," Rosemary said.

Jamie's hazel eyes, which had inherited her long thick lashes, lit up. "*Sí, sí,* mama!"

Rosemary smiled and hugged the little round body. "'Tis raising a bilingual child I am, Rita."

"This I should hope, Señora Rhodes! Jamie shall have a very difficult time being governor, no, if he does not speak the Spanish?"

Rita was gently poking fun at Stephen's plan that his son would go to law school in the East and return to govern the Territory, or state, as everyone hoped it would soon be. Yet Rosemary knew Rita was technically right, for the legislature in Santa Fe was carried on primarily in Spanish. Even official documents were still recorded in Spanish, although English records of transactions were now a requisite.

It was a perfect day for a picnic with a light breeze to rustle the pungent cottonwood leaves warmed by the July sun. Consuela's lemonade and cornbread baked with squash seeds and topped with honey went untouched for almost an hour as the two women and children laughed and tumbled and talked. Rosemary could almost forget the tiny mound on the far side of the cottonwood. There was only a small stone slab to indicate that there had been a previous child.

Both she and Rita laughed at how Stephanie drew in her breath each time the unfamiliar sensation of the wind played across the baby's skin. Jamie and Inez, whose serene beauty grew more evident each day though only a child of three, chased the butterfly that swooped down to rest on the field of wild hyacinth that painted the knoll. *Palomas,* or doves, sang in the tree's branches above them.

But the pleasure of the afternoon was soon spoiled for Rosemary at the sight of Stephen riding up the drive from the village. There was something even about the way he sat on his bay that suggested the man's certainty of his power. With him rode Cody, who in Lario's absence served as *caporal,* though he was rather young and inexperienced to handle the workings of such a tremendous enterprise as the Cambria Ranch.

Cody, Rosemary was glad to see, but not the Mexican who rode on Stephen's right. Ignacio was a fat sluggard she absolutely loathed and was happy that Stephen kept the man with him in Santa Fe most of the time. At least Stephen left her alone, but she had the distinct feeling that Ignacio would not should the situation arise to his advantage.

With only the barest greeting to herself and a polite *"Buenos días"* to Rita, Stephen dismounted and swept up Jamie who immediately stiffened in the gruff embrace. "Tickle. Tickle," he said of Stephen's mustache and tried to squirm out of his father's arms. But Stephen sat the boy astride his large bay stallion. "We'll ride back to the house," he told Rosemary.

She saw the fear leap in Jamie's eyes. "Let him finish his lunch, Stephen."

"Lunch with a passel of women!" her husband said and grinned proudly at his son. "Hell, no! Right, Jamie? We be having men's things to do!"

He swung up behind his son. The bay began to dance, and at once Jamie's little face screwed up, and he started to cry.

"Stephen, put him down! You know he doesn't like horses."

Stephen's furious gaze hit Rosemary like a fist. "I'll not have you raising a sissy. Don't ever be telling me what to do
79

with me son." His glare took in the bits of grass in her messed hair and the twill skirt, which without the support of hoops, clung to her curves, and he suddenly wanted her. "I see I shall have to stay home more."

He brought his quirt down across the bay's rump, and the horse shot forward. Rosemary could hear the cries of her son even though the churned-up dust now obscured the riders. It was the first time Stephen had ever shown disrespect in public, and Cody directed a curious look at Rosemary before reluctantly following Stephen and Ignacio.

"I'm sorry," she told Rita, who tried to cover her embarrassment by lowering her face to smell the clump of grass Inez held out to her like a bouquet of flowers.

"Ni modo, mi amiga. It's all right."

But it was not all right. Neither for Jamie nor Rosemary. Stephen was home again to make their lives miserable. Stephanie he flatly ignored, though there would be a time when the little minx would not allow it.

However, Stephanie did serve Stephen's purpose only a few days later when Yellow Dog and some of his men returned for their visit. Cody rode in on a lathered horse with the news just ahead of Yellow Dog. Unfortunately Rosemary happened to be in the yard with Stephanie, letting the baby take the sun.

"Get Stephen," she told Cody and scrambled to her knees, snatching up both the pallet and a protesting Stephanie. But too soon she spotted Yellow Dog and his warriors and knew he had seen her also. She noticed that Yellow Dog's son now rode a pony of his own, though the boy could not be more than four or five.

She could not run now and let Yellow Dog see her cowardice. She held her ground as the braves approached. Where was Stephen?

Then Stephen was there, brushing past her as he called in a loud, hearty voice, "Yellow Dog! It is the time for a smoke and big talk, is it not?"

"Sheegee," Yellow Dog said, addressing Stephen in the salute to a close friend. *"Noshti*—the big smoke. We are ready."

And for all the gifts you can carry off, Rosemary thought. Stephen turned to her. "Bring the whiskey, several bottles." He could just as easily have ordered Cody or called one of the house servants to go for the liquor, but Rosemary had been around Indians long enough now to know that Stephen would have lost face if his wife did not wait on him.

She set Stephanie down on the pallet again, well away from the stomping, snorting ponies, and went inside. When she returned, with one of the house servants helping her carry the bottles, she saw Yellow Dog's son sitting with Stephanie on the blanket. The boy reached out and touched the baby's head, which resembled an orange ball of fluffy cotton. Rosemary's breath sucked in, but the boy smiled—a smile that did not reach his eyes.

Rosemary hurried to Stephanie, who stretched out an inquisitive hand toward the bright red bandana about the Indian boy's head. Setting down the bottles, she swooped up her daughter. She did not care how inhospitable or rude Yellow Dog thought her.

Only later that night, when Yellow Dog's band rode away, thoroughly drunk and half-hanging onto their ponies, did she realize the impact of her actions. Stephen pushed open her bedroom door without knocking. "What the bloody hell did you think you were doing out there? Your rudeness angered Yellow Dog!"

Rosemary paused in brushing the rats from her hair. "I don't care, Stephen. You can barter all you want with those savages, but I'll not risk one of them taking a fancy to Stephanie's hair and making a souvenir of her scalp!"

Stephen laughed shortly, his florid face a deeper pink, and she realized he was as drunk as the Indians. "That's one thing you don't have to worry about."

His eyes told her he had unpleasant news, news that he enjoyed delivering. "I've promised Stephanie to Yellow Dog's son in sixteen summers in return for continued peace here at Cambria."

"No!" Rosemary screamed. She flew at Stephen and beat at him, one hand still clutching her brush. Stephen's fist came crashing against her temple, stunning her.

But the fight with his wife had sexually stimulated Stephen as nothing before had in a long time. And he pushed her face down on the bed.

16

"For a woman of twenty, you are very dry, me dear," Stephen crudely told Rosemary when his efforts to enter her had been frustrated. "'Tis a brittle, old woman you shall be before your time."

"I hope so!" she snapped back. "Maybe then you'll be leaving me alone!"

Stephen turned from where he preened himself before the long French Pier mirror, admiring his still-flat stomach. "Ahh, but you've grown so beautiful in your child-bearing years, I cannot be helping meself."

And it was true, he thought. There was a softness to her regally contoured face, a luminous glow to the creamy skin, a sensual fullness to her breasts and hips. And the taut stomach and long slender legs still held their suppleness.

He had married above himself when he took Rosemary Gallagher to wife, and in more ways than one she had proven his choice a correct one. From what he could tell of the ledgers Rosemary kept for Cambria's trading post, she was turning a better profit than that of his own Stanta Fe Trading Post. Every visitor who came to the Castle's table went away with the highest praise and respect for his charming wife. She had a head on her shoulders, and he had to acknowledge his wife's shrewdness in dealing with the lowliest peon to the governor himself.

Stephen crossed over to the bed and leaned over Rosemary resting his hands on either side of her head. His fingers toyed with one of the silken curls, and he pretended not to see the revulsion in her eyes. "Jiraldo and Rita shall be here for Stephanie's birthday next week, won't they? Why don't you and Rita take the children into Santa Fe for a shopping trip? It'll be doing you good to get away."

Rosemary's blue-green eyes searched her husband's face. "All right," she said at last. There was a purpose to everything Stephen did, and she knew sooner or later she would discover the reason behind it.

For right now it was enough to be out of his gimlet gaze for even a day, but for five days of shopping, it was wonderful. Since the summer before when Stephen had raped her, and that was the only thing Rosemary could call it, he had taken perverse delight in resuming his sexual rights, in seeing the fear and hatred that burned in her eyes.

"Rosemary and Rita can meet the coach out of Fort Union at Las Vegas," Stephen told Jiraldo at dinner the next week.

"It would be completely safe," Rita added, hoping to persuade her taciturn husband. "After all, there has been no trouble with these Confederates in over a year. And this Kit Carson, he has halted the horrible Indian attacks, no?"

Rosemary smiled. "I think Grant would claim he was responsible for the cessation of the Indian attacks." And she thought of Lario for the first time in months, feeling only a hollow emptiness within her.

"They can stay at the Governor's Palace when they reach Santa Fe," Stephen said.

Jiraldo quietly chewed the baked squash, but his hooded eyes watched his wife. Rita was young and vivacious. Too vivacious for a man of sixty.

"Jiraldo," Stephen said, sensing the reason for the hidalgo's reluctance, "I want them to listen—to find out what that Territorial Auditor be doing going through the Treasury Books."

"Esteban, I would advise you to go yourself," he said. *"Cortar en flor*—nip this in the bud, as you have often enough advised others."

"You should know yourself, Jiraldo, it never does to alert the enemy. With all the legislature gone home for the term, that auditor should not be there."

The old man thoughtfully swirled the red wine in his glass. *"Está bien,"* he said at last with a shrug of his bony shoulders

By sunrise of the following day the two women and three children were aboard the wagon. It would have been a pleasant one-day journey to Las Vegas but for the presence of Ignacio, who drove the buckboard. His body reeked of months without washing. Rosemary would have preferred Cody, but he was at the Wild Cat Camp.

Ignacio kept a percussion cap rifle in the crook of one arm and a dangerous-looking Green River knife at his belt. Stephen was taking no chances. "Don't leave Jamie alone for a minute," were his last words as he grabbed up his son and tossed him in the air. The boy caught his breath but did not cry. At three Jamie was learning what his father expected of him.

Inez and Jamie sat in the wagon bed, alternately playing and dozing under the warm spring sunshine. Rita and Rosemary took turns holding Stephanie on the front seat, with one or the other holding a yellow frilly parasol against the sun's bright glare. The April sun was unusually warm and Rosemary discarded her gray traveling jacket and fancy straw bonnet with its yellow muslin roses.

She had outmaneuvered her friend so that Rita was forced to sit in the middle next to Ignacio. Each time a breeze rose, Rita would wrinkle her nose at the odor, and both women would try desperately not to burst out in laughter.

Late afternoon brought the first in a series of events that would change Rosemary's life. The wagon passed through a cluster of ramshackle cabins and adobes with peeling gypsum whitewash. These were the outskirts of Las Vegas, the last stop on the old Santa Fe Trail. It was in that bustling city of twenty-three saloons that General Kearny declared the Territory of New Mexico a possession of the United States.

Excitement filled the two older children when Rita told them there was only a half-hour or so left before they reached Las Vegas and boarded their first stagecoach. But their shouts and laughter were suddenly cut off as the wagon topped a rocky rise to encounter a staggering line of Indians, mostly women and children.

The women looked old beyond their years, the children emaciated, and the few men—the mighty warriors that Rosemary had often heard spoken about—wore the vacuous look of beasts of burden. Their buckskin britches and calico shirts and blouses were worn through in spots, and their faces, dull and apathetic, were coated with dust. Rosemary glanced quickly along the line to see if any of the Indians could be Lario, because for some reason his presence seemed stronger than ever. But she did not find his face among the vacant ones trodding before her.

Five mounted soldiers in blue flanked the group of twenty-five or thirty Indians and prodded them as they would cattle with their rifle stocks, urging them forward with demeaning shouts. But the people were only able to shuffle along at a weary gait.

As the wagon drew near, a young soldier who seemed to be in command ordered the Indians off to the side of the road to allow the wagon to pass. Rosemary commanded Ignacio to halt. Before the *vaquero* or Rita could prevent her, she sprang from the seat with Stephanie balanced precariously at her hip. "These Indians, Sergeant, where did they come from?"

The sergeant seemed as surprised as she herself was at her outburst. He tilted the brim of his cavalry hat back, saying, "Fort Defiance, ma'am—in the Arizona Territory. We're taking them to the Bosque Redondo Reservation at Fort Sumner."

"My God, they've walked the whole way?" She was shocked, and her gaze switched back to the people who stood waiting dully for the sergeant's command to move on. One thin mother slumped down where she stood to suckle her baby at a shriveled breast.

"Ma'am," he said, trying to explain, "these people are nomads. They're used to walking. Why, the bucks can outdistance a horse."

"I don't notice you walking. Are you admitting to inferiority?"

The man drew a deep breath, but when he looked at her she saw the shame in his troubled eyes. "Ma'am, I am disobeying orders as it is. General Carleton issued orders that every—"

"I know," Rosemary said. She remembered the previous year when she had first visited Fort Sumner and seen the barren, desolate Pecos prairie that was to be the reservation—and she remembered not really believing Grant's words to Lario...that every man, woman, and child resisting the move to the Bosque Redondo would be killed.

The sergeant nodded his head toward one Indian, a wrinkled, bony old man with matted long white hair who wore chains at his wrists. "That's Chief Manuelito's father-in-law. Twice he tried to drive a knife into my men—and he would not move even after we subdued him. I had to threaten to take his grandson's life—the papoose nursing there—to get the old man to accede."

Rosemary looked over at the old Indian. Impassiveness etched the brown, aged face, but in the cavernous eyes lurked agony and sadness. "Perhaps it would have been kinder to kill him," she said softly and looked up to see the surprise on the sergeant's face...a surprise that slid into blankness as he suddenly toppled from his horse. She saw the brightly plumed arrow buried between the young man's shoulder blades at the same moment the hideous screams, like those of a panther, exploded about them.

Instinctively she whirled, with Stephanie gathered to her breast, and began to run back toward the wagon. But even as fiercely painted warriors plunged down out of the wooded hills, Ignacio snapped the whip over the team's rumps, and the horses jerked forward in galloping terror. Rosemary heard Jamie shout, "Mama! Mama!" in his little boy's high-pitched voice.

The Indians did not bother to stop the fleeing wagon but swiftly dispatched the remaining four soldiers. The fight was

85

over as quickly as it had begun. And Rosemary found herself standing among the former prisoners, the only white person.

As the warriors began removing the soldiers' boots and rounding up the horses, strange harsh words of joy and relief broke about her, yet she could only hear the trip-hammer beat of her heart. She knew she could face death, perhaps not as bravely as the stoic Indian. Under torture she might die screaming until there was no voice left. But then death came to everyone.

What she could not endure would be to watch the death of her daughter. The mental torture of seeing those savages kill her baby would be as great as a knife-blade cutting out her own still-beating heart.

She clutched the child tightly to her as one brave in a military shirt and slouch cap bounded from his pony and advanced on her. *No, dear God, no!* she wanted to scream but found the words locked in her throat. She clutched the child tightly to her and began to back away.

The brave tore the baby from her grasp. Rosemary's scream was wrenched from her lungs as he clasped the baby's small, pudgy ankles in one hand and began swinging his trophy. Rosemary lunged forward, but hands grabbed her from behind, and she squeezed her eyes shut in another guttural scream. She could not watch Stephanie's tiny head bashed against the rocks. She struggled, kicking and biting at the hands that held her.

A harsh command ripped through the air. All movement ceased. Rosemary's teeth clenched in the effort to force her eyes open. Her daughter still hung suspended by her ankles, crying. Then Rosemary noted the familiar chestnut Arab before her—and its swarthy rider. Lario.

His dark gaze swung on her, with an impact like the blow of a tomahawk. Unlike the warriors clad in the breechcloth and knee-high moccasins, he wore buckskin pants and a collarless blue velveteen shirt. But the red flannel bandana about his forehead was the same as those worn by the others. "You are as foolish as ever, Señora. Why did you not stay with your party?"

His dark eyes flickered to the brave who held Stephanie, then to the older Indian who rode at his side. The man's face was massive with a heavy high-bridged nose and deep furrows confining the wide lips. From under the blue turban wisps of bone-white hair could be seen. Lario addressed the older man as "Manuelito," and the Indian shook his head negatively to whatever it was Lario had asked him.

"They are angry, they want revenge," Lario told her, his eyes on the child. "I don't know what I can do to—"

"She's your daughter, Lario!" Rosemary screamed.

Lario's gaze slashed back to Rosemary. It searched her face for the truth. His Navajo words, so foreign to her, were directed at the brave holding Stephanie, waiting. The still-wailing infant was passed up to Lario. Rosemary thought his face looked as Solomon's must have when he judged the rights of the two opposing mothers for the child.

Lario noted the red hair, the same shade as Rosemary's, not Stephen's. He saw the fair skin, as light as dawn's first pink streaks. Then his gaze halted on the black eyes—deep, deep black. Almond-shaped eyes of the Navajo people. His piercing gaze met and held that of Rosemary's. After what seemed an eternity of slow-ticking minutes to her, he said, "You tell the truth."

Rosemary released her breath, as Lario first spoke softly to the Indians the soldiers had captured, then rapped out a command to his own men. When he looked back to Rosemary, his eyes were as cold as the frozen snow on the Sangre de Cristos' peaks. "You are to be released unharmed. The town of Las Vegas is not far. But the child goes with me."

He whirled his mount, and Rosemary broke free. Her hands latched onto the horse's bridle. "No!" she shouted as the horse danced about in confusion. "I won't let you!"

Lario tried to shove her from him but was hampered by the child held in his arms. Something hit Rosemary's head from behind, and she fell to the ground, dazed. For a few moments she lay there. Her vision was blurred, like the heat waves rising off the earth. She blinked her eyes. Her vision began to clear. The Indians, led by Lario and his braves, were already at least a quarter of a mile away, moving to the southwest, away from the wagon-rutted road.

Rosemary pushed herself to her feet. "No!" she screamed. "Wait!" Tears streamed down her face. Las Vegas and safety—and Jamie. But abandon Stephanie?

She began moving, sometimes trotting, sometimes stumbling on her cumbersome skirts, toward the southwest.

Beneath the scanty shade of a white-flowered saguaro cactus Rosemary paused to rest. Her breath sounded ragged in her ears against the utter quiet of the empty country about her. Only an occasional greasewood bush, its rank, olive-green stems waving high yellow or orange blooms, added relief to the desolation. Immediately before her glided the shadow of a swooping hawk.

And far ahead moved the dark forms, slowly outdistancing her. How long had she been walking? All night and part of another day? A frosty rocking-chair moon had illuminated the band of Indians during the long night, but now the sun, glaring like a twenty-dollar gold piece in the sky, hurt her eyes, and she had to squint to follow their receding figures. Didn't they ever stop to rest or eat, and what *did* they find to eat in that godforsaken wilderness?

The sole of one kid dress boot had worn through, and the heel of the other had snapped off. Her feet were a mass of bubbling blisters. The hem of her gray serge skirt was frayed by the pebbled floor of the plateau and torn in several places by the low-growing cholla cactus. Realizing that the skirt deterred her progress as much as her blistered feet, Rosemary ripped away the material below her knees where her high-top boots ended.

She drew a deep breath and straightened her shoulders. Stepping out from the lonely, protective shade of the saguaro, she forced one foot in front of another, concentrating not on the shapes she followed but only on each yard of ochre-hued sand directly in front of her. She would not allow herself the luxury of weakness, of fainting. Not with Stephanie stolen from her arms. She had experienced Lario's underlying gentleness, but it did not stop the talons of anger and fear for Stephanie that clutched at her heart. How would he feed the baby? The one nursing mother she had seen had not enough milk for her own infant.

First one foot, and then the other, Rosemary repeated to herself in a drone, keeping her eyes on terrain that was slowly changing to a rough and stony landscape. The shadow that fell across the narrowed range of her vision did not at first seep into her dulled senses. But as the shadow moved steadily with Rosemary's own shadow, so grew her perception that she was not alone. With an effort she turned her face upward, but the blinding sun hid the face of the phantom who rode at her side. A mirage? Determined not to succumb to collapse, she continued walking, a procession of stumbling steps, and focused her gaze once more directly before her. But the shadow followed along beside her.

As the afternoon wore on, her condition deteriorated. Her hair hung in lank strands about her shoulders. Perspiration soaked her dress. The skin of her face was burnt a bright pink. Her feet were raw flesh. She tottered, stopped, moved forward again. But now the mass of figures had disappeared from her sight.

"Are you ready to go back?" the voice at her side asked.

"No!" she croaked. Was she talking to herself; had she already lost her reason? No matter. Nothing mattered but that she continue moving. And Stephanie.

After a while she stumbled over a rock and pitched forward. The gritty sand abraded her face, and she lay there. She knew she could not get up again.

Arms encircled her, lifted her. She was once more cradled in Lario's arms. A dream, she told herself—a recurring memory of the first time Lario had found her when she had run away from Stephen. But she said in a raspy voice irritated by its dryness, "If you take me back to Las Vegas, I'll just turn around and follow you again."

"You are stubborn, Turquoise Woman," he said. But she noticed in spite of her lightheadedness that he did not leave her and that he had addressed her in Indian fashion. Then she let herself sink into a comatose sleep.

The jarring awoke her. Lario's horse scrambled up the steep side of a barranca like a mule deer and followed a narrow trail hemmed in on both sides by sheer sandstone walls. The trail wound about, ribboning ever upward until it emerged into one of the many small canyons hidden in the Sandia Mountains. There, thickets of cedar, aspen, and pine partially hid the score or so of brush-covered shelters. The sounds of domesticity—children laughing, someone chopping wood, women calling to each other, and a dog barking—reached her ears.

Lario halted before one hogan nestled among a grove of firs. "You insisted on coming," he said, his breath warm against her ear. "So you must be content to exist as we do. You will not be welcomed here by many because of the treatment suffered at the hands of your people. Never leave the hogan unless one of my family or Adala is with you."

But Rosemary was impatient. "Stephanie—where is my baby?" she demanded.

Lario dismounted. *"Our* baby," he corrected, "is within."

He did not attempt to help Rosemary down but strode toward the hogan. Rosemary heard the joyous cry, "Lario!" and saw the young girl, Adala, step from the hogan's entrance. Even in the evening's dusk, she could see the radiance that suffused the girl's face. Then Rosemary saw that Adala held Stephanie in her arms, and her anger exploded that another woman should hold her child. She tried to shove herself from the horse's back, but her skirts impeded her. She fell to the earth with a thud that knocked the breath out of her.

There was a sudden silence, as if each Indian there saw the Anglo woman's ignominious fall. Worse, when Rosemary scrambled to her knees she saw the laughter in Lario's eyes.

Always those laughing eyes. How she hated them now!

But Lario's well-defined lips were straight and firm when he turned back to Adala and took Stephanie, sharing words with the Indian girl that made her smile before she re-entered the hogan. Then in English to the baby, "It is time you knew your father, Sin-they."

"Her name is Stephanie!" Rosemary sputtered, advancing on Lario. A mixture of rage and indignation coursed through her. Lario held the chubby infant out of her reach, and Stephanie, unlike Jamie, laughed at the action. She held out tiny hands to clutch the bright crimson bandana about Lario's head, and Rosemary was furious that her child should betray her by taking a liking for the enemy; for Rosemary, peeved, refused to admit that he was also the child's father. He was simply The Enemy.

Lario handed the child to her. "Sin-they needs to be fed," he said and pushed aside the blanket over the doorway, stepping inside.

Rosemary had no recourse but to follow, hobbling on painfully sore feet. She recognized Lario's mother and grandfather, who were in the midst of eating, scooping with their fingers some kind of shredded meat and thick gravy from broken pottery. She nodded her head in response to their own polite nods and wondered if they realized she was to be their unwilling guest and if Lario had informed them for how long. His sister, Toysei, glanced up from where she spread a blanket over her son then looked away, her face as expressionless as Lario's could be.

Two young braves, who Rosemary learned were Lario's brothers, Hasteen and Guayo, reposed on the far side of the firepit, seemingly oblivious to her presence as they accepted the food Adala ladled into their bowls. The older, Hasteen, wore a mustache, which gave lie to the dictum Indians had no facial hair. Guayo possessed the same fine features as Lario—a younger version of Lario at eighteen and therefore lacking the strength of character found in Lario's face.

Adala handed Lario a bowl of the delicious-smelling meat with a shy smile and looked to Rosemary in question. "Do you wish to eat?" Lario asked her.

Rosemary could barely control the saliva that threatened to overflow her lips. Dear Lord, was she hungry—and thirsty! "Aye," she managed to whisper.

She settled herself far from the light of the fragrant fire that burned in the hogan's center. As if in response to Lario's question of eating, Stephanie began howling, and automatically Rosemary's fingers went to the buttons of her blouse, only to halt. No eyes watched her, but suddenly she was embarrassed in front of Lario. This is ridiculous, she thought. I have known this man's body. I have carried his child. Still, she maneuvered herself so that her back was partially to the others and put Stephanie to her breast.

Adala came over and silently placed a bowl before Rosemary. Rosemary forced herself to return the young woman's soft smile. After all, it was not Adala's fault that she and Stephanie were there against her will.

Soon Stephanie's eyelids grew heavy. Rosemary laid the child on the blanket that Adala had provided and hungrily turned to her now-cold stew. When she looked up again, Lario and his brothers had gone and their mother and grandfather were already stretched out on the blankets to sleep, their feet toward the warming fire. Toysei and Adala talked quietly. Rosemary did not doubt but they discussed her. But she was too tired to really care what they said or what they planned to do with her. She stretched out alongside of Stephanie, half asleep before her eyelids even closed.

She felt as if she could sleep for a solid week, but something awoke her during the night although there was no noise to interrupt the deep silence of the hogan. Embers smoldered in the firepit. From outside there wafted the sweet smell of the spring night's dampness as the hogan's flap fell in place.

Rosemary rolled to one elbow and glanced about the darkened shelter. Two blankets were empty. To her left lay Toysei. But among the sleeping forms clustered about the firepit that of Adala's was not to be found...only two empty blankets.

Rosemary turned on her stomach and buried her face in

her arms. If the other empty blanket belonged to Lario—well, it was none of her business. Soon she and Stephanie would be gone from those miserable hovels, would return to the secure warmth of her beloved Cambria.

18

A hot, stiff August wind blew down through Arizona's deep Canyon de Chelly, and Rosemary turned her face away from its furnacelike blast. She had just filled two large clay water jars, or *tus* as Lario insisted she call them, using the Navajo word, and they weighed heavily in her arms.

As she started back up the stream's rugged, rocky bank toward the newest *rancheria*, she reflected disgustedly that in the space of four months of living with the Navajo she was daily becoming more like an Indian woman. She wore the clumsy silver-buttoned knee-high moccasins with the calico skirt and hot velveteen blouse; she braided her hair in rolls over her ears; she was even learning to weave blankets and rugs on the upright loom made from the forked branch of a juniper tree, though she had not the patience to struggle with the stubborn warp or the monotonous spinning.

She crossed to the hogan Adala had helped her build. The young girl had worked patiently with Rosemary, showing how the thick evergreen brush was interwoven with the bent frame of stout piñon poles, leaving enough open space for the smoke hole in the roof's center.

When she had finished the hogan, Rosemary looked in through the wide door, seeing the cool darkness flecked with tiny spots of light and the sun shafting warmly through the smoke hole, and she was proud of her accomplishment. The hogan had not the strength and security of Cambria, but nevertheless it was something she had made herself.

The hogan belonged to Lario, for it had become obvious the first week of Rosemary's arrival that the one hogan would not be large enough to accommodate the entire family.

"But why must I stay in your hogan?" she had demanded of Lario after he had informed her of his plans. She had trailed him to a stump some two hundred feet away from his mother's hogan, and they were alone for the first time, if the spotted dog that yapped at Rosemary's heels and the three naked children that played in the stream just beyond could be discounted.

"I want my daughter with me." He resumed sharpening his hunting knife with the whetstone, as if she were dismissed, and that irritated her even more.

"But I am not your wife."

His keen eyes fixed on her. "I do not treat you as such, do I?"

Instantly she realized he had trapped her. "No. But others think that."

"Do you wish it so?"

Rosemary stamped her foot in frustration. "No. You will have Adala, so do not be planning to add me to your list of wives!"

"Ahhh." His mouth quirked in comprehension at her defensive action. "But Adala had no place to go after the soldiers captured her parents last month," he pointed out. "And she is not yet my wife."

"You are refusing to understand me!" she had exclaimed and spun away, leaving him smiling.

Rosemary shifted the water jars in her arms as she reached the hogan and gingerly set them down before she began to string one jar from a willow rafter to keep the insects out. She was relieved that she would be alone for another night, for Lario had gone out on one of his "rescue missions" as she referred to them.

She would not have to lie awake on her own pallet and hear the steady cadence of Lario's breathing. She wondered if sometimes he thought about that one night they had made love during the sandstorm . . . and if he still desired her. Was it their daughter who slept at her side that prevented him from coming to her in the night—or was it his love for the delicate, lovely Adala?

And from there Rosemary's thoughts conjured visions of Lario's dusky hands and generous lips making love to Adala as he had to her, and she felt the bite of jealousy. Ridiculous! she reminded herself. Lario is but an Indian. It is only that he is educated that makes him seem more—more what? Human?

How bigoted she was! Why not admit she wanted him? But she knew she never could submit to Lario, could never be one of many wives, as was the Navajo practice. If nothing else there was always the specter of the Sepoy Rebellion to loom between them.

Rosemary realized how absurd her speculation was, for Lario had never intimated he wanted her for a wife. Or that he even wanted her. She was angry with herself, realizing that even with him gone most of the time, she still thought about him. It would be better, she chided herself, to think instead about escaping from the canyon and making her way back to Cambria and Jamie.

She should try while Lario was away. In another day or so, she knew he would be returning, probably bringing back several dozen more Indians that had been captives bound for the Bosque Redondo Reservation. But she might as well be separated from Cambria by an ocean so little did she know about finding her way back. Better to wait and hope for rescue.

And then the thought struck her that Lario might not return. What would become of her and Stephanie? Would the Navajo turn on her then?

But for some reason she felt that Lario would always come back. He and his brother Hasteen were fighters, survivors. The youngest brother she worried about more, for Guayo was neither as powerfully built as Lario nor as experienced as the rebellious Hasteen in battle. Guayo was a shepherd by nature whose gentle manner earned Rosemary's reluctant friendship. She had even given him the bracelet Lario had made for her that first Christmas after Guayo saved Stephanie when she tumbled into a mountain stream.

Having strung both water jars from the rafters, Rosemary stepped outside in search of Adala, who had kindly offered to take Stephanie with her for the day to tend sheep. Rosemary was coming to genuinely like the young Indian girl, though she could not understand her complacent acceptance of another woman sharing her future husband. But then that was the way the Indian women were brought up from childhood. Of all the tribes, the Navajo men were most notorious for their polygamy. Rosemary was sure if she loved a man as Adala loved Lario she would scratch the woman's eyes out. Yet Adala treated her as a *deezi*, a sister.

Rosemary shielded her eyes from the bright sunlight. More and more hogans now dotted the canyon as the numbers of liberated Indians brought back by Lario and Manuelito mushroomed. But only a few women and children moved among the hogans, the rest still tending the sheep in the higher ranges where the grass grew more tender. Rosemary thought about taking the opportunity for privacy to go down to the cold, rushing stream and bathe, but she had no sooner returned to her hogan for the amole root the Indians used for soap when there was a commotion from the direction where the ponies were picketed.

Once more she stepped outside. The men were back! Seven or eight new Indians, mostly Navajo, but Rosemary recognized two as Apaches, were looking about the *ranchería* at what would be their new home. Lario strode toward the hogan with his two brothers falling in behind him. Hasteen raised his fist in an angry gesture and said something that Rosemary could not catch. Guayo turned away as the men reached their mother's hogan, but Hasteen caught sight of Rosemary and pointed at her, saying something now that Rosemary, with her limited knowledge of Navajo, did not comprehend, then... "You are wrong, Lario!"

She stepped back, allowing Lario to enter. "What was that all about?" she asked in English, enjoying the rare opportunity to use her native language. He looked tired. The cheekbones were emphasized by the gauntness beneath them, and a cut beaded with fresh blood drops across his upper left arm. "You're hurt!"

Lario shrugged and threw his long frame on the blanket. "Some of the soldiers did not wish to give up their prisoners."

She came over and looked down at him. "Are you admitting that it bothers you to kill?"

His gaze slashed up to hers. "Don't try to provoke an argument. I am too tired."

But he propped himself on one elbow, and she saw the pained effort it cost him as he winced. "Yes," he answered her. "It does bother me. But it is worse to watch my people die senselessly. And no amount of argument for or against can change what is bound to happen."

"Then why bother to make these forays?" she demanded, her abhorrence for killing charging her anger anew. "If you cannot change what will happen, your attempts are just as senseless!"

Lario reclined again and put one arm over his forehead. "I know," he said.

Suddenly Rosemary felt contrite. The enormity of the burden he carried hit her... that through his education he was able to see what the future held for his people, to see the futility of his efforts but unable to cease working, to cease hoping. "I'm sorry," she said. "I know it must be difficult for you."

She took a gourd hung from the wall with other utensils and filled it with water from one of the suspended jars before returning to kneel at Lario's side. "I have been lazy today," she confessed. "There is no food ready for you."

She was fully aware of the magnitude of her confession. In another hogan such laxity could be grounds for a beating.

But Lario she knew took into account that she was not accustomed to serving but to being served and was therefore more lenient with her.

He took the gourd from her, saying, "My stomach does not hunger for food this moment." Then, "An Indian child stepped in the way of the gunfire. The same age as Sin-they."

Rosemary now more thoroughly understood Lario's despondency. Despite the apparent hopelessness of his purpose, his effort was worth it for every captive he freed. But to lose a child— She put out a hand to touch his shoulder. "But there were many others you brought back, Lario."

He switched his intent gaze on her, and she blushed...a blush that turned to anger that she should capitulate so easily to her enforced captivity. Her long lashes snapped upward, and her gaze met his in fierce combat. "Let me go! When winter comes, there won't be enough to feed everyone here. Why keep me?"

Taut silence stretched the moment like a drawn bowstring. Then, "You are free to go."

Her eyes widened. "You mean it?" she whispered.

His black eyes were shuttered. He handed the gourd back to her, empty. "Yes. But Sin-they stays."

"Why?" Rosemary cried out. Then she took a different tack. "Would you deny her the education you had? Would you watch her starve through a freezing winter? Or go shoeless and lose toes to frostbite? Would you have her grow up like this?"

"There is love here for her," he said quietly.

"There is love for her at Cambria!"

"Is there? Let me ask you...would you want your daughter bedded by your husband when she had ten summers—or nine, or eight?"

"But she's his—"

"It would not make any difference," Lario snapped. "You know the kind of man he is." He grabbed Rosemary's free wrist. "And what do you think will happen to Sin-they should Rhodes discover she is not his child?"

"I'd make certain he never found out."

"Would you take that kind of chance with our child?"

Rosemary pulled her arm away. She kept her eyes on the reddened skin about her wrist where Lario had gripped her, for she could not meet his gaze. She was as trapped by circumstances as he was. And as if he sensed and understood her dilemma, his hand came up to cup her chin. He tilted her face so that she could see his searching gaze.

"It has taken me many years to learn there are some things I cannot change."

Rosemary's lips curled scornfully. "Yet you keep trying, do you not? And so will I."

"Were you any happier at Cambria?"

"But it is my home. The only home I have."

"Your home is here—with your child."

Can you not see that I am a white woman, she wanted to scream. That I don't fit in. You ask too much for me to lie in the darkness at night and listen as you take Adala to your bed.

But she stifled her mutinous thoughts and rose, saying, "I will bandage your cut."

With a high-pitched shout of "Da!" Stephanie came toddling into the hogan, a broad smile dimpling her rosy cheeks. Twice she almost tottered off balance before she fell laughing into Lario's outstretched arms. Rosemary watched Lario's hand tousle the bright red-gold curls and felt a moment of deep contentment. But Adala's shadow in the doorway dispelled the peace.

How long before Lario took the young woman for his wife?

19

Rosemary pitched the last of the wood chips onto the dying faggots. The wood of the quaking asp gave off almost no smoke for enemy eyes to detect. She held her hands to the warmth that leaped from the sudden flicker of orange-red flame. Beneath the gray woolen blanket wrapped about her, Stephanie snuggled in sleep close to her side. Her daughter's little body was toasty-warm, unlike Rosemary's cold toes and nose.

The February snow blew in through the small chinks in the mud and stick walls of the new hogan to settle in little drifts that quickly dissipated with the next draft of wind. Lario had been gone six days now, two days longer than he had planned, and Rosemary was worried. What if he lay bleeding to death from a bullet? Or was lost in the blizzard that roared in from the north the day before?

There was a swishing sound behind her, and she jerked about in surprise. Hasteen stood in the doorway. A limp rabbit dangled from one hand. Snowflakes glistened in his hair and on his eyelashes. "The deer and the antelope have moved further south," he said.

"Thank you, *shee-kizzen*," she said, using the Navajo word for brother. All she could think was that at least they were not yet reduced to eating the camp dogs.

Hasteen continued to regard her with unwavering gaze, and she realized how much of a man he had grown to be in the year that she had been at the *rancheria*. What was he, twenty-three? The mustache he affected made him seem older. Like Lario, he wore his hair in a *chongo*, back from his long, somewhat rawboned face. But his eyes were more slanted, more Oriental with none of the brilliant lights she found in those of Lario. And his nose and chin were longer, almost pointed.

When Hasteen did not look away, as he usually did when he was in her presence, she suddenly wondered if something was wrong, if Hasteen knew something she did not. "What is it?" she demanded.

"I am not a brother to you."

"You are Lario's brother," she began, not yet understanding.

He moved forward into the hogan and dropped the rabbit at her feet. The pelt sparkled with a thousand tiny crystals, and the velvety brown eyes were glazed over. Rosemary was so hungry she thought she could eat the rabbit raw. "But you are not his wife," Hasteen said. "And I bring you food. I offer my shield as your protection."

She tilted her head far back to look up into the hard countenance. "Hasteen, your brother asked this of you—to protect the *rancheria* while he and Manuelito were gone." Then Rosemary thought she caught the implication in Hasteen's words. "Oh, I see," she said, hurt. "It is that I am not of the *rancheria*—not a Navajo."

"It is that Adala will have sixteen summers the rising of the next full moon. Lario will take her to his bed for his wife."

A muscle flickered in Rosemary's cheek. Otherwise she did not betray the fear that now clutched at her heart. When Lario married Adala, she knew she would no longer be able to stay in his hogan. But where would she go? What would she do? Lario would never let her take Stephanie with her. And she would not leave without her.

Her arm slipped down to pull Stephanie closer to her. "I have known that this day would come."

For some seconds Hasteen said nothing. Rosemary did not break her gaze with him, for it would have been impolite.

At last Hasteen said, "I have taken two ponies in raids. They are outside. For Lario." He noted Rosemary's frown of confusion and explained. "I wish to pay him for taking you as my wife."

Rosemary's mouth dropped open. After a naked moment she said, "I already have a husband, Hasteen."

His lips thinned out in disgust. "Señor Esteban—the *Dine'é* know what kind of man he is!"

"But he is still my husband." Rosemary saw the hard glint in Hasteen's eyes. She could not afford to offend him. "I will have to think on your offer."

Hasteen's eyes were suddenly alert, and he spun about just as Lario stepped through the doorway. "What offer?" Lario asked, looking from Rosemary to his brother.

"Hasteen wants to take me as his wife," Rosemary said. "I have told him I already have a husband."

"Her husband is as the dead," Hasteen said. "He does not exist for her here."

Lario walked by both of them, stepping over the rabbit's carcass. He pulled the soggy poncho over his head and dropped it near the fire to dry. "She does not want to take a husband here, maybe."

"You keep her—but not as a wife. If you do not wish to offer her your protection, then I offer her mine. She must make a choice." Hasteen turned on her.

Lario cocked a brow at Rosemary. She drew the blanket tighter about her in frustration. Obviously Lario did not intend to help her in making the decision. "Stephanie?" she asked in desperation.

"Sin-they will be here as always at the *ranchería,*" Lario said. "Loved by all the *Dine'é.*"

Rosemary wanted to strike back at Lario's dispassionate attitude, to say she would accept Hasteen's offer. But the idea of bedding with Hasteen was repugnant. Unlike Lario, he did not bathe except on ceremonial days—the same as did most Navajo. She could not settle for either—being less than first and only with Lario, or being first with Hasteen.

She knew then she could wait no longer for rescue. She would have to try to escape the *ranchería.* There was no other choice. "Give me the days of one complete moon to consider on this," she told the men. "I shall have my answer then."

"Enju—it is well," Hasteen answered and left the hogan.

Lario dipped the gourd into the water and turned to Rosemary. "I have hunger."

That did it. She had never liked skinning rabbits. A deer she could—but not the small furry rabbit. She slipped out of

99

the blanket, forgetting her sleeping child in her anger, and crossed to stand before Lario. Her hands balled into fists. "Then you prepare the rabbit! As Hasteen said, I am not your wife!"

Laughter lurked in Lario's eyes. "But you are my *yisnááh*— my captive. I could make you."

Rosemary's eyes narrowed. "You wouldn't!"

Lario continued with a shrug. "But then I am welcome at the cooking pots of other hogans. I will not go hungry. But what of you?"

"What do you care?" she cried. She jerked the water jar from its rawhide ropes and shoved it at Lario.

The clay jar shattered on the ground in fragments. At the sound Stephanie turned fitfully, then settled again into a peaceful sleep, blissfully unaware of the fury that crackled like electricity between her parents.

Lario took a step toward Rosemary, and her eyes widened in fright at what she had done. His shirt clung to him, dripping water, and his damp buckskin britches molded his narrow hips and muscled thighs. She began to back away from the anger that smoked his eyes.

Lario shrugged out of his shirt and took another purposeful step toward her. In the firelight his bare chest gleamed like polished copper. Then he began to work at the loops that buttoned his pants. Rosemary's fingers flew to her lips. Despite the fact they shared the hogan, they had yet to undress before each other. Most of the time he was away, and the few evenings he spent in the hogan the fire had either already burned low or Rosemary had turned away in feigned sleep.

Perhaps it was the strain of the two of them living together, but not as man and wife, or maybe it was the tension that flared between them now, but suddenly Rosemary felt panicky laughter bubbling in her throat. Now her hands clamped over her mouth, as the laughter threatened to spill out, and she moved to put the firepit between her and Lario.

The buckskins slid to the floor. Lario's body was beautiful. He was tall and sinewy and lean with the physical fitness of a man who lived off the land. Rosemary's hands dropped from her mouth in open awe, but there was still the smile of laughter on her lips.

Lario saw it, and the faintest smile twitched at the corner of his mouth. "The doe has no fear of the hunter?" he asked and moved toward her.

"No, it's—" Then Rosemary started to laugh in spite of her determination not to. She turned and ran around the mound of blanket that wrapped their child. "No, Lario!" she tried to cry out as he took up the chase, but the fits of laughter choked her and tears sprang to her eyes.

Lario grabbed her about the waist and swung her up into his arms. "You must be taught the proper respect for the man. It is time you learned to act like a Navajo woman."

Rosemary kicked her legs and flailed her arms, all the time laughing—only to stop short as Lario's teeth tugged at one ear lobe. The slight prick of pain darted shivers throughout her. She ceased her struggling now but went rigid in expectation.

"And it is time you learned to better speak the Navajo tongue." His lips brushed her forehead as he sat her on his own pallet of robes and blankets. *"Táh,"* he said softly, while his lips once more brushed her temple. "Say it—*táh,* temple." He knelt beside her, gathering her close.

"Táh," Rosemary murmured as excitement streaked through her like lightning.

Lario lifted her hand. *"'lá*—finger."

"'lá," she repeated.

His brown fingers touched her stomach. *"Cŏs*—belly."

Rosemary's stomach fluttered like hundreds of hummingbird wings. She was achingly aware of his nudity and the warm hardness of his body. She had only to drop her gaze... *"Cŏs."*

He touched her breast, and she felt the scorching of his touch through her velveteen blouse. *"Be."*

"Be." She lifted her eyes to meet his smoldering gaze. Her hand crept out, and her fingers rested tremulously on his penis.

Lario shuddered with desire, but his gaze never relinquished hers. *"Zeh,"* he told her.

The same white-hot flame of desire leaped to life within Rosemary. Why not? she thought wildly. What difference if he does not love me? I'll be leaving soon—going back to Cambria.

The revulsion of the thought of Stephen dissolved her last reserve, and she leaned forward, hesitantly brushing her lips across those of Lario. She did not know what he would do... if he would be affronted by the Anglo form of foreplay as she sensed he had been that first time they came together or if he would be disgusted by her wantonness. But she could not help herself.

Lario drew away, and each saw in the other's eyes the memory of the first time, knew that the other had not forgotten that night of shared love. *"Íih,"* Lario whispered, as

101

he drew her down beside him, and Rosemary thrilled to the Navajo endearment.

His fingers slipped loose the buttons of her blouse even as his lips closed over her own. Rosemary realized it was a special offering, like no ordinary kiss between lovers. But her amazement at this special gift was drowned out by the maelstrom of passion his kiss incited. She forgot all else, forgot that it would be Adala he would be taking to bed as his wife, forgot that she would be returning to an empty life with Stephen.

Lario sat in the large ceremonial hogan that had been erected to the north of the brush corral. The hogan represented the universe. Across from Lario, Manuelito drew on a cigarette made of a poor-grade Mexican tobacco and wrapped in corn husks. The smoke curled upward through the conical hole in the hogan's roof. "The *ga'han,* the mountain spirits," he told the younger man, "will be pleased with your union with Adala."

Lario exhaled slowly on his own cigarette, his eyes narrowed as if watching the smoke's spiraling path. He said nothing...for what could he say? Outside could be heard the steady beat of the cottonwood drum and the clacking of the tortoiseshell rattlers. He knew at that moment Adala was being painted white to represent the Changing Woman. The puberty ceremony had lasted five days with feasting, during which time he had not seen her. That night a small brush fire would be lit around the interior of the corral, and pollen, representing growth and vitality, would be thrown in the four directions, followed by four painted dancers with masks and elaborate headdresses.

And tomorrow...tomorrow, Lario thought, Adala would be ready for marriage. But it was not Adala's soft deer-eyes he thought of but blue-green eyes that enchanted like the sacred turquoise stone. And at that he thought of making a squash blossom necklace for *her,* using the precious turquoise throughout his silver design. He could see in the eye of his craftsman's mind the beauty of his design and counted the hours of work it might take.

His straight dark brows came together in a frown. To even think about *her,* Turquoise Woman, was asking for anger from the Enemy Gods. She was not one of them, not of the *Dine'é.*

He had kept her with him too long, using their daughter to hold her. And he had finally violated his resolution to leave her untouched. But sleeping in the same hogan with her, hearing her soft, even breathing...returning home to her vitality after days of blood and death (it was the only way he could rid himself of her—to throw himself into battle)...he was as possessed by her as *Yusn,* the Giver-of-Life, possessed the body.

He wondered if the *ga'han* were truly satisfied with his pending marriage to Adala. Guayo cast calf-eyes at Adala and thought no one noticed. And though Lario knew Adala adored himself, he wondered if it was not the adoration reserved for an older brother.

Through the haze of smoke that filled the hogan Lario felt the older man's eyes on him and looked up. "Your heart does not beat for Adala," Manuelito said.

"She is as my sister, *shee-kizzen.*"

"And the Anglo woman?"

Lario's lips formed a wry smile. "Your eyes, Manuelito, are like those of the eagle." He drew deeply on his cigarette then said, "Her heart longs for her home and her boy child."

And maybe for Grant Raffin? At one time he would have thought so. But those past few weeks when she had welcomed him freely into her arms...he was no longer so sure.

20

Lario stopped only long enough at his mother's hogan to find Guayo. His mother's and Toysei's eyes widened in surprise that he had deserted the ceremonial hogan. The despondent Guayo sat cleaning his rifle, not even bothering to look up when Lario entered.

"Guayo," he said, "the six pintos outside the ceremonial hogan—they are yours. To give for Adala." Confusion clouded the youngest brother's face. "I know the love you bear her," Lario explained. "It is time you courted her."

"But, Lario," Toysei began, "what—"

"Silence, granddaughter," Maspha said. He continued to sprinkle the sand, his bony fingers moving the grains of the painting about, and said, "In good time everything will be known."

The mother nodded her gray-white head, saying nothing as was her custom. But her watery eyes were thoughtful as she trained her gaze on the beaded moccasins she stitched. One summer day as she had sat beneath the *ramada* working on her loom she had seen the Anglo woman bearing a load of firewood strapped to her back. And she had seen her eldest son lighten the woman's load, something that would have shamed any other Navajo man. Packing wood was a woman's work.

The old woman shook her head as she added another bead to her string of sinew. She could see no good that could come out of this love...but then that was wrong, for there was the special child, Sin-they. Sin-they was as no other child, a dancing flame to warm the heart.

Guayo rose. Like most Navajo men he was only of medium height, and his head barely reached Lario's shoulder. "Your words are not clear to me, brother."

"It is another my heart yearns for," Lario said and left before his family could detain him with further questions.

Hasteen—where was he? Even now was he with Rosemary? Courting her? But there were still three days left until the new moon, and Rosemary had said she would wait.

Lario loped down the incline and up the next rise to the hogan that stood alone at the bottom of the bluff, away from the other hogans. At the time he had not given thought to why he had picked that spot for the hogan, but now he knew. He had isolated the three of them—Rosemary, Sin-they, and himself—from the others. They belonged neither with the Navajo, nor the Anglo. Was there a place for the three of them?

And what if Rosemary would have no part of what he wanted? What if already she had accepted Hasteen?

Lario hesitated outside the curtained doorway. The March wind howled like the coyotes that closed in on the *rancheria* at nightfall, but he could not force himself to go inside just yet. The sound of Hasteen's voice did not reach his ears, but there came the exuberant, joyful laughter of his daughter. He pulled aside the curtain. Before him Rosemary, her back to him, and Sin-they sat opposite one another, horsehide playing cards held in their hands. Rosemary laid one card on the dirt-packed earth, and Sin-they threw another on top with a triumphant whoop.

As if she sensed another presence, Rosemary's back stiffened. Her head turned slowly. "Lario," she whispered.

Sin-they bounded to her feet and threw her tiny arms around one of Lario's leather-encased legs. Playfully he jerked one of her copper braids before going to take her place across from Rosemary. The child settled herself in his lap, content to feel his broad chest behind her.

Lario did not know how to begin, and Rosemary's lips grew taut at his silence. She wondered if the singer had already performed the ceremony for she had thought it still three days distant. She knew she should have left by now, but she kept postponing her departure. One more day, she would tell herself.

"You've come to tell me to leave," she said, making it more a statement than a question.

"No. I want you to stay."

Rosemary sprang to her feet. Sudden tears filled her eyes. "I can't stay here! Not with you and she...together!" She turned her back to him so he would not see the tears fall.

Lario set Sin-they aside and rose, coming to stand behind Rosemary. He turned her around, his hands clasping her shoulders. His lips kissed away the tears, and one forefinger stole up to gently rub the smallpox pit that rode high on her left cheek. "I want no other woman to share the hogan. I want you, Turquoise Woman."

Rosemary's lips quivered, not quite believing she understood Lario correctly. But she saw the truth in the depths of his eyes. She saw the love shining there. He might never tell her he loved her, but this was enough. "There is no other place for me but where you are, Lario."

"Me a woman, too!" Sin-they squeaked and squirmed between the closely pressed bodies of her parents. "Me stay here, too!"

They laughed and drew her up into their arms. Lario's nose burrowed into his daughter's rosy, plump cheek. "You and your mother, then, will be the only two—" He broke off, staring at something beyond Rosemary's shoulder.

She turned to find Hasteen in the doorway. His eyes blazed like the fires of a war dance. He whirled, and the curtain swung closed as if he had never been there.

"Josho!" Rosemary cursed beneath her breath as she thumped the batten down on the weft of her loom with grim determination. Four times more in the next ten minutes she struggled with her stubborn warp, then swore in English, but somehow the English no longer yielded quite the satisfaction of a good Navajo curse.

The monotonous weaving of the blanket was sheer torture for her. She often wondered why she bothered but knew she did it for Lario. So with her natural Irish stubbornness she gritted her teeth and forced her full concentration on the pattern which seemed to escape her with a leprechaun's resourcefulness. Her spine and her arms grew numb. At last, just before noon, she finished the weaving, carefully leaving a break in her pattern for the Navajo's evil spirits to escape. She cut the pitiful blanket from the loom and held it from her, squinting at it. It was a hopeless mess.

Rapidly she folded it and tucked it under her arm. It would never go beneath Lario's saddle. She would have to destroy it. Her feet slowed as she made her way from the *ramada* back toward her hogan. She could hear Lario's hammer ringing against his anvil.

As she topped the slight rise, she saw him working just outside their hogan. He was clad only in the Indian breechcloth, and the sun glistened off the sheen of perspiration that coated his coppery skin. As always now, when she would see him after an absence of a few hours, excitement bubbled up deep within her like a river under desert sands.

Without looking, the Indian in Lario told him she was there watching him. He put away his hammer and crossed to her. He ignored the blanket rolled under her arm. "You are the *bik'é hojoni*, Turquoise Woman," he said quietly. "The Trail of Beauty."

The tension and frustration eased from Rosemary, and her hand came up to caress Lario's jaw only to drop in case strange eyes watched. As if by mutual agreement they began walking toward their hogan together. Their conversation seemed banal enough. "Where is Sin-they?" Lario asked casually even as his black eyes boldly made love to her breasts.

"With your sister's child," Rosemary replied, blushing still after more than a year of living with this remarkable man. "You know how much Stephanie adores Lucero. She follows the four-year-old everywhere."

At the doorway Lario took the blanket from her and held it up, and Rosemary cringed, shutting her eyes. "The skill is something that must be mastered with much work, as a mustang must be mastered," he said softly. "But you have an eye for design and color. One day your blankets will bring much wampum."

Rosemary looked up at Lario through narrowed lids, but he was not mocking her. She saw only love for her in his serious expression. Then his well-defined lips curved slightly. "I can think of good use to put this blanket."

Rosemary grinned. "But 'tis only the middle of the day!" she said with pretended shock. Nevertheless she took the hand he held out to her and let him pull her inside the cool dark shelter into the welcome security of his embrace.

September brought news to the steadily growing, peaceful *rancheria*—the War Between the States was over, had been over in fact almost five months. At every station the telegraph wires linked, there had been celebration. Except when the news was relayed to Lario Santiago.

During the night the news of the War's end had come, Rosemary turned over on the blanket several times only to find that Lario had left their bed and not yet returned. At last she could pretend no longer to be the dutiful Navajo wife. Rather than wait passively for her man's return, Rosemary rose, checking first to see if Stephanie slept, and went in search of him. She knew many things weighed heavily on his heart, the largest, most difficult burden being the defection of Hasteen shortly after Guayo took Adala for his wife.

Rosemary had hoped that the happiness obvious in the faces of the youngest brother and Adala and the fact they expected a child in the spring would ease Lario's despondency over Hasteen's disappearance. She even blamed herself for the friction which had erupted between the two older brothers. She should have told Hasteen at once she could never be his wife rather than allow him hope.

The air was warmly spiced with the scent of the creosote bush and the late-night dampness, and the crystal-clear sky seemed to snap and crackle with a thousand stars as Rosemary made her way down toward the arroyo, the only place she knew to look for Lario. In the darkness her moccasined feet lightly sought the sure footholds of the shale-covered slope. Except for the heavy blanket which lent a peculiar stiffness to her slender body, she moved as quietly and surely upon the rocks as a mountain goat.

Still Lario was aware of her coming. "You would never surprise a deer," he said.

She spun to her left, her eyes searching among the overgrowth of the cedarbrake. She heard the smile in his voice and could well imagine his laughing eyes. Then he stepped out of the shadows of a boulder, and she ran to him.

"Don't leave me alone like that, Lario. If you must leave, wake me and tell me. I no longer have family or friends. I have no one but you and Stephanie."

He tilted her chin up. "You know I cannot always be with you, that I will not always be with you."

Rosemary wanted to cry out, "No!" But she only nodded her head, whispering, "I know."

It was the fatalist in him. He knew the path he had chosen and where it would probably lead, and they both knew he would not desert the path. And Rosemary knew her love for him would not be as great were Lario to be any other way. She would accept the joy she was given for the moment. Later...later when the will of Lario's gods was carried out...then she would begin the task of living without him.

Together they sank to sit on the pebbly bank, Rosemary's back against Lario's chest, his arms about her. "You worry about the news today?"

"With the war over, the Star Chief—General Carleton—will have more men available to hunt us down...more soldiers than stars in the sky."

It was something that Rosemary could not understand—the two-faced policy of the United States government, protecting the Indians through the civilian Department of Interior and exterminating them through their military Department of War. She longed to be able to offer a solution—and there was none; to say that everything would work out all right—when they both knew it probably would not.

She turned her head so she could look up into his dark face. "The *ga'han* have given us these moments, Lario. Let us not spoil the gift by demanding more."

She saw the gentle curve of the lips she loved so much. "*Íih,*" he said softly, using the Navajo endearment, "you are my life. You are a survivor. You are much more accepting than I. You should have been born an Indian."

Rosemary turned, nestling in the crook of his arm, and pressed her head against his chest. The steady beat of his heart was reassuring. She reached up and touched his face, wanting to remember its line and texture if the day came when...

And she did not let herself think beyond that or the gentle kiss that Lario pressed upon her eyelids. "Boy Chasing His Arrow has moved far across the sky," Lario said. "We should return."

But neither made a move to leave. Lario pulled Rosemary against him, his body and spirit seeking hers. And she gave him of herself, taking him into her, clutching him to her as she gave him the release he sought. She wanted to keep him with her, to be filled with him.

The second time, as his hands slowly stroked and caressed each part of her and his lips tasted of the warm nectar of her loins, loving her with a passion she had never experienced—this was his gift to her.

The attack, when it came three months later in the semi-darkness of an early January dawn in 1866, was so unex-

108

pected, so swift, that the ninety-five unarmed women, children, and old men asleep in their hogans had little chance to escape the slaughter that followed.

Rosemary, whose hogan was away from the others, almost out of sight of the *rancheria,* was awakened from an already troubled sleep by the heartrending screams. Her first incoherent thought was the men were returning from their hunting expedition, for with the winter the antelope and deer had migrated further south again.

By the time she reached the hogan's doorway, soldiers swarmed over the *rancheria* like ravaging locusts. They were all black men, the first Rosemary had ever seen, from the Ninth and Tenth Cavalry Regiments. These Buffalo Soldiers, as the Plains Indians called them, used their rifles and pistols on the women and children who tried to flee into the surrounding mountains. The camp became a shambles. Wounded children cried for mercy, and Rosemary, paralyzed by horror, watched as one soldier with black woolly hair swung a rifle butt against Lucero's head. Where was Toysei, she wondered wildly, and Adala and War Blanket? Within mere seconds the ground was strewn with Navajo dead. Crimson decorated the snow-covered ground.

Intruding into the scene of horror rode Hasteen, and Rosemary knew at once how the Buffalo Soldiers had found their camp. Even as she whirled to gather up a crying Stephanie, Hasteen charged his horse toward her hogan. Half-sliding, half-slipping, Rosemary fled down the slope of the arroyo with Stephanie in tow. On the stream's other side was a crevice in the canyon wall that opened into a narrow passageway. If she could make it there before Hasteen, there was a chance.

The water was shockingly cold when she and Stephanie plunged into the stream and waded across. As she pushed her way through the greenbriar that patched the far bank, she heard the scraping of horse hooves descending like a rolling boulder down the slope and into the stream. Then she felt the pain as her hair was jerked suddenly from behind.

"Run, Stephanie!" she yelled and tried to twist loose from Hasteen's grip. His horse lost its footing on the slippery shale, and Hasteen fell upon her, knocking the breath from her lungs.

"Murderer!" she shouted when she broke free, gasping. Then she glimpsed the pain that stamped his face and knew in that instant he had not expected the carnage to accompany his betrayal.

She turned and scrambled upward, but he grabbed at her legs, and she slid back down. The sharp rocks grazed her thighs. At the same instant she kicked out at him, Hasteen went rigid. He pitched forward, not crumpling but falling like a toppling statue. At the far side of the bank a bewhiskered soldier quickly reloaded his Springfield, and Rosemary realized the man had not recognized Hasteen as their informer.

She struggled out from under his body and threw herself into the greenbriar-covered crevice as the rifle cracked. The bullet impacted with rock just beyond and above her head. An arm's distance away Stephanie sat whimpering, her forefinger jammed in her mouth.

"For God's sake, hush, pet!" Rosemary begged. But the din of massacring drowned out the child's hiccoughs of tears.

Little by little Rosemary edged forward on her elbows until she was next to Stephanie. "We're going to race, all right? When I tell you to go, you must run as fast as you can."

The two raced down the narrow corridor of redstone. Rosemary, hearing the laughter of her daughter, thought how macabre and ironical it sounded as it mingled with the screams and gunfire behind them.

21

For three days Rosemary and Stephanie existed on piñon nuts and juniper berries. Exhaustion showed in Rosemary's face, the hollow cheeks and the shadows beneath the eyes. She slept in snatches, awakening at the rustle of leaves or the snap of twigs. Sometimes a tree popped with the cold, cracking like a rifle shot. Immediately she would gather Stephanie's little body close to her for reassurance.

Where was Lario? And the fear that haunted her returned —dead!

She kept moving, confining her steps to the rocks and streams by instinct. She was a hunted animal with no thought to the future. Only the survival of the moment. And that looked doubtful to her as she watched the tiny snowflakes begin to fall again the afternoon of the third day. The sawtoothed peaks of the Chuska Mountains blocked off the gray shafts of the winter sun, leaving Rosemary and Stephanie to huddle in chilling shadows of approaching night.

Wedged between a boulder and a trachyte-porphyry ridge and banked by rabbit brush the two were partially protected from the fierce winds that drove down the canyon that night. But it did not stop the icy moisture that numbed Rosemary's hands and feet. She stretched out her hands for Stephanie and looked in horror at the blue that colored them. Next black and then frostbite, she thought.

Her hands felt alien as she gathered Stephanie against her to conserve their body heat and tried to rub her daughter's tiny hands and feet, which fortunately still had some color in them. Rosemary's movements decelerated as she grew sleepier with each passing moment.

I must not sleep!

"Stephanie! Stephanie!" She shook her daughter. "Wake up!" The child's heavy lids lifted and then closed, and Rosemary shook her again. "I have a story to tell you—about the Gate of the Clashing Rocks and the Slayer of Enemy Gods."

Once more the little girl's eyelids fluttered open. Rosemary began the Indian tale of how the bear, Usen, had been the ruler of all the earth he walked, but soon she heard her voice slur. Stephanie was curled up against her, asleep. *What is the use? Perhaps 'tis easier this way than what we face if we are caught.*

She let her eyelids fall. Curiously, the cold no longer bothered her.

Heat. The heat stung. Rosemary opened her eyes. She was still alive! The falling snow almost obliterated the patches of sky visible through the brush above her. Slowly she turned her head. She was lying in a lean-to, hastily erected, from what her recent experience could discern. Nearby a fire burned. A small smile touched her lips. Piñon—the Indian panacea. The resinous wood would burn in the wettest weather.

The stinging of her feet drew her attention back to her immediate person. There sat Lario, briskly massaging the soles of her feet, then each toe. "This is a woman's work for her brave," he said with a wry smile, but she saw the relief that leaped into his eyes.

"I should have known you would find us." Was that her voice that sounded so much like a croak?

"You left a trail that even a white man could follow." He took patches of her calico skirt from his pocket. "I collected these—before someone else could."

His smile faded, and she knew what he was thinking. "Are they—is everyone dead?"

He nodded, and Rosemary, who had thought her heart was as dry as dust, welled up inside with tears for the dead women

111

and children. And suddenly she remembered their own child. "Stephanie!" Her head twisted about frantically, her eyes searching.

"Sin-they is all right," Lario said. He turned his head to where his poncho lay in a heap. "She is sleeping."

Reassured, Rosemary sighed. Lario continued. "Manuelito has surrendered. At Fort Wingate with the twenty-three men we have left. Guayo went with Manuelito after he learned of Adala's death."

His hand stopped the massaging of her feet. "Only the Apaches are left who still refuse to be imprisoned at Bosque Redondo. I am going to join the Warm Springs chief, Victorio."

Rosemary jerked her foot away. She sat up. "I'm going with you, Lario. Stephanie and I."

He shook his head. In the flickering firelight she could see the weary lines that creased each side of his mouth. "No. I have kept the two of you with me—and almost lost you to the *Yeibechai*. I would rather not have you and at least know that you are alive somewhere...that your thoughts hear and speak with mine, though maybe I will never see you again."

Rosemary moved next to Lario. She laid her head on his chest, nuzzling the hollow of his neck with her lips. "You tried to leave me behind once before, Lario Santiago. You did not succeed then—and you won't now."

Her breath tickled his skin. He wound his fingers in her silky hair and tilted her head back. "You are as delicate as the blade of my knife, Turquoise Woman... and as enduring."

She knew he meant it as a compliment. "With you, for you," she whispered, "I can be strong," and she offered him the sanctuary of her lips. Later they made love, slowly, leisurely, drawing from each other sustenance, like water from a well, renewing their life's strength. The pleasure of giving, of hearing Lario's hoarse cry, was equal to the pleasure his knowing brown hands brought to her own body.

Rosemary knew they had created something indestructible, a love far more enduring than their bodies. She lay there in the cradle of Lario's arms, drifting in the savage sweetness of release and thought that some of Lario's fatalism was claiming her. Outside the warmth of the firelight the *Yeibechai* were waiting, the gods of the Supernatural, of death. But as long as she and Lario remained together, the light of their love would keep the *Yeibechai* at bay.

The fleas were worse than ever that August. Rosemary finally relented and took Stephanie to the stream one morning to anoint her scalp with a mud plaster that suffocated the pests. The child loved it. She dabbled in the mud and spread it on her naked sun-browned body.

Looking at the mud-caked skin and the coppery curls stiffly packed with the plaster, Rosemary had to laugh. She was reminded of the Buffalo Soldiers and their wiry black hair. But the curve of the woman's lips disappeared with the recollection of that tragic afternoon the soldiers attacked the *ranchería*.

A chill coursed up her spine, and Rosemary looked about her at the Apache camp. It had taken Lario more than three weeks and almost six hundred miles to lead his wife and child back into the New Mexico Territory to Victorio's camp.

The camp lacked the friendliness and warmth of the Navajo *ranchería*. It was because it was not as clean, Rosemary told herself. There were the thin, mangy dogs that roamed the camp, seeking a tuft of green to lie on; the flimsy hovels that the Apache squaws erected in minutes, leaving them and moving to newer ones when they became filthy and flea-ridden. And there was the impermanence of the camp—always moving in and out of the rugged and impassable canyons that converged and twisted through the Mongollon Mountains.

Or perhaps she felt more a stranger at the camp because of the Warm Spring Apaches themselves—the *Chihinne* or Red People they called themselves because of the band of red clay painted across their faces. The women carried knives and some of them had ammunition belts and rifles. Then there was always the sight of a squaw braiding a bridle with the hair of some scalped victim.

Rosemary found it difficult to adjust to these more barbaric customs of the Apache. It was bad enough that the men braided animal pelts in their hair, but when an Apache woman wanted to tattoo Rosemary's forehead and chin Lario had to explain as tactfully as he could that Rosemary's customs forbade tattooing. All of which together went to make her and Lario outcasts in Victorio's camp.

But what Rosemary found most intolerable was the fact that Stephanie readily and successfully adapted to the Apache way of life. The child spoke Apache better than English, and often Rosemary would have to ask her daughter's help in communicating. Wistfully, Rosemary realized how happy she had been at the Navajo *ranchería*. Only the nights when she and Lario came together in the privacy of their wickiup did she experience the hours of contentment, the moments of ecstasy, that made all else worthwhile.

Rosemary calculated that enough time had elapsed to suffocate the fleas and began to wash off the dried mud in the rushing water with the soap from the *sotol*, a yuccalike plant. Stephanie squirmed and kicked, and when Rosemary finally released her, she scrambled to her feet and planted both her tiny fists on her naked hips in imitation of the *caique*, Victorio.

"No more water!" she sputtered. Her golden-red curls were plastered to her face, and her grubby hands pushed them out of her eyes. Then once more in good humor, she began to laugh as the water dripped on her small potbelly.

Rosemary could not help but compare her with Jamie— Jamie with the even disposition, sweet and considerate. And Stephanie—explosive, mercurial, gregarious, and terribly spoiled by the other Indian children who, out of admiration, allowed her to have her way. Though barely three, she tried to keep up with them in their games and loved *cooncan*, which was played with hoops. And she was quite fearless on a pony. She should have been Stephen's daughter, Rosemary thought— or son.

With the thought of Stephen Rosemary automatically recalled Cambria and its beauty, with the Pecos lacing the green valley like a blue satiny ribbon. The loss of Cambria was like the loss of a child to her; yet it was a grief she would willingly bear for the privilege of being near Lario.

The bathing over, Rosemary started back to camp. Her heart quickened when she saw Lario in conversation with Victorio but she continued her pace. It would never do for the lowly wife to interrupt her husband even in greeting.

Wife! She was not Lario's wife. But she belonged more to him than she ever could to Stephen. Just looking at Lario made her pulse race with excitement. He was much taller than Victorio, who was of average height and already graying. The Apache men were built like deer, with small hands and feet, slender sinewy arms and legs, and full-chested lithe bodies. Like the Apaches, Lario wore only the breechcloth and knee-high moccasins, and when Rosemary glimpsed his muscle-corded thighs and back, she blushed with the memory of their nights of love. For this she would cede Cambria to Stephen.

She knew that at the moment Lario was disagreeing with Victorio's policy, for rather than attempting to set free imprisoned Navajo and Apaches and establish a more permanent camp Victorio preferred a "strike and run" type of operation. His warriors would lie in wait along portions of routes remote from settlements for small parties and unprotected wagon trains, and having plundered both travelers and wagons, would rapidly retreat to the fastnesses of the mountains.

Victorio was an intrepid warrior and, so Rosemary thought, would have made an excellent general. And while she did not like his policy of revenge on sometimes innocent settlers, she knew the aging man to be at least a compassionate one, which was evident even in the way he teased Stephanie about her hair, telling her she painted her curls with red dye when no one was looking.

There lived among the Warm Spring Apaches for a time a young Chiricahua Apache called Gokliya, whom Rosemary thoroughly detested. The Apache would as soon kick a sleeping dog out of his way than step over it. He was a troublemaker and a braggart. Worse, he refused to follow Victorio, wanting to be a leader himself, thereby causing a rift in the camp. Rosemary made sure she and Stephanie stayed out of his way when he was at the camp.

Eventually Victorio ousted Gokliya. But neither Rosemary nor the rest of the Territory had heard the last of the Chiricahua Apache, for later in a battle with Mexican Rurales he established himself as a reputable war chief under the name of Geronimo.

The passage of time, like the growth of Stephanie, could not be seen. The sun moved a little more to the north, the child was a little taller. For Rosemary time moved like the sluggard Pecos beneath the shade of the tamarisks and poplars.

She wanted desperately to leave Victorio's camp. She was tired of playing the *soldadera,* a miscast role for the woman who hated killing in all its forms. She wanted the permanence of a home and an orderly life. Thoughts of Cambria and Jamie crowded more often into her mind. What did Jamie look like now? Did he remember and miss her?

Then one crisp autumn evening after she had tucked a sleeping Stephanie between the warmth of her buffalo robes and returned to grinding the small amount of corn kernels left, for it seemed she never had enough time to finish her work, she saw from the corner of her eye Lario stiffen, as if he were listening to or for something.

She put away the *mano,* a stone slab, and moved over next to him. In the light of the fire's dying embers his bronzed face was as pale as the gypsum whitewash. "What is it, Lario?"

His black eyes raised to hers. "You don't hear it, do you?"

She paused. "No."

"Tecolate, the Owl. He calls."

Rosemary's head canted. Did she hear the dismal hoo-hooing of an owl, the bird of ill fortune, or was it a trick of the wind on her imagination? Her hand cupped his jaw. "I won't let omens decide my life for me!" she said with a fierceness born of desperation.

Lario's hand caught hers and brushed his lips against the inside of her wrist. "You are the strong one, *áád*," he whispered. *Áád*, the Navajo word for wife!

That night they did not make love but held each other throughout the hours of darkness. Toward dawn Lario kissed Rosemary's temple, saying, "I love you."

She had known for a long time now of his love though he had never uttered the words to her. And now she understood its full depth.

22

In February a late winter screamed down upon Victorio's camp with all the fury of a trading-post whore. The grazing for the paltry flock of sheep and herd of cattle was insufficient, and the dry bitter cold forced the camp to move down out of the Mongollon Mountains closer to the more fertile Rio Grande Valley—a warmer climate and better grazing range but more exposed to the danger of discovery by the Fourth U.S. Cavalry.

But it was not the weather but a visit of a sub-chief that had precipitated this latest move. Barboncito and several of his warriors had escaped late the summer before from Bosque Redondo, and the frightening tale they brought back convinced otherwise those who entertained thoughts of giving themselves up in exchange for food and shelter at the Bosque Redondo.

Rosemary remembered Barboncito as he had sat talking with Lario two days earlier. The chief's face with the strong nose and hooded eyes was ravaged with grief. "It is a miserable place," he told Lario in a hoarse, almost inaudible voice. "We are prodded with bayonets and herded into adobe corrals where they are always counting us and marking numbers in small books.

"The *Naat'aani* promise us blankets and clothing and better food, but we never get them. All the mesquite and cottonwood have been chopped down so that only roots are left for firewood. And there is nothing to protect us from the rain and sun, and we have to dig holes in the ground and cover ourselves with grass mats. We live like prairie dogs in burrows! We are crowded together like penned sheep! There are many others like ourselves risking their lives to get away."

When Lario questioned Barboncito about Guayo, the subchief knew nothing, for there were seven thousand Indians closely watched and it was impossible to move out of an allotted area.

In preparation to leave, Rosemary packed the few belongings they had on the travois secured to the back of a calico pony. She was not sorry to be leaving the camp, but she wished she and Stephanie and Lario were leaving the Apaches—where the three of them could go, she did not know.

Lario came up and held the pony's bridle, steadying the horse. "The wires talk of Grant Raffin," he said, and she knew he was watching her. She turned and faced him, waiting. "He has been made Colonel of the Fourth Cavalry," Lario continued, his eyes never releasing her. "He claims he will not rest until the last Navajo, the last Apache, is wiped from the Territory."

At last Lario looked away, saying, "When we reach the Rio Grande, I am sending you home. A war camp is no place for a woman—" And then he smiled at her, adding, "Not even a squaw."

Rosemary turned her back on him and began strapping the remainder of the articles on the travois. "I will not go back."

He jerked her about, and for the first time ever she saw emotion blazing in his face. His grip hurt her arms, but she did not cry out. "I don't want you here. You are in my way. You are going home!"

Rosemary's words were almost lost in the wind's howling. "You are my home, Lario."

He swung away, and she wanted to cry out to him, but she knew that this time she could not yield.

She found Stephanie playing with the horsehide cards with another child, a game her daughter was almost as good at as a Mississippi riverboat gambler. She bundled Stephanie in the thick blanket, which, though smoky and smelly, had no holes and put her on the back of the pony. With Rosemary leading the pony, they fell in line with the rest of the women, and the band began to move out.

Somewhere ahead of them Lario and the other braves reconnoitered the terrain while the older children and the men too old to fight brought up the rear, driving the remaining sheep and cattle.

For two days the band fought the bitter cold that slammed against their faces like doors of ice as they picked their way down along the treacherous trails out of the Mongollons. Several times a sheep or cow, precious sustenance to the camp, strayed off.

At night Lario and Rosemary slept together but not touching despite the cold. Both remained adamant in their decisions. Come morning Rosemary would see Lario's stony countenance and sorrow would knife through her. Soon they would reach the basin, and it appeared that there could only be a bleak resolution to their personal battle, regardless of who was the victor.

However, the forces of nature were the main foe to be immediately dealt with. The previous summers had been dry ones, and the last two winters had not brought enough snow in the mountains to water the dry arroyos of the semi-arid plateaus. Now when the caravan of Indians reached the basin, they found only dry waterholes, saw only flats of alkali.

Rosemary watched the single-file string of gaunt steers approach an arid wallow or a Navajo mother suckle a lamb at her breast and knew what it was to cry in one's heart. And when Stephanie's lips cracked with the bite of the dry cold, she was tempted to approach one of the adobe houses she saw in the distance, looking dingy and delapidated without whitewash. But the fear of civilization held her back.

There was no mush to be had from the mescal plant nor bear or fish meat, for the latter two were taboo to the Indian, and so the band continued its nomadic life, migrating steadily eastward toward the Rio Grande out of necessity.

One afternoon, as Rosemary watched the awkward speed of a fleeing roadrunner, she saw the dust churning against the northern horizon. An hour later a scout lathered his pony toward the band of women and children. "Many soldiers! Many *petiltows*—rifles! Flee!"

Like a well-organized army the band of women and children swerved back and began their retreat toward the foothills of the San Mateo Range. All but Rosemary. She stood next to the calico pony as the horde streamed past her in flight. Then she began walking toward the dust cloud that billowed on the horizon. Without the others to break the sweep of frigid wind she found each step forward more difficult.

"Mama," Stephanie wailed from beneath the protective layer of the blanket, "I'm cold!"

Rosemary looked back at her daughter who rode the pony bareback as well as any Apache child. "We shall be warm soon," she shouted.

Muffled by the blanket Rosemary leaned into the wind, ducking her head. Each step took her closer now to the Fourth Cavalry, to civilization. And to Lario. Her heart beat faster with the fear that even now he might be dead. But some instinct told her he was not. Not yet. She would know, she would feel it deep within her heart. If he managed to escape the soldiers, he would return for Stephanie and her. And if he was taken captive...then she would find him.

The sergeant saluted the officer behind the pine-paneled desk. "Colonel Raffin, sir. There's a squaw outside who demands to speak with you. Says she's a citizen of the United States." He paused, then added, "She does speak English."

It was late in the evening, well after eight, and Grant was tired. Libby would be peeved that he was late again. What he needed was a stout whiskey. But he'd have to forego that if his physique was to be kept trim.

Grant sighed and set aside the report the lieutenant had brought him on the last detail. The engagement with the Apache would result in the complete subjugation of the warring tribes. Only Victorio had eluded him, but it would not be long now before the wily chief, without the aid of his warriors, submitted.

Grant's troops had known neither summer rest nor winter quarters but had pursued the Indian foe relentlessly month after month, night and day, over mesas and deserts and rivers, under boiling suns and rough winter snows, killing and capturing them in their most chosen retreats.

Now, with all but Victorio and a few renegades incarcerated, the Apaches' and Navajos' spirit would be broken. Grant glanced again at the figures—over seven thousand Navajo and four hundred Apache living on the Bosque Redondo Reservation, a tract of land forty miles square with six thousand acres of arable land. It had been a successful campaign, resulting in, he hoped, his appointment to succeed General Carleton as Commander of the Department of New Mexico.

"Ahhm."

Grant looked up at the sergeant. He had completely forgotten the soldier's presence. His fingers massaged his forehead. Too many days and night spent at the damned fort. He needed to get into Santa Fe. Look up Doña Lura or, better, one of her girls. "Send the squaw in, Barstow," he said tiredly.

When next Grant glanced up, a rail-thin woman stood

119

before him. She had the high cheekbones found in the Athabascan tribes, but her straggly, lank hair, a dirty shade of brown, was not dark enough for a Navajo or Apache. Perhaps a stray Pueblo caught in the roundup, he thought, looking at the haggard woman. Well, he'd get this over with and get to bed. "Yes?" he snapped.

"Grant."

It was such a hoarse whisper that he did not think he heard correctly. His eyes narrowed. "What was it you said?"

Rosemary put a hand on the desk to steady herself. She saw Grant's distaste as he eyed the ragged and dirty fingernails, saw his nose wrinkle as the odor of her unwashed body hit him. She had walked nearly three hundred miles. Bloody tracks made a path on the puncheon floor from the door. She had to smile at her accomplishment, at the fact she had managed to survive; and the sight of her macabre grin, which resembled the ghostly grimace of a skull, startled Grant.

His fastidiousness caused him to shrink inwardly from the woman across from him. He had a horror of the diseases the squalid Indians carried. "What is it you want?" he asked impatiently. What was it the sergeant said, something about her claiming to be a United States citizen? Impossible!

"I want your help, Grant," she managed to get out. "I want to find Lario Santiago."

His blue eyes widened then narrowed disbelievingly. "Rosemary?"

She looked down at herself with a smile of self-derision. "Aye," she replied, looking back to Grant. "'Tis the same."

"Good God, Rosemary!" He hurried from around the desk and pulled out a chair for her. "We believed you dead these last three years."

"Sergeant!" he bellowed. The young man stepped inside, and Grant said, "Rouse the cook. I want a hot meal within the hour."

When the sergeant left, he quickly went to his desk and pulled out the bottle of whiskey and poured a glassful, handing it to Rosemary. Even now he could not bring himself to touch her as she accepted the glass. "Now's not the time for questions. I'll have Libby find clothing for you. A bath and you'll be your old self."

Grant rattled on, disconcerted by Rosemary's own composure in the face of what she must have gone through, and he realized she would never be her old self. Finally, as he told her that Stephen, still grieving over her supposed death, had not remarried, she broke in, saying, "Jamie—how is he? What does he look like now?"

"He's doing fine, Rosemary. We—Libby and I and our son Wayne, he was born not long after your disappearance—were at Cambria last month with Rita and Jiraldo to celebrate Jamie's fifth birthday. He's a tall lad—I guess he got that from you."

For the first time Rosemary took a sip of the whiskey. It burned all the way down, but it warmed her where she thought she would never be warm again...and it steadied her for what news Grant would give her of Lario. Dear God, don't let him be dead, she prayed.

She had been kept separate from the warriors taken in the cavalry's surprise attack and had been put with prisoners taken in previous roundups and marched to Fort Sumner. She had asked, upon arriving, of both the Navajo and the Apache she met if they knew of Lario's fate. But no one knew anything, much less cared. Their apathy stunned her.

"What do you know of Lario Santiago?" she asked with sudden directness.

Grant poured himself a glass and took a deep swallow. So that was how it was. Incredible! She was in love with the Navajo. An Indian! He looked into the large eyes, always before so expressive. Now it was like looking at a wall. Had she lost her reasoning? Gone loco living among the savages? He considered lying to her, telling her the buck was dead, but decided against it.

"I'll check the roster of prisoners as soon as the captain completes it, Rosemary. But you must understand if Lario survived the attack, he will be executed along with the other Indian males within the week."

"You can't! He's done nothing that you haven't done, Grant. He's fighting for his survival! Is that so wrong?" The whiskey sloshed from her glass, and she set it on the desk with a trembling hand.

"That's Carleton's policy—either they yield to removal to the reservation or be exterminated. Too many peace treaties have been broken because they declare it's bad Indians doing the killing and stealing. They've got to know we mean business this time."

Rosemary sagged in the chair. Grant put his own glass down in alarm. "I'll take you home. You can eat there. The quarters aren't much, but they're the best the fort has to offer."

It was only a large, round wooden bucket, and Rosemary had to stand while she washed, but to feel the lye soap and

121

hot water, the first in three years, cleanse away the accumulated dirt—it was an almost unbearable pleasure.

Libby poked her head inside the bedroom door, and Rosemary did not miss the gloating look that settled on the woman's now-plump face as she took in Rosemary's emaciated body. "I got you a dress. But it's certain sure going to hang on you."

Rosemary refused to cover herself. "Thank you, Libby. Do you have anything that Stephanie could wear?" So many words at once. She had forgotten how talkative the Anglo race was.

In the corner of the room stood a Wabash bedstead. On it lay Stephanie in exhausted sleep. Libby glanced at the child, whose long gangling legs stuck out from beneath the blanket. Looks just like an Indian brat, she thought. But it was her Christian duty to help the heathen, and God only knew what kind of fallen woman Rosemary Rhodes was after living with the savages for three years.

Libby sighed at the burden that had been placed on her shoulders. "I don't think my Wayne's knee pants would fit your daughter," she said, her mouth pulled tightly as if she had tasted a lemon. Privately she thought she would rather not have her son's clothing contaminated by the Rhodes child. No telling what varmints were crawling all over her. Still, the girl was the daughter of the most powerful man in the Territory. For Grant's sake she would have to silently endure their visitors. "The commissary clerk's wife—her girl died of the croup last year. She might still have clothing that'd fit the child."

After Stephanie had awakened and she had been washed and dressed, Rosemary and her daughter joined Grant and Libby and Wayne at the long puncheon table for dinner. Rosemary felt awkward handling the utensils and had no desire for food, not until she learned of Lario's fate. But Stephanie dug into the roasted venison, ripping the meat with her teeth and hands. Rosemary saw Libby eye Grant in horror at the child's table manners.

I won't apologize! If their son had lived as we had, he would know no better either!

Grant touched his napkin to his lips. "Rosemary..." He hesitated and looked around the table. "The—ah, friend you asked about is here."

She nodded, but he saw the blue-green eyes cloud over like the murky waters of a lagoon. "He has two weeks," he said.

Rosemary drew a shaky breath. "And there is nothing I can do to change the orders?"

"What are you two talking about?" Libby asked. She had never liked the intimacy that had existed between the two, that seemed to still exist in spite of Rosemary's haggard appearance.

"An old friend," Grant said, and for the first time Rosemary actually liked Grant. Perhaps there existed a spark of compassion in Stephen's protégé after all. It gave her hope.

Now that Stephanie's stomach was full, she began to look around at the strange surroundings, her eyes wide with interest but wary at the same time. And her eyes crossed the inquisitive gaze of Wayne, only to come back. The boy, four months younger than she, was the most beautiful creature she had ever beheld. Below golden curls that seemed to her as bright as the sun were vivid blue eyes in the pale face that made her want to reach and touch them to see if such a color was real.

When he continued to eye her steadily, she became uneasy, wondering if there were something wrong with her. Had she sprouted antlers as old War Blanket had promised she would if she spoke with untruths? Stephanie stuck out her tongue at the boy and grinned at the frown that suddenly crinkled his face.

Losing interest in him, she finished inventorying the room with its hard, colorless walls, then turned to her mother, asking in a very grown-up tone, "Where is my father?"

"Your father's in Santa Fe," Grant said.

With a start Rosemary realized Stephanie meant Lario. She forestalled her daughter from any further questions, saying, "Stephanie, 'tis bedtime."

"But, mama, I just woke up." However, her lids were having a difficult time staying open. She yawned, stretched, and wandered off into the other room without any further protest.

"Stephen won't return to Cambria for two more weeks, I understand," Grant said. "Why don't you stay with us? I'll send a courier to Cambria to leave word for Stephen to come for you."

Rosemary saw Libby grimace at Grant's invitation to stay with them. But that did not make any difference to her.

She had two weeks to make Grant change the orders regarding his captive.

23

"It must have been awful for you, dear," the quartermaster's wife ventured. Her protruding eyes darted a furtive glance at Rosemary and quickly returned to fix their attention on the blanket she quilted.

"It was difficult at times, Mrs. Pettigrew," Rosemary said in a noncommittal tone. She jerked on the thread of the gown's hem she was letting out. The dress, Libby's, would still be too short, but it would serve its purpose for the rest of the week.

One week left. Dear God, what was she going to do?

Molly Mallam, the fort's washerwoman, put down her patchwork. Her small mouth pursed in indecision, then opened to blurt out, "Were you—that is, did they..." She broke off and looked about the sewing circle for assistance.

"No, I was not raped," Rosemary replied, each word falling like a drumbeat in the silence of the avid listeners.

"You hear about them doing such horrible things to women," Libby said, unwilling to let the subject drop.

"I suppose so," Rosemary said. Her stony gaze went from one lady to the next in the circle. "But then I personally saw atrocities committed against the Indians by our glorious soldiers. Things like..." And Rosemary halted, seeing the skepticism that claimed the women before she had even begun. She realized they did not want to know. Surely they had seen for themselves the suffering the Indians were enduring right there on the Bosque Redondo Reservation.

The memory was clear enough in her mind from when Grant had driven her out to the reservation earlier that week. The insects that swarmed in spite of the cold, almost devouring the babies. There was no game, no food except the unfit maggoty beef issued them by the Indian Agent—and Rosemary gritted her teeth at that thought, for it was Stephen who supplied the beef to the Indian Agent.

The Navajo and Apache tried to be farmers, like the Pueblo, but they were pastoral—sheepherders and cattlemen—and the worms ate their corn. Grant mentioned that the trading post Stephen had established on the reservation was selling liquor; and if that was not bad enough, smallpox had broken out, so that Grant refused to let her go among the Indians in search of Guayo and Lario in spite of her protest that she had already had the dreaded disease.

Guayo had disappeared from the reservation several months earlier and no one knew if he had succumbed to the disease and famine or if he had escaped. But Grant had located Lario from among the eight thousand Indians and had summoned him to the trading post. And that was the worst of all.

The trading post was set on a flat, bare buttress of sand and rock. It was an L-shaped, one-story house of adobe and stone with a corrugated iron roof. Around it was nothing green. Behind it was a corral with six-foot-high sides.

With Grant, Rosemary waited inside, nervously warming herself before the pot-belly black-iron stove sitting in a sandbox that also served as a spittoon. Grant had dismissed the old clerk so that the two of them were alone when they heard the smart knock at the door. Rosemary jumped. The door opened and a grizzled soldier saluted Grant. "I have the prisoner here, sir."

"That'll be all, private. Dismissed."

Rosemary watched the doorway, unaware of the bleak wind that swept through it to rustle her hoop skirts. Her heart pounded like a locomotive. She heard him before she saw him. With shuffling steps Lario stepped into the doorway. Iron clamps riveted his ankles and wrists.

"Your days of striking and running are at an end, Santiago," Grant said, and Rosemary saw the delight play on his handsome face, delight that he had at last outmaneuvered the Indian.

Lario said nothing, his bronze face maintaining its Indian sang-froid. Nevertheless, Rosemary recognized with a start the deep hate that flared in the eyes that were as black as the smoke of hell.

And the hate was directed at herself!

Seeing her at Grant's side, he believed she had betrayed him. Suddenly she could think of nothing to say, nothing that she wanted Grant to hear. "Could we be alone for a few minutes, Grant?"

One blond brow arched. "A lovers' tryst? I suppose so. I'll wait outside."

"No," Lario had said, speaking for the first time. "It is ended." He had turned his back on them and begun to move away. Rosemary had opened her mouth to call out, and Grant had said, "Don't, Rosemary. At least leave him his pride."

Rosemary looked around the sewing circle now and said, "I'm sure you would be more interested in figures and facts

125

than my own personal observations." Her gaze halted on Libby's face. "Your husband informed me that the United States government has spent nearly thirty million dollars so far in its war to exterminate the Apache and Navajo and has actually succeeded in exterminating less than two hundred, including women, children, and old men. Two hundred out of seven thousand. Your tax money is being wasted."

As Rosemary tasted the spicy potato soup that evening at dinner, she became aware that Grant's gaze followed her. She had looked in Libby's tarnished mirror that morning and was almost satisfied with what she saw. Another week of forced eating and her weight would be back to normal; no more protruding pelvic bones or prominent ribs exposed. The gauntness and haggard look were easing into supple and firm lines. Before dinner she had pinched some color into her cheeks.

Now, if no one looked into her eyes and saw the numbness that grew in her heart like mold in the dark, they would never suspect her life was nothing more than an existence. It could never be more if Lario were executed.

One week left.

"Grant," she began. "There are people, Apaches, I wish to say good-bye to before I return to Cambria. Could you arrange for me to visit the reservation once more?"

The way Grant's gaze moved over her, her feminine instinct told her he would accede to her request. If only Libby would not ask to go along. Rosemary held her breath, but Libby relieved her fears, saying, "I don't see how you can stand to be around those filthy people. All those flies—and the odor. It's just horrible!" She pressed her napkin to her nose as if she could actually smell the reservation's stench.

Surprisingly, Rosemary found herself almost enjoying the ride in the spring wagon the next day...if she did not let herself think about the task that lay ahead of her. Since the March air was brisk, she wore a woolen shawl, but there was the hint of spring everywhere. The sun burst forth like a glorious yellow daisy. Froths of wild plum blossoms relieved the majestic desolation of the russet-hued landscape. There was a primal charm about the country that served Rosemary's purpose.

Grant had driven from the fort, out of sight of the watchtowers, and then she saw it—the barn that was really nothing more than a lean-to. The first time she and Grant had passed that way the week before, it had almost escaped her attention. But later she had recalled it. It was perfect for her purpose.

"Grant," she said and laid her hand on his, which held the loosely gathered lines. "Stop," she said when he looked at her questioningly.

The wagon rolled to a halt, and Rosemary looked about her, satisfied with the place. The Pecos wound closer to the road there so that the few stunted cottonwoods partially shielded the small barn. "Can we walk, Grant? I—I want to talk to you."

"All right." He edged the wagon off the dirt road between the cluster of trees.

Rosemary managed to get down from the wagon on her own, avoiding Grant's proffered hand. Taking her time, she walked on ahead of him in the direction of the barn. Inside the ramshackle structure shafts of sunlight streamed through the roof's cracks, and there was the warm smell of manure and hay.

Grant caught her arm and turned her to face him. "What is it you have in mind, Rosemary?"

Her eyes searched the arrogant, brash face. Excitement glistened in his dark blue eyes. She did not need to pretend then. "Seduction," she said with a derisive smile.

His eyes narrowed, as if not quite believing her. He caught her to him. "You mean it?"

She placed her hand against his chest, feeling the scratchy sky-blue kersey greatcoat, which, flapped back over the other shoulder, made a gallant display. Her voice warned him of her serious intent. "I'm negotiating a business deal with you, Grant. Much as you and Stephen do with your bankers, your politicians, your flunkies."

"It's Lario, isn't it?" She nodded, never taking her eyes from his, and he said, "You must love him terribly—to come to me like this."

She saw the pain in his eyes. "I do. But I respect you enough to be honest. I would not use you. I am giving you what you want. In exchange for what I want...his life spared."

His smile just as derisive, Grant set her from him. "I'll match your honesty. I'll accept your—bribe. But you must fully realize I cannot promise anything. Only that I'll try."

Rosemary's fingers went to the buttons at her throat. She had chosen not to wear hoops and stays. She wanted to get the affair over as quickly as possible. Grant laid aside his belt and saber. But when he removed his clothes, she was surprised. She had been prepared to martyr herself, to endure Grant as she had Stephen. But Grant was superbly built, like a Greek statue, all golden rather than copper.

127

And that made the coming act that much worse. To actually enjoy making love to Grant would be a betrayal of Lario. She closed her eyes as he came to her, lifting her in his arms and laying her on a mound of musty hay. The contact of his skin sent shivers through her.

"Jesus, but you're beautiful!" he whispered, his voice husky with passion. He stroked her body, her long, rigid back, her hips that curved softly, the small but perfectly rounded breasts.

Her eyes flew open. "No, Grant," she protested as he began to kiss her all over.

"Yes. I want you completely. No holding back. It must be a fair exchange," he reminded her.

She closed her eyes and willed her mind to be a complete blank. But Grant would not let her off that easily. His hands and lips teased her. He forced himself to be patient, to wait for her. He might never have this chance again, and he meant for her to remember it, as he meant to remember it.

"I didn't want it to be like—"

"Sweet Jesus, Rosie, you should have been a courtesan!"

"Ohh!" Her breath caught short and in the midst of her shuddering she wished the pleasurable feeling could last forever.

When it was all over, when they lay spent, drawing deep breaths and drenched in steaming perspiration in spite of the coolness, Rosemary knew that it had changed her, for better or worse. She had to acknowledge that she had enjoyed it, as she never had with Stephen. It was to be the burden of guilt she was to bear.

Yet a small spark inside her flickered and burst into a steady flame, fanned by the knowledge that, though her body had responded to Grant's undeniable expertise in lovemaking, her heart, her spirit, had remained dormant.

She waited to be reignited by Lario's fire.

24

Rosemary put her hand above her eyes, shielding them from the sun's glare. Two figures stood on the veranda and waved their arms.

"Must be Rita," Stephen said. "When the news came you were alive, she came over to wait for your return."

He pulled in on the buggy's reins and turned to her. "See here, Rosemary, if anyone asks—well, I've told everyone that the Navajo sold you and Stephanie to a Mexican family in El Paso. And that the Cavalry found you after you had escaped—wandering the Tularosa Valley." His sharp eyes fastened on her. "I told them that you were well treated...in all respects."

"Then that should satisfy their curiosity about my matronly virtue, should it not? No breath of scandal must touch the Rhodes name. 'Tis a pity we dinna die, is it not? It would have saved you explanations. I am surprised you took us back."

But she really was not. As long as she was alive, there was the chance she would inherit Lord Almsley's fortune.

Stephen's thin lips stretched tightly. "A husband rejecting his wife is not a good image for the Rhodes name—or I would have."

She laughed shortly. "And bribery and misuse of tax funds is? Tell me, Stephen, how did you resolve that matter? Buy off the Territorial Auditor?"

His smile was frightening. "I did not need to. Mr. Stewart met with an accident."

Rosemary drew back, realizing only at that moment the extent of Stephen's power. "This is the kind of empire you be building for our son?" she asked in a horrified whisper.

"Mama, mama," Stephanie demanded, pulling on Rosemary's sleeve. "That boy on the veranda—is that my brother? Is that Jamie?"

Some of the tension slipped from Rosemary. She had carefully coached Stephanie before Stephen's arrival at Fort Sumner...that she was not to mention her father, Lario, under any circumstances, that she had a brother and another home. But when it came to teaching Stephanie to call Stephen "father," it was more than Rosemary could do. Stephen would just have to accept the fact she had been too young to remember him, which was true when they were taken by the Indians.

"That be Jamie," Stephen answered. "Look at the boy—he be almost as tall as Rita and not even six yet!"

Rosemary had forgotten how short Rita was until she stood on the veranda with her arm about the woman. Her friend's head barely cleared Rosemary's shoulder. *"Bienvenido, mi amiga, mi hermana!"* Rita said with tears glistening in her eyes.

Rosemary found it difficult to speak with the emotion that choked her. "I've missed you, Rita."

She turned to Jamie, who had backed off at her approach. "Jamie, come here," she pleaded. She held out her arms, and the tears came to her eyes for the first time since her return.

Jamie shook his brownish red curls. "I don't have a mother. She left me."

Rosemary whirled on Stephen. "Is that what you told him?" she demanded.

Stephen scowled. "Should I have told him you be dead? How did I know you weren't?"

"It would have been better if he thought I were dead," she exclaimed, "than to believe I dinna care enough to stay with him!"

Rita went over to Jamie and took his hand. "Jamie, Tía Rita has never lied to you before. This is your mother, believe me—and your sister. They couldn't help it that the Indians took them."

"She kept *her* with her," he declared, pointing accusingly at Stephanie. "Why didn't she keep me?" And he spun out of Rita's hands and ran around the corner of the veranda, out of sight.

Rosemary bit back her cry, dropped her outstretched hand. It had been three years since she had last seen him, she told herself. It might take that long to make him remember her, to make him forgive her.

Later that evening, after an uncommunicative dinner with Stephen, Rosemary and Rita sought out the privacy of Rosemary's office. For a long time Rosemary only rocked, letting the repetitive motion of the rocker ease away the pain and difficulty of adjusting once more to what Libby had called civilization. She only half-listened to what Rita told her about the things that had happened in the three years of her absence.

"We now have daily mail service with the East, *amiga*. And the Sisters of Loretto are building an academy for young women in Las Vegas, imagine! Did you know that a Captain Martin, or was it Miller, he drilled a well in the Jornada del Muerto and discovered water? Oh, and did Esteban tell you that the Goldmans sold out their half of the Santa Fe Trading Post to him and moved back to the States—*gracias a Dios!*"

Rosemary let her ramble on. She knew her friend was trying to make it easier for her and thought she had no wish to talk about what had happened. But Rosemary felt she had to talk to someone or she would go crazy from worry. And at last Rita broke off her discourse, seeing Rosemary's preoccupation.

"What is it, Rosita?" She laid a comforting hand on Rosemary's, now browner than her own. "If you wish to tell me anything, you know your words will be safe."

"Rita, those three years I was away, I—Stephanie and I—we lived with the Navajo first, then the Apache...not as slaves in a Mexican household. And for all purposes I was Lario's wife those three years."

Rita's lips formed an *O,* and Rosemary had to smile. "You told me to take a lover, did you not? As I recall, you even mentioned Lario."

"Dios mío," Rita breathed. "If Esteban ever found that out, he would—"

"He would have me flayed alive. He could never forgive that I willingly preferred an Indian over him."

Rosemary proceeded to tell her friend what had transpired the past three years, everything but the fact that Stephanie was Lario's daughter. If Rita ever inadvertently let that knowledge slip out, if Stephen ever discovered the truth, Rosemary knew he would kill the bastard girl as easily and with as little compunction as he had had the auditor, Stewart, killed.

No, she would keep that one secret until the time came that she could join Lario—once he was freed. But this time, she would take both Stephanie *and* Jamie with her. Together she and Lario would find a place where they could live safely from society's vindictiveness.

She never let herself think that Lario would not be set free, that he could be executed, hanged or shot before a firing squad. Grant had promised her he would try.

So she waited with trepidation as the month's end came and April arrived and she still received no word of Lario's fate. She did know that most of the military telegraph lines were finally completed and that Grant should have been able to contact Brigadier General Carleton, who was in Arizona Territory at that time.

She found herself making errors in the ledgers, dropping stitches if she knitted (which frustrated her worse now than rug-weaving had), and speaking sharply with the servants and children—something she never had done before and which even Stephen noticed. One evening at dinner when she snapped at Stephanie for climbing to the top of a tamarisk and ripping the sash off her dress, Stephen said, "You be awfully touchy, Rosemary."

His scrutiny disconcerted her, and she looked away. "I suppose I am. After so many years away, 'tis difficult adjusting to life again at Cambria."

Stephen inhaled on his dundeen. "Then it's time you put in an appearance at Sante Fe."

"Why would I want to go there?" she asked listlessly.

"For one, it would be killing the people's curiosity and getting your mind off things."

"I don't care what other people be thinking!" she snapped.

"For another," Stephen continued, "I've just been appointed president of the First Santa Fe Bank. I've been thinking about letting a place there for six months—just so I can be keeping my finger in the pie. Besides, I want Jamie to get an idea about what politics is all about. What better place than the Territory's capital to learn?"

Rosemary glanced at Jamie, who sat silently pushing his food around on the plate. He had inherited the Welsh dark looks. But none of their explosiveness. Her heart went out to her lonely son, who feared his father and hated his mother.

"I really think it'd be better if we stayed here," she said. "'Tis peaceful, and I think we all need to adjust to each other before we try the capital. Besides," she added, "who would run Cambria while we're gone for six months?"

"Cody's been running it for three years now and done a bloody good job of it. Hasn't he kept the cattle rustlers off Cambria?" But Stephen did not press her further as he remembered the pleasures he had enjoyed in her absence—staying up all night playing monte or chuza, betting an entire flock of sheep against a land grant when he felt reckless. And then there had been the children found in the *jacales*, the thatched-roof huts, of Santa Fe's poor district who were easily bought for a night of pleasure.

And the month before he had installed his most recent henchman in the office of Territorial District Attorney—as easily as dealing a deck of cards. There was nothing to stop him now. He controlled the major businessmen and politicians. His dynasty was keeping up with the timetable he had set. If only Rosemary would be more cooperative and play er part. It would look better if she appeared with him. Damn, he didn't need so much money to keep the wheels turning. till, there *was* something desirable about her that had not een there before.

"Jiraldo and Rita will be in Santa Fe," he said persuavely. "A bill to approve his land grant will be up before the cond session of the legislature. And Grant and Libby are ere now, house-hunting."

Rosemary knocked her wineglass over and hurried to clean p the spreading purple stain. "What—why are they house-unting?"

"Didn't I tell you? Heard the news at Las Vegas yesterday. he government is closing Fort Sumner and the reservation ere. President Johnson has appointed Grant Territorial ssociate Chief Justice. It'll most likely be in this week's *anta Fe New Mexican.*"

Why had Grant not told her anything before he left? Even ow was Lario's body lying beneath the sandy earth, decomsing? Rosemary spread her hands, gesturing to the spilt ine. "I suppose I am a bit nervous these days. Perhaps you're ght, perhaps we should put in an appearance in Sante Fe."

<h1 style="text-align:center">25</h1>

osemary refused to stay in Santa Fe's Exchange Hotel, in ite of Stephen's angry demands. "'Tis no place for a boy mie's age," she told Stephen the first night they arrived Santa Fe. From down the hallway at the monte tables me the drunken shouts of the gamblers who had hit a lucky reak or lost a fortune in sheep. From the richest to the orest, all were caught up in the fascination of the exciting ce.

Occasionally the burst of gunfire could be heard from the aza as a dispute was settled or a lady's reputation preserved. osemary had noticed the town had grown considerably, owg largely to the great numbers of men mustered out of the ilitary after the end of the Civil War. And most of these en seemed to come from Texas. "Big, handsome *vaqueros*," ita called the cowboys who sported the huge Stetson hats d Colt .44 pistols at each hip.

Stephen told Rosemary to find a place if she wanted to live mewhere else other than the hotel, knowing full well that with the legislative session about to begin, there was not a room to be let, much less a house, in that small mountain outpost. Nevertheless, Rosemary set out to hunt the third morning in Santa Fe, taking Stephanie and Jamie with her.

First, she tried several private residences that fronted the plaza. She met with no success, but everywhere she went the men moved out of their way for her, tipped their sombreros, derbies, or Stetsons. At last she realized she was the only woman in the plaza whose face was not shielded by the rebozo.

The men, who had come into the Territory for various reasons—rumor of new gold and silver deposits, flight from the long arm of the law, or search for work at the growing number of cattle ranches—were all avid for the sight of a woman. And especially an Anglo woman. Even the sight of a child brought gentleness to the most hardened hearts.

Stephanie behaved like a little coquette. "Stephanie, you must not wave at every man that looks at you," Rosemary told her daughter when an old man in a battered hat and long, white matted beard staggered out of the *calabozo*, or jail, and swept the child a parody of a courtly bow.

"But, mama, they like to look at me," Stephanie said with an irresistible grin. And Rosemary thought it was so. With the red hair, and black, almond-shaped eyes, the child possessed a unique appearance that bordered on beauty. But it was more than that. Already, though she was only four, there was an aura of vitality, a spirited animation about her, that was almost tangible.

Jamie eyed his sister. "That's because you're different looking." But there was no malice intended. While he continued to remain aloof from Rosemary despite her gentle attempts to win him back to her, she sensed the awe he held for his sister.

It took two more days of looking, but Rosemary finally chanced upon an observer-sergeant in the United States Signal Corps who had just accepted a job as Indian Agent for the San Carlos Reservation in Arizona. He had two rooms he rented, one above the other, in the rear of the Staab's Store on the plaza, and he arranged for her to rent them before anyone else had the opportunity.

With that taken care of, Rosemary had only one purpose now...to talk with Grant Raffin. She had to be circumspect, she knew; she could not just appear at Libby's door, asking for him. Curiously enough, it was Stephen who suggested they accompany Grant and Libby to a dinner party being held for the influential businessmen of the city and the new legislature.

"You mean for the Santa Fe Ring—The House," she said, not bothering to hide her sarcasm.

Stephen paused in adjusting the stiff collar onto the boiled shirt and glared at her. "That's something you'd best not mention."

"Why not, Stephen?" she asked with a mocking smile. "Everyone knows about the Ring."

He resumed his dressing, draping the huge gold chain across his flower-brocaded vest. "Then you should also know it's the Ring that puts the clothes on your back." He glanced at the off-the-shoulder dinner gown of lilac-colored satin with sprigs of violet linen flowers on the voluminous skirts. Rosemary did not miss the desire that lit the black eyes, and she turned away.

Both angered and aroused by her indifference, he came up behind her and took her shoulders. His walrus mustache tickled her bare shoulders. "Much better than the cheap calico—or smelly buckskins you wore, wouldn't you say?"

"Are you suddenly taking an interest in my past, Stephen?" she asked and shrugged out of his grasp. She found it peculiar he never asked about the three years she lived with the Indians. His unconcern piqued her, but she knew she should be only grateful he was not curious. She had learned the extent of his power with the assassination of the Territorial Auditor. If he ever found out about Lario, about Stephanie, she knew his rage would know no limits.

"You've been in one Indian camp," he answered, "you've been in them all. I have no interest in the dirty, stinking camps you lived in."

Rosemary cast him a sidelong glance. She could not help herself. The temptation to put a dent in his smugness was overwhelming. "Nor the stinking men I slept with?"

"Nor the stinking men you slept with, my dear." Stephen was one step ahead of her, as usual. "For once I pity the poor savage who took you to his bed. A lump of coal is more responsive."

Rosemary thought of several replies she would have loved to snap back with, but she was treading on perilous ground. She picked up the long white evening gloves and ivory fan, asking lightly, "Was there any particular reason you wanted us to go with the Raffins tonight?"

Stephen smiled at her retreat. No lady liked to be reminded of her sexual degradation, he thought. "Grant's sending Wayne off to a boys' school in St. Louis. I wanted to know more about St. Mark's. I be thinking it would be good for Jamie."

135

Rosemary gasped and turned back to Stephen. "Jamie's not old enough to go away yet."

Stephen raised his bushy brows. "He be two years older than Wayne."

"You know what I meant. Jamie's not as mature. Besides, Stephen, Jamie and I are just beginning to get acquainted with one another again. Please," she begged. "He's my son also."

"Don't be foolish. You'll smother the boy with all the attention." He picked up the new malachite walking cane and silk top hat which had put the fur trappers out of business when it replaced beaver hats. "Let's go. We're late."

Rosemary and Stephen sat behind Grant and Libby in the surrey. Libby chattered on about the new governor's private home, a pink adobe in the Barrio de Analco, one of the earliest settlements in the United States. The governor's wife, whom Stephen wanted Rosemary to cultivate, had given a tea several days before, and Libby had attended. She could not say enough about the walls that were covered with paintings by well-known American artists, the hand-painted window shades, and the small melodeon.

Stephen's boredom was obvious as he openly yawned. Rosemary's fingers played nervously with her fan. Across from her Grant looked uneasy, though several times Rosemary caught his veiled gaze on her before he looked away to the large adobe homes that irregularly walled the winding, cobblestone road.

The dinner seemed interminable to Rosemary. Indian boys dressed in white cotton *camisas* and *calzones* served silver trays arranged with *pollo marengo* and thick pork chops in Madeira wine sauce. The new governor, William Mitchell, made several lengthy speeches followed by as many toasts to the new administration.

At last it was time for the men to light up their favorite cigars and the women to retire from the room. The men rose from their chairs as the ladies passed by. Rosemary let the fan slip from her hand as she passed Grant's chair. "I have to see you," she whispered below the hum of conversation as he bent to retrieve the fan. "In half an hour—in the courtyard."

Rosemary endured the chatter of the women for the next thirty minutes, responding with polite answers to the questions directed her way. Then she quietly made her excuses to the hostess at a time when the wives were occupied in a debate over the merits of beeswax candles versus tallow candles, telling the governor's wife, "It must have been the amount of food I ate, Mrs. Mitchell. It was so delicious, I dinna stop. Do you mind if I step outside for a breath of air?"

Rosemary knew that as soon as she left the room she would probably be the topic of discussion—*poor Mrs. Rhodes, what horrors she must have endured!* But she did not care. Her waiting had reached its end. *Lario.* The name sang through her blood as she slipped through the veranda doors which, like all the rooms in a Mexican home, opened onto the central courtyard.

The spring night was shadowy with a cloud-streaked moon. Carefully Rosemary avoided the *macetas,* the large pots containing hibiscus plants, and made her way across the flagstones to the Moorish fountain. "Grant?" she called softly. But there came only the splash of the water cascading over the gray stones. A hand touched her shoulder, and she gasped and whirled.

"If I'm found out here alone with you, it'll ruin my career," Grant said. But he took her in his arms and pulled her to him. "I haven't stopped thinking of you. Not since that day in the barn."

Rosemary leaned back, placing her hands against his chest to separate them. "You'd better forget, Grant. There was nothing to that day but a business arrangement."

Yet she knew that was not true. No matter what her intention had been, the incident changed Grant—changed her. She had no illusions about their relationship that day, but she was honest enough to admit that the common act had transformed them, the circumstances, their thoughts into something that was essentially nonphysical, which lasted beyond the act.

"I want to know about Lario. Please," she said in desperation as a hardness gripped Grant's countenance. "Where is he?" She clutched frantically at the lapels of Grant's gray frock coat. "He is still alive, isn't he?"

"Forget him, Rosemary." He grasped her wrists in a painful hold. "The best I could do was to get him transferred to the Santa Rita Copper Mines."

Rosemary gasped. She knew the mines were in the far southwest quadrant of the New Mexico Territory—where hell opened up on earth some said. "For how long?" she asked in a whisper.

"It doesn't matter. If he was released in two months or

twenty years, he wouldn't be the same. Whatever kind of man he was is gone now. Accept it and forget him."

"No! I won't accept it. I'll wait for him to return, Grant. Twenty years if need be!"

"If he ever returns, Rosemary, it'll be to kill me—and you."

Part Two

26

**Wild Cat Camp
Cambria, New Mexico Territory
July, 1873**

Cautiously the ten-year-old climbed the slats of the corral.
At the corral's far side the steely blue mustang pawed at the
dirt nervously. Its small ears lay flat against its bony head.
Its nostrils dilated at the scent of the human. The stallion
had been ridden only once, and he was alert and wary, ready
to defend himself as viciously as he would defend his sovereignty over his band of mares against another intruding stallion.

The girl, who looked more like a boy dressed as she was
in her brother's overalls with her strawberry braids tucked
up under the floppy felt hat, perched on the corral's top slat
and watched the mustang prance about the corral in agitation.

It was a beautiful horse, she thought, with gleaming round
quarters and bunched muscles at the chest. Although Cody
Strahan had ridden it the day before, the stallion was not yet
ready for any other human to try its back. Which was all the
more reason why Stephanie meant to ride the animal.

She figured by now her mother would have already discovered she was not in her room studying. No matter, by the
time she had finished riding Malcreado and made the two
hours' journey back to the Castle maybe her mother would
be getting just worried enough to forget her anger. And her
father—maybe he would come out of his office, his gruff face
for once beaming with pride, and say, "That's my daughter!"

She slid down off the slat and began walking toward the
horse. "Hello there, my fancy steed," she said softly, gently,
imitating Cody's manner as she approached Malcreado. "You
and me are going to be the best of friends."

The stallion snorted and danced off to one side, but Stephanie continued to talk as she steadily walked toward him.
"Folks'll say, 'My, aren't they a handsome pair,' when they
see us. And that bratty Wayne Raffin will have to make good
his wager," she added triumphantly.

She was almost there now, within grasping distance of the
gray-blue matted mane. Slowly her hand came out. The
horse's eyes rolled. With no warning it reared; its sharp
hooves pawed the air. To Stephanie it looked like some great

140

beast. She began to back away. Malcreado came down only to rear again as it advanced on her.

"No!" Stephanie cried out and turned to run. Her boot heel caught in a dirt clod, and she went sprawling. Above her the horse hooves came down, and she rolled to one side, screaming. On all fours now she scrambled through the flurrying dust for the corral's far side. But Malcreado pursued her, its one intention to destroy the intruding enemy. When the sharp hooves came flailing up this time, Stephanie knew there was no hope for her to reach the safety of the corral's slats.

Then there came the sharp ricocheting retort of gunfire, and Stephanie felt the impact of the horse's boulderlike weight. The breath whooshed from her. Blackness charged with streaks of reds and blues inundated her, though she was dimly aware of the heavy weight being removed, of hands that ran along her legs, her arms, her rib cage, feeling, moving her wrists and ankles.

"Yyowl!" she grimaced, as the fingers poked at her eyelids. "You're hurting me!"

"I'd like to take a razorstrap to you!" Cody grunted. But his hands were gentle as he lifted her and carried her toward the one-room cabin of native stone that served as a bunkhouse for the cowpunchers of the Wild Cat Camp. "What in hell's hot furnace did you think you were doing, you little pisser!"

"None of your business!" Stephanie mumbled as he eased her onto the narrow, rawhide slung bunk. Her eyes flew open. "Malcreado—what happened to—?"

Cody's expression went flat. "Dead," he said and turned away. He crossed to a shelf that held tins of coffee, flour, and sugar along with jars and bottles. "I take it your maw doesn't know you're here?"

The tears that stung Stephanie's eyes prevented her from answering. The beautiful animal was dead, and it was her fault. "She's gonna string you up by your braids when she finds out," Cody went on.

"You...you won't tell her, will you?"

He paused from searching through the bottles and cocked a brow at the child. "When you're hobbling around tomorrow morning, she's gonna suspect something. Why'd you do it, kid?"

Stephanie shook her head, her lips folded tightly. Already she hurt, feeling like she had been trampled by a herd of stampeding buffalo.

Cody came back to her carrying a bottle of Dr. Walker's Horse Liniment. "I see," he said. He sat down beside her. "Shuck your clothes. We'll see what can be done."

141

Stephanie stiffened. "Ain't going to."

Cody sighed. "Look, kid, I gotta get on to those mossbacks. It's either the liniment or hole up in bed for a week."

Wiping her dirty nose across her sleeve, Stephanie weighed the alternative and concluded that the burden of her mother's disapproval was the worse of the two.

With unladylike groans she painfully dropped her britches and shrugged out of the faded red cotton shirt. She stretched out on her stomach, resting her head on folded arms.

As Cody worked at the muscles at the back of her calves and thighs and massaged her back and her arms, the liniment penetrated into her body, warming her. Drowsily she thought of Wayne and how she would yet make him acknowledge she was as capable as any boy, though why she should care she could not imagine.

Finally the pleasure of Cody's sure hands massaging away the aches lulled her into sleep.

27

**Philadelphia
May, 1880**

Stephanie posed in front of the gilt-framed mirror and readjusted the ruchings of her brown and tan plaid silk dress over her bustle, then tilted the beribboned and beflowered bonnet at a saucy angle over her right brow.

"Of course, I've kissed him," she told the three girls who sat on her bed and watched her in breathless silence. "Every summer when I go back, Wayne's there to meet me at the Las Vegas depot and take me home to Cambria."

She saw the three pairs of wide eyes in the mirror, waiting. "And...and we kiss. We kiss a lot."

"Stephanie!" Lottie breathed in horrified delight. Her plump hand crept up to rest at her neck. "What would your father say?"

Stephanie reached for the daguerreotype stuck in the rim of the oval mirror. Her brother had given her the picture the previous summer before Stephanie returned to Mrs. Goddard's Women's Academy for the fall session. She held the well-worn cardboard frame between her fingers, but there was no need to look at the picture. She could envision it with her eyes closed. The two young men, Jamie sitting on the university's low wall, his face wistful, his dark looks a perfect

142

foil for Wayne's fairness—and Wayne lounging next to her brother, all his father's arrogance evident in his own brooding good looks.

"My father doesn't mind. He spends most of his time in Santa Fe. So, he doesn't really know how wild Wayne is about me."

Stephanie jammed the daguerreotype in her reticule. Maybe, just maybe, Wayne would really be at the train depot this time. And she could not help but wish that things could have been as they were when she was a child, when Wayne came to spend the summers at Cambria. He was always taunting her, spurring her into one misadventure after another. She remembered wryly the summer he had challenged her into riding Malcreado. Cody had kept her secret, and she had told Jamie and Wayne that she had ridden the stallion. She suspected her mother somehow found out, for that fall her mother packed her off to finishing school, saying, "'Tis time you learned to be a lady, my pet."

Along with Wayne's taunts and mockery there had been the companionship of the three of them—she, Wayne, and Jamie. The laughter and fun of their childhood had created a camaraderie she badly missed as she grew into a young lady. Now, when she thought of Wayne as a polished lawyer, she feared she might still seem the gawky tomboy despite the fact she had spent eight years at Mrs. Goddard's academy acquiring both an education and gracious deportment.

Stephanie turned to face the three spellbound schoolgirls. "Besides," she declared, "I'm eighteen now. Old enough to get married."

"Oh, Lottie," Betty Jo squeaked, "can you imagine being married to someone like Wayne Raffin?" Her little face with the round mouth and button eyes screwed up in a gesture of ecstasy. "It—it'd be like marrying Adonis!"

"I don't believe you, Stephanie Rhodes!" Priscilla said. Her hair, like Stephanie's, was red but a washed-out shade—not the vibrant hue of blazing fire, and it was kinky. "Why, I bet Wayne Raffin's never once looked your way. There's no more truth to you marrying him than there is to your yarns about rattlesnakes swallowing their babies and Cambria being the size of Rhode Island. You're just a liar, Stephanie Rhodes!"

Stephanie's black eyes narrowed until they looked like two small obsidian rocks. She ached to jump on the prim Priscilla Broadbent. "I could tell you tales about the Indians, Miss Smart-aleck, that'd make your hair straight as a tooth-pick!" Her fingers uncurled from their fists, and she relaxed, secure at least in her knowledge of the wild New Mexican frontier. And secure in the knowledge that she would be leaving the academy for the last time, never to return.

She crossed to the doorway and picked up the two calfskin suitcases and her reticule. She faced the three girls. "If you don't believe anything I've told you, Priscilla," she said smiling, "you're welcome to visit Cambria any time you wish. I'll even send you our wedding invitation."

The boast had been foolish, she knew. Yet later, as Stephanie squirmed on the train's uncomfortable seat, she realized she had meant it. She *would* wed Wayne Raffin. And Priscilla Broadbent would receive the first invitation. Just how she would accomplish the feat, she did not know. She was half afraid he would not come back this time from Virginia where he and Jamie were reading law.

The heat in the car was unbearable, and the coal dust and smoke blew through the car's open windows. Still, Stephanie was able to follow the sweep of the terrain as the train took her further into her beloved Southwest. After the train chugged over the steep Raton Pass and down into the high plains of the New Mexico Territory she watched the mustang ponies as they raced alongside the train, their manes and tails flying. Occasionally she sighted a buffalo, but their herds of fifteen thousand were depleted mightily from almost a decade before when she could remember taking three days to ride through one herd. Thinking back, she estimated there must have been between two and three million in that one bunch.

Stephanie had forgotten how much she missed the wide expanse of prairie, like a sea of grass, and the limitless sky that was bluer, clearer, than any she had seen in the East...but most of all she missed the mulberry blue mountains. There was something about their majestic heights that she found reassuring. She remembered them dimly from her childhood, remembered moving about in their maze of canyons from one Indian camp to another.

Once she had questioned her mother about those years they had spent with the Indians, but it seemed to her that her mother had been reticent, telling her merely of their abduction and their final return to Cambria three years later. Stephanie could only reason that those years of captivity brought back agonizing memories her mother did not wish to recall.

No more than she herself wished to, she thought, as her glance strayed across the aisle to the fat squaw with the irritatingly stupid face. Her memories of the Indians were ones of flies and dirt and fleas. Her association with the

Indians had been one thing she had been too ashamed to speak of when she entertained the girls at the academy with stories of the wild West.

Off to the train's left Stephanie could make out the dark basalt foothills called Wagon Mound, a formation that closely resembled a covered wagon pulled by a team of horses—or was it mules, she was never quite sure. But she did know that once Wagon Mound came in sight it would be only a little while longer before the train pulled into the Las Vegas depot and she saw her family again. And maybe Wayne.

As the train chugged to a halt before the frame depot with its nine-stall roundhouse for servicing the locomotives, Wayne Raffin's imposing figure was nowhere to be seen. Did she really expect him to be there?

Stephanie joined the other passengers in the car's aisle. She was careful to keep her skirts, extended by wire hoops, from touching the old squaw who trod off in the direction of the Fred Harvey Diner where *girls* worked as waitresses— though with the short supply of women they did not remain long but soon married.

Then Stephanie saw her mother. The locomotive's steam surged about her skirts, making her look like some celestial figure. With her were Inez and Rita, who was a little plumper than the previous summer but still wearing the exotic look possessed by all Mexican women. Every summer the Rhodes and Sanchez families reunited in Las Vegas where Inez attended Our Lady of Sorrows Convent school and Jamie and Stephanie disembarked from trains arriving from the East. And from Las Vegas the two families usually journeyed on to Cambria to spend several weeks filling everyone in on the nine-months' gap away from home.

Stephanie hugged Inez first. "You haven't changed," she told her friend. "Only taller—and still just as pretty."

A becoming blush tinted Inez's tea-rose complexion. "And you, Stephanie, still blaze as brightly as the sun."

Stephanie laughed. "Then why haven't we been besieged by suitors if we're such great catches!" She turned to Rita. "Tiarita," she asked, "have you been keeping my mother busy in naughty things?"

Rita hugged Stephanie, saying, "*Sí, chiquita.* Lately I've been trying to teach her to smoke *punche.*" The woman laughed and rolled her eyes. "But even such a mild tobacco makes *tu mama* cough!"

Stephanie saved the last greeting for her mother. She thought she might find some sign of age to make her seem more of a—a mother. But the woman stood before her, her

145

eyes shimmering with abiding love, and Stephanie knew that her mother was more special than other women—and knew she would always envy her mother for her qualities.

Beneath her mother's cool, ladylike reserve, Stephanie had sometimes caught glimpses of Rita's impishness and impulsiveness and Inez's sweet, loving disposition. But the way she unobtrusively ran Cambria in Stephen's absence told of Rosemary's durability.

She would never age like other women, Stephanie thought. The blue-green eyes were still as bright and sparkling, the cinnamon red hair held no trace of gray, and her figure curved like that of a young girl's. Stephanie calculated her mother's age and realized that her mother was nearly thirty-six years old, a terribly old age it seemed to her. She also noted as they stepped out onto Railroad Avenue that the men stopped to stare, and more than half the glances, she grudgingly conceded, were directed at her mother.

Rita hailed one of the six-passenger rockaways as Rosemary explained they were not going directly to Cambria but would stay in Las Vegas several days. "Your father has invested in a two-hundred-and-seventy-room hotel, the Montezuma, that was just completed last winter. 'Tis six miles out of town, but Rita and I thought it would be fun to try the curative baths at the hot springs there before your father and Jiraldo come to take us back to Cambria."

Normally Stephanie would have been eager to visit in Las Vegas, to see the changes and meet old friends. But now she did not even bother to glance at the new flimsy frame buildings they passed, barely even heard Rita chattering. It was beginning to dawn on her that this time she was back in the New Mexican wilderness for good. Once she left Las Vegas it would be her last touch with civilization, except for the occasional visits exchanged with the Sanchezes and the few brief shopping trips into Santa Fe.

And she would never have the chance to try her wiles on Wayne.

There would be only Jamie to while away her loneliness. Jamie, who accepted her mercurial moods. And for the first time she noted his absence. He usually arrived from Richmond a day or two earlier than she. "Mama, where is Jamie?"

"The classes were a month late in letting out. He and Wayne should be arriving tomorrow or the next day." Rosemary smiled fondly at her daughter. "I thought you two deserved a holiday, and the Montezuma seemed just the place. I even brought a bathing suit for you."

Stephanie tried to keep her voice casual. "And Wayne—

146

will he be going on through to Santa Fe or staying at the Montezuma also?"

Rosemary's discerning glance fell on her daughter. "I don't know. I suppose we could ask him to stay over for a day or so."

Shrugging carelessly in an effort to contain her joy, Stephanie turned to Inez and asked, "Will you be returning to Our Lady of Sorrows or is this your last year also?"

Inez smiled. "Not if mother has her way. She would keep me in the convent forever if it would prevent me from getting married."

"Men—bah!" Rita said, waving her fan in dismissal. "They bring only trouble. And besides, *hija*, there is no man your father would have you marry. He would keep you a *virgen, no es verdad?*"

A becoming blush suffused Inez's dusky skin, but Stephanie, watching her friend, suspected there was more to Inez's discomposure than was apparent. She glanced to see if her mother had intercepted the flustered look on Inez's face and was startled to see her mother frowning at a letter she held in her gloved hand. "What is it, mama?"

Rosemary quickly folded the letter and put it with the rest of the mail she had picked up at the Las Vegas post office before meeting the train. "Nothing, dear. Only some items your father asked me to take care of."

But Stephanie noted the envelope bore Grant Raffin's return address.

28

The Montezuma, set before the Gallinas River with the pine-shrubbed Sangre de Cristo foothills as a backdrop, was a redstone hotel with casino, stables, and even a hospital—and, of course, the famed bathhouses that could accommodate three hundred persons a day. The hotel's name derived from the legend that Montezuma and the Aztecs of old Mexico made journeys there.

Built in the Queen Anne style with towers and gables and stained-glass windows, the hotel had all the conveniences found in the East, contrasting with the rustic scenery of the mountains and canyons of the West. And it was this contrast that attracted the leisure section of nouveau riche growing

147

in America—and which attracted Stephanie. "Oh, mama, it's lovely," she said, when they stopped at the reservation desk that evening. "It's the best of two worlds!"

"I thought you would be liking it, pet," Rosemary said and took the room key from the desk clerk.

The next day went quickly for Stephanie as the four women covered the hotel grounds—touring the conservatory reached by an arcade, the gardens of blooming rare flowers and splashing tile fountains, and finally the baths themselves.

They bypassed the mud bathhouse, which was nothing more than a long, low wooden shed, in favor of the mineral waters bath which was housed in a sandstone building of Neoclassic style. There in the large steamy portion reserved for females, the four women lounged about in discreet alpaca bathing suits with attached bloomers and detachable skirts that fell below the knees. Stephanie seriously considered discarding the cumbersome skirt but knew she would probably shock the other bathers. What would the dowagers think, she wondered with delight, if they knew she went swimming in a stock tank every summer in the nude?

Rita related the most recent gossip, keeping the other three laughing at her hyperbolic descriptions. "And Libby, she has put on so much weight! Grant must think it is a grizzly he kisses each morning, if he does kiss her. Do you know that her corset popped during a dinner and knocked the wine-glass out of her hand —*si, por la Virgen Santa*, it is the truth!"

Stephanie happened to glance at her mother and caught in her expression, rather than the silent humor which usually curved her lips, a fleeting trace of melancholy. Rita went on, saying, "You must make your mother leave Cambria more often, *chiquita*. I will not stay at our hacienda so long a time now. Santa Fe is the place to be. It's more alive. Something happens every night! *¡Ejoli!* Last week I gambled away three of my best fringed shawls, did I not, Inez? No, I will not let Jiraldo hide me away at the hacienda!" She snapped her fingers. "He goes—I go!"

The following afternoon, as the women prepared to go to the depot to meet Jamie and Wayne, Stephanie had a sudden surge of a nervous headache. She could not believe it—that she, the tomboy, would have weak knees and sweaty palms. "I'll wait here, mama, if you don't mind." Her mother's thoughtful gaze searched her face, and she added, "I guess I'm still worn out from the trip."

Rosemary brushed aside a wisp of hair that had escaped

148

from the cluster of curls behind each of her daughter's ears. "You haven't started having your dream again, have you?"

Stephanie had to smile. "That was kidstuff. I'm a grown lady now, remember?" But she was half afraid the dream would resume, as it always had before, whenever she returned home. It was a silly dream, she thought, for it was only a face that wove in and out of her sleep... but it was the cruelty that glazed the oblique eyes, the mouth that was almost lipless and grimaced like a gargoyle that had caused her to wake up screaming as a child and later, as she grew older, to wake with terrible headaches.

"I remember, far too easily, that 'tis a grown lady you are now," her mother said, smiling. "But perhaps it's resting you should be. Then you'll be fresh when Jamie arrives."

And Wayne, Stephanie thought. However, she could not lie down. Excitement drove her every few minutes to the window that overlooked the curved drive. Would Wayne notice she had grown into a lady in the intervening years?

At last she spotted a tilbury rolling up the drive past the summer cottages that had sprung up with the construction of the hotel. Its occupants descended from the carriage, and Stephanie's hungry gaze sought out the taller, more slender, of the two men. He removed the straw planter's hat, and she saw Wayne's silver-blond hair and the mustache that matured his raffishly handsome face. He also had grown up in the intervening years.

She hurried to the mirror and fluffed the curls behind her ears, wishing she had sugar and water to give more spring to her hair, which Rita said was as straight as an Indian's. She tilted the brim of the feathered hat low over one eye and pulled on her gloves. As she smoothed the wrinkles from her shamrock green organdy dress her mother entered.

"Stephanie, 'tis beautiful enough you are," she said, the amusement enriching her lilting Irish voice. "Come along, everyone is in the dining room, waiting. Jamie's asking about you."

Stephanie stretched out a hand to her mother's elbow. "Mama, I—I'm a bit nervous. I'll be down in just a few moments."

Rosemary searched her daughter's face that mirrored so much of her own unique beauty. "'Tis Wayne, isn't it?" she asked slowly.

Stephanie nodded. "I think I've been in love with him since that first day at Fort Sumner, when we stayed at the Raffin quarters. What was I—four, five? But I can still remember the way his blue eyes glared at me. And I hated him then. Now, mama...now I want to marry him."

Rosemary bit her lip. "Stephanie, you don't know anything about him. If he snores, or drinks himself to sleep, or—or whatever!"

Stephanie laughed, relieved now that she had unburdened herself of her secret. "Oh, mama! You crossed an ocean and half a continent to wed papa. And what did you know about him? Less than I do about Wayne. You'd never even seen papa. And I dare say you're as happy as most couples."

Rosemary turned her face from her daughter, pretending to look out the window at the park below which, besides its free-form bluegrass lawns and graveled walks, even had a section for croquet and lawn tennis. But Rosemary's mind was not on the two men engaged in the tennis game but on the letter she had received earlier that week.

She hesitated, wondering if she should tell her daughter of the letter's contents. It was not the fact she would be betraying Grant's confidential request that held her tongue—nor the bitter knowledge that she, of all people, should be the last to give advice on choosing a husband. What cautioned her was the fear of opening avenues of questions to Stephanie, possibly revealing her long-kept secret...or worse, endangering a life. Was he still alive? He had to be, she would know if it were otherwise.

With the fervent hope that Stephanie would come to change her mind by summer's end, Rosemary made an attempt at smiling. "If your regard for Wayne is your only problem, then I shan't be too worried."

The dining room, with its painted ceiling showing the faces of the four directions and its magnificent iron chandelier, was filled to capacity—soldiers returning to Fort Union, politicians on their way to Santa Fe, and the sickly who intended to settle in the mild, dry climate. In one corner was a Russian samovar for making tea. In another corner an old man with an ivory-white goatee and long hair played at an elegant Knabe piano.

All of this Stephanie perceived indirectly. Her senses were attuned to only one person in the room. And though the dining room echoed with the noise of muted conversation and soft music, for her there existed only the sight of Wayne. He was dashingly dressed in gambler's striped pants and a fawn-colored frockcoat. She moved toward him in a dreamlike state, oblivious of the greetings once she reached the table.

She heard only his voice, deep with laughter, as he took her hand, saying, "Since last I've seen you, Stephanie Rhodes, our hair has gone up and your dress has gone down." The smile beneath the clipped mustache was gently mocking, even if it never reached the opaque eyes. "The little fighter has grown into a beautiful young lady."

Stephanie heard her own voice and was surprised at its light, bantering tone. "You've never forgiven me for biting you, have you!"

Everyone laughed, and Wayne said, "I deserved it. Stephanie wanted to ride my pony," he explained to the others, "and when I wouldn't let her, she took a hunk out of my arm." He fixed his disconcerting gaze on her. His voice held a note of self-derision. "As it turned out, you were a better rider than I."

Quickly Stephanie turned to Jamie and hugged him. In the arms of her brother she regained her old self-possession. "You're taller, James Gallagher!" She saw the warmth shining in his hazel eyes, and her hand affectionately slipped up to cup his cheek. "And still as handsome."

And indeed he was, she thought, especially dressed as he was in the fashionably cut blue-serge suit. Though he had not the saturnine good looks and irresistible charm that Wayne possessed, a charm that made every female in the room yearn to be the object of his attention, there was about Jamie a boyish handsomeness, a gentleness and sensitivity.

The six settled down to their dinner of roasted duck and creamed spinach with wine, and the talk turned to school with Jamie declaring the next year would be his last. "We should be admitted to the bar by then, shouldn't we, Wayne?"

Wayne glanced at Rosemary. "Hopefully." He turned to Stephanie. "Your mother and I've been talking about the need for an extra hand at Cambria this summer. Myself, if Cody'll hire me."

Stephanie cast her mother a glance of appreciation, but Rosemary's countenance was noncommittal. Jamie gave Stephanie a knowing smile and said, "I've been trying the entire year to get Wayne to come home with us this summer, but he kept putting *me* off."

Stephanie met Wayne's all-consuming gaze that was like a physical assault, and her composure splintered inside her like shattered crystal. "Your mother's persuasiveness—and other things—changed my mind," he said.

Rita winked at Rosemary, then said, "Why don't you two young ladies show Jamie and Wayne the hotel's grounds? And I shall show Rosita how to play *chuska* at the casino tables. It is time she enjoyed some wicked games, no?"

The octagonal gazebo seemed the natural place to end the

tour. The stars were barely visible in the still-light sky; however, there was enough light for the four of them to sit on the stone benches and talk of their childhood days. But Stephanie found herself tongue-tied. Just knowing that Wayne's arm rested behind her on the bench excited her. There were probably at least fifty young women competing for his attention at Richmond University and in Santa Fe, she thought miserably, and *she* could think of nothing to say.

She cast a glance at Jamie and Inez who talked eagerly. Inez's long, dark lashes swept down modestly at something Jamie said, and suddenly it came to Stephanie that the two were in love. She wondered that she had not noticed it before. Had she been blind to everything but her seemingly hopeless love for Wayne?

"So, you've noticed it also?" Wayne whispered at her ear, nodding at her brother and Inez. "When Jamie would talk about Inez at school, I often wondered if I could ever come to care for a woman like that."

"Did you?" Stephanie asked in a small voice.

"I never met a woman I thought I could love. But always at the back of my mind was a little hoyden—a childhood friend. Does she still exist?"

Stephanie bit her bottom lip. What Wayne offered was better than nothing. And she had almost the entire summer to make him see her as something besides a childhood friend. "Did I ever teach you how to play *chuska*," she asked, managing to smile.

Wayne shook his head, laughing, and Stephanie stood up. "Then come on," she said and tugged at his hand, "we've some wagers to make at the casino."

29

"Wayne was marvelous, father," Jamie said. "The way he summed up the case for the professors left everyone in the classroom stunned. It's no wonder he's already caught up with me. He's a great orator, and I'm sure the Territorial District Attorney will want to recruit him as soon as he's admitted to the Bar."

Stephen flicked the reins, keeping his eye on the potted road that ran between Las Vegas and Cambria. "Don't be getting ideas in your head about working *for* the government, son. I want you to make the government work for *you*. It's why I sent you to school instead of putting you to work to learn the land—so that when land grabbers start snapping at your heels, we won't have to be doing what Chisum's doing—hiring a pipsqueak killer like Billy Bonney. Your knowledge of the law will be Cambria's guns. Cambria's more important than wealth, honor, lo—" Stephen broke off. "It's in the blood, son. Cambria will be here a hundred years from now for our sons to enjoy when everything else is gone."

In the rear of the new Studebaker wagon Stephanie sighed and saw her mother's sidelong glance. But it was impossible, Stephanie thought, not to feel some resentment. What was it about her father that made him so indifferent to her?

She thought it ironic she had her father's same love for Cambria, while Jamie had always wanted to be a doctor. She could ride astride as well as any of the ranchhands and could even lasso a calf sitting sidesaddle. She'd like to see a wrangler do that! And the summer before, Cody had taught her to ride point and drag on a trailherd.

She turned her head to the left on the pretext of watching a hawk swoop down and clutch a sidewinder in its talons, but her gaze covertly traveled to the wagon behind. With Don Jiraldo getting on in years, Wayne had volunteered to drive the Sanchez wagon. Her expert eye took in how well he handled the matched bays. The summers he had spent at Cambria had taught him well. But he did not belong there. He was not a backward ranchhand to be roasted and wrinkled by the elements. He belonged in a courtroom—and later in the Governor's Palace. And when that happened, Stephanie meant to be at his side.

While Stephen and Jamie argued the merits of the new Land Settlement Act, Stephanie seized the opportunity to thank her mother for inviting Wayne to Cambria for the summer.

"I dinna do it for you, Stephanie." Rosemary placed a hand over her daughter's. "I fear you may get your heart broken."

"Horsefeathers! I'm not so naive that I don't know what a rake Wayne might be with the women, mama. But don't forget I'm a Rhodes." She saw her mother's eyes cloud over, and she quickly added, "You know Cambria wouldn't interest Wayne. The Raffins are doing very well as it is in the political arena." She turned and looked straight ahead, her lips tight. "Besides," she said after a moment, "he's not even interested in me."

Rosemary smiled gently. "'Tis difficult being young, isn't it?"

Stephanie looked at her mother out of the corner of her eye. Her pouting lips eased into a grin. "I can't imagine life ever being difficult for you, mama. You seem to sail easily through troubled waters. I'm sure you were born knowing just what to do, when to, and how to do whatever you set your mind to."

Rosemary laughed, recalling the frightened young girl who made her first stagecoach trip across the western wilderness. "I'm afraid I had to earn my strength like everyone else. And adversity does wonders as a character builder."

Stephanie made a face. "Thanks, but I'll skip the adversity and settle for a shallow character."

Rosemary's laughter pealed like an altar bell. "Oh, Stephanie! I don't think I was ever as young at heart as you are!" She hugged her daughter. "'Tis so good to have you home again. And you're stronger than you realize. You just haven't had a chance to test your strength."

It *was* good to be home again. In her quieter moments at the finishing school Stephanie often thought that as she grew older Cambria would diminish in size and grandeur. But set in a land whose canyons seemed to gouge the earth's center, whose prairies stretched beyond vision, and whose mountains climbed into the heavens, Cambria held its own—because there was nothing that could compete with its uniqueness for a thousand miles in any direction. It was as much a part of the New Mexican grandeur as were the canyons, deserts, and mountains.

The wagon edged over the rise in the prairieland, and Stephanie could see the low-lying bluffs now, stretched out like a sleeping giant. Not much longer until the carriage rounded the rear of the giant's head, and there, sitting on the knoll overlooking the bend of the Pecos, would be the Castle.

When the mammoth house finally came into view, Stephanie blinked back tears. She swore each time she returned she would not get emotional. But here was home. Excitement, security, danger, warmth. A contradiction of abstractions that made Cambria what it was...a life lived for each moment, not the stale existence of the effete East.

As they passed through the town, children waved and men removed their hats. Miguel stood in front of the store, and she blew the old man a kiss. The winding road crested the knoll where several of the Mexican women were sweeping the driveway. On the veranda railing Cody sat waiting for them. He smoked one of those horrible-smelling Mexican cigarettes, and Stephanie smiled, thinking of the gift she had for him, a package of the new Hooks Machine Cigarettes—a continuous roll of cigarettes that could be cut into separate lengths.

She often wondered how Cody knew to expect them. But it was just like everything else—he seemed to be attuned to some natural telegraph that told him when it was going to rain, what time of day or night it was, where the puma lay in wait.

Consuela came out on the veranda and shielded her eyes against the setting sun as she watched the wagon's progress. Cody tossed his cigarette away, and together the two employees came down the veranda steps to greet everyone.

"¡Nietos!" Consuela cried, addressing Stephanie and Jamie as if they were indeed her own grandchildren and wrapping her ponderous arms about them. But as always her concerned gaze sought out her mistress, reassuring herself that *La Patrona* was all right.

Stephanie pulled away from Consuela and said, "I've brought you a timer, Consuela—a clock that will tell you when to remove the bread from the oven. This way you won't burn it anymore."

"*Ejoli, nieta,* I never burn the bread!"

Stephanie laughed at the old cook's pretended indignation and turned to Cody. "I've a gift for you also."

Cody's slate-gray eyes smiled out of his leathery countenance. Tall, gaunt, with fine squint lines fanning out from the corners of his eyes, he had the longest legs, and Stephanie had called him High-pockets as a child. He removed his worn Stetson to wipe away the perspiration with his sleeve. The forehead above the sweatband line was white, his skin below the line the color and texture of rawhide.

At her four years of age, his twenty-one years had seemed very old to Stephanie. Now, at eighteen, she looked at Cody Strahan from a different viewpoint. He was only a year younger than her mother. She wondered if he, like every man that met Rosemary Rhodes, was infatuated with her. And somehow the idea piqued Stephanie, for Cody seemed to always have been especially hers, like a well-worn teddy bear.

"If your gift's that pomade you tried to get me to use on your last trip home, forget it, kid." He chucked her under her chin, then after greeting the rest of the family, turned to Jamie, who pumped his hand.

"Cody Strahan, you old bronc-buster! Are you going to ride the hell out of me and Wayne this summer?"

Cody's brows quirked. "Wayne?" He watched as the tall,

slender man got out of the Sanchez wagon. "Grant's boy's back?"

"He's not a boy anymore," Stephanie said.

Cody laughed and clamped his hat over her head. "So that's how the land lies, eh?"

"Cody, I hope you don't mind," Rosemary said. "I thought with the Murphy-Dolan gang rustling cattle and that bear killing off the sheep, you could use another hand."

"'Course he doesn't mind," Stephanie said.

Wayne extended his hand. "Good evening, Strahan."

"Evening," Cody said. His light, keen eyes took in the handsome young man who had grown almost as tall as his own six-foot four-inch frame. And he knew why Stephanie had fallen for the young man. Cody told himself that it was none of his business, that he ought to keep his personal opinion out of it. Still, he had ridden herd on the girl for so long he couldn't get out of the habit of keeping check on her. His glance flickered to that of Rosemary's, and he saw the troubled look that mirrored his own.

Stephanie drummed her fingers on the windowsill. The window was so deeply set in the thick sandstone wall it made a perfect seat in which to curl up. But she was in no mood for sitting or leafing through the Montgomery Ward's catalogue her mother had picked up at the Las Vegas post office.

After three minutes of idly turning the pages she flung herself from the window seat to once more pace the room. Her divided riding skirt of soft leather swirled about her cowhide boots as she suddenly spun about and stalked out the door.

Her mother looked up from the ledger as Stephanie rushed into the small office. "Mama, why didn't you let me go with the men after the bear? Papa would have if he were here."

"But your father and Don Jiraldo are back in Santa Fe," Rosemary said patiently. She turned her chair around to face Stephanie and laid aside her pen. "I know you're bored, but there's the Fourth of July dance at Fort Union next Saturday."

"That's five days away, mama!"

"You're not needed at the bear hunt, Stephanie! Let Cody and the boys take care of that. You could better apply your time sewing on the gowns you and Inez will be wearing."

"But Inez isn't sewing," Stephanie persisted. "She and Tiarita are taking siestas, and you know I dislike siestas as much as you do. It's because you hate killing, isn't it?" she challenged.

156

"That has nothing to do with it." Rosemary sighed and looked away. Perhaps she was doing the wrong thing in trying to protect Stephanie. "All right. Go ahead, pet. But please be careful."

Stephanie hugged her mother and ran from the room. She knew where to find the three men. If they had not tracked down the bear yet, Cody would call a halt for lunch at the Conchos buffalo wallow. She took a breech-loading shotgun from the gun cabinet and went to the stables to saddle her notch-eared roan.

Within half an hour she was in the foothills. Her excitement mounted as she neared the watering place. She would make Wayne notice her this time! Every time she saw him her breath was taken away, as if someone had slammed a fist in her stomach. If only his work did not take up so much of his time. And at night either her father or Don Jiraldo monopolized Wayne's time with talk of politics. A month of the summer already gone and Wayne had yet to kiss her!

Her horse topped the rim of the Conchos, and she spotted the three men squatted beneath the sparse shade of a scrubby juniper. The three pairs of eyes watched her approach. Cody wore a frown of irritation, though Stephanie could not imagine why. Before, he had always been as permissive as her father in allowing her to do anything the men did.

All three rose when she dismounted, and Jamie said, "Sis, you shouldn't be here."

"What, you too!" She turned angrily on them. "What's going on around here?"

Cody took the reins from her, saying, "You might as well eat now that you're here. There's some cold beans and jerky in the pack over there."

"No!" Stephanie snapped. "I want to know why you don't want me along. A week ago you were all for me riding fence with you."

"Sis, this is a killer bear. He's not going to run and hide when he sees you."

"I can shoot as well as any of you—and you know it!"

Wayne handed her a rope of jerky. "Why not tell her?" he asked the other two. The brim of his hat shadowed his eyes, but she saw the cynical twist of his lips. "As of two weeks ago you were put on the marriage market."

"What?" Stephanie dropped to the ground beneath the juniper and tugged off her Spanish crowned hat. Her expression was wary as she looked from one face to the next, expecting a joke. "What do you mean!"

Cody hunkered before her. "The Apaches have taken up

157

the warclub again. Geronimo's been seen in the vicinity—
and one of his sub-chiefs is Satana."

"Yellow Dog's son?" Stephanie shuddered, remembering
the old chief's annual visit two weeks back. Her father still
plied Yellow Dog with gifts, though there seemed no longer
any reason to fear the murder and depredation of earlier
years from his band. Now it was only a matter of protecting
herds of cattle and flocks of sheep from the pilfering Apaches.
"But what has this to do with me?"

"On his last visit Yellow Dog claimed the gift your father
promised him seventeen years earlier." Cody's eyes narrowed
so that the pupils looked like pure flint. *"You."*

Stephanie looked to Jamie, then Wayne. "I don't understand."

"He means your father promised you in marriage to his
son—this Satana," Wayne said. "In return for the continued
safety of Cambria. My God, it sounds like something Bret
Harte would write—a dirty redskin and an English heiress."

Stephanie's gaze flicked from Jamie to Cody. "Papa would
do this—just give me away to Indians? I don't believe it."

Jamie sighed. "I think father thought Yellow Dog would
forget. But the point is, Sis, Yellow Dog did not forget. And
that means we've got to keep you hidden when Yellow Dog
comes back for you next month. Mom felt that by then she
would have a solution to all this mess."

Stephanie smiled. "I already do. I'll simply go back East
with you."

"You'd hide in the East forever?" Jamie asked. "Give up
Cambria?"

Stephanie put on her hat and tightened the chin strap.
"I don't intend to hide. But..." she shrugged her shoulders,
"other things could happen between now and then. Now, are
we going to hunt a bear?"

30

Jamie wiped his sweaty palms on his canvas pants. He
watched as Cody ran sensitive fingertips over the animal
track. "It's the bear's?"

Cody rose. He squinted into the dying sun that just topped
the spires of pine and aspen dotting the low mountain's hog-

back. "He's got maybe forty minutes on us." He swung up into the saddle. "Come on."

"Shouldn't we signal Wayne and Stephanie that we're on the trail?"

Cody's lips curled up on a one-sided grin. "It's not bear that she's hunting, Jamie boy."

Jamie drew a deep breath that eased out in a weary and nervous sigh. Perhaps he should warn Stephanie about Wayne, even if Wayne were his friend. She was so inexperienced. Well, her virtue might not be at stake at the moment, but his own courage was. "I'm ready," he answered and kneed his pinto into a trot behind Cody.

When first Jamie glimpsed the bear standing at a distance, he thought he must be mistaken, for it looked like an oak tree. The black bear, more cinnamon than black, was the largest he had ever seen. At that distance Jamie estimated the bear must be at least eight feet tall and weigh five hundred pounds. The click of a shell being shoved in Cody's rifle told him that Cody already had spotted the bear.

In his heart Jamie knew that Inez would not feel him any more the man should he lay the bearskin at her feet. She didn't measure a man's worth by his courage to kill. Yet the blood that coursed through Jamie's veins sang that this was something he must do himself. A melody that he heard over and over again, drumming in his temples. *You are not afraid. You are not afraid. You are a man.*

And as he slid his own shell into the rifle's chambers, he knew the song was for his father. That tough, unbreakable man who had always seemed larger than life. Taller than Cody, fiercer than Yellow Dog.

"Leave the horses here," Cody said beneath his breath. "If we miss him with the first shot, the horses will be useless in all this undergrowth. Take to a tree instead."

"Cody, he's mine. The bear. I want first shot."

The cowboy peered around at him, then nodded his head in assent. "He's yours, Jamie."

They moved forward, always keeping downwind of the animal. Once the animal reared to its full height, scratched its back against a cedar's shaggy bark, then ambled on. Several times it halted, raised its protruding snout to the air.

Jamie had always thought of bears as being clumsy animals. But this one was almost beautiful, if one could associate beauty with power. With its gleaming reddish-brown coat and splendid build, it was a magnificent beast, and Jamie hated to see it destroyed. But he heard the song again and
159

knew that only this way could he break away from his father's dominance.

The two were close enough now to fire. As though it sensed the impending danger, the bear reared and whirled around, almost as if it were dancing to the same song that played in Jamie's head. On its short, powerful legs it began moving toward the bush-tangled place where Jamie and Cody hid. Its forefeet with their long, heavy nails pawed the air.

"He's scented us," Cody said. He looked at Jamie. "Are you ready?"

Steadily Jamie returned his look. "Yes."

It moved with ponderous steps, each step like the heavy beat of the Indian cottonwood drum. Jamie watched with growing surprise as the rifle's sight began to tremor. It was as if he were totally disassociated from the rifle. He watched as the nervous spasm spread from the young man's stomach outward like a ripple in a disturbed pond.

He saw the beautiful beast moving ever nearer—and saw the image of the young man's father behind him, lip out-thrust, eyes flaring wide in disgusted anger.

The black bear loomed over Cody and Jamie, its shaggy coat blotting out the bright, white sun. It looked, Jamie thought, as the mammoth must have looked eons earlier, before the glaciers receded to the crests of the Sierras.

"Fire!" Cody hissed.

Stephanie knelt at the trickling stream and splashed the mossy water at her neck. She smoothed the loose hair back into its knot at the nape of her neck and pulled the broad-brim hat on her head before rising. All this took two and a half minutes. Long enough for Wayne to make some kind of overture.

When she could stall no longer, she turned and caught the brooding look that so captivated her. One day she knew she would be the woman to break through the shell of mystery that was also part of his charm. "Aren't you going to help me mount, Wayne?" Her voice was barely a raspy whisper.

Wayne smiled, a slow smile which she knew did not reach his heart. Maybe she was foolish to try and make him love her. But she could no more suppress her love for him than Jamie could hide his adoration of Inez. And she wondered why she tried. Why she had to pretend. No matter what the girls at the academy said, it seemed so unnatural to pretend indifference. She thought about her mother and knew that if her mother had ever loved anyone wildly, not the mild affection her mother had for her father, but loving beyond reason—she knew her mother would never have made the coy game of it.

Wayne cupped his hands for her boot. "I'm at your bidding, princess."

"Why do you call me that—princess?"

His lips twisted sardonically. "Aren't you the princess—of a kingdom larger than that of any fairy tale?"

"I'm still a woman, Wayne," she said huskily. She brushed his cupped hands aside. His arms slipped around her waist, pulling her against him, and his lips came down over hers. It was a hard, reckless kiss that left Stephanie trembling when he at last released her.

Her fingers reached up to touch the golden mustache above the warm lips, the lips she ached to kiss once more, and he caught her hand and pressed his lips against the hollow of her palm. Stephanie's breath sucked in at the exquisite sensation. She moved into his arms again, feeling her breasts turgid against his chest. Her arms wound about his neck. "Ah, Wayne, I want you so!"

Wayne's fingers dug into her hair, kneading her scalp. Dear God, if there was a woman for him, it was this one...part female, part wildcat-tomboy. Not some simpering ninny like his mother. How he hated the woman, always badgering his father, himself, making life a hell when he was home. It was no wonder as a child he headed every summer for Cambria...and Stephanie. She was the best of him. With her there might be hope.

He felt Stephanie's loins pressed against him, grinding urgently with her desire, and he forgot all else. "My God," he groaned, "you're a magnificent bitch, Stephanie!"

Stephanie reeled back as if slapped. Tears stung her eyes. Wayne grabbed her shoulders with an anguished moan. "I didn't mean that!"

Her glistening black eyes searched his face. "I don't understand you. I don't know what you want—or what you want me to be!"

"I don't—"

The sound of the rifle shot ricocheted about them. They broke apart. "The bear," Stephanie breathed. "They've found the bear!"

The fragile moment of their tryst was broken; yet both were relieved at the interruption—relieved for the time allowed them to sort out what had passed between them and gauge their feelings.

The next day, as they all sat around the oblong dining table toasting Jamie's successful kill, Stephanie reflected on that revealing moment with Wayne. Her woman's intuition told her that Wayne wanted her. She watched him across from her, saw the habitual cynicism claim the handsome face but realized that this time the curl of the lips was a result of something going on at the table. Forcibly she brought her attention back to the conversation.

"I promise you, son, the bearskin shall lie in my office before the desk," Stephen said at the table's far end. He and Don Jiraldo had returned that evening from Santa Fe and despite his weariness he was elated at the news of the kill. The walrus mustache and Prince Albert whiskers did not conceal the flush of inebriation. "And every man-jack who enters my office—from politician to peon—shall know my son can hold his own." He rose, swayed, and raised his glass in another toast. "To the only man fit to inherit the largest tract of land on the North American continent...James Gallagher Rhodes!"

Jamie, Wayne, her mother's face—Stephanie saw the same indefinable expression on each of them. Only Inez, Rita, and the nine or ten guests who had drifted in to sample the famed generosity of the Rhodes dining table seemed unaware of the tension in the room as they again raised their glasses of imported champagne in toast.

Jamie's chair suddenly tilted backward and fell over as he shot to his feet. His face wore a tortured look that was unbearable to watch. "I can't stand it! I can't take the credit, father. I couldn't kill that bear. I froze! Do you understand? Cody killed it. Not me!" With a strangled sob he spun from the table and ran from the room.

Stephen's florid face whitened. "You cowardly imbecile!" His voice thundered through the stunned silence.

31

Stephanie watched from the veranda on the Castle's west side as Ignacio and Julio shoveled the dirt from the pit they were digging beneath the cottonwood. Despite the perspiration that dotted her upper lip and riveleted the valley between her breasts, she shivered—whether from the fact it was her grave they were digging or just the sight of the two loathsome men, she did not know.

Bodyguards her father called the two men, who went with

him everywhere. Leeches, she called them...Ignacio, the fat bloodsucker, and Julio, the small, beetle-eyed tick. She would not hesitate to crunch both beneath her boot if she could. Cody would have fired them long before were they not personally hired by her father.

It was Cody who set the two henchmen to work, digging Stephanie's mock grave. "When Yellow Dog returns," he told her father, "tell him Stephanie died from cholera or whatever—make sure he sees the marker along with the other under the tree."

Stephen seemed satisfied with the deception. Not so Wayne. "It won't work," he said, coming up behind her. He stood in the veranda's shade, not touching her but so close she could hear his own irregular breathing. They had not talked since the day she had offered herself to him at the stream.

"Do you have a better suggestion?" she snapped. Why couldn't she make him want her—want her enough to marry her? "The idea is to stall for time."

"And then what?" he demanded.

Stephanie tore her gaze from Wayne's eyes, which burned blue-hot like the center of a flame. Another second beneath that mesmeric flame and she would foolishly throw herself at him like the proverbial moth. Instead she watched the progress of the digging. The July sun shimmered the air, and against the rising heat waves the two Mexicans looked like ghoulish creatures. "After that I don't know," she whispered.

Absently her hand slipped up to wipe at the perspiration that collected at the V-neck of her open blouse. She looked back to find Wayne's enigmatic gaze fastened on the curve of her breasts. Now perspiration dotted his temples. Her eyes dared his. "Unless you want to marry me."

Wayne moved against her, trapping her between him and the veranda post. His hand cupped her breast. "You don't understand, do you?" he asked before his mouth brutally possessed hers.

"Señor Raffin?" Pedro asked.

The two broke apart, and the houseservant looked at his sandaled feet with embarrassment. He had only recently taken a wife, and he was well aware of the grip of desire; still, he had known Stephanie since the day she was born and himself a boy of seven, and it was hard for him to accept her as old enough to know passion's hunger. "El Patron wishes to talk with you, Señor Raffin."

* * *

"Mother?"

Rosemary looked up from the book in her lap, opened at the poem "Lady Geraldine's Courtship." It was her favorite of Elizabeth Barrett Browning's poetry, and she sometimes wondered if she weren't being foolishly romantic after all the years.

And what lay before her but more years? Empty years. Why did she keep hoping?

She laid aside the book. "Come on in, Jamie. I'm not really reading. Just sort of daydreaming. Talk to me."

That was what Jamie admired about his mother most of all. Her patient love for him had been the bridge that spanned the bitterness that flowed through him like an underground stream. Never in all those years since her return had she ever been too busy to talk with him and to listen to his own daydreams of helping people recover from the thousand and one minor illnesses that seemed to claim their lives just as surely as a plague. An insignificant cough, a rusty nail, spoiled food. Instead, he had somehow ended up practicing law.

He stepped inside the doorway. "Mother, Inez is with me. We'd like to talk with you."

Rosemary smiled, relieved to see that Jamie had apparently put the previous evening out of his mind. She suspected Inez had something to do with restoring his equanimity. "Don't leave her standing there, Jamie. Inez, please come in." She turned to Jamie. "Shall I have Consuela make us something cool to drink?"

Jamie shook his head. He took Inez's hand and led her to the loveseat opposite his mother's bed. "This is something special. A secret to be kept for a while."

Rosemary looked at both their faces, bright with hope that only the youth seemed to have. "I think I can guess your secret. You two are in love and you want to get married."

"It's that obvious, is it?" Jamie asked, smiling.

Rosemary nodded, and Inez said in her softly accented voice, "We were afraid there would be objections because I am older than Jamie." Her fingers had been toying with the folds of her long, flounced skirts, but now her head snapped upward. With her dark brown hair piled high and held in place with a tortoiseshell comb, Inez looked as regal as a Spanish queen. "But it does not matter what anyone says. We love each other!"

Rosemary rose and crossed the room, bending to give first Inez, then Jamie, a kiss on the cheek. "I couldn't be happier, children. And I'm certain Rita will be very happy about the news."

"We knew you would feel that way," Jamie said. He paused

and looked at Inez, then went on. "We were hoping you two women might smooth the way with our fathers. I thought I'd ask Don Jiraldo for Inez's hand at the Fourth of July Ball tomorrow night. But father ..." Jamie frowned. "Well, you know, mother, we're not that close. But I would like his blessing."

Rosemary turned away. She moved to the window and, with her hands crossed about her elbows, stood looking out. She saw the great cottonwood where her firstborn was buried alongside Stephanie's grave. She saw the millhouse where Grant first kissed her. And she saw the village below where she spent many afternoons teaching and many nights watching over the sick. Almost a quarter of a century she had lived in this land. A land she had come to love despite her initial reservation. She was bound to this land, more so than Stephen could ever be!

Slowly she turned to face the two lovers, her decision made. "Jamie, your father will never give his blessing."

"Why not? Surely age can't be that important. And he and Don Jiraldo have been friends for years."

Rosemary held up her hand. "Let me finish." Her teeth played with her lower lip. "I don't know how to say this, because I care so much for you, Inez. But you see, Jamie's father brought me here from Ireland to be ..." she drew a deep breath and finished, "not so much a wife—but a breeder. Like a thoroughbred horse."

She saw the couple's faces register disbelief, then shock. Her lips twisted in a sad smile. "Actually, Inez, 'tis not so uncommon. Your father, who is a gachupine with the finest Spanish blood in his heritage, would never consider letting you marry a Mexican with Indian ancestry, a mestizo. Though he might be persuaded to let you marry Jamie ... I don't know. I do know that Stephen will never allow you to marry Inez, Jamie. He wants an empire ruled by pure Anglo blood."

Jamie bowed his head. His right fist ground into his left palm. When he looked up, Rosemary saw the fury that tore him inside out, the tears that symbolized years of frustration and anger and hurt. "I used to dream, mother—horrible dreams. Every night of the three years you were gone. And father was always in them. Yelling, shouting, bullying.

"After you came back the dreams eventually stopped. But not my hatred for what father stands for. A bigoted megalomaniac. He will control everything, everyone. He moves us like puppets. The puppeteer. But not me, mother. Not any longer. With—or without his blessing, I shall marry Inez!"

Rosemary stifled her urge to console her son. Her voice sounded harsh in her ears. "Jamie, your father merely has to give the word, and one hundred and thirty *vaqueros* are at his command, ready to do his bidding. And that's just here at Cambria. His hand controls the entire Territory."

Inez dropped to her knees at Rosemary's feet. Her hands clasped Rosemary's. *"Por favor*, Señora, help us. I love your son. And he loves me—and needs me. *¡Ayúdanos!* Help us!" Tears misted her eyes.

Rosemary lifted Inez to her feet. "The third floor of the mill," she began hesitantly as she made her plans. "Leave the dance tomorrow night—separately. I shall arrange for the Methodist circuit rider—he's at Las Vegas now I think—to meet you at the mill. It's two witnesses you'll be needing. Your mother, Inez, and Stephanie. I'll detain Stephen."

Jamie took his mother's face between his hands. "I love you, mother."

"And I love you. Now go, both of you. I've much to do before tomorrow night."

32

Stephanie looked up into Wayne's face and saw the grim lines carved at the corners of his mouth. She waited until he had whirled her past the musicians' platform, away from the twang of the banjo and the scrape of the fiddle and the watching eyes of the matrons and retired soldiers too old to dance any longer, content to watch the younger people dance, and dream of another era.

A strained smile came to Stephanie's lips. "I'm not forcing you to marry me, only seduce me. Am I that bad of a bargain, Wayne Raffin? After all, I am heiress to a kingdom, as you once reminded me. And I'm not that bad looking. Ask the master-sergeant over there. Already he's asked me to dance twice this evening."

Recalling the cloddish daughter of one of the homesteaders he had just danced the quadrille with, Wayne had to smile. "Are you trying to bribe me into marrying you, Stephanie?" he asked, attempting to match her humorous sparring. "If you are, it won't work. I've found I'm allergic to your bites."

Stephanie's smile leveled into a serious line. "Wayne, we'd be good together! Can't you see it?"

Embarrassment surfaced on Wayne's countenance. His

eyes looked past her head. "I know only that you're still a child in some ways, Stephanie. That you don't see beyond your own needs and wants."

Before the dance was even ending its last note, he dropped his arm from about her waist and escorted her back to her mother. Stephanie turned her back on him as he thanked her and rapidly began to fan herself. She was glad her mother was too preoccupied with Rita at the moment or she would have easily detected that something was wrong. But from the corner of her eye Stephanie hopelessly watched as Wayne bowed to Inez and heard him ask, in Jamie's absence, for a dance.

Stephanie wanted to cry and stamp her feet at the same time. She knew every pair of female eyes watched her, gloating at her frustration. She raised her head and glared at the nameless faces about her. Her defiant gaze swept by the women, herded together like sheep for security, and on to the men at the room's far side. She saw through their façade of nonchalance to their nervousness. And she saw Cody Strahan in lithe relaxation against a post, his watchful gaze on her.

With cool deliberation she snapped shut her fan and began walking across the sand-sprinkled puncheon floor that separated the two sexes like an enemy firing line. She heard the startled gasps even above the beginning strains of the music. She came to a halt before Cody, who raised one brow. "Will you dance with me, Cody?"

Cody took her in his arms and led her out onto the floor. It was the first time Stephanie had ever seen him dance, and she was surprised at his smoothness, for she had expected the usual awkwardness of the other cowpunchers she had danced with. Looking up at him now, she realized he was attractive in a rugged sort of way. He wore a dress-white linen shirt with the paper collar, and rather than his usual bandana knotted about his neck he had on a thin drawstring black tie.

"You're grinning like a opossum, kid," he said. "Does it hurt that much?"

Stephanie nodded, still smiling. "It shows, huh?"

He shrugged his shoulders. "I doubt the others know. I just been around you a lot maybe."

"You can read me like you can read bear tracks, Cody Strahan, and you know it." She looked up into the knowing gray eyes. "What am I going to do, Cody?" she asked in a pained whisper. "I want Wayne more than I've ever wanted anything in my life."

"And you've always gotten what you wanted, haven't you?"

Stephanie stiffened. "Are you against me also?"

"Nope. No one is. But you're headstrong. Like an unbroken colt."

"I've had to be, Cody!" Stephanie grated. "What do you think it's been like—growing up at Cambria where you count for nothing? Pet her, and she'll go away and leave you alone. That's my father's theory. It's always been Jamie this and Jamie that!"

"Are you jealous of Jamie?"

"No, no one could be. I love him, Cody, and I don't think he's been any happier with the life that's been forced upon him."

"So, you think you should've been the boy."

Stephanie looked away. "I never wanted to be. It just seems easier."

"Hey, kid—you're just as beautiful as your mom...but in a different way."

Stephanie looked up shyly at Cody. "You mean it?"

Cody laughed out loud. "Don't play the coquette with me, Stephanie Rhodes. I've known you too long, kid."

Stephanie laughed, enjoying herself in spite of Wayne's rejection. Too soon the waltz finished, and when Cody returned her to the benches of watching women, Rita was there with Inez.

"Cody—Inez, she does not feel so well," Rita said. "Maybe you and Stephanie can take us back to Cambria, no?"

Cody cocked an eyebrow at Inez, and indeed she seemed pale.

"Rosita can return with Esteban and Jiraldo tomorrow morning as planned," Rita continued.

"I'll clear it with mama and papa, Cody," Stephanie said, "while you bring the wagon around."

Cody caught her arm. "No, I'll clear it with them. You three wait."

Stephanie saw the knowledge in Cody's eyes that something was afoot. "Cody, please," she whispered. "This isn't for me. It's for Jamie."

He glanced at Rita, and she nodded imperceptibly. "Your mom and pop don't know about this?" he asked.

"Mama does. Please, Cody."

Cody hesitated, then said, "I'll be waiting outside. Make your good-byes."

Nervously Stephanie twisted the ends of her shawl as she approached her father. At her side Inez said, "I do feel so sick now, Stephanie. My stomach, it churns like butter."

"Good!"

168

"*¡Callados!*" Rita hissed. "Hush, you two. Inez, hang your head. *Chiquita,* I shall do the talking."

At the women's approach Stephen turned from the group of Las Vegas businessmen and their wives who surrounded him and Rosemary. He pinched his daughter's cheek. "You be looking as bonny as your mother did at your age."

"Why, Inez," Rosemary said, taking the girl's two frozen hands between her own, "you look like you don't feel well, doesn't she, Stephen?"

"*Con su permiso,* Esteban," Rita said, "we thought we'd return to Cambria early, if Cody could take us. Inez, she has been complaining of a *dolor de cabeza* all evening."

"A headache, huh," Stephen said. "Maybe we should rouse the fort's surgeon. Have him examine her."

"That probably would be unnecessary, Stephen," Rosemary said. "Inez just needs a little rest, I'm sure."

"I'll return with you, *mi amor,*" Don Jiraldo said. "These fiestas that last *todo las noches* are too much for a man my age."

Stephanie opened her mouth to protest, not knowing exactly what she would say, but her father spared her the worry, saying, "I'm sure Rosemary and Rita can take care of Inez, Jiraldo. Besides, we still haven't finished the deal on the Encino Silver Mines. Get with Hubbard and finish off the details while I walk the women to the wagon."

Outside there was the usual nip of coolness in the evening air, and the women hugged their shawls close about them. From nearby Las Vegas could be heard the explosion of fireworks. At noon that day Fort Union's cannon had fired thirty-eight salvos, one for each state in the Union.

Rita, Inez, and Stephanie climbed into the back seat of the wagon, and Stephen helped Rosemary in next to Cody. "Rosemary," he said, releasing her waist.

Rosemary heard the challenge in his voice. How many times had she faced it over the twenty years of their marriage, most of the time losing, sometimes winning? At times she thought Stephen had actually come to enjoy their marriage, enjoy the challenge she brought to it. "Aye, Stephen?"

"The Methodist circuit rider, Reverend—what's his name? He won't be at the millhouse."

Simultaneously the three women drew their breath in sharply. Stephen continued, "Oh, yes. I knew." Then to Rosemary, "You should know better after all these years than to underestimate me. Sending Pedro to Las Vegas to visit a clergyman—you should have realized it would not be going unnoticed."

"Does Jamie know?"

"To be sure. He and I had a father-to-son talk. I think he understands now I will never allow a marriage between him and Inez."

Rita bounded to her feet. "And for what reason? They are in love! Why do you stop them?"

"Because her background is not impeccable enough," Rosemary answered tiredly. "Her ancestry must be as Anglo as Stephen's Hereford cattle."

"*¡Mierda!*" Rita swore.

Inez cried out, "Where is Jamie? I go to him. No matter what you say!"

"I think not." Stephen's smile was benign below the calculating eyes. "It's already arranged between your father and Grant Raffin—you are to marry Wayne next year when he returns to practice law."

"No!" Stephanie screamed. She sprang up and threw herself at her father. "I won't let you control Wayne and myself. Not us, too!"

33

There came only the clip-clop of the horses' hooves on the grooved road that groped its way in the night between Fort Union's foothills and Cambria's high plains. Beneath the heavens' star-seamed canopy the wagon's five occupants sat in silence, each preoccupied with Jamie Rhodes, wondering where he had gone when he rode out from the fort into the night's concealing darkness an hour earlier.

"He's just angry at being thwarted," Stephen had said, mildly irritated at Rosemary's smothering concern for the boy. "When he realizes I've done the best thing for him, he'll turn up. Jiraldo and I will be coming home tomorrow sometime after we've finished business here with the Englishman Hubbard."

Occasionally Inez's muted crying would puncture the night's silence. "We must find Jamie!" she would beg of Cody.

Only Stephanie felt her worry surmounted by other feelings. Bitterness. Betrayal by Wayne, her father, and even her friend, though she fully realized Inez had no part in the betrayal; that Inez's love for Jamie was as deep as hers for Wayne. Still it hurt, like the sting of a scorpion, each time her imagination flashed a picture of Wayne and Inez sharing the bridal bed.

When the Castle finally came in sight, dawn tinted the sky a boiling orange. Inez and Rosemary did not wait for Cody to halt the wagon before the veranda steps but stumbled down from their seats as it was still rolling and ran into the house. Rita followed, cursing all the way. "Esteban and Jiraldo, they are *bastardos!* Pigs!"

Stephanie sat listlessly in the wagon, listening to Rita's epithets trail off into the great house. What could she say to her brother that would be of any consolation? Stephanie knew too well how he felt. Helpless frustration and a killing rage. Had she a pistol she would have shot her father at that moment; yet she felt greater anger and hurt toward Wayne. He had sold himself, she was sure. How much had her father paid Grant and Wayne Raffin to accept Inez Sanchez y Chavez into their family?

Her fingers curled, biting into her palms, and she was unaware of Cody lifting her down from the wagon, guiding her into the house that had come alive suddenly with lights. Her mother stood at the foot of the stairs, her face as white as the plastered walls. It was the first time Stephanie could remember seeing her mother so distracted. She whirled on Stephanie and Cody. "Consuela says Jamie has not been here at all."

Rita came out of Jamie's room and leaned over the banister. "There is nothing missing, Rosita. No clothes gone. His carpetbags are still here."

"Jamie would not leave without me," Inez said, coming up behind her mother. She bit her lip, looking at the man and two women below. "Where would he go?"

"It may be that he's not up to facing everyone right now," Cody offered. "He could be at one of the camps. I'll saddle up and look for him."

Rosemary put out a hand to Cody. "Calm him down. Tell him everything will work out all right."

Cody was already saddling his horse when Stephanie caught up with him. Cody eyed her blue satin gown bunched behind by the bustle. "Don't tell me you're going, too," he told her coldly.

"No, I'm telling you I don't think you need the horse!" she snapped. "I think I know where he is."

Cody sighed. "All right. Where?"

"At the millhouse. Remember how we used to hide out there when mama threatened to paddle us?"

Within minutes they covered the distance that separated the corral from the mill. It loomed dark and forbidding

171

against the morning sky. "He's here," Cody said and pointed to the grazing pinto. Cody looked down at Stephanie. "You wait here."

"Let me go with you."

"Not this time. A hysterical female ain't going to help his disposition none."

"You know I'm not that way."

Cody looked into her eyes. "No, I don't know that. Not anymore, at least. Now do as I say and stay put."

Stephanie fidgeted, feeling the cool morning air ice her clothes. Even her skin. The early dawn's mist cast an eerie haze over the sun. After a few moments she heard Cody's spurs clink on the mill's wooden stairs. Then another silence. Impatience seized Stephanie, and she ran inside. Whatever Jamie could tell about Wayne, she wanted to hear. The cornmeal dust coated her skirts as she ran up the first flight of stairs. On the second floor it was warmer.

"Cody? Jamie?" she called, out of breath. She could not see anyone in the darkness among the paraphernalia of rotted saddles, greasy blankets, and worn hides.

"For God's sake, Stephanie," Cody bellowed from the floor above, "go back downstairs!"

Stephanie heard the agitation in Cody's normally lazy drawl and took the stairs two at a time, ripping the lace at the hem of her dress.

"Dammit, I told you to—" But he broke off, knowing she had seen the horror he tried to conceal.

The scream tore through her, echoing again and again throughout the tower. From above and behind Cody's tall frame a man's body swung gently, suspended by a rope from the timbered ceiling.

The glass exploded in purple-dyed shards against the office wall, and Stephen's belligerent and drunken voice could be heard throughout the house. "Consuela! Linda! Pedro! Another wine bottle. *¡Ahorita!*"

Stephanie huddled deeper against the window seat. She had always considered herself brave though she stood in awe of her father's black Irish rages. Now, she felt only an angry grief as gloomy as the late summer rain that fell outside her window, streaking the panes in dusty rivulets.

For three weeks, since the morning after Jamie's burial beneath the cottonwood, she, along with the rest of the household, had listened to Stephen's drunken bellowing that mixed with his morose soliloquys and occasional bouts of crying.

Only her mother seemed unperturbed by Stephen's frightening behavior and dared enter his chamber of mourning.

For Stephanie it had been three weeks of a loneliness she had not known existed. All her life Cambria had been a fairytale land. Hundreds of her father's employees to adore her and thousands of acres to roam with no restrictions. Oh, the dreams she and Jamie and Wayne had created there. The buffalo they had shot and the Indians they had vanquished! The pirates they had dueled. When she had gone off to school, she had felt a pity mixed with dismay at the cloistered lives led by her schoolmates. Years of needlepoint, piano, and singing. Boring!

But now there was only the vast emptiness of the land to swallow up the house. Jamie was gone forever. And Wayne, back to Virginia. But then, after he finished law school, he would be returning to marry Inez. Inez and Rita had at least escaped the forlorn atmosphere that claimed the Castle like quagmire, pulling it and its occupants ever deeper into despair.

The weeks of accumulated inactivity were more than Stephanie could bear, and at last she sprang from the window seat and went to the wardrobe. There in the back of musty, long-unused clothing she found her yellow slicker. She would ride. Ride until she had ridden the bitterness and hurt and grief out of her system. She would let the rain wash away the ugliness that seemed to eat away her insides. Then, maybe then, she could think of Wayne without the terrible hurt.

Maybe then, and her spirits began to flicker with life again, she could think of a way out of all this, think of a way to regain Wayne. She would not accept her father's dictum for her as docilely as Inez accepted her ordained marriage to Wayne. Rita wrote that Inez had lost all will to live, walking about the hacienda like a zombie of All Souls' Day. Worse, Jiraldo had suffered a stroke and was not expected to survive.

As Stephanie passed by her mother's room the sound of her name on her mother's lips slowed her, and she paused at the open door, not comprehending at first.

"You never took the time to include Stephanie in your plans, did you, Stephen? You unwisely centered all your hopes and plans around Jamie. How unbusinesslike for a man such as yourself, placing all your eggs in one basket! I wonder if you even ever loved our son!"

Stephanie heard the tears of agony in her mother's voice and turned to leave, when her mother said, "But I won't let you do the same to Stephanie. I won't let her be used as you did Jamie!"

"I'll do what I bloody well please, Rosie! I haven't come

this far to fail now." He gave a short, mirthless laugh, and Stephanie shivered despite the warmth of the enveloping slicker. It was a cold laugh that warned like the rattle of the diamondback snake. "Stephanie'll marry that Englishman. With his wife dead three years, Hubbard'll be hot to bed Stephanie—given a wee push in the right direction."

"You bloody son-of-a-bitch." It was the first time Stephanie had ever heard her mother really swear. But her mother did not stop with that. "I've watched you manipulate all of us. You've used us as building blocks for your empire. But now 'tis all over, Stephen. Your pure Anglo empire ended with Jamie's death. Stephanie is not your daughter! Did you hear me!" Rosemary screamed. "She's not your daughter!"

"What the hell are you—"

Her laugh was almost maniacal. "'Tis good to see you stunned for once, Stephen. You, who always know everything keeping your finger on every person. But you did not know that Stephanie wasn't your daughter, did you? While you were out fighting your glorious Civil War, I was being raped by one of your friendly Apache tribes. Stephanie's a half-breed, Stephen!"

Something toppled to the floor. Stephanie heard her father's snarl, sounding like a cornered mountain lion. But she was finished listening. She spun from the door and ran down the stairs.

Old Miguel called out after her as her horse thundered through the mud-washed streets past the store, but she was oblivious to everything. Tears mingled with the drizzling rain that stung her face. It was not until she was safe within the forested foothills that she knew where she was going.

She would get roaring drunk in Las Vegas.

34

It was a glittering saloon, one of the better ones of the twenty seven saloons that jostled with the shops and office buildings for space around Las Vegas's plaza. Still, hand-hewn rafters crisscrossed the room at a low height, and the earthen floor was strewn with refuse. Lighted candles shimmered through the haze of smoke.

Every gambler there smoked, from the elegant caballero with his Havana cigar to the humble ranchero and hired do

174

mestics; from the clerks and cowboys who rolled their own *cigarros* to the titled lady furnished with her *tenazita de oro,* the little golden tongs which held a cigar and prevented her delicate fingers from being polluted with the scent and stain of tobacco.

Cody's eyes squinted through the haze. It was the fifth saloon he had tried that evening. And he worried now. Maybe the information that the Rhodes girl had been seen in one of the town's gambling establishments had been a false trail. But it didn't matter. If he didn't find her here, he would keep looking for until he did find her. He would have come looking for Stephanie whether Rosemary had asked him or not.

Cody thought of Stephen, and his anger rose again in him like black bile. The man was back in Las Vegas, winding up the Encino Silver Mine venture with the Englishman. Cody could only hope their paths did not cross, because he did not know what he would do. But ending up at the end of a rope for murder was not what he had in mind when he first came to Cambria. He had planned to kick about for a couple of years. Until the memory of his wife and daughter's deaths had faded from the homestead.

It had seemed to Cody then that his wife's lavender scent and his daughter's bright laughter had lingered about the one-room cabin like friendly and familiar ghosts. Perhaps that had been what first attracted him to Rosemary's daughter. The child's bubbling laughter. Her captivating smile, enchanting with just the hint of flirtation in it. Stephanie had inherited the smile from her mother but without that trace of sadness found in her mother's. Or at least sadness had not been present until this summer.

Cody grimaced, feeling again the anger. At men like Stephen and Wayne; maybe just at life in general. If he had any horse sense, he'd ride the hell out of Cambria, back to Loving's Bend and his ranch. But he knew he wouldn't go anywhere. Not leastways till Stephanie made up her mind what she wanted. He told himself he was too old to go a-courtin' again, 'specially a girl some seventeen years his junior. A babe. And a spoilt one at that.

At the far end of the saloon a man's woeful cry went up as the dealer in gartered sleeves and paper-billed cap raked in his winnings. It was then, just past the man who had lost his fortune, that Cody thought he sighted the flash of red hair. He shouldered his way through the crowd to reach a table at the rear of the saloon. A priest, two motley-looking cowpunchers, and an old man in owlish-looking glasses and suspenders sat with Stephanie.

Cody walked over to the table and stood behind her. He did not know if she had seen him coming; she gave no sign of it. But the others, they seemed to be aware of his more than passing interest in the game. He looked at Stephanie's cards, held fanwise in her sun-browned hand. She had pushed forward one silver Mexican 'dobe dollar. Cody felt it not enough, for the others were paying little attention to their cards. He threw down an eight-sided California gold piece.

One of the cowpunchers, a skinny youth, grinned and tossed in his hand. The others followed suit. Stephanie did not move, and Cody scraped in her winnings for her. Then he made an almost imperceptible motion of his head to the first cowpuncher, who promptly stood. The three others rose also and made their farewells. They were all gone.

Cody still stood behind Stephanie. Her low-crowned Spanish hat hung by its cords from her neck, and her head was bare. He laid his hand on the brilliant hair. "Let's go home, kid."

Stephanie leaned forward to escape his hand, then pushed at the table and stood, swinging around to face him. She was wearing britches and boots and a cambric shirt that did little to hid her ripe breasts. A leather belt accented her small waist. She dug her hands into the table behind her. "I have no home!"

"Your mother's waiting for you."

"That's not my home. Didn't you know," she spit, "didn't they tell you—I'm a half-breed! Ask my mother. Ask Stephen Rhodes!"

With a sigh Cody hooked his thumbs in his pants pockets. So the rumor had finally come home to roost. "I don't need to ask anyone—'cause I don't care one way or another. But your mother loves you and wants you to come home."

"So I can be bartered off?"

"You've never been made to do anything against your will."

"Then you haven't heard that I'm being traded from Satana to Hubbard?" she sneered. "Stephen—"

"Stephen Rhodes is here, in Las Vegas, and your mother's home worried about you." Cody grabbed up the slicker draped on the back of her chair. "Now come on, we're going home."

Stephanie shoved away his outstretched hand and turned from him.

"Hell's fires, kid, you're a stubborn cuss!" He grabbed her from behind, spun her around, and threw her over one shoulder. With Stephanie shouting and beating him on the back, he began to edge his way through the press of people.

"Damn you, Cody Strahan!" Several gamblers stopped to stare, some to laugh, but her shouts of "Help!" went unheeded. A lovers' tiff. More power to the wrangler who tamed the woman who tried to act like a man.

Once outside and away from the saloon, Cody set Stephanie on her feet. "Don't try to hightail it, 'cause I got longer legs and I'll take you down quicker than a jackrabbit."

Stephanie stood mute and stiff.

"Now, where's your horse stabled?" Cody demanded.

The new Pintsch gaslights illuminated the slow, wicked smile that dented the corners of her mouth. "Sold it—and the saddle, too. For a stake."

Cody closed his eyes and let out a grunt. "Come on," he said, grabbing her hand and pulling her along behind him. At the livery stable he roused the little Mexican urchin and paid him. Stephanie dropped to the straw-littered ground and watched Cody saddle his paint. "How'd you know where to find me?"

Cody grimaced. "You leave a trail like a city slicker. Thought I'd taught you better."

"Guess I just didn't care," Stephanie mumbled, chewing on a piece of hay.

Cody jerked hard on the girths. "Well, you'd best start caring. Geronimo and Satana are still toting the war hatchet."

Stephanie looked up at Cody. "You worried Satana is going to come for me?"

"One day he will. When he and Geronimo have shaken the soldiers off their tails."

Stephanie kept on. "And that worries you?"

"Anything that affects Cambria and my job worries me, kid. Now let's get moving. Dawn'll be here soon, and I don't want to be riding under Satana's sights."

He grabbed Stephanie about the waist and pitched her up into the saddle before she could protest, then swung up in front of her. Stephanie wrapped her arms about his lean waist and laid her head against his back, as she had often done as a child, and Cody uttered an inward sigh. It was going to be a long ride back.

The brisk August wind whipped about the paint and its two riders, and a stooped-back moon peeped through streaked clouds to cast dancing shadows over the rolling terrain. Stephanie hugged closer to Cody's brush jacket, feeling its rough warmness against her cheek. "Cody, were you ever in love?"

"Once."

"What happened?"

There was a silence, then, "I married her."

Stephanie raised her head and looked accusingly at his back. "You never said you were married."

"Not any longer. Maggie—and Becky, my daughter—

177

they're dead. Killed by a couple of Johnny Rebs. It happened a long time ago—when I was just a kid about your age."

"Oh." Stephanie laid her cheek against Cody's sheltering back once more. "I see."

But she didn't see, he thought. And was glad. Or else she would know what a damned idiot he was making of himself, loving her like he did.

Dawn found them coming down out of the scrub-tufted foothills, still halfway from Cambria. Cody knew Stephanie would never admit to weakness, especially to another ranch-hand. But the two weeks of whirlwind gambling and carousing showed in the shadows beneath her eyes and the new hollows beneath her cheekbones. "Let's ease up a spell," he said. "A siesta would do us both good."

Stephanie looked at him suspiciously. When Cody halted the paint in the lee of a mesa's wall, she said, "You never got tired before, Cody Strahan."

"No," he agreed, smiling. "But I never got old before."

Stephanie's eyes narrowed, watching the tall man as he settled back against the mesa's sandy slope, crossed his long legs, and tilted his hat brim down over his face.

She looked at him for the first time as a woman really looks at a man. The sinewy length of corded muscle, the uncompromising jaw and firm lips, the weather-browned face. But it was the eyes, shielded now by the Stetson's brim, that had captivated her ever since childhood.

The eyes were the entire man, she thought. A nondescript color of gray, they were nevertheless luminous, eloquent with the gentleness inside the man. She had always supposed his an ordinary face, but now she perceived the deep character sketched in its lines. So much he never talked about—and so much he knew. And so much time she had wasted when she could have been learning from him, getting to know him better.

She dropped down from the saddle and went over to stretch out next to him, at first self-conscious because of her awakened awareness of the man. But even this faded when she closed her eyes and the vision of Wayne's face returned to haunt her as it had each night for as long as she could remember—his golden good looks; the brooding, hot eyes; the reckless curve of his lips. And she knew she would not return home to be bartered off to the Englishman.

She waited until she heard Cody's breath, steady and even in sleep. She hated to leave him stranded there, but he was a survivor. He would make it back to Cambria. And maybe she would too someday. But not now. Not as long as there was hope for her and Wayne. Slowly she began to inch away from him, until she was far enough to crawl. After two more yards of tension-filled progress, she deemed it safe enough to spring up and make a dash for the paint.

The impact of Cody's body flattened her. He jerked her roughly around beneath him. Her lungs fought for breath. The red sand ground into her back where her shirt had pulled out of her britches. But she was aware only of Cody's eyes, a gun-metal gray now in their wrath. Always before there had been only the harsh flatness in the tone of Cody's voice to show his displeasure. Never had she seen him openly display anger and she was frightened.

"I said you're going back to Cambria," he said, his words clipped and hard, and she could feel the fury even in his warm breath.

"So I can be bartered off?" she bristled, her rage momentarily drowning out her fear. "Never!"

She buckled then, trying to roll from beneath him, but his body came down hard against hers, and his hands pinioned her wrists above her head. "Lackey!" she spit up at him. "You're Stephen Rhodes's lackey, just like everyone else!"

Cody's face tightened. "You've never been made to do anything against your will . . . before." His mouth closed ruthlessly over hers, the fierceness of his kiss parting her lips.

At first Stephanie was too surprised and remained immobile under the angry onslaught of his kiss. Her mind reacted with confusion to this first kiss, and then even it slowed to an opiumlike stupor as her emotions took over. Unconsciously her arms wound about his neck, wanting to draw the hard, lean body closer into her. Her hips undulated with their need. Somewhere in the distance she heard her low moans of desire.

Suddenly Cody pulled away. Stephanie's lids flew open, and she saw the passion in his face before it closed over like a mask. "You're going back to Cambria," he said huskily. "After you've talked with your mother, you can leave if you want to. But until then you have my word—you're safe from Stephen Rhodes."

"Just like I'm safe from you?" she sneered.

35

Stephanie's gaze followed Burton Hubbard's pale, slender hand as he smoothed the linen napkin into neat folds beside the heavy ironstone plate, and she thought again, as she had done so often those past three months since she had returned to Cambria, of Cody's weather-browned hands. From her childhood she recalled a summer day when she had been badly bruised by a mustang she had tried to ride...and Cody's sure, firm hands massaging away the pain. With a tingling in the pit of her stomach she remembered the melting warmth of languor that had flowed through her like warm rum.

"Stephanie!" Stephen snapped. "Mr. Hubbard asked you a question."

Miserably Stephanie lifted her gaze to meet Burton Hubbard's pinched face. The Englishman looked as uncomfortable as she. "I'm sorry," she murmured. "What were you saying?"

There was an awkward silence. Burton Hubbard cleared his throat, and his Adam's apple vibrated. "I was curious if you had seen the Gila Cliff Dwellings near Silver City. They're really supposed to be quite unique."

Stephanie saw the calf-love in Burton's eyes. So, he really was in love with her. It was not just Stephen Rhodes's promise of a kingdom. "No, Mr. Hubbard, I've never seen the cliff dwellings."

Listlessly she returned to eating. She wondered how much longer Stephen Rhodes would wait for his plans to come to their hoped-for fruition before he forced her into the marriage. So far in the five or six times Burton had stayed at Cambria he had yet to make an overture of marriage. But she knew it was coming.

Earlier that evening he had cornered her in the veranda swing. She had been, for all purposes, reading; but actually she had hoped to catch a glimpse of Cody. The few times their paths had crossed he had all but ignored her, something it seemed that Burton did not intend to do, for he had taken her hand between his clammy ones. Whatever he had been about to say, Stephanie could only guess, because at that same moment a servant appeared with the message her mother wanted to see her.

Stephen tossed down his glass of brandy. His florid face

was newly marked with purple veins. His eyes were almost continuously glazed with the increased amount of alcohol he consumed. He was a man robbed of his one dream. Still, he would not give up. He could yet make an Anglo dynasty for Cambria—at least three-quarters Anglo—and he would do it, by God, with Hubbard's bloodline and Hubbard's money. "I be thinking," he said loudly, "that mayhaps we could all take some sort of pleasure trip out to Silver City. To inspect our mines. It'd do you good to get away, Rosemary. And you, too, Stephanie. Mr. Hubbard here could act as our guide."

Stephanie rose from her chair and dropped her napkin beside her plate. "I really don't feel well!" She glared at Stephen then turned to Burton. "I'm so sorry, Mr. Hubbard. Excuse me," and with that hurried from the room.

Half an hour later her mother was at the door. "Stephanie?" She lit the lamp on the wall beside the dresser, and Stephanie's eyes blinked at the light.

"Are they still below, mama?"

Rosemary nodded. "Having their cigars and brandy." She went to sit beside Stephanie on the bed. Her daughter lay huddled in a fetal position, her flaming hair down about her shoulders like a blanket. Rosemary smoothed the stray wisps back from her daughter's face.

"Mama," Stephanie whispered, "what am I going to do? Papa—Stephen," she corrected bitterly, "will keep me a prisoner here at Cambria until I marry Hubbard."

Rosemary's green-blue eyes flared momentarily, then she said softly, "When Cody brought you back, I promised you that you wouldn't have to marry the Englishman. And you won't. I'll write your great-uncle in Ireland—Lord Gallagher—and ask him to call in all Stephen's notes."

Stephanie sat up. "You mean you could bankrupt him?"

Rosemary laughed curtly. "Hardly. But it would negate whatever financial reward he hopes to gain from the Encino Silver Mines...and your marriage. But until I hear from Lord Gallagher, I think it would be best if you stay out of your father's way. Perhaps a trip to San Francisco or maybe New Orleans."

"I'm not leaving, mama. Not as long as there's a chance Wayne will change his mind."

Rosemary's control shattered. She grabbed Stephanie by the shoulders and gently shook her. "Don't you see what sort of man Wayne is? A man that can be bought...among other things!"

Stephanie twisted free. "And what kind of woman does that make you, mama? Tell me! Didn't Stephen Rhodes buy you?" Her youthful face was rigid in rage. "How can you judge Wayne? Tell me, mama, how many men have you bedded with besides Stephen Rhodes and my father?"

Rosemary's hand lashed out, and Stephanie fell back on the mattress, the red imprint of her mother's hand across one cheek. "And don't you be judging me, Stephanie," Rosemary said in a low, tight voice. "Only when you've walked in my shoes will you have that right."

Stephanie rolled to one elbow. Tears stung her eyes. She reached out her hand toward her mother's in a conciliatory gesture, though it was not yet an integral part of her proud character to ask forgiveness. "What was my father like, mama? You never said. Who was he—I have to know!"

"He was a man," Rosemary said simply. "He possessed a courage that was tempered only by his gentle love. But who he was—I cannot tell you that. Not now. Maybe some day."

Right now it was enough for Rosemary to play Stephen's cat and mouse game. His new attitude of wait and watch strained her nerves like strung wire. How long could she keep Stephen from guessing the identity of her lover?

"Is my father still alive?"

"Aye." And though she had had no word of Lario Santiago for fourteen years, she knew she would know otherwise if he weren't. Her soul would know if he had died in the depths of the copper pits.

She closed her eyes, remembering the days and nights when she thought she would not survive one more moment without him. But she had. She still lived. No, change that, she thought. *I still exist. Inside I have dried up to a withered, cold woman...as dead and rootless as the tumbleweed.*

The same must not happen to Stephanie, she thought frantically. She looked at her daughter's willful face—the square chin, the inner determination that showed through the eyes' dancing lights, the firm mouth. Stephanie's spirit had not yet been quenched, and would not be if Rosemary could help it. "Obviously you wouldn't want to visit with Rita and Inez for a few months, would you?"

Stephanie shook her head, and Rosemary said, "Then I propose you ride the camps like you used to as a child. It will at least keep you out of Stephen's way for a while. And Cody will see to it the hands do not get out of line."

Stephanie doubted if anyone ever knew the exact boundaries of Cambria in the early days when it was the DeVega Land Grant. The confusion as to the boundaries still existed in spite of the surveys made by civil engineers with the Land Department.

The Wild Cat Camp cabin where she and Cody wintered with several other wranglers lay below a spring that bubbled from a hillside five hundred feet away—at almost the exact point where four sections met. Over the years the spring had been claimed by different owners, each of whom had attempted to validate his claim by various cornerstones.

Within Stephanie's memory the wandering cornerstone, a well-known marvel in the Territory, had made a circle around Wild Cat Springs. The cornerstone was a small mound of rocks with markings chiseled into the rough surface of one of them, like a cat's claw. Hence the Wild Cat Camp, though by now the protection of the questionable boundary did not matter, since Stephen Rhodes had acquired it all in the course of the years.

Still, in Stephen's absence the year before, Rosemary had decided on Cody's advice to string barbwire. Few weeks had gone by that some Texas cattleman did not drive his herd to market in Colorado over the waterholes and buffalo grass of Cambria. Now with the boundaries fenced there was less chance of cows wandering and cattle rustling than on the open range. And Rosemary never questioned if the fencing happened to take in a few more acres than previously accounted for.

Stephanie tacked the last string of barbwire to the lone post and slumped down against it with a sigh. The post did little to protect her from the blustery February wind, but at that point she was too tired to care. She peeled the leather gauntlets from her chilled hands and looked at the raw spots where the barbs had pierced through the gloves to her skin.

What man would want a roughened woman as she was, she wondered ruefully. Skin tanned brown by the sun and wind; body honed to a lean firmness with none of the opulent curves to entice. No, there was not a man, especially Wayne, who would find her desirable in her present condition. And at that moment she didn't give a damn. She wanted only to rinse the dirt and grime away and crawl into her bunk. Thank God there was only one prickly hoop more to string that day.

Oh, hell! she thought. It could wait until tomorrow. She'd get back to the bunkhouse and maybe get in a hot bath before the others rode in. It seemed like months, though it had been only weeks since she'd last been up to the Castle and had a real bath in the white enameled steel bathtub. For now the wooden tub at the bunkhouse would have to serve. With more

183

energy than she thought she had left Stephanie swung up on her piebald and struck out for the camp.

Set just above the stockpond and maze of corrals, the stone cabin was a welcome sight. A refuge from the cold. After toting two buckets of water from the tank, she rapidly shed her gauntlets and sheepskin jacket along with her woolen shirt, britches, and boots. Nude, she knelt before the caliche fireplace and fanned the morning's banked embers.

While the water heated in the big Dutch kettle, she unbraided her hair and brushed the accumulated dust from it. At last the water was hot, and she poured it into the round tub. The tub was so small she had to stand to bathe, but it did not matter. With a sigh of rapture she stepped into the water, feeling its cleansing warmth as she held the sodden washrag to her breasts and let the water flow down the length of her body.

The door flew open and let in a gust of frigid air. "Shit, it's colder than a witch's—" Cody broke off as he beheld Stephanie, all glistening and golden in the sheen of the leaping fire.

"Cody!" The name burst from Stephanie's lips as her hands flew to shield her nakedness. The foreman turned his back, but not before she saw the desire that flickered like a flame in his eyes. In the three months she had ridden the camps with Cody, he had politely ignored her, speaking to her only when giving an order. The tension between the two of them had strained her presence with the other men as never before. She was no longer just one of the hands.

Each time she looked at Cody not only did she feel shame at her wanton response to his kiss the day he had brought her back from Las Vegas, but she felt an anger that she should want to feel the heat and weight of his body on hers again, to feel the searing touch of his hands, when she loved another man. What kind of woman did that make her? A woman like her mother who shared the bed of more than one man?

"I'm sorry," she murmured to Cody's back. "I didn't expect anyone to return this soon."

Cody kept his gaze on the red flowering geranium plant in the old lard can that Stephanie had placed on the table the week before. Fishing out a thin piece of paper from the jappaned tin in his pocket, he sprinkled black flakes into the paper's fold and began to roll it. "Billy and Clem are repairing the corral over at Coon's Draw and will be late," he said evenly. He shoved the tin back in his pocket and snapped a sulphur match across the door's bar. "I'll finish setting out the stock salt." His hand went to the latch.

184

"Cody...could you pass me the blanket—there on the bunk?"

Only a fractional moment of silence followed. Then he turned to face her. In the fire's flickering light his gray eyes blazed with an anger that Stephanie was unaccustomed to seeing in the man. "I'm too old for games, kid—and you are, too."

Stephanie said nothing, confused by the conflicting emotions that bombarded her. Should she act naive and let the moment pass? Or brazen it out and discover just what it was that was so special about the act of intercourse? She had grown up on Cambria and had been initiated early into the mating of the animals. Was it so very different with humans?

Her eyes took in Cody's tall, lean frame, hard and weathered as her own. The rawboned face. It had none of Wayne's handsomeness. But the slate-hued eyes—they glowed, held her almost transfixed. "Pass me the blanket," she whispered hoarsely.

"Do you know what you're doing?" he demanded.

"Are you afraid of me, Cody Strahan?" It was a taunt to hide her growing fear. Her knees quivered like jelly. It was the hot bath that had enervated her, she told herself. Still, she marveled at her boldness as unflinchingly she faced the penetrating gaze that seemed to burn her like a branding iron. Challengingly her hands fell to her sides, displaying the firm, round breasts and triangular patch of red-brown curls.

Cody dropped the bar over the door's latch, then jerked the blanket from the bunk. But when he faced her, his wrath was bridled. He wrapped the scratchy blanket about her rigid form, never taking his gaze from her large, dilated eyes. Sweeping her up into his arms, he crossed to the bunk and laid her on the fluffy wool mattress. For a moment he posed above her, then his gaze relinquished hers as he shucked his clothing.

Stephanie had thought that when the moment came she would be sensuous, as seductive as the naked lady in the painting above the bar of one of Las Vegas's saloons. But when Cody slid his long, whip-corded frame next to hers, she giggled. "You smell like a cow, Cody!"

But she liked his scent—a mixture of old leather, sweet tobacco, and piñon smoke. She tried to recall Wayne, the intoxicating scent of his cologne and pomade, but everything about Cody overpowered her. From his own husky laugh to the work-toughened hand that lay lightly on her hip.

Cody smiled. "I think a damned rutting bull would hit the mark." His lips feathered across her temple. "Scared, kid?"

Stephanie nodded. "Yes, but I never figured to go about

it like this, Cody. But I don't want to change my mind," she added quickly.

Cody laughed again, and the warm sound of it gentled her. "I don't know of any other way," he told her as she snuggled closer, laying her hand across his matted chest.

His gentle teasing relaxed her, and there was no fear, no stiffness, as his hands caressed the supple curves of her woman's body, sliding down to entangle themselves in the mound of hair that was as downy as lamb's fleece.

Stephanie gasped, and her eyes snapped open.

"It's part of it," he said gently as his tongue teased the bowlike line of her upper lip. "It's part of loving."

Stephanie's lips parted beneath the insistence of his tongue. For a moment she lay lax as his tongue sought and captured hers, but a warm stirring in her belly rippled like suddenly disturbed pond water so that the very outermost parts of her were soon awash with the sensuous feeling. When he at last freed her, her body trembled with unquenched desire. "I didn't know—" she began.

"There's a lot you don't know," he said huskily. "We're just beginning." But he had to smile as he caught her gaze lowering past his small, hard nipples nestled in the mat of curls. "Yes, I'm different—but that's something you should know." He took her hand, guiding it to him.

Stephanie forgot her embarrassment as her fingers traced with wonderment the beauty of the man's physique. And when Cody's breath sucked in at her own rhythmic caresses she knew the great pleasure of giving.

His hand closed over hers. "Not yet. There's time." And he rolled away so that he could see the whole of her, watch the soft expression on her face give way to passion's demand as his hands and lips made love to her. When he touched and kissed the softest, most hidden part of her body, her head lolled to one side and she moaned at the unbearable pleasure that racked her body.

At last when she lay quivering like a spent bowstring beneath his knowing fingers, he slid up and over her. Her eyes closed, her tangled lashes lying over her high cheekbones. Her body arched against his, seeking once again the love he was giving her, the love he had hidden for so many years.

Their passion mounted with the tempo of their lovemaking so that they both gasped as one at the incredible pleasure that exploded between them. "Look at me," Cody told her during the brief, sustained moment of ecstasy. "I love you, Stephanie Rhodes."

36

The attraction that crackled between Stephanie and Cody like summer lightning was obvious, though none of the cowhands dared mention the fact—not only out of respect for Stephanie but also from a healthy fear of Cody's reaction.

And in concern for Stephanie's reputation Cody was careful that the two of them were never again alone, usually sending Jack or Charly, two of the old-timers, out with Stephanie on the line ride. Cody knew Stephanie's mercurial nature and waited with watchful patience to see if her attraction for him was a thing of the moment, a substitute for Wayne, or if it held a deeper significance.

The waning days of winter, marked by warm days and frosty nights, meant that soon the line riding would be over and it would be time to return to prepare for spring roundup. Spurred by this knowledge and driven by the more primitive instinct of mating that came with spring's approach, Stephanie trailed Cody to an outlying water tank. Cody never looked up from where he knelt at the bank washing the grime from his face, but as he wrung the water from his bandana, he said, "You're about as quiet as a riled buffalo, Stephanie."

Stephanie watched the way his thick, leather-brown hair curled at the nape of his neck and knew the wild desire to run her fingers through it again, to kiss the tanned, corded neck once more. Just watching Cody's movements made her weak with a passion that continued to amaze her. She wondered if she was like one of the wanton women that the cowhands often joked about, the kind of women who lived in the barrio districts of Las Vegas and Santa Fe.

How could she want one man so much and continue to love another, one who obviously cared nothing for her? She knew she was a fool . . . and knew there was nothing she could do about it. Since her childhood Wayne had been a fever in her blood as much as gold fevered a prospector.

"Why don't you ever take me seriously, Cody?" she asked as she dismounted and looped her piebald's reins about the wooden rungs of the dilapidated windmill. "Cody!" she said desperately when he did not answer her. "I don't want to go back!"

Cody rose and knotted the damp bandana about his neck.

"You can't hide out forever, Stephanie. Sooner or later you're gonna have to face what you're running from."

Stephanie wrinkled her nose in impatience and began to fan herself with her hat. "If I go back, papa—Stephen—will start in again about me marrying Hubbard. And I won't do it!" She sounded convincing, but both knew that she was evading the issue.

Still Cody said nothing. He swung up into the saddle. "I promised your mother I'd bring you back when spring roundup began. By that time hopefully your Englishman will have lost interest. Besides," he said, looking down into the inky depths of her eyes, "I'm leaving soon—after the branding is over."

Stephanie caught his bridle. "What do you mean you're leaving?"

"I've been running, too, kid. For too long. It's time I started making my own life again."

Stephanie stuttered, not knowing what to say. "But you've always been—I thought you were happy here."

Cody eyed Stephanie, his lids narrowing to slits. He wished he could understand her. "Happiness isn't guaranteed," he began and was saved an explanation by his inborn sixth sense that responded to a presence before he ever heard the tell-tale movement of other horses through the tall grass.

"What is it?" Stephanie asked as he rapidly drew the Spencer carbine from the saddle scabbard and shouldered it. Her untrained ear still heard nothing. But within seconds three horsemen appeared on the next rise. Stephanie gasped. "Satana!"

"I've been waiting for the coyote to show his face!"

"You knew he was around?"

"I didn't think he'd go for the story about your death," Cody replied as he watched the three horsemen slowly approach. "Came back to see for himself, I guess."

Satana raised his hand, halting his party within yards of Cody and Stephanie. His lank hair hung about his shoulders. His buckskins were black with grease. Only the charcoal black eyes seemed alive in the cruel face that was the color of dead leaves. Stephanie repressed a shudder as her mind tried to recall something from the past.

"Your spirit I see has not left the earth," he told her with a smirk.

Cody matched his smile. "She didn't wish to marry one who runs with the dogs, Satana."

Satana's hand slid to the knife at his waist. The other two went for their outdated flintlock rifles, and Cody said, "It would give me great pleasure to kill you."

"Paren!" Satana said, nodding to the two warriors to halt. He looked back to Stephanie. The lust gleamed in his eyes. Lust for the unobtainable. The white woman. This white woman whose look of loathing he did not miss. He remembered her as a child, with hair the color of the sacred fire, and remembered how her mother had jerked her from him, as if he were something unclean. He did not take his eyes from the young woman now, though he addressed her man. "I will come for her, white man. And when I do, I will take your hair with me for her to mourn over."

He dug into his pony's flanks and wheeled about, and Cody said, "You're going back home, kid."

Rosemary fingered the embossed invitation before passing it to Stephanie. "We do not have to go. We can take that trip to Ireland you've been putting off. Stephan would never dare deny you the trip, not with your great-uncle ill as he is."

With the arrival of her aunt's letter informing her of Lord Gallagher's stroke, all hope that he might be able to call in Stephen's notes was temporarily suspended. And if he died, what then? Rosemary wondered as the seeds of panic sprang to life within her. All hold over Stephen would be gone.

"Gracias," she told Consuela, taking the cup of hot chocolate the woman handed her. She took a sip and looked at her daughter over the cup's rim. "Well, shall we go to Ireland?"

Stephanie returned the invitation and sauntered over to the sink. Her back was to her mother as she rolled up her blouse's sleeves and began pumping water. "And have everyone think me a coward, mama?" she answered flippantly while she washed her hands. "No, I'm going to the wedding."

She would see Wayne again, if only for a moment. She would not give up. She would wait until that last moment when the padre encircled the couple with the bridal rope and blessed them as man and wife.

The Rhodes family left for Las Vegas the first day of June, five days before the wedding, which was to be held in the stately flagstone Church of Our Lady of Sorrows. While Stephen negotiated with a Charles Blanchard to introduce the first telephones in New Mexico, Stephanie and Rosemary shopped among the boutiques hidden in small alcoves off the plaza. At last Stephanie found the dress she wanted, and it needed only a few alterations.

She knew it was daring to consider wearing the dress to Inez's wedding—white eyelet cotton over batiste, but it was too beautiful to pass up. As she dressed for the wedding she realized she had forgotten the pleasure of a woman's beguiling fi-

189

nery. Beneath her lace-ruffled underskirts and wire darb, suspendered garters held up fine silk-embroidered hose. Her wide-brim leghorn hat, abounding in magnolia blossoms of silk and organdy, was tilted at just the right angle over her face. Long white-laced gloves set off the picturesque summery dress.

When Rosemary entered Stephanie's room, she carefully shut the door behind her, leaning against it, and took in her daughter's dazzling beauty. There was sadness in her face, and Stephanie asked, "What is it, mama? Don't I look pretty?" She twirled so that her voluminous skirts flew out. "Well?"

"You know you do. And you also know that these days white is reserved for the bride. I should never have let you purchase the dress."

Stephanie's lower lip thrust out in a pout. "It's time someone broke the tradition. What's so wrong with wearing white? Cody would chuckle if he could see me now." She suddenly wished she could have persuaded him to come with them to Las Vegas. She needed his company, his open admiration now more than ever. Facing Inez and Wayne alone would be difficult.

"Cody's always admired your daring," Rosemary said carefully. "But Inez has been your friend since childhood. This would hurt her."

Stephen knocked and entered the room. "It's gorgeous you look, Stephanie!" He crossed to her and caught her chin between thumb and forefinger. "You shall make a lovely bride, me dearest."

Stephanie smelled the liquor that seemed to perpetually scent his breath those days. "Getting married today was not what I had in mind," she said and twisted her chin free of his grasp.

Stephen flicked a glance to Rosemary who sat on the bed watching him with a dispassion that was a continual source of irritation to him. "You've your mother's beauty," he said never taking his red-rimmed eyes from Rosemary, "but not her guile. Why not admit it, Stephanie—you're hankering after Wayne Raffin."

Stephanie cast her mother a worried glance. "No," she began.

"Don't be trying to pull the wool over me eyes. Go ahead and hanker after Wayne. Nothing wrong with it. Just don't get caught. And especially by Hubbard. 'Cause you *are* going to marry him." He grinned and pinched Stephanie's pale cheek. "As soon as he returns from his Colorado mining exploration. I'll not let you postpone the marriage any longer."

After Stephen and Rosemary left the room, Stephanie

clenched and unclenched her hands, letting the circulation flow back in painful pricks. She had been aware of her mother's warning look that she must not betray their hope for Lord Gallagher's intervention. But it made no difference. She would never marry Burton Hubbard.

She poured herself a glass of wine that had been left in the room, compliments of The Exchange Hotel management. With a vow she would make Wayne want her she drank the glass dry. Did she not know the ways of a man now? Wayne could never want Inez after having her. They could run away together and laugh at everyone who stood waiting at the cathedral for what would never happen.

There were still two hours left before the wedding. Stephanie filled the glass and drained it once more before she left her room and headed down the hall to the room Wayne occupied. Only then did it occur to her that his father or mother might be inside with him, but it was too late to change her mind, for Wayne opened the door at her first hesitant knock.

His starched, ruffled white shirt lay open, his golden locks tousled. "Wayne," she breathed, the pain at seeing him again hurting like a blow to her stomach. She threw her arms about his neck. "I can't stand it, Wayne. Don't do it. You don't love her! I know you don't!"

Wayne tried to disengage her hands. "Stephanie, it won't work. Not even with you. There's no hope!"

Stephanie pulled his face down to meet hers, her lips offering him her love. "My God," he groaned, pulling away. "You don't understand. I—"

A polite "ahmmm," interrupted them.

Stephanie whirled to see a small-boned but debonair man watching from the overstuffed chair in the far corner. "A touching scene," he lisped.

Stephanie's glance flew back to lock with Wayne's. "My best man, Stephanie," he said, his voice tight and hard. "John Duncan, my roommate at Richmond University."

Stephanie spun away and ran blindly down the dimly lit hall. She wanted to hide, to cry. Now it'd be out all over the Territory about how Stephanie Rhodes had thrown herself at Wayne Raffin. Her hands groped for her own doorknob. She let herself in and collapsed across the bed. Her shoulders heaved with tears she would not let herself shed. She wanted more than ever the safety and security of Cambria. But she would not run away. She would go to the wedding. And dare anyone to say anything.

37

Instantly Cody came awake. His hand slid under the pillow to grasp the Peacemaker. Slowly, quietly, his thumb cocked the hammer. In the cabin's darkness his eyes perceived the slightest light of moonlight seep through the door's aperture. A shadow interposed itself, moving closer to him. With cool deliberation born of years of daily facing danger, Cody raised the pistol.

"Cody," Stephanie whispered.

"Kid! What the hell are you doing here?"

She reached out in the darkness for him, and his arms encircled her, bringing her safely to his bed. "I haven't been able to sleep," she told him, her body sliding to fit in the familiar curves of his nude one. "Not for a week now."

"Since Santa Fe, eh? That's a long time to go without sleep."

"Don't, Cody," she said, her voice tremulous. "I came for consolation. Not to be teased."

Cody slipped his arm around her shoulder; his fingers played with her unbound hair. "It's that bad. Want to tell me?"

Yes, she wanted to tell him and knew she could not. Not everything. Not how the want for Wayne was eating away at her soul and body and mind, so that it seemed she was nothing but an empty shell. "Cody, do you love me?"

"Is that what you wanted to say?"

She twisted her head, trying to make out the strong line of his profile in the dark. "Why haven't you asked me to marry you? You're only thirty-six. Stephen was much older than that when he married mother." She paused, then asked, "Are you still in love with her—your wife?"

His voice was calm, dispassionate. "I have no wife, Stephanie. Only a memory. I told you, she's dead." He raised up on one elbow, and she could make out now, from the shadows of his face, the beautiful, compassionate eyes. "And as for why I haven't asked you to marry me—I've been waiting for you to find out just what it is you want. Now, my lack of proposing," he went on, "hasn't been what's kept you awake. So, what's the trouble?"

Stephanie's fingers slipped up to touch the chiseled lips

and moved on to wander through his thick hair. "Cody, Stephen's determined he's going to make me marry Burton Hubbard—and you know what he's like!"

Cody chuckled. "You could be getting a lot worse, kid."

"I'm serious. And stop calling me kid! I'm a woman!"

"I know, I know." Involuntarily his lips brushed her neck. "You've made me well aware of that."

Stephanie's breath caught at the sudden pleasure that coursed through her, the same kind of funny feeling she used to get as a kid when she and Jamie and Wayne would sneak a light of the foul-smelling, wretched-tasting jimson weed. Invariably she would later become ill at her stomach and swear off the stuff for another summer.

But the pleasure that Cody gave her never left any nauseous aftereffects. Only the wild desire that could not be satiated. When he touched her, he made her come alive, made her fully aware of her woman's body as something earthy and wonderful. Why then could she not love him, why did it have to be Wayne?

Cody raised his head, releasing her lips. "So, what are you going to do?"

"I...damn it! You know what I'm trying to say. Stop making me squirm, Cody Strahan!"

Cody sighed. "You'll manage to wriggle out of the wedding some way. If I thought you were in love with me, Stephanie, I'd marry you quicker than a coyote on a rabbit. But you aren't—and I'm not going to make things worse than they are. Like it is—I can leave here with...warm memories."

"Memories!" Stephanie hissed. "Is that all I am to you? A good tumble in the hay till you can get back to your precious ranch? My God, you've been living off your wife's memories all these years! Aren't you man enough to take on something real?"

She felt the constriction of his muscles. "You'd better go climb in someone else's bed, kid."

Stephanie's fingers came up to rake down his cheek. But lights exploded behind her eyes as Cody lashed back, his hand snapping her head to one side. Stephanie lay stunned for a moment. Tears rushed to her eyes. Never in all the years she had adored Cody had he been anything but gentle.

His fingertips brushed away the tears that rolled from the corners of her eyes. "I'm sorry, Stephanie," he whispered. "Hurting you was the last thing I wanted to do. I guess it's better I move on. I never figured to hurt you."

Stephanie clutched at his hand, holding it between her breasts. "Cody, don't leave me. I don't know what to do.

Please. There's the ranch. It'd be yours someday, if you married me."

He sighed. "You don't know me at all, do you?" He pulled her into his arms and lay back beside her. "Tell me, is escape from marriage with this Hubbard guy the only reason you want to marry me?"

"You mean am I—am I carrying your child?"

"That'd do for a start."

After a silence, Stephanie said, "No, I thought about lying to you, but I couldn't. Besides, you'd find out sooner or later."

"Glad to hear that decision. Is that all? Is there anything else you want to tell me?"

Now was her chance. But fear that Cody might change his mind made her hedge. "Should there be anything else?"

"I'm asking you."

Stephanie raised her head and softly kissed his lips. "Only that I want to hear you tell me you love me."

Cody crushed her to him. "You're a little pisser!" he growled, but nevertheless his hands were gentle as he gave her what she wanted and showed her what he wanted, hoping beyond expectation she might come to understand what lay behind the giving of himself. And when she did not, as he had known she wouldn't, he rode her hard, draining her of all her frustrations so she was at least at peace with herself.

Stephen leaned back in his chair and looked across the desk at his foreman whose length was stretched out in the leather-stuffed chair next to the desk. He ignored his daughter who sat, skirts spread demurely, on the sofa. He had been expecting it for some time now. Ignacio and Julio didn't miss much. And he hated it because Strahan was his best employee. "What's on your mind, Strahan?"

"Stephen," Stephanie began stiltedly. She rarely addressed him these days if she could avoid it. She saw the black eyes squint, making them seem small and hard and unyielding. But she would not give ground. Not this time.

"Stephanie," Cody said. Quietly and firmly. Stephanie bit her lip but deferred to Cody.

"I'd like to marry Stephanie," Cody said. "With your blessing."

Stephen raised a grizzly brow. "And if I say no?"

"I'll marry her with—or without your approval. But I'd like to have it. It'd get our marriage off on the right foot."

Stephen smiled. "I didn't take you to be ambitious, Cody. Seems I was wrong."

The muscles in Cody's jaws flickered but his voice was unruffled, smooth as a summer breeze on the Pecos. "You *are* wrong. After the wedding, I'm taking Stephanie back with me to Loving's Bend."

Stephen laughed out loud. "You be thinking that way? Do you think, man, I'd let Stephanie marry some two-bit cow-poke?" Stephen's fist came down on the desk. The smile erupted into a snarl. "As far as the Territory's concerned, she's a Rhodes! Do you know what that name means in New Mexico?"

"I don't care what the name means, Rhodes. I care about Stephanie. Can you say that much?"

Stephen rose to his feet. Both fists rested on the desktop, the knuckles rigid and white. "How far do you think you'd get with her? There are one hundred and thirty men out there to fill you full of holes if I give the word."

Cody rose. He towered over the shorter man. "Most of those men have never even seen your face, Rhodes. Most of those men have fought by my side—the Indians, nasty weather, a stampede. You name it. We're *compadres*. A word I doubt you'd understand."

Stephen shook now, something he had never done before he had begun drinking so heavily. His dark face looked sallow. "Get out! Get off Cambria! And if I even hear of you in this Territory, I'll see to it you're strung up to the nearest windmill!"

Cody clamped his hat on his head. "I'm not sneaking off with Stephanie like some horse thief. I'm riding to Las Vegas for a minister—a priest, if need be. And I'll be back tomorrow for Stephanie."

Rosemary really was not asleep. Behind the closed lids frightening scenes played out so realistically that the speed of her heartbeat increased, her mouth grew dry, her palms sweaty.

For years, how many years...twenty-one, twenty-two... she had endured Stephen's ruthlessness, his megalomania. The dutiful wife. He had destroyed their son, almost destroyed herself, and now...was Stephanie the next sacrifice for the Rhodes empire?

Stephanie deserved her chance, and Cody could give it to her.

Rosemary saw again her son's limp body, the bluish face. Was that ever her son? The tiny, soft form, with dimpled knees and elbows, that she had held to her breast? The pudgy fingers and pot belly? What hopes one has for their children, she thought. For the future.

Her future was gone. And Jamie's. Yet there was still hope

that Stephanie might survive Stephen's manipulations. But how? Rosemary swallowed. Her mouth felt like cotton. Maybe she would slip downstairs for some fresh water. What if she awoke Stephen? She could not take it, not tonight.

Warm air stirred about her. She opened her eyes, thinking she ought to close the shutters. The insects seemed to be worse than usual.

A hand clamped over her mouth. Something sharp pricked at her throat. Black eyes gleamed above her.

Lario!

No! It couldn't be! Fifteen years!

Even in the darkness the shape of his face was unmistakable. Why shouldn't it be? She had memorized it every night of her life. The wide cheekbones, the flaring nostrils, the generous lips—and the oblique eyes that always had seemed to see clear through her. And the memory of another night flashed before her, when she had awakened in Lario's hogan after running away from Stephen. That night, like this one, she opened her eyes to the sight of Lario's brilliant black ones. Black eyes that could be as soft as velvet in making love or as hard as jet in anger.

His voice came quietly, harshly. "For years I have thought how I would kill first Raffin, then you. After a while, after months of sores and hunger and beatings, I realized how much better to kill Raffin—and leave you to live without him—to tear out your hair and cut your face and rub in the wounds the ashes of a widow's grief."

Rosemary lay there. Her eyes devoured him. Her body trembled. But Lario saw no fear. And the anger that had festered over the years like sores took hold of him, destroyed his caution. He grabbed her shoulders and shook her, so that her head jerked back and forth like a rag doll's. "Bitch! Whore!"

Rosemary managed to grasp both sides of Lario's face. Despite the violent way he shook her, she pulled his face down to hers. "Lario, you must listen to me. It was for you I played the whore. Grant promised to save your life if I—"

His hand lashed downward, and her head snapped sideways with the impact. "Life! Death would've been better than the hellhole where you two sent me!"

Her eyes smarted with tears. Yet her hands crept up to encircle his neck. "Lario," she whispered hoarsely. "I love you."

With an almost pantherish snarl of rage his hands went around her neck. "Damn your soul to the white man's hell! Every night of my life, every breath of mine dust I ate and breathed reminded me—like a drum beating in my head—how I would kill you."

196

Rosemary did not struggle. Instead she pressed her body against the length of his. "Then kill me," she gasped.

Surprised, Lario's fingers relaxed only barely, and Rosemary seized the opportunity to find his lips with her own. Her fingers dug into his long, thick hair, caressed the muscled back ridged by scars. Her hips moved against him, taunting with passion.

Damn, what was she doing? He had thought—no, hoped —she would beg, grovel for her life, for Grant's. He had wanted to kill her, now he was returning her kisses like a man too long starved. She had meant trouble for him since that first day in San Antonio when she had unflinchingly met his mocking scrutiny. And he thought of the sandpainting, of his grandfather's warning, and groaned, forgetting even that as her small tongue darted in to tantalize his own. It was just like all the other times.

With one hand he ripped the cotton nightgown from her while his other fumbled at the buttons of the canvas pants. But her own hands were there, loosening, sliding them below his hips. Her lips seared his belly. "Damn you!" he growled.

His fingers buried in her hair, pulled her back to him. And she was ready. No urging, no preliminaries were needed between them. It was as they had known it would be, as they had both dreamed over the long years. The vortex of their passion unleashed upon them like one thunderous, giant whirlwind.

38

He lay at her side, propped up on one elbow. Almost absent-mindedly his hand caressed her pale silken flesh as he listened to the lilt of her still-Irish voice.

"Sin-they?" she replied. She had not thought of Stephanie as Sin-they in such a long time. "Your daughter is much as you are. Stubborn. Headstrong. Willful. And loving and sensitive."

"And does she have her mother's beauty?" His brown hand rested on the slight curvature of her stomach.

Rosemary blushed with pleasure. So long since she had heard words of adoration. She could almost feel her life's juices flowing, singing through her veins. Feeling young again when she was almost forty! Was it possible?

"She has her own special beauty, Lario. 'Tis a kind of beauty that makes people want to look at her again. You would be really proud of her. She is very self-sufficient. As capable as any squaw."

In the mauve light of dawn that tinted the bedroom, she saw his smile and gloried in it. "There is a man who is in love with her. A good, strong-willed man much like yourself." Her fingers crept up to touch his warm lips, and she felt the renewing of her desire for him. It would never be quenched. This passion, this love.

Lario teased her fingertips with the tip of his tongue. "And does she love him?"

"She could... in time. She has agreed to marry him." Rosemary sighed. "But at the present she is blinded by infatuation for..." Her words trailed away. Time was too precious to waste on the tenuous moment.

"Lario, it'd work, I know it. Take me with you. We could go to Mexico. Live there."

Lario scowled. "And what kind of life would you have? What kind did you have when you lived with me? Hunger. Death. Filth. Always running."

Rosemary's fingers dug into his arm. "And what kind of life do you think I have here? 'Tis useless I am! A leaf that has withered and fallen by the wayside. At least with you I am alive! Lario, I followed you once—and you couldn't turn me back. I shall do it this time if I have to!"

Lario pulled her against him. "You are my curse... and my heart's blood. It was only the thought of you—the hate and love for you—that kept me going."

He could not tell her about the black rages of jealousy that had sometimes swept over him... and one rage in particular when he had envisioned her fair slender body entwined with Grant's golden one, had imagined her fresh rosewater scent, and had felt her delicate tremor of ecstasy. The murderous rage had sent adrenalin rushing through his body like a flash flood through a desert barranca, and he had gone for one of the guards with his pickax in his frenzy to be free, to make his way back to Grant and Rosemary. For that one moment of incaution he had almost been executed on the spot.

"I'll hide you here until tomorrow evening." Excitement began to color Rosemary's voice as she made the plans. A frown creased a line in her otherwise smooth complexion. Only the small, faint lines at the corners of her eyes betrayed any sign of aging; still she wished they were not there—that she could be for Lario as she had been at sixteen. "I wish—" she began.

Sensing her thoughts, he smiled at her feminine vanity. "You were like one of our *Kachina* dolls—not completely made yet. You are fully whole now."

Rosemary smiled and rubbed her nose against the hollow of his neck. She could not get enough of him. She wanted him to make love to her again, but she recalled what it was that was worrying her. "Tomorrow Cody is supposed to return for Stephanie—even though Stephen has warned him he'll have him killed first. I'm frightened for Stephanie and Cody, Lario. I don't know what Stephen is planning, but he's obsessed with the idea of his Anglo empire for Cambria, and I know he will not let Cody take Stephanie away."

"So I am to meet this man Cody who loves my daughter?" Rosemary looked at him with surprise.

"Do you think I'd leave Sin-they to Rhodes's control?" Lario asked. "We will wait. When Rhodes makes his move tomorrow, I will be ready."

Consuela continued to peel the waxy red skins from the steamed chili peppers, pretending not to notice Stephanie's nervousness. The girl had already drank two glasses of water and was now pumping more water, splashing it over her face and neck.

"It's so damned hot!" Stephanie muttered. She patted her face dry and rebuttoned the top of her blouse. Her head canted as the Queen Cathedral clock in the parlor chimed the fourth hour of the afternoon. Cody would have been there by now, she was sure. Unless something happened.

She whirled and stalked from the kitchen. She would have it out with Stephen and get it over with. She would force him to let her go away with Cody. But first she went to her room and took the Smith & Wesson .22 out of the tiny alligator leather holster that hung from one corner of her bureau mirror. She had had no need to use the little pistol once in all the trips she made to and from Philadelphia. But now...could she outbluff Stephen Rhodes, an incorrigible gambler himself?

She paused at the open door to his office. His feet were propped on his massive desk as he read a yellowed copy of the *Las Vegas Gazette*. In his left hand he held the ubiquitous glass of brandy. He looked up at her. "Railroad stocks are up," he said with a toast of his glass. "That might mean a trip for us all—maybe back to Wales to see where I came from."

As half drunk as he seemed to stay these days, there was still something powerfully menacing about his presence to Stephanie. She kept the hand that held the .22 behind her back, calmly saying, "I'm not going anywhere. Unless it's with Cody."

Stephen laughed shortly. He set down his glass and with an equal calm folded his newspaper, laying it aside. "By this time," he at last said, "Juan and some of the others have waylaid your fiancé outside of Las Vegas and are escorting him to the Texas border."

Stephanie laughed contemptuously. "You think he won't be back?"

Stephen smiled. "Juan has instructions to nail Cody's hands to his saddle. He'll never use them again."

Stephanie gasped, and he went on. "I be thinking that Cody is smart enough to realize I mean what I say. And I hope you are."

Stephanie whipped the pistol from behind her. But her anger and fear caused the shot to go wild. And then Stephen knocked the breath from her as he shoved her to the floor and wrestled the gun from her. He stood over her, his breath coming in deep gasps from the exertion. "You bloody fool! Even your mother has more intelligence than you. She has learned the futility of crossing my will. Why can't you?"

"I'll never submit to you! And I won't kill myself like Jamie did either!" She saw him wince, and she said, "I'll fight you until you have to kill me yourself. But I'll never give in!"

Stephen opened his mouth to say something, then thought better of it. His face looked old, tired, and Stephanie could not imagine what had made him seem so omnipotent only minutes before. Stephanie stood up, but as she turned to leave the room, Stephen said, "Don't be thinking about leaving. You won't be getting past the Cambria boundaries."

Stephanie flung him a look of utter hatred before running up the flight of stairs to her mother's room. "Mama?" she asked, knocking at the door. Imprisoned. It was unbelievable! She realized her hands were clenched into fists and made them relax. She raised her hand to knock again, and the knob turned, the door opened partially.

"What is it, Stephanie?" her mother asked quietly.

"Mama, I need to talk to you. You must help me get away. Stephen—" She tried to fight the rising panic in her voice. "I think he's had Cody killed!"

A silence. "Wait for me below in the parlor. I'll be only a moment."

200

"Mama, you don't understand. Stephen's insane!" She pushed past her mother. "He's a mad—"

A man, an Indian, stood behind the door. Stephanie opened her mouth to scream, and at once his hand was about her mouth. She kicked her legs and flailed her arms, but his free arm held her locked to him.

"Stephanie! Stephanie!" Rosemary said. "Listen to me. Stop struggling. This man will help us. Lario is—our friend."

Stephanie went limp, and at Rosemary's nod Lario released her. Pulling away, Stephanie twisted around so she could see the Indian's face. Her face knitted as her eyes searched the stonelike countenance. The image of the man flashed before her in another scene...of her mother and him laughing, holding one another. And her squeezing between them, wanting to be a part of the love that bound the two. "I know you," she said slowly. "You were with us...when we lived with the Indians."

Lario looked to Rosemary. Tears shone in her eyes. He was no longer sure of the right thing to do. The young girl before him, proud and comely as any Indian maiden, shared his blood. Dare he tell her? She was also an Anglo and had as much right to claim her mother's bloodline. At last he said, "You are my daughter. You are Sin-they."

Stephanie's pupils expanded, then narrowed to slits. "So it was you who made me a half-breed," she whispered. "You're the Indian."

Half-breed—Indian. How many times he had heard the words, heard the contempt expressed with them. He turned now from the look of self-disgust that crossed his daughter's face. He went to look out the window—at the expanse of land that had once been the *Dine'és*'. What had made him ever think he would fit in the white man's world?

Rosemary saw the anger that boiled in Lario—and the deep sadness. And fear choked her, sealing her windpipe like a cork. Lario was thinking about leaving, she knew; he would leave her behind.

She forgot her daughter and crossed to face Lario, grabbing his arm. "I won't let you! I haven't waited for nothing. If it's fighting and getting yourself killed you be wanting—well, that's all right. But I'm still going with you!"

"My, my," Stephen mocked from the doorway. "So the whore follows the cur like a bitch in heat."

All three whirled to look at Stephen. The worst of Rosemary's fears were now realized—the confrontation between Stephen and Lario. Tiny hairs at the nape of her neck prickled in frightened anticipation. Her husband's voice, like his face, was calm. But the demented rage was nevertheless there to see. It glittered in the eyes. It exploded in his lungs, causing his chest to rise and fall like a panting coyote. Behind him stood Ignacio and Julio, eager as two dogs on the scent of a wounded buck.

Lario swung around, meaning to escape through the second-story window, but Rosemary blocked his path. "Get him!" Stephen ordered.

Rosemary found herself knocked to the floor as the two men dove for Lario. He kicked one off, catching him on the jaw. Half-in, half-out of the window, Lario struggled with Ignacio. Rosemary came to her feet, pulling at the man's head. Her fingernails clawed his fat cheeks, but still he held on—until Stephen crashed the oil lamp over Lario's head. Lario slumped over and fell in a heap at Rosemary's feet.

"String the thief up!" Stephen commanded. "He tried to steal my wife's jewelry."

"No!" Rosemary cried. "You can't kill him!"

Purple veins stood out at Stephen's temples. He watched Ignacio and Julio drag Lario's inert body through the door, then said to Rosemary, "Oh, I don't plan to kill him. Just make certain he doesn't spread any more of his bastards about." His spiteful, consuming gaze encompassed the two women. "I shall be dealing with you later." He closed the door, locking them in.

Rosemary threw herself against the door. Her fists pounded on the heavy wood. "Dear God, help me! Don't let Stephen do this!"

Stephanie walked slowly over to the bed like an old woman and stretched out, one arm thrown across her forehead. "It's useless, mama. You have brought us to this."

But Rosemary did not hear her. She ran to the window. A crowd of men and some of the wives and children had gathered at the corral reserved for branding. She could not see what was happening. She raised the window and leaned out. Someone shouted something, and the children scurried away and the women, hiding their faces in their rebozos, quickly followed their children.

Then Rosemary saw what the men had clustered to watch. Lario lay spread-eagled in the corral's center. His bronzed body, so beautifully made, was naked, glistening pink with the dying sun's last rays. Or was it blood?

The bedroom door swung open. Stephen stood there. Fury contorted his face so that he looked like an ogre out of some ghoulish fairy tale for children. "No, don't turn away," he said. "I want you to watch. You, too, Sin-they—isn't that what the red man called you?"

He jerked her up and shoved her toward the window. "Watch!" He grabbed Rosemary's chin and yanked her head about so that she was forced to stare at the man below.

Her man. So many years. She really did not know the man staked out below. Surely he had changed. Surely he was not the man she had come to love. And she had changed. Yet she did know him. She would know Lario no matter how many years, how many centuries, were to pass.

"Watch, whore!" Stephen ordered again. "It's remembering I want you to be every waking moment of your life!"

Rosemary forced her eyes open. She had braved many things through the years. The worst—and she thought that if she could survive that, she could survive anything—had been Jamie's death. She would be no less brave now. But, oh God, she was such a coward! Her sin—how many times had she paid for it, and innocents with her...Jamie, Stephanie, and Lario?

Ignacio stepped out of the surrounding group of men. The knife blade gleamed. The guillotine must have looked just so to the aristocrats trussed in the carts like swine bound for the butcher, she thought. It was a butchering knife. One from the kitchen. Rosemary saw the perspiration glistening over Lario's muscles. Saw them strain at Ignacio's approach, saw the mouth stretch taut and tight. Always the brave warrior. No sound will come from his lips, no screaming, no begging.

Slowly, obviously taking great delight in his performance, Ignacio began to saw away at the exposed genitals, hacking when the sinewy skin and tendons did not give.

A scream. Stephanie screamed and screamed. Surprisingly it was Rosemary who slapped her into silence. "Do not embarrass your father, Sin-they!" she hissed. "Give him at least this dignity."

Like a bell the words repeated themselves in Rosemary's mind...and she remembered in that awful moment Grant once saying the same to her. Steely-eyed, she turned her gaze back to the scene below.

The bound man twitched in spite of his enormous self-control. Blood poured between the rigid thighs and oozed into the dirt. Then the body went limp.

Stephen looked at the two women. His jaws were clenched with still unfulfilled fury. A muscle throbbed in his cheek. Rosemary faced him. Daring him. Hoping? she wondered. For what was left of her, and of the human being below who was once a man. And she knew.

203

Stephen whirled from her and stalked from the room. And she knew what was left to do.

39

The Springfield rested in its usual place in the gun cabinet. In the house's darkness it was barely visible, only the blue-black gleam of the long barrel. Nevertheless, Rosemary had no trouble in locating and removing it from its place. The smooth stock felt cool against her hands, the parquet floor cold beneath her bare feet.

The heavy front door gave way with a squeak that made her breath catch. She waited. No one stirred in the sleeping house. Outside in the brisk air of the late autumn night only the dust squeezing between her toes was warm. She moved quietly toward the center of the branding corral. Lario was still there, staked out for the morrow's buzzards, but only for torture. She knew Stephen had no intention of letting Lario die.

Lario's pallor shone in the cloud-streaked night. Yet his senses were alert as ever. He had known she was there, his eyes watching her as she knelt over his prone figure. "Lario," she whispered. Her voice coughed out in a croak. Her hand smoothed back the damp hair from his forehead, and she felt the tears at his temples.

His tears were for her, she knew. But she would not let herself cry. Not then.

"You know what I want, Turquoise Woman?" he whispered thickly between swollen lips.

She nodded.

"Then do it quickly."

She bent and kissed the feverish lips. And she was crying anyway. "Good-bye, my beloved."

Swiftly, before she lost her courage, she moved off to stand in the shadow of the nearest shed, a tack house. The rifle barrel came up. Its sight fixed on the dark form on the ground. The trigger pulled back smoothly. An ear-shattering blast. The recoil of the rifle. Once more, another shot that caused the body to jerk with the impact.

Rosemary quickly crossed to the house, fading into the shadows of the hollyhock that laced one wall. She waited, hidden, for what seemed like eternal seconds. Already, men, shrugging into their pants, came running from the bunk-houses.

And at last Stephen stumbled out the front door. His long-johns gleamed starkly white against the night's darkness. Rosemary put the rifle to her cheek and fired at his back. He was lifted up, as if caught in the whirl of a dust devil, spun, and dropped at the bottom of the veranda steps.

Calmly she moved out of entwining shrubbery, walked past his twitching body into the house, and replaced the rifle. She heard Consuela collide with one of the house servants in the hall, a muttered oath in Spanish, her daughter at the top of the stairs calling, "Mama?"

"I'm here, Stephanie. What happened? I heard a gunshot." They surged past her now out onto the veranda. Stephanie came to her side, and they followed the others.

"*¡Dios mío!*" Consuela backed away and saw Rosemary at the door. "*¡Por favor, Señora, no mira!*" She took her *patrona*'s arm gently. "Go back inside. *El Patrón*—he has been shot."

"Then I need to be with him," Rosemary said and shrugged off Consuela's restraining arm. "Send Ignacio for a doctor at once."

She followed two cowhands as they lifted the sagging body and brought it inside. "This way," she said, leading them toward Stephen's room.

She stood on one side of the bed as they laid Stephen down. His eyes were open. They moved toward her. And she saw the incredible amount of agony—and hate—imprisoned behind them. But the coarse features never changed.

"I fear he is *paralítico*—paralyzed, Señora," Consuela said.

Rosemary's gaze flickered over to meet the cook's rheumy eyes. *She knows. And she says nothing.* Rosemary knelt at the side of her husband. Her hand took his limp one. "I will wait . . . and pray . . . until a doctor can be brought."

The men turned to go, shuffling out in single file past Stephanie who watched apathetically from the doorway. One turned back, Pedro. "*Patrona*, the Navajo outside—" He faltered with pained embarrassment. "He has been shot, also. *Está muerto.*"

"Bury him," Rosemary said curtly. "Beneath the cotton-wood."

Next to Jamie and the stillborn infant. Rosemary's chin dropped to her chest, her lids shut tightly. The graves of the people she had loved were fast accumulating.

Rosemary noticed that Consuela had cleaned the Spring-field in the gun cabinet. Other than that, there had been no inquiry, no interest raised in the mysterious visitor who had killed Lario Santiago and sought to kill Stephen Rhodes. It was more or less presumed it was the work of avenging Indians, perhaps Geronimo's renegades—maybe even Satana himself.

Only Stephen Rhodes knew the killer's identity, and, of course, he was totally paralyzed.

In every face Rosemary read the sympathy for her, except in the faces of Ignacio and Julio when she fired them the next day. "I am accusing you two of theft," she said, sitting in Stephen's office, behind his desk. "It's three days you have to ride clear of Cambria. After that I am instructing my hands to shoot you on sight."

The two Mexicans looked shocked and angry, but they wasted no time in gathering their gear and leaving.

The word had spread rapidly after the doctor from Las Vegas had departed. *El Patrón* will never walk! He cannot move a muscle! Imagine—not being able to speak! The women looked at Rosemary and thought—poor thing, to spend the rest of one's days waiting on a bedridden husband. And the men, they looked and thought—how lonely her bed will be. Will she ever take someone to share it? And had her husband shared it? He was old, you know. How can such a woman exist without—and they would eye each other and wink in spite of their deep respect for the Anglo woman.

Stephanie never said anything. It was all she could do to force herself to come into Stephen's room. To look at the dry skin, the shriveled body. The room smelled. And she thought it was not just from decay. Could hatred have a smell, for surely it seemed almost tangible in the air? Stephen Rhodes's eyes burned when she entered, and she thought the intensity of their hatred would blister her skin.

She felt no pity, only revulsion. And she was ashamed of herself for the pleasure she took in his helplessness the few times she fed him, watching the food drool from the flaccid lips.

Only a week had passed since the shootings; yet it seemed already like a year. Eternity loomed before Stephanie's mind. An eternity of rising, waiting out the hours of the day, and sleeping. To this she and her mother were condemned.

Even her anger at her mother was gone now, replaced by a great vacuum.

The urge to escape was so overpowering at that moment, to run—anywhere—that Stephanie set the bowl of vegetable soup on the bedstand, ignoring the questioning in Stephen Rhodes's eyes, and ran from the room out onto the veranda. Fresh, clean air. She had to have it. Her chest heaved as she sucked in the air in great gulps. She heard the sobs welling from deep in her chest, gurgling upward like the filling of a water keg.

Stop it! Get control of yourself. You're a grown woman. No longer a child.

Weakly she leaned back against the veranda post, feeling now only a self-disgust. She felt unclean. Soiled. A dirty half-breed. Wasn't that what people like her were called? What man would want her now? Not fastidious Wayne. She would have even been his mistress had he wanted her; but not now. He could only look at her with revulsion.

And Cody? Would he have still wanted her had he known about her Indian heritage? Was he alive, perhaps at his ranch now...or were his bones slowly being bleached by the torturous New Mexican sun?

Through heavy lids her gaze swept the sun-beaten countryside. If intense longing could produce a mirage, it seemed to her that what her gaze encountered that moment had to be. She straightened to her feet, her hand shielding her eyes. But the mirage continued to move closer. Too many times Stephanie had sat on the veranda steps as a child and watched the man ride toward her, his weather-stained hat slouched down over his eyes in just the same fashion.

"Cody!" she cried. She picked up her skirts and ran toward the approaching rider.

Cody dismounted and opened his arms as she threw herself against him. "Stephanie," he rasped against her ear. His arms wrapped about her, though his hands were held awkwardly away from her body. It was when she pulled away to look at that wonderfully craggy face of his that she noticed the bandaged hands, the dirt-crusted strips no longer white. Her face paled.

"They did it then?" she whispered, taking one of his hands between the two of hers. "Stephen told me what he planned. It must have hurt terribly!"

Cody nodded. A grim smile settled on his face. He recalled the ambush, and the excruciating agony that followed as skin and muscle tissue tore and shredded when at last he pulled himself free from the embedded nails. "It didn't hurt much more than what Juan Jesus and Dick are undergoing right now."

Stephanie raised a questioning brow, and he said, "I never made it to Las Vegas. After I got free, it took me two days to catch up with them, and when I did I wasn't in too good a shape, but the Spencer carbine—it made me more nearly equal. I didn't kill them, but their miserable souls were hanging by threads when I left them—staked out on the Alkali Flats."

The words "staked out" reminded Stephanie. "Cody, things have happened since you left."

"Fill me in," he said, putting his arm about her shoulders as they walked toward the house.

By the time they reached the veranda Stephanie had related the shooting of Lario and her father's subsequent shooting and resulting paralysis. "And no one knows who's responsible?" he asked.

Pedro's approach saved her from answering. While the young man and two more wranglers heartily pounded Cody on the back, Stephanie waited aside, listening as Cody lightly shrugged off their concern for his hands by explaining they had been rope-burned. She wondered if she should reveal the discovery of her father to Cody. But she was afraid that would open an avenue to other questions that might easily lead to the identity of Lario's murderer—of which she was not entirely certain herself.

That night, after the few visitors who had drifted through Cambria left the dinner table, Cody told Rosemary, "I want to take Stephanie back with me to Loving's Bend. We've got to start somewhere on our own. And here, working for Cambria..." he looked down into the dark liquid in his coffee cup, "here there'd always be talk I married Stephanie for Cambria." He looked up, and his somber eyes met those of Rosemary's. "I hope you understand."

Rosemary was silent as her fingertip traced the curve of her coffee cup. "I don't know how I shall be getting along without you after all these years, Cody. You be like a younger brother. But I shall manage. Pedro's experienced enough to take your place now. With time," she smiled and shrugged her delicately rounded shoulders, "perhaps we shall make it."

"What about Stephen?" Cody asked. It was the first time the name had been mentioned except when Cody first offered his condolences.

Rosemary took a sip from her cup, waiting for the warming tea to go down, buying time. "Stephen's helplessness should not keep Stephanie from the happiness she deserves. And I shall be happy here at Cambria. It's what I want." She turned to her daughter. "What I want to know—is this what you want? Running away never solves anything."

So Rosemary knew, Cody thought, feeling the old despair eat away at his stomach. Ulcers, an aged ranchhand had diagnosed, but Cody knew better. Funny how your body'll turn on you when it's pining away for something it can't have. Still, Cody's face never mirrored its anxiety as he calmly waited for Stephanie to deny her love for Wayne.

At last Stephanie looked at him. "It's what I want."

It was supposed to be a small, simple wedding that took place two weeks later in Cambria's old adobe chapel. But it seemed that every breathing soul in the northeastern part of the Territory had turned out for the wedding, so that when Cody, dressed handsomely in a black frockcoat, and Stephanie, gowned in her mother's rose-satin wedding dress, exited arm in arm from the chapel there was a sea of faces to greet them. Stephanie laughed, turning her radiant face up to Cody's. "It *was* a simple ceremony," she said.

Father Felipe had ridden all the way from Las Vegas on his prized cream-colored mule to officiate at the wedding. Later, after he removed his vestments and put away his sacred vessels, he came in to join the friends Rosemary had invited to share in the celebration. Rita, a wealthy widow now, was among them. Rosemary looked forward to the evening's end when she and Rita could talk over a glass of wine, as they had in the old times.

Rita was now quite plump, and her blue-black hair was streaked with gray. Still, with the lines of laughter dimpling her skin and the twinkling eyes that always looked for the positive in everything, it was an arresting face. Yes, the two of them would have much to talk about... except for the subject of Wayne and Inez. Rosemary longed to ask if Inez was happy and sincerely hoped her godchild was, though she had her private doubts. It was, of course, best for everyone concerned that Wayne had sent his apologies expressing his and Inez's disappointment at not being able to attend.

And Grant. Rosemary's gaze moved to him and Libby. In middle-age Grant was even more distinguished. Silver highlighted the golden hair at his temples. Rosemary thought she could detect a certain look of melancholy in the bright blue eyes, making him seem more human than he had in his youth when his features were Apollo-like. And she smiled as she noted the way he held in his stomach. Yes, he would definitely have a problem with a paunch in not too many years. She looked at stodgy Libby at his side, who had not changed, then turned back to Father Felipe as he toasted the newlyweds with the imported champagne.

Rosemary looked at the bride, flesh of her own flesh. Forgive me, my child. I have loved you so much. And hurt you so much. Why? Is it true we hurt the ones we love the most? I must tell her and Cody before they leave tomorrow that I am keeping Cambria for them . . . and their grandchildren

209

. . . if they should change their minds.

And Rosemary thought of Stephen, alone in his room listening to the noise of the wedding celebration, and knew that bile as black as miasma must be rising up in his throat to choke him. So many years, so many people maneuvered and trampled on to gain one end . . . and now the hopes of a pure Anglo to rule the Cambria kingdom had been thwarted.

"What were you saying, Father? I'm sorry."

"Disgraceful!" the old priest shouted at her ear as near-deaf people have a habit of doing. "There is no reverence for anything sacred anymore. At the last Novena of High Masses would you believe a gang of cowboys out of the Lazy B Ranch rode right into the Cathedral and defiled the font! Urinated on it!"

"Disgraceful!" Rosemary agreed in a polite murmur. But her attention had already moved to the stairway where Stephanie, with her back turned, tossed her bouquet of baby's-breath to the crowd of young ladies, mostly daughters of the Cambria employees. There were shouts of chivalry and song, and an accordian and harmonica played riotously as Stephanie shyly placed her hand in Cody's and let him lead her up to the bedroom they would share on their wedding night.

"That could have—should have—been us twenty years ago," Grant said quietly, suddenly at her side.

40

It was only a mild intoxicant, the bubbly champagne. Still, Stephanie's blood thundered in her ears. From outside came the noise of shouts and pistol shots as cowboys circled the house in the traditional chivaree. Her lids lifted and closed heavily. She tried to make her eyes focus on Cody as he extinguished the gas lamp and came toward her, the paleness of his sinewy body gleaming in the room's sudden darkness.

In the two times they had come together she had known the quickening of her heart, the singing of her blood, the ache of desire in her loins. Cody had that sexual power over her that made her weak just in waiting for him to come to her. And on this night, mixed with the passion, there should have been a special joy, she thought. But she felt only a pervading sadness, like the slow seep of oil from the ground. It's the champagne, she told herself, as her hands slipped around his taut waist and slid up to the corded shoulders.

But she knew it had been the sight of Wayne's father and Inez's mother that had brought back all the frustration, all the years of wanting and yearning, to culminate now in a marriage with a man she did not love. I'll learn to love Cody, she thought. He's a good man, and he loves me.

And as Cody gently kissed her lips, his mouth searching, asking, Stephanie felt the shame of her treachery wash over her. How could she condemn her mother's adultery when she was just as adulterous?

Ah, Wayne, would you come to me now, knowing the taint I carry in my blood? A half-breed? A bastard? An adulteress, if not in thought, then deed?

The hopelessness of her life stretched out like a frozen, barren land behind her closed lids. Yet as Cody drew his lips from the hollow of her neck, moving lower to tease one full breast, Stephanie felt herself responding against her will, felt as if it were Wayne she was betraying with the soft, purring moans. Or was it Cody she was betraying? All the champagne—she couldn't think straight. She could only think now of the mounting pleasure as Cody's tongue lashed relentlessly at the small, hard core of her femininity. At last, when she could wait no longer, he slid up over her. His lean body, hardened by the years of range riding, began to move against hers, first in a gentle, slow tempo. And then, as her own body arched to meet his with each stroke, the cadence of their passion increased. Pounding, throbbing, rising, falling ...*Wayne, Wayne, Wayne!* her body cried out, matching the tempo of her growing ecstasy.

Brilliant colors exploded behind her lids, coinciding with the tremors that racked her, one after another. "Wayne, Wayne!" she gasped. "Oh, don't let it stop now!"

Cody pulled away from her. The darkness hid the hurt in his eyes, but not in his voice. "Damn your cheating soul!" He left her spent and shaken body alone on the bed as he dressed and left the room. The cool night breeze poured through the fluttering chintz curtains to chill Stephanie's bare flesh and dry the tears on her cheeks.

"You're a fool, Stephanie!"

Rosemary bit back her railing. Her gaze rested sorrowfully on the bent head and thin shoulders of her daughter, who sat hunched over, her chin buried against her knees. Stephanie, who had been the stronger willed of her two children, was wast-

211

ing away before Rosemary's eyes; going each day to sit beneath the cottonwood and look out upon the sweep of the Pecos.

Did people actually die of heartbreak? Rosemary wondered. She had survived more than fifteen years of heartbreak. Or had she? Some part inside her had died, withered away with Lario's imprisonment. And the rest of her...her soul, her heart, her spirit, whatever one called it...had begun to decay the day Stephen had castrated Lario. Regardless of how wrong what she subsequently did might have been, the vengeance she took did dilute the bitterness that poisoned her.

Perhaps she should take her own life, ease the agony that greeted each morning she awoke. Yet, she knew she could not. Something in her fought back, would continue to fight. Life was too precious. It was a gift that should never be taken for granted.

There had been many brief moments of happiness for her over the years. Stephanie's first words, "I love you"; Jamie's graduation from law school, her deep friendship with Rita. These were things to be treasured.

But perhaps because of her own numb heart, she could not understand her daughter's suffering. Rosemary sat down beside Stephanie, spreading her skirts over the grass that grew sparsely beneath the tree's thick branches. She waited, letting the moment stretch into peaceful silence. A dove chirped out his song from a branch high above, a buzzard soared lazily beneath the midday sun, and Stephanie's fingers listlessly plucked at a lone brown leaf.

Fall was fast approaching, Rosemary thought. Then winter and another year. And another. What do I want for my own life? And without looking she saw the Castle behind her, as clearly as the first day she had seen it as Stephen's young bride. She knew then that the love for Cambria had been as strong as her love for Lario. Only in a different form.

And she knew that Stephen, bedridden—a shell of the once-powerful man—had triumphed in his own way. Her love for Cambria would consume her life now.

Satisfied with the realization of the direction her life would take, she leaned her head back against the narrow girth of the cottonwood trunk. She closed her eyes, seeing the face of the man she had loved for so long and knew that she must set his daughter free.

Perhaps it would be Stephanie's children, Lario's grandchildren, who would return to live at Cambria. A smile touched her upturned lips. What a twist of irony...Cambria owned, controlled by an Indian's tainted blood.

"Stephanie," she began, unsure of what to say. Was not the truth always simplest? She laid her hand on her daughter's shoulder.

Stephanie jumped, torn from her stupor of despondency. "Mama, what's left for me?"

It was a desperate whispered plea for help, and Rosemary sighed inwardly with relief. "You can stop pining away for something that doesn't exist," she said softly. "Wayne—the man you've painted in your mind since childhood is just that...a one-dimensional caricature that does not exist anywhere except on the mind's canvas. The truth about Wayne is—"

Stephanie raised her eyes to meet her mother's hard gaze. "Mama, don't. I know I am a fool. I know Wayne's a weakling."

And more, Rosemary thought.

"But I don't know what to do, where to start. For days now I have felt like I've been in a deep hole. I'm so confused!" Stephanie buried her head in her arms. "I'd like to wipe out that last night..." she faltered.

"Why don't you go to him—to Cody. Loving's Bend isn't that far."

Stephanie looked up. Her lips trembled. "What if he doesn't want me?"

A hundred questions popped at her. What ifs...what if Cody didn't go back to his ranch, what if she got to Loving's Bend and no one knew where his ranch was, what if there was another woman already?

Tired and dusty from two days of traveling in the stagecoach, for the railroad did not follow the Pecos River that far south yet, Stephanie found it difficult to converse politely with the other occupants—two elderly sisters making their second daring trip to Mexico City and a middle-aged man in a black derby with a worn, black case in his lap. A traveling salesman—a drummer—Stephanie was sure.

The rocking and swaying of the coach made Stephanie drowsy. She tried to forget the perspiration that dotted her upper lip. Her smartly tailored, blue-striped taffeta traveling dress was really too warm for the hot September sun. The two sisters did not make the trip any more pleasant either. Once they discovered she was the "Rhodes girl," they kept up a steady stream of chatter.

"Yes, yes—I am visiting a relative in Loving's Bend," Stephanie responded. "No, I've never been there before."

She listened as Lizzie Burns described the wicked Fandango dance the brazen women of Mexico City performed—

213

"lascivious"—and how the women—and even children—smoked cigarettes. And Charity Burns told of the beautiful missions there and the enormous bull arena.

The man sat stone-faced, and Stephanie wondered if he were not a preacher or lawyer instead.

But when the talk turned to the trouble the Territory had been having with Indians, especially Geronimo, and why General Crook had not done anything about the worsening situation, the man, introducing himself as Hiram Wharton, began a tirade. "Savages! Every last one of them. Dirty heathens! Every man, woman—and yes, child—should be destroyed, lest they breed like rabbits and rise up in revolution. Filthy scum they are!"

A part of Stephanie began to shrivel inside. At Cambria she had been safe with the love of her mother and the people of Cambria to protect her. But out here, what would happen if the raving man found out she was a half-breed?

She felt dirty, her pride destroyed. But a flicker of her old spirit flamed up at the man's castigation of the Indians. "You talk as if you know the Indians well," she said, addressing him. "Perhaps you lived with them for a while?"

Lizze and Charity tittered. The man's lips folded tightly beneath his bulbous nose. "I spent one hour with them, Miss—which was enough!" He doffed his derby to expose a balding pate crisscrossed with scars. "Lifted my scalp, the dogs did!"

"Oh!" the two old maids gasped in unison.

But Stephanie did not have a chance to reply, for her attention was turned to the coach's left where cliffs gouged by the now dry channels of the Pecos River crept down to within only half a mile or so of the rocky road. From crevices of these ridges Indians galloped their mounts at full speed toward the coach. From above came the messenger's shout, "Apaches!"

Impossible! Stephanie thought as cries of alarm went up inside the coach. There were no warring tribes that side of the Guadalupe Mountains. And Geronimo and his band were still reported roaming the Ojo Caliente area.

She smiled grimly at Hiram Wharton's sudden pallor but felt pity for the fear that caused the two sisters to clutch one another with trembling, bony hands. She reached out a hand to reassure the two women but halted midway as the first war whoop reached her. A yell that curdled the blood like buttermilk. She had heard it as a child.

And as she watched the riders draw near, their vermilion painted faces hideous in the hot sunlight, she knew that the Indian cry was woven in her destiny. She knew it when she recognized the face of Satana.

And Satana knew. For this was no chance encounter but a planned expedition which had required the Indian's unlimited patience. Months of watching the white woman's every move, of endless waiting for a time when she would be alone— far enough away from possible help, had finally culminated in the success of the day's attack.

Rifle shots shattered the air. One pony tumbled head first into the dust, trapping its rider beneath it. Another rider pitched backward out of the saddle. And still Satana kept coming. That face. It had haunted her dreams. The cruelty that glazed the oblique eyes. The mouth that was almost lipless, that grimaced like a gargoyle.

These are my people!

The coach rocked and careened over the rough terrain. Amidst the war whoops there was another burst of gunfire, and the messenger toppled from his perch and bounced to the ground like an India rubber ball. "Hah! Hah!" the driver yelled at his team and flicked his lash over their backs. But already the lather foamed at their mouths.

The road veered sharply around a sloping bluff, and Stephanie grabbed at the tug strap, knowing the coach would not make the curve. The wild team plunged around the bend, and the coach slid off the road and smashed into the outcrop of boulders on the far side. Stephanie tumbled against the body next to her, that of Hiram Wharton's. An arrow pierced the double chin.

The coach rolled twice more, and when it stopped with a final splintering crash, she groped for her reticule and scrambled from the wreckage. The small Smith & Wesson glinted in her hand. One shot. For herself—or the Indian who loped toward her—Satana? His triumphant grin was terrible. Like looking at a death's skull, she thought distractedly, and raised the pistol and calmly fired into Satana's face.

An animal howl of rage. Her blood-soaked adversary leaped upon her, knocking her to the ground. He whipped the knife from the band at his breechcloth. And Stephanie welcomed the quickness and mercifulness of death. Her neck arched to receive the blade.

Satana suddenly smiled. "I will not take your life," he told her in the Apache language she had learned as a child.

And Stephanie knew a fear greater than at any other time in her life.

She could hear the carnage being performed on the other three occupants of the coach. The screams from the two sisters who had unfortunately survived the coach's crash; the hasty chopping of fingers for rings; the unwieldy slash of the knife through the scalp of the struggling coach driver.

Satana was missing out on the scavenging. With a sharp blow of his knife butt, he struck Stephanie across the temple. She slumped to the ground in blackness. When next she came to, she was slung like a sack of booty across a pony led by Satana. Craning her neck, she could see him on the pony in front. A black derby sat on his head, a cravat about his bull-like neck.

Thirst parched her throat, and sweat gathered at her armpits. The pony's steamy flanks reeked. Her muscles, stretched abnormally, ached. It was all a nightmare. And this was just the beginning, she thought, swallowing the fear that threatened to choke her.

The camp was reached by a tortuously winding path through a maze of arroyos and canyons carved by the varying courses of the Pecos. She noted it was a makeshift camp, for the short sparse grass was still untrampled before the tepees. A thin stream meandered through the camp and out through another shallow canyon.

Stephanie cringed as the squaws screamed like harpies at the sight of Satana's captive. They pinched her, and one old hag spat upon her. Satana yanked her from the pony and dragged her, hobbled as she was, through the opening of the tepee. In its darkness she could make out a grossly fat squaw bent over a kettle that boiled on the firepit.

Satana sent Stephanie reeling to the ground. "You will be my second wife and wait on Little Chipmunk."

The fat squaw, Little Chipmunk, turned and grinned at the news, displaying missing teeth.

"I can't be your wife," Stephanie replied in Apache. "I already have a husband."

A frown ceased the greasy face. A gleam of intelligence flickered behind the eyes. "You know the language," he said. "That is well."

Stephanie nodded, waiting. Something told her she must not underestimate the Indian.

"Then you also know," he continued, "that you were promised to me by our fathers."

"But I did not make that promise."

Satana shrugged. "That is no matter. You have lain with another man. You have been unfaithful, yes? For this, we mark such a woman, as you must know."

Stephanie shuddered, little tremors that increased to great heavings of her body while Satana advanced on her.

Above Little Chipmunk's urging cries of "Hiyah! Hiyah!" she heard her own piteous screams.

Part Three

41

The two men, delegates to the Territory's Constitutional Convention, stood in the shadows of the Mess Hall as the children of the Santa Fe Boarding School for Indians filed in groups of platoons for breakfast, the first of their allotted two daily meals.

Normally the two men would not have been allowed past the main building that housed the Indian Bureau's office for the school. But they had not asked. And in the dawn's half light their gray Prince Albert coats blended with the steel gray of the ramshackle Mess Hall so that few were aware of their presence.

"My God, Cody!" the dapper Swanbeck said. "I wouldn't have believed it. A government boarding school—it looks more like a prison farm!"

Cody followed the direction of the man's glance and saw the thin boy in tattered corduroy knickers who shuffled along with the others but carried a heavy lead ball maybe six inches in diameter with a chain attached to his chafed ankle.

It was worse than he had expected. He knew of the Indian Bureau's kidnappings—taking children from their parents to the schools, so that the parents would go three and four years without seeing their children; of the food deficiency; of the poor health service . . . all the horror tales that were whispered and never really believed. But he had not expected this—or the sight of two children digging furtively in the trash barrel for food, their skeletal look, the rags that clothed them.

Yes, he had expected it, he corrected himself. He was just getting old. Nearly sixty-five. I don't want to face life's ugliness anymore, he told himself. I'm tired.

Then what had prompted him to suggest this visit to the Territory's Senate Investigating Committee? He could recall his pompous words, "We were turned down in '68 because of our slavery stand. Do you think the United States Congress will grant us statehood this time if the condition of the treatment of the Indians was known?"

And the murmured denials . . . "A few isolated cases of the Indian Bureau's mismanagement"; "the Indians are rich, they can afford better schools and doctors if they wanted them."

Cody knew differently, as everyone did. The IBA's fraud was rampant. But no one else concerned himself with the appalling treatment of the Indians. So why did he have to involve himself?

But he knew the answer to that. The nightmare that had haunted him for so long...how long now? Almost twenty-five years, wasn't it, since Geronimo and his men surrendered to General Miles? Twenty-five years since he learned that Stephanie was alive.

And that was where the nightmare had started. The guilt that had driven him to the Mescalero Indian Reservation in 1886 where the government had moved some of Geronimo's warriors and their families. It had been Rosemary's letter that had lured him out of his ranch recluse after four years.

"The government reports a white woman with the band, Cody, a captive for four years," Rosemary had written. *"It has to be Stephanie, for it was four years ago when she left Cambria to find you!"*

For four years he had believed his wife had died in Satana's raid on the Las Vegas–Chihuahua Stagecoach. And when he finally set out for the reservation with Rosemary, both of them nervous with excitement, he kept reminding himself that there would be adjustments for Stephanie to face, that it would not be easy for either her or him. But his spirits rose with each mile. After all those years of wanting and loving Stephanie, she had at last returned that love, had at last sought him out. And now they were to be together again.

But they were not. Stephanie refused to return with them, refused in fact to even see them.

"It's that bastard, Satana!" Cody had grated. "He won't let her see us!"

He had pushed past the Apache scout reservation policeman, who also acted as an interpreter, and entered the tepee belonging to Satana. It was dark inside. But he heard the sudden intake of breath. "Stephanie?" He paused. "It's me, Cody. Are you alone?"

The silence seemed to stretch through an eternity. Then, an almost inaudible, "Yes."

"Stephanie!" He started toward where the voice came from, his hands outstretched. Tears filled his eyes, and he was glad for the darkness. "You don't know how I've hated myself, kid. How I've pun—"

"No! Get away! Get out!" The words came in staccato syllables, as if she had to recall each word.

Cody halted. There was real panic in her voice. Fear. He let his hands drop to his sides and began talking to her gently, as he would to a frightened horse. "I love you, kid. Even when I knew all the time you loved Wayne, I couldn't help but love you. I'd never hurt you. But I won't leave here without you. Do you understand?"

"Please," she whispered, and he heard her voice catch in a sob. "Please—go away. I'm not your Stephanie...not any more."

Cody could imagine the degradation she had been subjected to and the humiliation she had endured. He had seen and heard of captives treated worse than slaves, like animals. "Stephanie," he said, talking slowly as if to a child, "no matter what has happened—we can work it out. Please give my love a chance to make everything up to you."

She stepped out of the shadows then, nearer the shaft of sunlight that peeked through the entrance's flap. "Do you really mean that, Cody?" she taunted, her voice raspy with its old mockery. "Take a good look—and tell me if I'm the girl of your dreams."

Cody's stomach knotted and turned over. He thought he was going to be ill. Stephanie's nose had been cut away, all the fleshy end gone. Both nostrils were wide open, denuded of flesh. "It's not very pretty, is it? Still want to take me back to Loving's Bend as your wife?"

Jesus help him, he wanted only to run. To hide and cry like a boy for all that was lost. But still, he tried. "It wasn't your beauty I loved. It was your spirit. What's on the inside."

Stephanie laughed sharply and sneered. "That spirit is dead. Now get, white man. Run, before I change my mind!"

The nausea was acrid on his tongue. He turned on his heel and left with her mocking laughter following him. Rosemary brushed past the reservation policeman toward him. She grabbed at his lapels. "She's not coming, Cody?"

He took her hands. "It's not her, Rosemary. I asked the woman if she had heard of Stephanie, but—she didn't know of another white captive with the Chiricahuas."

Yes, Jesus help him, he thought, as he stood and watched the pathetic Indian children file past him. His guilt had hounded him, driven him there to the school, after twenty-five years, to somehow atone. How many more reservation schools did he have to visit, how many Indians did he have to beg absolution from before Stephanie would put his tortured soul to rest? And was she still alive? He mentally calculated what her age would be. Forty-seven.

He shook his head slowly. He was a stupid old fool. Going back into the past like that. Still, as the last child stepped inside the mess hall, he turned to his companion. "Let's go inside."

The stout woman looked up from where she stood at the head of the three rows of wooden tables. Her thin mouth parted in surprise at the sight of the two strangers. She unfolded her arms and swooped down on them, looking, Cody thought, like a giant crow, dressed as she was all in black. "What are you two doing here? Do you have a pass? You'll have to be reported at once to the office!"

"We're with the New Mexico Congress," Cody said calmly. "And are here, with the Governor's knowledge, to observe government boarding school conditions."

There was a silence in the room as all the small heads turned to watch the interruption, something that was unusual in the school, which was run in a military fashion. The matron clapped her hands. "Back to your breakfast!"

At once the round faces ducked in compliance. She turned back to the two men. "I'm sorry," she began again, a meant-to-be-charming smile plastered on her square face. "There are rules we must follow, you understand. If you'll come with me, I'm quite sure the superintendent can arrange a tour for you."

Cody ignored the thick hand that gestured toward the doorway. "This is as good a place to start a tour as any." He brushed past her and began walking down the aisles between the tables. It was worse than he had expected. The children were drinking coffee and eating hard bread—at least he thought it was. The loaves were so covered with flies it was difficult to be sure.

He snapped around. "We'll see the superintendent now," he told the other delegate, disregarding the matron who stomped along behind him.

Superintendent Jackson removed his glasses and wiped his forehead with his handkerchief. "Gentlemen," he said in a reedy voice, "you must understand. We do the best we can with the little we're allotted."

"The treasury records indicate otherwise, Jackson," Cody said. "In fact, they show the apportionment out of the Indians' reserves for food to be quite large."

A band of sweat broke out again on the little man's forehead. "But you must understand. We've clerks and secretaries and cooks' salaries to pay out of this."

"What of teachers and nurses?" Swanbeck asked with a grimace. "It doesn't appear that your students are in the best of health."

"Teachers and nurses won't work for that kind of salary," Jackson whined. "We're doing the best we can."

221

"I don't believe you are," Cody said. "We saw one child, a boy of not more than five or six years, dragging a ball and chain about his ankle. A ball and chain, my God!" Cody was surprised at how incensed he was over the matter. I'm getting old, he thought. Used to be, nothing rattled me.

"He's a problem child. Chase-the-Wind has been running away continually since he came here six months ago. On top of that Mrs. Duffy—our matron—reports he's a bed-wetter."

"Get him," Cody said.

"What?"

"You heard me. We want to talk to some of these children ourselves."

The superintendent searched for Chase-the-Wind's files while the boy was being sent for. Cody pulled out his pocket watch. He was almost sorry he had suggested the investigation. If they didn't hurry, they'd miss the season's opening of the Santa Fe Opera House that evening, one of the few pleasures he allowed himself when he came to Santa Fe. That evening Texas Guinan, a vivacious woman who reminded him much of Stephanie, was playing in *The Gay Musician*.

The boy stumbled in, followed by the matron. Beneath his razor-cropped black hair his black eyes moved warily from Swanbeck to the superintendent to Cody before they abruptly shuttered over. The little brown face seemed to rigidify with hatred.

Cody undid his lanky frame from the chair and crossed over to the boy, stooping so that he was eye level with him. "Tell me, Chase-the-Wind, why do you run away from here?" he asked gently.

The boy bared his teeth at Cody, then spat into his face.

"See!" Jackson exclaimed. "They're savages! You can't civilize them. You can put pants on them, but 'fore you know it, they've gone back to the blanket."

The child stepped back, apparently expecting Cody to strike him, but Cody calmly pulled out his handkerchief and wiped the spittle away, all the while watching the boy's face. By the time he stuffed the handkerchief back in his coat pocket, his hand was shaking. There was something about the look in the boy's eyes. The daring, the impudence, the flash of spirit. Still kneeling before the boy, he said, "Tell me what's written in the boy's file."

The old man looked from Cody to Swanbeck with raised brows and shook his head in bewilderment. He opened the file. "Hmmm. Not much. Father, an Apache sub-chief. Died last year of trachoma. Boy'll be five next February—big for his age, ain't he?"

"The mother?" Cody prompted.

"Let's see. Not much that way either. Never is. Here—mother died at birth. Hemorrhaging."

"Was there a doctor present?" Swanbeck asked.

"Well, of course. But those things do happen. Even to a white woman. And look here—" the man's knotty fingers flicked the folder's pages, "she was forty-three when she had the kid, her firstborn. That ain't young. Specially for an Indian. Why they looked like mummies by the time they reach twenty-five."

Cody had begun to tremble. The boy's eyes were steady on him. The solemn mouth turned upward in contempt. He saw the white man's weakness.

"The mother—" Cody's voice came out in a croak, and he tried again. "What was the mother's name?"

The superintendent licked his thumb and turned a page. "No Nose." He looked at the two men with a knowing grin and winked. "A camp whore, no doubt. That's what the bucks do to the ones that sleep around—chop off their noses. Had one myself one time. Real grateful they are to a white man."

A rage built in Cody. He wanted to spring at the old man. But he never took his eyes from the boy's piercing gaze. "What tribe?" he demanded.

"Doesn't say. So most likely a half-breed."

"The father's name?"

"What is it?" Swanbeck asked Cody, sensing there was more to Cody's questioning than just the casual investigation the man had proposed.

"The father's name?" Cody repeated. Stuffy air permeated the cluttered room. Cody could feel the perspiration break out in his mustache and at his temples.

The superintendent's finger ran down the page, then stopped. "Yes, here it is!" he said, glad to finally find some concrete information. "Satana."

Cody rocked on the balls of his feet. His heart slammed against his chest, then missed a beat. He forced himself to relinquish Chase-the-Wind's gaze and rose to steady himself. "I want the boy released to me."

Both Jackson and Swanbeck gasped simultaneously. "That—it can't be done, Mr. Strahan. I mean there's red tape of all sorts. I mean it's just not the sort of thing that's done."

"Then today will be a first," Cody said.

"Cody, have you lost your mind?" Swanbeck asked, his bullhead jutting forward in disbelief.

"No, I haven't. I may have finally found it again." He hunkered down before the boy again. "My name is Cody Strahan," he said very slowly. "I knew your mother before she was a *yisnááh*, a captive. Do you understand me?"

The boy's eyes widened at the sound of the Indian word but he gave no other indication he understood Cody. But Cody knew. "I want to help you. I will take you with me. Give you all the food you want. Clothes." And sudden inspiration made Cody add, "A horse—a pinto pony. Do you understand? *Lá áá?*"

The eyes blinked. But still not a word.

"You can't do this. Everything has to be cleared first with the Indian Commissioner!"

"Then do it!" Cody ordered. He looked at Chase-the-Wind. "I shall return next week for you—Monday. But you must not run away. It·doesn't solve anything." Cody smiled wryly and added, "If you want to change things for the better, become a politician." He held out his hand. The boy looked from Cody's face at last to the outstretched hand. "You have my word," Cody prompted.

Cautiously the boy's thin, grimy hand stole out to lay in Cody's big one. Cody smiled. "Things are gonna be different for us two lost souls." But when Cody went to withdraw his hand, the boy would not turn it loose.

Cody knelt once more. "Here, son. Do you know what this is?" he asked, drawing forth his pocket watch. "It's very valuable and tells the time. It's yours. That way you know that I'll come back for you. *Lá áá*, all right?"

Slowly the boy nodded. Once, then twice. And Cody could have sworn a smile curved the stoic lips.

Friday, June 17, 1910

Dear Rosemary,

Four times now I've started this letter to you. I've followed your progress through the newspapers; learned of Stephen's death two years ago, your discovery of uranium on Cambria last year, your prized black angus winning world fame, and the contract with Phelps Dodge to mine coal on Cambria.

My own life has been in comparison relatively quiet, considering a quarter of a century has passed since last we saw one another. Quiet until last month, when I agreed to be a delegate to the Constitutional Convention. Which brings me to what I've been trying so unsuccessfully to tell you from the beginning.

While in Santa Fe I took a tour of the Santa Fe Government Boarding School for Indians. I found there—

and I hope you are prepared for a shock (you always were)—a boy whom I know to be your grandson. It's all on the file at the superintendent's office.

As you by now realize, it was Stephanie you and I found that day. But she refused to come back with me. Later I shall make a confession of the inexcusable reason for the lie. Right now I just wanted to prepare you. As soon as the convention is over, hopefully within the month, I shall be bringing Chase-the-Wind to Cambria to meet his grandmother and see the empire that will one day be his.

Cody

It was as if a great burden had been lifted from Cody as he slipped the letter in the envelope. He would address it then and give it to the landlady to post the next day. He had never been good at penmanship, but this was the most important missive of his life, and he carefully penned each letter on the envelope…and with each letter the joy grew in him. The joy of release—excitement that his life had meaning.

But the excitement became too much for him.

His heart began beating erratically as it had earlier that day in the superintendent's office. His hand trembled before he had even affixed the "Mrs." and "Rosemary," and with the first letter *R* of the surname, his hand slipped in a sliding down-stroke.

"No," Cody cried, "not yet!" though actually the words never reached the tip of his tongue, and his lids closed before his body thudded to the floor.

42

August, 1938
Ramah Navajo Indian Reservation

The sawmill and every inch of the thirty-one million feet of timber belonged to the Indians. And up until two years before the Indians cut and towed the timber along the Zuni River to Ramah for processing. Then Joseph Lomberg secured the exclusive right to operate lumber on the river—by agreeing to employ Indian labor in preference to other labor on equal terms.

Since that time old Lomberg began to bring in carloads of Austrians, Swedes, and Germans, and Ramah's population leaped from four hundred to eleven hundred. Now more white men lived on the Indian Reservation than Indians. Now the white men worked in the forests, and the Indians sat idly with their squaws.

Carefully Chase laid the length of the board against the sharp teeth of the edger. The sawdust flew through the heated room like snow, clogging his nostrils and powdering his raven hair. It coagulated with the rivulets of sweat which snaked down the brown-sheened, muscle-ridged torso that was naked from the waist up.

With each whir of the edger Chase imagined Lomberg's dwarflike body stretched out on the platform. The old man writhed and twisted as the sawtooth blade crept nearer to his ostrich neck. He begged, pleaded, cried out for forgiveness. And then the bright red blood spurted to mat on the floor with the sawdust.

The whistle sounded, and Chase finished the board he sawed and shut down the edger for the day. The other workers, mostly Zuni and Navajo, were already at the door, struggling into their shirts and jesting good-naturedly, for it was Friday. An hour would find them in one of the back canyons around El Morro and Inscription Rock, having their after-work drinks. But the drinks would be fermented corn whiskey, not gin; and they would be drinking around a blackened firepit, not before a long oak bar in one of the speakeasies that, along with the bawdy houses and dance halls, flourished in the towns that bordered the reservation, places that were forbidden to the Indian.

Anxious to begin the weekend, the Indian workers clambered into the back of buckboards or buggies. No longer did they bother to invite Chase Strawhand with them. Chase, they agreed, was different—neither Indian nor white. Billy Whiteshield claimed Chase was a Pueblo, his father a cacique. No, George Caballo declared. He had to be Navajo. Look how much taller he was than most of the other Indians. Only the Navajo grew that tall. All agreed Chase Strawhand was quick-tempered and dangerous, especially with the hunting knife. And so they left him to himself, which was how he preferred it.

The hike from the sawmill to the closest border town, San Jose—which perched on the Continental Divide—took Chase a little over fifty minutes. Rather than return to the isolation of the log hogan he had built, he made the hike every Friday afternoon, arriving before the Blue Top Bar almost exactly to the minute at six o'clock. With his bottle of illegal but potent *tiswin* that old Mary Two-Cows sold him, he would plant himself on the granite boulder that jutted over the forested two-lane highway running in front of the bar. He would sprawl there, his back against a spruce, and watch in the late afternoon sunlight as the tough lumberjacks and railroad men began to arrive in their battered Packard and Ford pickups.

He listened to the way the loggers talked and swore, watched the way they walked—how their steps went unplanned—and noted the type of clothing they wore, only slightly different but enough to set them apart from their Indian counterparts. He missed his former job as a logger that took him outdoors—the freedom of the sun and the wind on his face. But those highly paid, much-desired jobs belonged now to those Anglos.

And as he weekly watched those Anglos go in and out of the Blue Top, his resentment of the white race grew, increased by each swallow of the *tiswin*. The white matron who had beat him with the rubber hose each time he wet the bed, the white man who had promised him the world and had given him nothing but a pocketwatch, and the half-white woman who had given birth to him but denied him a birthright... the desire to bring revenge down upon the white race, the *bilagaana,* was as bitter and as strong as the *tiswin*. The thirst for revenge consumed his every waking moment, even burrowing like a mole into his dream-tossed sleep.

The snap of a twig warned Chase that Deborah had arrived, but he remained where he lay stretched, his sharp eyes riveted on the Blue Top.

"Ahalani, deezi—greetings, little sister," Chase said at last when the small, slender young woman had dropped down beside him with her sketch pad and charcoal pencils. He cast a cursory glance at the oval face with its fine features framed by the coil of braids over each ear, then returned his interest to the Blue Top as he took another swallow of the powerful *tiswin*.

Deborah wrinkled her small nose at Chase in exasperation. She wondered why she continued to meet him, leaving the laundry as soon as old Clyde Barstow dropped the dusty blinds over the store's window each Friday evening at six. Chase never would really pose for her. She sighed as she rummaged through her purse. She'd be much better off sketching the usual portraits of the leathery old Navajo men and women that the other art students did.

She found the package of cigarettes and lit one, sticking it between Chase's lips. "It's a Chesterfield," she said. "A man left them inside the pocket of a suit he brought in to be cleaned."

Chase quirked one brow. "Since when did you start to smoke?"

Deborah tossed her head with a disdainful gesture, but she could not conceal the ever-present curves that clung to the corners of her lips even in her rare moods of ill humor. "Stop playing Big Brother, Chase Strawhand. I'm old enough, eighteen—almost nineteen."

Chase grinned, a rakish smile that sent delicious chills through every female who happened to be with him—all but Deborah. She and Chase, she had learned as a child—to her disappointment—were from the same Navajo clan—the Tahtchini. And that was practically the same as being brother and sister.

Chase inhaled, then blew the smoke out in a slow spiral. "Nice cigarette. Who in San Jose wears suits and smokes these?"

"Turn your face more toward me," she said impatiently. "There—that's it," and she began to stroke the pencil across the pad, hoping this Friday she would capture the elusive electric quality of Chase's angular face—the mobile lips, the flaring nostrils that suggested sensuality, and the masked eyes. It was the eyes that always caught her artist's imagination. One would have sworn they were blacker than Hades, but actually the pupils were a sky blue—the hue found in a good turquoise.

"There are some who wear suits," she said in answer to his question, letting her words fall with each deliberate stroke of the pencil. "The banker's son, Orville Barnham, for instance. He tipped me a dollar last week for having his suit ready early." From beneath the tangled lacework of lashes she peered at him. "Do you think Harry will be jealous?"

Chase's laugh was short as he recalled her brother-in-law's cousin who had set up his own business, a shop of hand-woven blankets and rugs that was bringing in the tourists by the droves. Her father was urging her to marry the smart Indian.

Chase rolled on his side and looked at her now, seeing the rose-hued skin, the almond-shaped eyes that teased, and the petite but shapely body. She reminded him of a playful kitten. "I don't think you give a sheep's turd about Harry Gray Fox."

Deborah's hand moved furiously across the page. The evening's light was fading fast. "That's not true," she said, only half concentrating on her strokes now. Chase's face was so near she could smell the bittersweet odor of the *tiswin* on his breath. Funny, she thought, he could drink old Mary Two-Cows dry of her *tiswin* and still never show a sign of rowdy drunkenness as the other Indians did.

228

"It's just that I wanted to finish art school first," she continued defensively, though now she was having doubts about her ability. She could not even capture the essence of Chase's powerful male virility on her sketch pad no matter how many times that summer she had tried. However, she did come close one time, back in July during the hottest part of the year.

Chase had shucked his shirt. Rivulets of perspiration ran down his corded neck and drained off into the channels created by the gray welts that crisscrossed his back—souvenirs of the Indian boarding school they had both attended. Her memories of him then, when she had been five and he eighteen, were of a much different man. Rail-thin, his young face had not yet evidenced the uncompromising features—the hard jaw, the mocking lips, the shuttered eyes. But his near-naked body last July had been sculpted by years of lumber-jacking into a network of sinewy muscles. She had gazed at the magnificent physique with open admiration until she remembered she was supposed to be sketching.

Deborah decided now was as good a time as ever to broach her subject. "Chase, do you recall that photographer in Santa Fe—Roger Zamazloski, the one who asked me to pose for the jewelry advertisement?"

Chase raked a brow but said nothing. He waited patiently with those watchful eyes that never seemed to miss anything.

Deborah hurried on. "Well, he's offered me a morning job—as a photographer's assistant. I'm thinking of taking it. I'd work in a room that has a view to heaven and back, and he lights a fire every morning and serves Chinese tea in English bone china at 10:30...then when I'm through inventorying his work and dry mounting and wrapping the photos, I'm free to work on my drawings." She drew a breath. "Well, what do you think?"

Chase came lithely to his feet. "I think if you're going to work in Santa Fe's art colony, you better get rid of those bobby socks and dirty saddle oxfords. Come on," he said, pulling her to her feet, "let's get you back home before your father starts a war dance."

Chagrined that he refused to take her seriously, Deborah gathered her purse and art supplies and fell in step with Chase's longer stride. He never walked her any further than the old part of the reservation where the blanket Indians lived, the ones who still preferred the hogan to the tinlike barracks and their modern conveniences; for her father, fat and wrinkled with age, thought Chase a malcontent who would bring only more trouble to the Navajo.

But her mother—Deborah smiled at the thought of the

229

wiry little woman—her mother, she suspected, had half-succumbed to that hard, virile quality that attracted women to Chase. And, damn it, Deborah didn't know what it was herself. Maybe it was that after years of taking dole-out from the United States government, the Indian male seemed emasculated, while beneath Chase's cold detachment flowed a fierceness that was almost tangible.

When Chase paused to turn back at the edge of the Little Horse Camp, Deborah put out a restraining hand. "Chase, the part-time job I had in Santa Fe last year—the one with the American Indian Defense Association—it's open."

Chase jammed his hands in his pants pockets. "You're suggesting I apply?"

"The AID's attorney needs an assistant—someone fluent in both English and the Indian languages—to do research and things like that. You've completed high school, and you're intelligent—and it'd be a way to help our people."

There it was—that mocking, cynical smile. "Why would I want to help out our people? They're where they are because they were too ignorant and too trustful. Don't attribute any noble motives to me, Deborah."

Deborah's wing-tipped brows lowered. "All right, I won't," she hissed. "But you're just as ignorant! You sit watching the white men every Friday with bitterness and hatred brewing like old Mary Two-Cows's *tiswin* still. You want revenge. Oh, I know you do," she said, shaking a finger up at his surprised face.

"But do you ever bother to do anything about it? No! In Santa Fe you could learn their ways and beat them at their own games. Why you could even go to law school. The University of Albuquerque has opened its night class. Sure, it's sixty miles," she rushed on, now that she had his complete attention for once, "but you could find a way to commute two or three times a week. You could do it, Chase. I know you could if you really wanted to!"

She was breathless now, her energy expended.

Chase could only feel anger at both of them that he even let himself consider the possibility. After all those years of being taken in by the white man's honeyed words of promise, he'd have to be a fool to think about entering their world.

Deborah suddenly surprised him by standing on tiptoe and kissing him on the cheek. "Think about college and the job—and don't tell me you're a coward, Chase Strawhand!"

Chase watched her whirl and run toward the compound of hogans. He watched the way her small, rounded hips swayed beneath the gingham skirt. The desire that suddenly ached in him was almost incestuous. He reminded himself that she was of his mother's clan, of the Tahtchini. He put both Deborah and the AID job from his mind.

One idea was as absurdly foolish as the other.

43

Wilbur Fairchild, attorney for the American Indian Defense Association, sat at his notched, cigarette-burned desk. He looked at the man across from him and assessed him as quickly as he had assessed potential jurors over the forty-one years he had served on the bar.

Male Indian, late twenties or early thirties; ruggedly healthy with the look and movement, a feline grace, of the outdoors; shoulder-length hair denoting a rebel; worn overalls and plaid shirt and brogans; intelligence...that was debatable, Fairchild thought as he tried to see past the hooded eyes.

He hooked his thumbs under his suspenders and tried to study the man more impartially, without Deborah's idolatry to bias him. In spite of her praise, he had been expecting a savage, and from the looks of the man he was. Yet behind that calm animal detachment...yes, perhaps there was a gleam of intelligence.

"Deborah has told me you'd like to work for AID and go to college part-time. I assume you can read and write?"

Chase looked across at the old man with the shock of snowy hair falling across his forehead and the sharp blue eyes that mocked him, and he felt the heat of anger begin to beat at his temples. How had he ever let Deborah talk him into this? He could break the frail man in two with his bare hands, but it was a white man's job and he'd play it the white man's way. His long lips turned up almost imperceptibly in a cynical smile. "You might say that, Mr. Fairchild."

Will eyed the Indian, mildly surprised he had not been able to penetrate the man's lithe relaxation. He leaned back in his swivel chair. "If you were to work for me, Mr. Strawhand, you'd have to have some understanding of legislative policy, some knowledge of political science. You see, I was really hoping to find someone more qualified—"

Chase flexed his brown hands, then met the old lawyer's challenging glare. "Your job with AID, Mr. Fairchild—as I understand it our Tribal Council hired you to protect us from our protectors, the Federal government's Indian Bureau Agency. What have you done in the way of formulating new policy? Of investigation?"

Will's seamed lips tightened. "I was under the impression that I was doing the interviewing, Mr. Strawhand."

"Which proves that you don't want to hire me any more than I want to be hired." Chase rose to go.

"Then what are you doing here?"

Chase paused. His brow furrowed. "I don't know. I suppose a wily young woman in braids and saddle oxfords tricked me into this," he said with a sigh.

"Tell me, Mr. Strawhand—by the way, does your surname have a Navajo equivalent? I haven't heard the name before."

Chase's brief moment of affability faded into his previously cold reserve like a New Mexican glacier. "Strawhand has no Indian derivative."

No, he thought bitterly, the surname Strawhand was a constant reminder of the white man's treachery. It was the nearest he could recollect to twenty-six years prior when a man with the first name of Cody and the last name with the sound of something like Strawhand had promised to return for him.

"Well, tell me—Chase—what reforms would you recommend if you were to bring suit against the Indian Bureau Agency?"

The memory of a large, drab gray truck rolling into the reservation, taking Chase and the other children away from the only home they had ever known, carting them two hundred miles to attend an Indian boarding school, flashed through his brain, searing it as it had that day.

Some of the children had not survived the internment at the boarding school. He distinctly remembered the nauseous odor, the horrible feeling of suffocation, as they were lined up against the walls of the huts and sprayed, like cattle, for lice, tics, and nits. Two children had died that evening.

"Whatever is attempted for the Indian betterment," Chase said at last, "will come too late for the old ones. And they will find change hard as hell. Begin with the children. The Indians should be given schools on their reservations, near their homes. And no more messing around with their religious—" Chase broke off and shrugged. It was all hypothetical. "But all that's your problem, Mr. Fairchild. You're the one getting paid to help those poor sons-of-bitches."

He turned on his heel, and Will said, "No, it's your problem now, Chase. You're getting paid to investigate these malpractices of the IBA."

Slowly Chase turned back and looked at the old man,

looked past the bright blue eyes, trying to look into the man himself. Was it another trick? But he saw only a tiredness there. The same tiredness with life that he himself felt.

"Get yourself a jacket," Will ordered, embarrassed and confused at his sudden softening. "One that matches some pants. And get that horse's mane cropped. Next thing I know those artsy boys up on Camino del Monte Sol will be prancing round here looking for a job."

For the first time Chase smiled, an authentic smile, and Will snapped, "I want you to meet me at the Capitol tomorrow for the afternoon session. The Senate Finance Committee's reviewing Senate Bill 263."

The twill jacket was too tight across Chase's broad shoulders and certainly did not match his faded overalls. And the haircut he had gotten—it felt odd not to feel the hair brushing his shoulders—now curled at the nape of his neck, still too long by civilized standards.

Chase left the house on Castillos Street where he had rented an attic room the day before and set off in search of the State Capitol Building. During the thirteen years he had spent at the Indian Boarding School he had been outside the grounds only twice and knew little of Santa Fe's maze of winding streets. And he had too much pride to ask where Galisteo Street crossed Montezuma.

Finally with only five minutes remaining before the opening of the afternoon session he came upon the Capitol, a magnificent structure composed of two wings and a large central dome. In spite of all his scorn for civilization, he stood in awe before the building. It represented all the greatness, all the power the white man was capable of wielding.

This was his enemy. This was what would break him, as it had so many of his people; this symbol of the white man's laws would reduce him to the groveling dregs of humanity that so often wound up on the suicide lists—if he did not break this enemy first. A surge, almost like the feeling from one's first kill, swept through him, and he took the shallow steps three at a time in anticipation of the confrontation.

It was exactly three o'clock when he found Room 205. *The Senate Finance Committee* it read on the door, with a schedule of the times the different Senate bills were to be considered for that day. Chase ran his finger down the list to the time marked 3:00 P.M. and found SB263, the Conservancy Act.

Quietly he opened the door to a smoke-congested room. A U-shaped table dominated it. About this table were men in suspenders and vests, their long sleeves rolled up. Chase felt

233

conspicuous in his ill-fitting jacket. The men, maybe sixteen or seventeen of them, appeared to be listening to the testimony of a plump man who sat at a small, square table before them. To the rear of the room were several rows of wooden folding chairs, and Chase spotted Will there signaling to him.

"Much better," Will whispered, eyeing the chopped haircut as Chase took the empty seat next to him. "We're up after the next recess."

The bill presently before the Senate Finance Committee dealt with the Labor and Industrial Commission, and Chase found himself spellbound by the manipulations, the innuendos, and the intricacies that went into its consideration, so that when someone made the motion the bill be passed, followed by a second and the scraping of chairs as the Senators prepared to recess, Chase sat dazed.

"Chase!" Will said, and Chase turned his head to find Will shaking his shoulder. "Let's get some coffee. We're next to face the Solid Seventeen."

In the dingy cafeteria Will anxiously went over his notes, muttering to himself and making a check at some crucial points he wanted to stress. Chase listened as Will made comments, but his attention was distracted by the noisy entrance of a man of medium height. Reporters' flashbulbs exploded about the man, and a barrage of questions was hurled at him. Square-set with powerfully built shoulders, his face had an intelligent forcefulness about it that caught the eye.

But it was the woman at his side who riveted Chase's attention. Tall and slim, she possessed the same fair features as her companion. The silver gilt hair was long, in a page boy that fell over one brow, so Chase could not see her eyes. And suddenly it seemed to him the most important thing in the world to look into those eyes.

Her movements were fluid, like liquid silver, her smile dazzling, as she took the coffee cup her companion handed her. As if she sensed the intensity of Chase's gaze, her head turned slightly. From behind the peek-a-boo wave her glance met that of Chase's. The eyes above the sculptured cheekbones were a pale green in contrast to the tanned skin, and Chase thought it was like looking at a mountain meadow covered by frost. Their gazes held for a naked half-second before she turned her interest back to whatever it was her companion was saying.

"Who is that?" Chase asked Will.

"What?" Will looked up from his notes and took a hasty sip of the cold coffee. "Oh, that's Philip Masters—the Senate Finance Chairman. A charming man when he wants to be.

Unfortunately most of the time objects rather than people interest him. Power and profit are the clues to his—shall I say—dynamic personality."

"No, not him—the woman with him."

Will chuckled. "I *am* getting old." Then, "So it's not Deborah."

It was Chase's turn to ask, "What?"

Will shook his shaggy head and gulped the rest of the coffee. "Nothing. In answer to your question, the woman is Christina Raffin. She's old man Raffin's daughter. And in case you don't know who Wayne Raffin is, he's a retired senator and still the most influential man in Santa Fe county—and probably the State for that matter."

"I don't want to know about him. It's his daughter I'm interested in."

"Obviously," Will said dryly. "If a stare could undress a woman, Christina Raffin would be naked by now—a highly unlikely state since she's as closely guarded as Fort Knox."

"How old is she?" Chase asked, his intense gaze never leaving the couple. "And is she married?"

"She's twenty-two or three, she lives with her father in a mansion in the Barrio de Analco, and she's a registered lobbyist for the Labor Unions—the only woman lobbyist. And no, she's not married. Anything else?"

Later, when Chase sat at the small table before the Senate Finance Committee with Will and Senator Katchmeyer, who had reluctantly agreed to sponsor the bill, he spotted Christina in a serious conversation with another of the Senate Finance members, but Philip Masters called the Committee to order, and she took a seat at the rear of the room behind Chase.

He forced his attention now to the case Will was presenting against the Conservancy Act. "The Santa Fe Railroad's scheme is fraught with menace to the Rio Grande Valley Indians by taking almost half of their arable land and leasing it to white men and applying all the rental fees on the Indians' debt for their part in the flood control works.

"The result of this action will be to alienate the land for two more centuries from the Indians who have tilled its soil long before Leif Ericson ever sighted the North Atlantic."

Chase thought the speech eloquent, reminiscent of the Navajo War Chieftains. He had not yet made up his mind about Wilbur Fairchild—if the old man was only out for a piece of the action, or if he truly cared about the Indian cause.

One senator leaned and whispered to the man on his right, who promptly motioned the bill be temporarily tabled. "We've gotten a reprieve," Will said, as he gathered his papers and rose to go. "Now it's your turn. I want you to dig up some facts for me. You can start at the University's law library. Then..."

But Chase was not listening. His gaze was fixed on Christina Raffin's delightful curve of buttocks beneath the silk sheath dress as she leaned over the table to say something to old Senator Farrell. He felt the stirring in his groin, and he had the great urge to take her there on the table and mount her like a stud horse an untried mare before the whole bunch of damned sanctimonious senators who would deny having such lustful thoughts.

Chase shook his head. He'd better high-tail it to the nearest reservation because he knew he was hard up when he started sniffing out pale flesh.

44

Chase ran his long fingers through his hair. The letters and words blurred before him. Twelve years of schooling and all the white man had wanted to teach him were harnessmaking and horseshoeing—dying trades.

His hawklike face scowled at the words that seemed so alien. He flexed his shoulders. He ached to be out of the musty and confining library. In the open. He needed to be swinging an ax again, getting the kinks out of his muscles, feeling the hot sun on his back.

Once more his eyes scanned the notes he had taken, hoping it was what Will wanted. He felt his own rage mount as he reviewed again the notes he had taken from the "Hearings before a Subcommittee, February 17, 1938."

The Indian Bureau, as a guardian of its Indian wards, had agreed to the cost per acre of $67.50 in constructing the flood control works, when it knew the same work could be done for $35 or $40. Further, it countenanced without even a questioning expression the newer figure of $109.50 despite the second provision of the Tribal Council prohibiting it. And furthermore, it was a higher charge than was made against the acres of the whites.

Chase closed the large volume, *Congressional Records*, with a thud. He was bone tired after a year of working six days a week and trying to make the classes two nights a week in Albuquerque. He pulled out the smoothly worn pocketwatch. Eight forty-five. He had already missed the last train out to Santa Fe. He shrugged. He could not afford the fare anyway.

As Chase shoved the watch back in his pocket, his fingertips brushed the initials *CJS* grooved into the gold-filled case, and he was reminded of the white man's last words to him—that if he wanted something changed, become a politician. Chase knew then he was tired...if he could actually be contemplating becoming a politician.

It just was not done. Not by an Indian anyway. Thirty-eight percent of the population, over one-third, was of Indian origin, yet they were excluded from state citizenship by the New Mexico constitution. He'd have to be crazy to think about mounting a one-man campaign to change the law.

Damn the white man's law!

Out in the open, away from the confines of the library, Chase came alive again, inhaling the rain-freshened October evening. He shrugged into the patched woolen sweater and set out at a steady trot along Albuquerque's darkened streets. Only twice before had he missed the Santa Fe train. Once a fruit truck had picked him up, but the other time he had trotted the entire sixty miles, making it in a little less than seven hours. The next day he had fallen asleep at the desk of AID's small, seedy office.

With the same cat-footed grace of his ancestors, he ran smoothly, wasting no breath. The University's grounds were three miles behind him when he heard the hum of an approaching car. He veered off to the road's edge, waiting for the car to pass, but the decreased revolutions in the motor told him the car was slowing alongside of him.

He laughed to himself, hoping it was one of the local college toughs spoiling for a fight with a red man. He had seen their looks of disdain and knew by their sneers that he had violated a sacred Anglo institution by registering for classes. Not only was he older than the others, he was an Indian.

The muscles rippled beneath Chase's shirt and sweater in keen expectation of a fight. He wanted to pulverize every bone in their snotty, white-fished bodies. They revolted him as much as he did them.

When still there was no sudden snap of a door swung open, Chase, never losing the rhythm of his pace, slanted a glance to his right at the roadster that moved along with him. He recognized the sleek lines of the 1937 silver Mercedes Benz, having seen it in the Capitol parking lot several times. And when the husky voice asked, "Want a ride, Mr. Strawhand?" he knew the driver's identity.

He halted. His eyes pierced the darkness, making out the pale iridescent beauty of Christina Raffin. He put a foot on the running board. A sleek woman for a sleek car. What was she doing out that late alone? "Is this 'do a good turn for an Indian' night?"

She laughed. "Don't try to frighten me with your Indian scowl, Mr. Strawhand. The Indian Wars ended with Geronimo's capture. Besides, I don't frighten easily."

Chase's gaze was clamped on Christina's knees, where the dahlia-blue crepe dress had ridden up to expose the long legs encased in silk hosiery. He could well imagine the pale flesh beneath that molded all the way along the thigh bone, and the blood began to roar in his ears. Nothing but a humping buck, he thought. He did not know if he trusted himself to get in the car. Never before had he needed to bother about restraining his impulsive libido, but obviously Christina Raffin knew nothing about rape. She was an emancipated female, career and all.

Chase groaned inwardly and swung open the door, hoping the darkness concealed the bulge in his pants. "Once in a While" drifted up from the car's radio. Christina reached over and flicked it off, and Chase caught the subtle scent of her L'Aimant perfume.

"You're either very trusting or very stupid," he said.

"I never trust any man . . . or I wouldn't be where I am now. Look behind us—the Chevrolet—the men in it work for my father. I learned at a very early age, Mr. Strawhand, just how much power my father's money will buy. And I like the knowledge. Want a cigarette?"

Chase took the cigarette and noticed by the passing light of a street lamp that the cigarette had been especially made for her. The paper bore her name and the scent of perfume. He wanted badly to shake her self-confidence. When he inclined his head to light up the cigarette, he said, his face close to hers, "A man who has something to lose would be damned stupid to upset Senator Raffin. But I, Miss Raffin, have nothing to lose."

He saw her pale eyes flare before the shadowed lids narrowed and noted the way her breasts rose slightly in agitation, and he felt the taste of pleasure that he had managed to disconcert her, however briefly.

Christina inhaled on the cigarette and blew a slow stream of smoke before replying. "We've never been formally introduced, but as we both seem to know the other's name, it would be silly to pretend ignorance. I've noticed you up at the Capitol. Someone told me you work for AID."

Chase slumped back in the seat, enjoying the ride in the luxury car. "I'm impressed you took the time to find out," he said idly.

"Don't be. I make it my business to know everyone and everything in Santa Fe. It makes me a more effective lobbyist." She softened her statement with a smile, saying, "There might be a time when I'd want your support, Mr. Strawhand."

He knew the last thing she thought she would need from him was political support, since the Indian did not have the franchise. "That's a bunch of sheep manure, Miss Raffin. Why not admit I'm different from your fancy dudes that tiptoe through the Capitol?"

Christina laughed, and Chase liked the unpretentious sound of her laughter. But she wrinkled her nose then, as if smelling something distasteful. "That you are—a diversion, my magnificent Indian. Tell me, did your family raise sheep?"

The hackles on Chase's neck rose. She had bested him. "No, they scalped and murdered the pale-skinned intruders. You can let me out here."

Christina slammed on the brakes. "Leave the window down," she said sweetly when he opened the door. "The fresh air will clean the car."

Two more months passed, and it was the week before Christmas when next Chase saw Christina. The senate had been working late, and Chase had decided to attend the session rather than take the train to Albuquerque. He was half afraid testimony regarding the Conservancy Act would be presented, and either he or Will should be there. As it turned out his effort was worthless—worthless, he thought, unless he counted the sight of Christina Raffin's long legs encased in Du Pont's new nylon hosiery.

From the rear row he had watched her enter the room, stop here and there to exchange a few words and smiles with those attending the session, and had watched every male in the room caress her with a covetous glance. She never gave any indication she noticed him though she did wink pertly at Masters who was chairing the session before she took a seat one row away from Chase.

But later, after the session was over, with the people beginning to disperse, and Chase headed toward the Capitol lobby and outdoors, Christina caught up with him. "You're taking more than a casual interest in politics, aren't you?" she asked breathlessly as they descended the multitude of steps.

Light snow fell about them, and her long golden lashes glistened with the melting flakes. She looked ravishing with her silver hair draped over the red-gold fox fur coat wrapped about her. Chase let the air build in his lungs before replying. "Nope, just don't want the bill to get through. Not at $105 an acre."

Christina stopped him, placing a hand on his arm. It was like the feverish heat of a sudden cold rocketing through him, but she did not seem to notice his reaction. The last of the stragglers passed the two of them by, and they were left alone beneath the Capitol's spotlights. "Chase, you know I'm lobbying for the Labor Union. They want this bill to pass. It'll mean more jobs—and ultimately more revenue for the State."

"And less money for the dumb Indian's pocket."

"You know I didn't mean it like that."

"But that's what you and your kind intend, isn't it?"

"Chase, give up on this. Let the Indian Bureau take care of its own."

"I'm one of its own—and I don't like the way they took care of me."

Christina moved closer. "Then let me help," she said softly. "My father could get you a job with the Legislative Council that pays more than AID does."

"Don't think so, Christina." It was the first time he had used her given name aloud, and he liked the sound of it on his lips. "Then I'd be passing the buck."

She smiled at his pun. "Maybe you'll change your mind. I—I'd offer you a ride home tonight, but I've another appointment to keep."

Chase looked past her to Masters coming toward them. The man frowned but offered his hand as Christina introduced them. Chase watched the two of them disappear into the night, feeling that old bitterness eating at his gut. Christina was a white woman, his age-old enemy.

So, why did he want her?

Deborah took another sip of the steaming Chinese tea to ward off the September chill which seeped into Roger Zamazloski's studio despite the fire that blazed in the corner fireplace. Her gaze scanned the headlines that basically had not changed since June when Germany occupied Paris and Italy declared war on the Allies.

But for a change it was not the world crises that interested Deborah, and she thumbed through the pages until she found the large photo of the lovely young lady in the daring strapless evening gown on the front page of the society section. *European Exile Courts Our Christina* read the large type, and beneath, the story gossiped of Prince Serge Kaminsky who

240

had jilted the New York "celebutante," as Elsa Maxwell had dubbed her—Brenda Frazier—for the Princess of Santa Fe Society, Christina Raffin. Even the black and white photo could not obscure the woman's vibrant beauty—the creamy skin and the pale shade of eyes set off by the vivid lipstick she had made the rage in Santa Fe—"Hothouse Red."

The week before, another picture of her had dominated the *Santa Fean*. *Raffins Host Bête Noire Ball* had read the caption beneath the picture of Christina and her distinguished father standing at the head of the receiving line. The "pet hate" ball had been held in the Raffin Victorian mansion for the opening of the new legislative session, and half the politicians had shown up with short-clipped mustaches and khaki uniforms in imitation of Germany's Adolph Hitler. A close second was the glasses and cigarette holder of Roosevelt with the imitators arriving in everything from wheelchairs to crutches and canes.

But it was the tall man photographed dancing with Christina in a smaller photo on the same page that had caught Deborah's attention. It was Chase dressed in the letter-sweater attire of the popular radio and comic-strip figure, the All-American Boy, Jack Armstrong. She had had to smile at Chase's audacious mockery of the Anglo superhero type despite the funny feeling she had in her stomach at seeing him holding the lovely woman who was dressed as the gun moll, Bonnie Parker.

A sister's jealousy, she told herself. Being from the same clan, though he shared only half her Navajo blood, made her want the best for him.

The door's tiny bell tinkled as Roger Zamazloski entered his studio and shut the door. The short, balding man shed his raccoon coat and rubbed his hands and blew on them. "I moved here from Boston for the sunshine. Where did it go?"

Deborah put away the newspaper and rose to pour her employer a cup of tea. "Come back in three months," she said, laughing. "That's when the Navajo's Changing Woman brings the spring and your sunshine."

Roger took the cup of tea and sat down at a large table littered with wrapping paper and string, and papers ready for filing. He was a middle-aged man with graceful gestures who, Deborah decided long ago, was neither straight nor homosexual like some of the artists and writers who inhabited Camino del Monte Sol. To her way of thinking he was neuter, with no sexual preference. After the first months of working for him, his odd feminine gestures no longer bothered her, for she actually enjoyed his witty personality and his sincere friendship and encouraging interest in her work.

"Are you still hoping one day to have your own one-woman art exhibition?" he asked her now between sips of tea.

Deborah paused in stacking the filing papers to one side of the table. Roger was watching her with an intensity that disconcerted her. "One day," she answered carefully. "When my paintings have gained greater acceptance by the critics."

Roger reached in his pocket and fished out a telegram. "It's from CBS," he said, handing it to her.

She looked from Roger to the yellow piece of paper addressed to him. NEED CORRESPONDENT TO PHOTOGRAPH WAR PROGRESS IN EUROPE STOP ARE YOU INTERESTED STOP REPLY BY JANUARY FIRST STOP.

"I've no interest in giving up my practice," Roger said. "It's taken me too long to get it established."

"I don't blame you," she said, handing him back the telegram. "Still, it'd be exciting to cover something of that magnitude."

"I was hoping you'd feel that way. I thought I'd recommend you."

"Me?" she squeaked.

"Why not? The first female photographer to cover the war would be quite a coup."

Deborah sat down in a daze. "But I know very little about photography."

Roger uncrossed his legs and leaned forward. Excitement danced in his young-old eyes. "I've watched you crop my photos. You have a photographer's sense of the unusual—and an artist's eye for the essentials."

"I—I don't know. Santa Fe's the biggest town I've ever been in. It's difficult to imagine moving to Europe—being on my own."

"If nothing else, think of the great publicity your Navajo Indians would receive. It'd show the nation that the Indian is no longer the primitive savage the Tom Mix movies make him—or her," he said, smiling, "out to be."

Deborah thought of the photo she had seen on the society page that morning. And then there was the young Indian sculptor she had recently met, Greg Red Bird. Did she really want to leave? "I'd have to think about it, Roger."

"I was hoping you'd at least give it a chance. You've got until the first of the year to decide."

45

It was as if the boring hum of conversation did not exist, as if the hired musicians had taken a break from the evening's entertainment, as if there were not another man in the room but Chase Strawhand...at least, thought Christina, as far as every woman in the Palace Hotel's Grand Ballroom was concerned.

He stood in the wide, open doorway, magnificently virile in spite of the civilized trappings of the black tuxedo, which Christina was certain he had rented, and every woman present came alert—like bitches in heat, she thought. Evelyn Addison, the Mayor's wife, patted her sausage curls. A senator's wife, Wanda Greiner, smoothed over her fat-padded hips the tight red sequined dress that flared at her knees. It seemed that every female gaze swiveled like magnets toward Chase Strawhand.

And I'm no better, she told herself. After almost two years of studied politeness toward him, of suffering Kaminsky's tiresome courtship, of involving herself so deeply in her work that she fell in bed at night like a zombie, she still could not get Chase out of her system. Seeing him at the Capitol or at an occasional party was not enough. She wanted him. She wanted him to make love to her so that things like lacquered nails and permanented waves and the next committee meeting would be driven from her mind. She wanted him to be the first, for in spite of her image as the worldly wise and sophisticated young socialite and businesswoman, she was still inexperienced in lovemaking.

It was not only that the eligible men acted either awkward or exceedingly polite in her presence, as did Philip Masters, who she knew was only biding his time. It was also the host of feelings left over from childhood...the years of listening to her parents argue, her mother's desertion of her father and herself for a man more her age, and her father's coldness and reluctance to demonstrate affection. The whole idea of love and its ensuing sex act was something she had not wanted to ever get involved in and had settled for the challenge of a career in a man's world.

Then she had seen Chase Strawhand, felt the intense heat of his gaze that first day in the Capitol cafeteria. And after that, each time they were thrown together she was surprised at the lack of control over her body, over the way her nipples hardened and her loins flowed with aching desire.

From across the room Chase's gaze met hers and locked. She shivered with his infuriatingly lazy grin...and the secret message his eyes held. Suddenly she was tired of listening to Governor McDonald's praise of the Democratic re-election campaign and his opinion on the war in Europe and Roosevelt's recall of the arms embargo and what it meant at home. She wanted only one thing.

"Excuse me, Fred," she said to her Princeton escort. "I need to repair my make-up." As she made her way past the tables toward the door she nodded here and there at the party's workers who had earned their ticket to the New Year's Inaugural Ball. Impatience to reach Chase before he was swallowed up by a gaggle of socialites made her short with the sycophants who sought to detain her.

"Hello, Chase," she said quietly, ignoring Margaret Maxwell, the prominent patron of the arts and founder of the Maxwell Galleries. The bleached blond, with a half-empty champagne glass in one hand, was seductively tracing the folds of Chase's red cummerbund with the forefinger of her free hand while she talked about what the Democratic Party could do for AID.

"Hello, Christina," he said. "I take it I owe you a thanks for the invitation?"

Christina turned to the woman who blinked with surprise at the interruption. "Isn't that your husband over there on the dance floor, Marge? I think he's motioning for you to join him in the Conga Line."

When the woman had departed in a huff, Christina said, "I thought you might enjoy the New Year's party." The way his inky-black eyes watched her—it made her nervous. And the way his raking gaze moved down the plunge of her cleavage, she wondered if he even noticed the $750 frothy lilac gown from John-Frederics. "I didn't think you would come," she blurted. Then, "You're bored, aren't you?"

Chase slanted a brow. "Aren't you?"

Christina surveyed the crowded room. Wasn't this what she had worked for—the power so long denied the woman in politics? She looked back to Chase, tilting her head up in spite of her five feet ten inches. "Good Lord, yes—and I'm just realizing it!"

"Come on," he said, taking her wrist. "We're missing a better party."

The band was playing a swing rendition of Glen Miller's

"Blueberry Hill," and from the corner of her eye she could see Fred making his way toward her. Wordlessly she nodded her head at Chase. Chase took her glass and handed it to a passing waiter in purple livery. "Let's go."

Chase did not need to take his eyes off the winding Cerro Gordo Road to see the exhilaration that shone in Christina's eyes each time the flare from her cigarette lit up the elegant bones of her face. A woman of power and wealth and beauty. A dangerous combination. He would be a fool to let himself get involved with her. He imagined she would be like the female species of the whip vignaroon scorpion that inhabited the New Mexico alkaline flats—cohabitating with her mate, then stinging him to death. If the mate let her.

Chase's long lips flattened out in a dry smile as the realization occurred to him that he was looking forward to a duel with this woman. He felt her eyes on him, and he glanced at her. "Where are we going?" she asked.

"I told you. A party. Of sorts. We're going to an Enemyway Chant—a squaw dance."

Christina laughed. "Are you going to make a squaw out of me?"

"I think that would be difficult. We won't be seeing what the ordinary tourists see. We've a special invitation to the medicine hogan."

"What's going to happen there?"

"That's where the Native American Church meets."

"A church meeting!" Christina's eyes narrowed. "You dragged me away from the party of the year to attend a church meeting?"

Chase's smile was crooked. "You said you were bored. Wait. If you change your mind, I'll see that you get back."

Christina did not miss the implications in his words. Chase Strawhand was not a man to be gelded. He would probably send her back with some fat, blanketed chief with a stovepipe hat jammed on his head. Well, this is what she had wanted. And being out under the stars with a man like Chase, even if he was not wild for her like Serge, was better than suffocating at the tedious ball. And where was Serge? she wondered. The latest gossip had it that he had followed up her rejection by pursuing Barbara Hutton, the Woolworth heiress—or was it the movie actress, Alice Faye?

Chase maneuvered his Torpedo Ford through the flow of horses and buckboards, past the main grounds of the pueblo where most of the tourists would be found on a weekend snapping away with their Kodak Brownies. "We're not stopping here?" Christina asked.

Chase shook his head. "Un-uhh. Further back in the canyon of the pueblo reservation is a small band of Navajos. They'll be having their own ceremony tonight."

"At the church?" she asked, somewhat skeptically.

"Mmm-huh." Chase kept his attention on the road as the Ford bounced over a series of ruts.

The January air was colder there where it whistled down the narrow valleys, and Christina shivered despite the heavy mink coat. Then, back in the trees a dim light flickered, growing steadier as they neared a log and mud hogan. Four or five ponies and a Model-T were off to the hogan's left near a lean-to.

Christina's desire for the warmth of the cabin drained as Chase switched off the engine. A ribbon of mist swirled about the hogan. From inside came mournful wailing occasionally broken by a shrill chant. "Will they be angry—that you've brought me?"

Chase's smile was unfathomable. "I think the shaman's expecting you."

Christina smiled, uncertain if Chase was joking. And Chase was not sure himself. The previous summer he had made a cursory tour of the pueblos along the Rio Grande to get a better idea of how much of the flood control project was involved in the Conservancy Act. At one pueblo he had stopped before an old shaman who was sandpainting. Half-fascinated—half-derisive, Chase had stood with the crowd of tourists and watched the old man dribble the colored powders on the ground, painting some ancient divinity.

The chanting that accompanied the sandpainting meant little to Chase. But there was something commanding about the shaman who looked almost mummified. Furrows ribbed the taut skin about the great hawklike nose, and long, straggly, bone-white hair framed the arresting face. About one veined wrist was an unusually designed bracelet of silver and turquoise.

After some minutes Chase realized the old man's piercing gaze had singled him out from the crowd of tourists. Still in a sing-song chant, the shaman began to speak to Chase in the common Navajo. "There is a medicine hogan—not meant for tourists' eyes. Come some evening, and I shall tell you of the Long Walk made by your mother's mother."

Chase's laugh had been mocking. "Your hocus-pocus won't work on me, grandfather," he replied, uncaring that the tourists stared at him now during this interchange. "My mother's mother was a white woman." That much he knew for sure, reluctantly revealed to him by his father. That and the information that his mother's father had been a Navajo of the Tahtchini clan.

The shaman let the sand play out between his horny fingers, never looking at the form the grains made. "Nevertheless your mother's mother made the Long Walk. You will make the Long Walk." His eyes at last released Chase, and Chase felt as if a hypnotist had snapped his fingers.

"You are old, grandfather. You don't know what you say."

Without looking up this time from the sandpainting he continued to make, the old man said, "Bring the woman of the moon. Her pale beams reflect on your past."

Glad that he had broken away from the traditional superstition that bound so many of his people to ignorance, Chase had turned away with a half-pitying, half-scornful laugh for the old-timer, who was known as Guayo Santiago.

But, curiously, over the past months he had been drawn back to the medicine hogan on the few weekends he had no assignments due or research work needed for AID. And each time the old man had mentioned the pale moon woman.

No one looked up when Chase and Christina entered. Seven other people lined the sides of the octagonal log hogan. Smoke drifted up from the firepit through the smoke vent in the center of the hogan. But it was not the smoke that pervaded the small room with the acrid smell.

The smell was that of peyote. Although the possession of peyote was a crime under New Mexican law, the Indians were subject only to federal law, and under federal ruling peyote was not a narcotic and could thus be used in the religious ceremonies of the Native American Church.

On the room's west side the old shaman sat near a half-formed sandpainting. To his left was another Indian with a massive, bulldog face. "That is Cedar Chief," Chase whispered. "He will help the Road Priest, the old man making the sandpainting, by sprinkling powdered juniper on the fire. Before Road Chief is the altar—there, with the large peyote blossom."

Christina wrinkled her nose at the bitter smell, and he said, "It's the peyote you smell. Later, when the Road Chief readies the kettle drum and the ceremonial praying and singing begin, you'll smoke the peyote."

"I think I'd rather have one of my own cigarettes, thank you."

Chase shrugged with a mysterious smile. "You might change your mind. Wait." He took a seat on the dirt floor, cross-legged, and Christina did likewise, carefully arranging her skirts and floor-length fur coat around her.

Sacramental food was passed around, a *pozole* of corn, and

247

the mournful wailing began again. A person here, an old woman there. "They are confessing their sins," Chase explained in a whisper.

A middle-aged woman with a rebozo covering her head began weeping, and Christina said, "Good Lord, if I began confessing my sins we'd be here all night."

"We will be."

Christina rolled her eyes upward, wondering what she had gotten into. It was certainly a different experience. The old man whom Chase had named Road Chief began stopping before each person with a shallow basket filled with what appeared to be rolled cigarettes.

"Take one," Chase advised. "You're about to begin your journey on the Peyote Road."

"And Daddy warned me against smoking," Christina said with a mocking sigh as she took one.

Road Chief returned to his place before the sand-painting. Cedar Chief began the slow, steady beat of the hollow, deep kettle drum. It was eerie—the weeping and wailing of confession, the ceremonial praying, the singing and smoking. Christina thought the cigarette pleasant but not as strong as she had expected. But shortly after midnight the old Road Chief passed about peyote buds that had been sliced and dried.

One bite, and Christina knew she was taking her Road Trip. It was like a series of timed depth charges. Chase, watching her, could judge her progress from his own past experience. The unsettling of the stomach, and thirty minutes later, the flushed face. Pupils dilating, salivation increasing. Christina's eyes grew wider, and she smiled—a slow smile, and he knew she was experiencing a sense of exhilaration, like the swift intake of pure oxygen.

His own exhilaration was more muted, more reverent. The old Religion of the Gods formed more a part of his introspective thoughts than he realized—despite the fact he had denied both the old gods and the white man's God the missionaries at the Indian boarding school had so vainly tried to instill in him.

He could tell by Christina's closed eyes that she was focusing her own energies inward. Ideas seemed to flow as rapidly in Chase's head as the hummingbird. He was on an intense plateau, and his thoughts were uncannily luminous. He would rule the white man, not the other way around. He would make the laws. He would rule with the white woman beside him. Of course, that was what Road Chief, Guayo Santiago, had been telling him!

It was a dawn to dusk affair, and with the first light of

the sun the religious services ended. The attendants moved awkwardly, but there were no aftereffects. Chase helped Christina to the Ford. Her lovely pale-green eyes were glazed, but he could not tell if it was from the lack of sleep or the shock of her experience.

"Whhew!" she breathed after she had settled her long skirts inside the car and tucked her loose wisps of hair back into the fashionable pompadour. She flashed him a smile that was touched with embarrassment. "'Leaping Lizards,' as Little Orphan Annie would say. That was some experience! I knew I had the solution to the world's problems sometime during the night, but it seems to have slipped away."

"It's customary now to take a steam bath to purify yourself," Chase said as he whipped the car around and headed back down the bumpy, overgrown road.

A pulse beat in the hollow of Christina's throat. Her father would probably have the state police out searching for her, but she had shared something very personal with Chase, and she was not ready for it to end.

Chase was not yet ready for the night to end either. He wanted Christina now more than he had ever wanted anything, and it had nothing to do with the peyote experience. She was the embodiment of beauty, womanhood, and power; she possessed the strength and grace of the female puma...and he would tame her.

"There is a summer hogan," he said slowly as the idea took shape in his head. "Not a sweathouse like our people use. But it's empty now with the winter here. However, we could manage to sweat away our impurities there."

His smile was wicked now, all male, and Christina thrilled to it. She thought she could hardly wait until they reached the place. She made no complaint even though Chase half-dragged her through rough undershrub when the Ford could go no further, tearing the frothy organdy and net gown.

A cool mist still hovered in the morning air. Further through the trees Christina spotted the summer hogan. Beehive-shaped, it was formed of stout piñon poles overlaid with thick evergreens. Looking in through the wide door she was conscious of a warm darkness broken by shafts of dawn's light that poked through the leaves and filled the central smoke-hole. Inside the sweet smell of the night's dampness pervaded everything.

Christina let the mink coat slide to the earthen floor and turned to face Chase. Her heart thudded loudly as he loomed over her, the essence of male, and she was afraid—a thrilling

249

kind of fear, knowing that this time, finally, she would be the one to be mastered.

Chase buried his hands in her hair, tearing loose the carefully arranged rolls of curls. He hurt her, but she trembled with the pain and pleasure and the expectation of what was to come.

The gown tore away easily beneath Chase's impatient hands, and Christina wondered how she would ever get past her father's gimlet eye. "I'm a grown woman," she thought rebelliously. "I don't have to answer to him."

Then all thought was driven from her mind as Chase's mouth scorched a passionate path from her parted lips to her eyelids and brushed the dainty shell of her ear before nuzzling the hollow at the base of her neck. Her head lolled backward. "Oh, love me, Chase," she whispered when his head moved lower to the bare breasts exposed above the wire strapless bra.

She watched breathlessly as Chase pulled away and shed his tuxedo—and the last vestiges of civilization. Petting in the rumble seat after a date at the ice cream parlor had revealed to Christina the composition of the male sex. But Chase's coppery physique, corded with muscles by years of hard work during the summer in the Kansas beet fields as a child and later, after he had graduated, as a lumberjack, made that of her college dates seem immature in comparison.

Her fingers fumbled at the waistband of her long silk slip, and her nylons, garter belt, and panties fell away—as the remnants of her reticence fell away. After twenty-four years of waiting, Christina was ready now. Ready for Chase. Wanting him, needing him, immediately. She wrapped her arms about his shoulders, pulling him down into her own soft, sweet dampness.

Chase took her there on the deep, luxuriant fur of her mink coat with a pounding, driving tempo that wracked her body, so that the initial pain was diluted by the intensity of their need. Perspiration rolled off both of them to fall on the fur. Christina thought she could not get enough of him. The mounting ecstasy was more than she thought she could stand, and she wanted to cry out. But his lips silenced hers, driving her into a forgetfulness.

For Chase all thought was heightened, like the effects of the jimson weed, like the peyote bud. He envisioned the old gods, the Yé'ii, frowning down upon him for betraying his people, for coupling with the unclean pale-skinned woman. He had had other Anglo women, mostly the lower class who had frequented the reservation's bordertowns, and one or two society matrons since coming to Santa Fe, women who found him a novelty.

As perhaps Christina did—a diversion. But she was unlike any Anglo woman he had possessed before. She was the White Queen, the Woman of the Moon.

And he would not let the primitive, ignorant fear of the Ye'ii's revenge keep him from having her.

46

Chase and Will bent over the map of New Mexico as Chase's blunt finger traced the course of the Rio Grande River that divided the state in half. "This plat—and here, this plat—those there...these are the acreage that Bill 263 will tax. With Elephant Butte Reservoir going—"

The door of the office opened, and Deborah came in. It was the first time in two months Chase had seen her, since Christmas when she had come by the AID office with a gift for him, a sweater she had knitted to replaced his hole-filled one. She had stayed only a moment, but Chase had been slightly surprised at the change in her. There was still a gamine expression to her childlike face. But there all resemblance to a child ended.

Her lovely dark brown hair was no longer coiled in braids but hung loose, touching the small of her back, with the sides and front rolled away from her face, emphasizing the full cheekbones and tilted cinnamon-brown eyes. And she had been dressed in spiked heels and a wraparound print dress that displayed her soft curves and shapely legs.

Today her small figure was outlined in a tightly fitting paprika-colored sweater and men's khaki trousers. "What do you think?" she asked the two men as she twirled for them. "It's the latest rage."

"Then it's true?" Will asked with a straight face. "Eleanor Roosevelt's doing away with the female sex?"

Deborah made a face at Will. "No! And besides the slacks make it easier to work with the outdoor props that Roger's photographing—which brings me to why I'm here."

She turned pleading eyes on the two men. "I'm running up to Taos to set up an exhibition for Roger at one of the galleries, and I thought you two—and May, if she can get away from the kitchen long enough, Will—would like to go along. I've got Roger's Stutz Bearcat, and I thought we could stop off at the Picuris pueblo on the way. They're holding a ceremonial dance tonight—the last of the season."

"Count me out," Will said. "'Gangbusters' is on tonight, and you couldn't pry me away from the radio with a crowbar."

Deborah looked at Chase and flashed an elfin smile. "It's a Mountain Chant. Say you'll come."

Chase slid down in the swivel chair, his hands clasped behind his head. He wanted nothing better than to go back to his attic room and crash for the night. But there stirred in his blood the childhood memory of the mysterious Mountain Chants—the succession of ceremonial dances, the jugglery and legerdemain that took place around a huge fire from sundown to dawn, the eerie shadows that leaped and the wild beat of the rattle and the drum.

And there stirred in his blood the more recent memory of the New Year's Peyote Ceremony held in a back canyon. Eight weeks had passed since that night—eight weeks of seeing Christina's aloof expression at the Capitol or occasionally at the nearby Tapatio Restaurant where many politicians met for lunch or an after-work drink; and always Chase wondered what Christina was thinking behind that mask of cool control.

She had avoided him the one time he had happened to meet her alone—in one of the Capitol's corridors. She had drawn away from him as if his touch burned her. But Chase had pinned her against the tiled wall, his hands on either side of her as his mouth angrily took hers, and her hands had slipped up around his neck to entwine in his collar-length hair. Yet when Senator Folley had called out for her, Christina had seemed relieved the spell was broken.

Chase grabbed his corduroy hunting coat. "See you tomorrow, Will."

They made one stop, at the St. Vincent's Sanitarium where Deborah lived. "The good sisters have more rooms than patients," she explained, laughing at Chase's surprised expression. "And besides, they offer excellent accommodations and good food for a modest sum. I'll be just a moment—I've some paintings I have to cart up to Taos for Roger."

When she returned to the car, a good-looking young Indian with clean-cut brown-black hair and a friendly face helped her with the paper-wrapped paintings. "Gregory Red Bird," she said, introducing him to Chase.

The young man, who was of medium height, took Chase's hand.

"Greg's taken the room down the hall from me. His sculpturing class was called off, and I invited him along."

Greg smiled wryly at Chase. "I'm a full-blooded Navajo, but you'd never know it. I've never seen a night chant before, so Deborah thought it was time."

Deborah's enthusiasm was contagious, and Chase could only agree, though as he shifted the Stutz into second he could not figure out why the man's presence should irritate him. He found himself feeling more than ever like Deborah's big brother, and when Greg put his arm on the seat behind Deborah who sat between the two of them, he felt like asking just what Greg's intentions were.

As Chase maneuvered the Stutz around the hairpin curves and along the narrow Highway 68, Deborah explained to Greg the nature of what he would see that evening. From that point their conversation turned to exhibitions and galleries and New Mexico's creative giants like Ellis, Weston, and Lawrence.

The sunset was a brilliant hue of purples and oranges when Chase finally wheeled the Stutz off the main highway onto a rock-studded road that twisted through several ridges dotted with cottonwoods and junipers and littered with tin cans and beer bottles—products of the white tourist. But tonight few white men would witness this ceremony. As the car neared the enormous clearing, surrounded by walls of evergreens, the road became crowded with other Indians, most from Picuris, arriving by burro, an occasional pickup, and on foot.

Nearly a thousand Indians were standing and sitting as the first of the spectacular performances commenced. It was a fire dance, with the dancers' bodies painted white with clay to ward off the heat as they raced around the blazing bonfire. Each clutched a burning brand and struck the dancer ahead. They circled wildly, coming closer and closer to the leaping flames.

Chase and Greg, with Deborah between them, shouldered their way through the Indians to find an empty place on the ground to sit. A blanket-wrapped Indian moved past them, juggling rounded stones. To their left a clown burlesqued the priests, dancing out of step, and the children laughed at his antics. The sight of the families, the close-knit clans, awakened in Chase a yearning for the family he had missed as a child.

Toward midnight, as the more sacred ceremonial dances began, small bowls of *penole* and *piki* began to circulate among the group along with the ubiquitous *tiswin*. The night air had turned cold, and Chase noticed that Greg had taken the opportunity to put his arm around Deborah possessively. Chase's eyes, shielded by lazy lids, turned away to watch the barbaric splendor of the primitive dances. The rattle of the tortoiseshell and the thud of the cottonwood drum lured him back to a primeval time.

Deborah felt the same stirring in her blood, watching the rites, letting the savage sounds fill her until there existed nothing else; a stirring, she thought, that Christina Raffin and her kind could never know. She wanted to spring up, loose the fetters of Greg's arm, and lose herself in the ever-quickening tempo of the dance. But she willed the stoic calm in herself, watched Greg as he partook of the *tiswin*, noting that Chase drank little.

One dance faded into another, children grew sleepy and crawled up in their mothers' arms, the ancient wandered off to exchange a beer and tales of their youth while the younger ones took up the passionate beat of the dance.

Toward dawn Greg's arm fell away as he slipped into a nodding doze. Now was the time, she thought, the real purpose for which she had invited Chase. She turned to him. He would not be able to hear her above the throbbing music. She touched his shoulder and rose. Chase looked up, as if disturbed from a trance. She mouthed the words, "Follow me."

The two of them wove their way through the sleeping mounds and huddled bodies, deeper into the encircling forest. The air was purer there, but the insistent pagan music, though muted, still followed them. The pine needles crushed beneath Deborah's espadrilles, whispering seductively, as she followed the trail that led to the Rio Grande's banks.

Chase caught up with her and took her arm, and she turned to face him. "What's this all about?" he asked.

Although the darkness surrounded them, she could still see the concern that showed in his self-contained countenance. "Chase, you're the only family I have near, and... and..." She broke off, not knowing how much to tell him.

Chase took her shoulders. "What is it?"

"Greg asked me to marry him yesterday."

Chase's hands fell away. "Oh. He seems—nice." He looked away into the darkness. "With your common interest in art, you should make a very happy couple."

"I—I was hoping you'd say that. I wanted your approval... being as you're like a brother."

"You have my best wishes, Deborah. When's the wedding?"

"There's something else I had to tell you, and tonight seemed as good a time as any. The wedding is six months away. After I return from a photographic tour of the European war front. Tonight is good-bye."

Chase grabbed her shoulders again. "You've gone and joined the white man's side?" He shook her, and her heavy hair swayed like a wind-ruffled curtain. "You dumb little shit!" He pulled her into his arms and held her. "Why'd you go off and do a cockeyed thing like that?" he asked over her head.

Deborah could feel the angry beat of his heart, though his hand was gentle as it mindlessly stroked her long hair. The safety and security of his arms were the home away from home that she had known since she was five and he had befriended her at the Indian boarding school. She could still remember the way his thin shoulders, clothed only in a threadbare shirt, hunched over against the bite of the winter wind as he directed her toward her dormitory. Her arms wrapped around his waist. "Oh, Chase, I wish I didn't have to go," she murmured. "But I do. I do."

At that moment she wondered why she *was* going. There would be other opportunities to perfect her craft. And it wasn't just because Greg and Roger had urged her to take the job.

Unconsciously the two clung together against the intrusion of the white man's world and his war, swaying with the distant throb of the drums that Deborah felt echoed the unidentifiable pain that pulsed somewhere inside her...until Greg's call of her name pulled them apart.

47

The roll had been called, followed by the prayer and the Pledge of Allegiance. With the reading of the journal and the introduction of legislation Christina began to breathe easier.

She had seen Will enter the Senate Gallery during the pledge, but without Chase. Maybe Chase wouldn't show up. Of course, he would find out sooner or later that she had been opposing his project from the start, using him and his information. But she'd rather not see his face, be in his presence when he realized the extent to which she had gone.

Because her efforts had backfired on her. She had fallen for the Indian and she was ashamed that she could be so silly, so feminine—and over an Indian! The Conservancy Act should have been wrapped up long before, during last year's session's actions. But she had stalled, soft-pedaled the issue to the politicians, which was unlike her.

As late as two weeks ago, when she had met Chase in the corridor—when he had made love to her in the Capitol, no less, and left her shaken, her legs weak—she had felt the compunction to contact Senators Folley and Ramsey, to tell them to go ahead with their support of AID, to vote against the Conservancy Bill. But she had a job to do. She could not she told herself, let sentiment stand in the way.

Christina knew she shouldn't be there on the chamber floor now. It was not protocol when legislature was in session But she had one last detail to attend to. Throwing back her padded shoulders, she nodded at the Sergeant-at-Arms as she passed and crossed to Senator Folley's chair, laying the envelope casually on his desk as she bent over to talk, to smile— making certain everyone saw her pleasant exchange of words. She knew it helped that her toast-colored crepe dress had ridden up, exposing the long expanse of leg between the knee and suede half-boot.

"The last half will be delivered at lunch—after you've cast your vote," she quietly told Folley, never letting her smile fade.

She stood up then, exchanging a few more words with the senators seated around Folley, for rather than listening to the Message from the House of Representatives they were loudly doing their own casual canvassing of the work-in-progress for the day.

As she prepared to leave, something prompted her to glance up into the gallery. Chase stood there, his face granite his eyes like black stones. She shivered and quickly turned away. She could hear the Reading Clerk delivering the third reading of the legislation. Then would come the voting of the bills. If she hurried, she could make it to the parking lot and be gone long before they reached the voting of Bill 263.

The "aye, aye, nay" echoed down the hall along with the click of her boot heels. Absurd to be afraid. But she was. He was an Indian. An Apache—or was it Navajo? Whatever tribe everyone knew the Indian still settled his feuds outside the boundaries of the law. With knife or pistol, it made no difference.

Christina's car key fumbled at the doorlock. She flipped through the set, frantically searching for another. A hand clamped on her wrist. She whirled around with a small cry

"Well, Puss n' Boots, you won."

Her gaze darted about the empty parking lot. Everyone seemed to be inside. "Chase, please," she whispered, frightened. "It wasn't what I wanted."

Chase's black gaze pinned her pitilessly where she stood "What did you want? A little diversion, as long as your job wasn't jeopardized?" He yanked the keys from her and opened the door. "Get in. We're going for a ride—to show you a diversion or two."

Christina clutched the armrest of her door and steadied herself with one hand against the dashboard as Chase wheeled the car out of the parking lot and drove out Cerro Gordo Road. The road passed the clay pits where the prisoners from the penitentiary were digging loads of clay to make bricks, then climbed and twisted back into the canyons; and in the daylight Christina recognized the road as the one that led to the old hogan Chase had taken her to on New Year's Eve.

Several times she thought Chase would hurl the car off into a gorge, that he wanted to kill them both. He said nothing the forty-some-odd minutes the trip took. Then she realized when he turned off onto another corduroy road, exactly where he was taking her.

He slammed on the brakes at the foot of the wooded trail that snaked upward. The Mercedes only missed a jackpine by inches as it slid on the pebbles to a halt. "This isn't a pickup!" she snapped, more bravely than she felt.

Chase jerked her from the car and both dragged and pushed her up the slight incline. Pine cones and needles tore at her stockings. "Chase, you're hurting me!" She stood in the hogan against the furthermost section of wall, rubbing her wrist. She bit her bottom lip, not knowing what to expect next. Her pulse hammered at her temples.

He crossed to her, and she began edging around the wall as he stalked her. "You were hungry for my embraces not so long ago. Has something changed since then?"

"Chase—no!" she cried out as he grabbed her shoulders and yanked her to him. His mouth closed over hers in a brutal kiss that had no passion; yet Christina, after a few moments of futile struggling, of trying to resist the kiss that was as narcotic as the peyote, trembled uncontrollably then sagged against the overpowering body as desire geysered through her like an oil well out of control.

Her arms entwined about his neck. "Oh, Chase, it's only you I wanted," she murmured breathlessly, incoherently. "I didn't . . . I don't know why . . ."

Chase broke away from the cold, white mouth that crept over him like a slug. Heedless of her crying, he left her and her car there and began walking. Where he was going, he did not know.

He felt only a repulsive emptiness—an emptiness that could be filled only by the rawest rotgut whiskey he could find. He was disgusted with himself and with every treacherous Anglo on the face of the earth. Whatever had made him think he would be accepted in the white man's world? Going to college, working for the government, loving a pale-skinned woman—these were things a white man did.

It took four days of drinking himself into a stupor with Taos Lightning. And three more days to pull himself back from oblivion. But when Chase finally managed to focus his eyes for more than half an hour and force some semblance of thought into his numbed but pounding brain, he found that he had joined the Marine Signal Corps.

Hawaii offered more green than Chase had ever seen. Even after three months at Pearl Harbor, he had not overcome his aversion to seeing only green around him and above him, hemming him in. He missed the expanse of the clear New Mexico skies, where the stars seemed so close you could reach up from your bedroll and touch them.

At divisional headquarters in Pearl Harbor he and twenty-nine other Navajo were processed and briefed in the drab government-green headquarters about their secret assignment. Though officially not at war with the Axis, the United States government was preparing for the possibility. One such project was the development of an indecipherable code—hence the idea of the Navajo Code Talkers.

The United States government had been apprised of the fact that even though an enemy should learn the exceedingly complex Navajo language, unintelligible even to other Indian tribes, it would be virtually impossible for the enemy's tongue and throat to make it sound correctly.

And it was this task of devising a code that fell to the Code Talkers. Placed in charge, Chase had to develop a code to stymie enemy cryptographers—words for military terms not in the Navajo language, an alphabet to spell out names not in their tongue such as Sicily, Libya, and Rumania, and words for the ranks of officers, organizations, communication systems, months, and so on.

After rigorous field exercises during the day and working on the code at night, Chase would fall exhausted into his bunk, already half asleep. But even his dreams were filled with cryptic words that he and the other Code Talkers were devising: Owl, *Ne-as-jah,* for observation plane; swallow, *Tas-chizzie,* for torpedo plane; eagle, *Atsah,* for transport; and beaver, *Cha,* for mine sweeper.

This taxing assignment accomplished what he had wanted—it occupied his mind totally so there was no room for thought of a woman with silver-gilt hair and eyes as pale green as Hawaii's lush lagoons.

Only once did he let himself think of the mainland—of New Mexico. It was the last day in May when Mail Call handed him the letter with the Santa Fe, New Mexico, postmark. He jammed it into his pocket, not wanting to read it but knowing he would.

Later that evening he was alone at his desk in the makeshift quonset hut. Before him were the briefings he was compiling for the Code Talkers on the care of their signal equipment—illustrations and explanations of the semaphores, field telephones, and hand-cranked generators. But his mind was not on the stack of papers but on the envelope in his pocket that burned like a hot coal.

At last he took it out. He was slightly disappointed—it was a letter from Will, reprimanding Chase for not letting him know where he had gone and the trouble Chase had caused him in tracking the marine down. The old lawyer sketched briefly the Santa Fe happenings that had occurred since Chase left in late February. He mentioned nothing about the failure to stop the passage of the Conservancy Act, nor Christina Raffin, though Chase was certain the discerning old man knew everything.

Will did enclose a photo of Deborah. Dressed in trousers with a camera slung over her shoulder, she was posed before a B-17, the Flying Fortress, at Nichols Field in the Philippines. She had been assigned, so Will wrote, to cover the Japanese assault on French Indochina. She was smiling, and, though her face was slightly indistinct, he knew those brown eyes were laughing.

Chase tucked the photo in his wallet, wondering if Deborah was faring any better in the white man's world than he. Because of his Indian heritage he was precluded from holding rank in the service, which made him just that more bitter. However, his year and a half of college did qualify him as coordinator for the Marine Signal Corps' special project. Yet he remained aloof from the Anglo companions—the *bilan-gaali*, as the Code Talkers called the white man. And he rarely fraternized with the Navajo Code Talkers. He was caught between two worlds, contemptuous of both.

The first of September he received his orders. To his irritation he found that, because of the standby alert in the Far East Theater, instead of being attached to a marine unit he would be reporting immediately, along with four other Code Talkers, to an army command.

He shipped out on the *President Pierce,* a luxury liner converted to an army troop transport that had sailed from San Francisco a week earlier. For Chase it seemed that the

259

Ye'ii had arranged his orders. Not only was the 200th Anti-Aircraft National Guard, part of which was the New Mexico National Guard, aboard the *Pierce,* but the *Pierce*'s destination was the Philippines and Nichols Field, Manila.

It would be one of life's implausible ironies, he thought, that he should travel halfway around the world to escape his past, only to meet with Deborah. However, his intention to find her once he reached the Philippines was temporarily shelved when he found himself assigned to the Decoding Room on the tiny rock island of Corregidor in Manila Bay.

After an indoctrination class on the area's operations, complete with a detailed map chock full of red tacks representing Japanese locations, Chase and the other new recruits, including the four Navajo Code Talkers, were directed to the company supply clerk and were issued jungle combat gear—everything a camouflage green again.

The first night in the barracks, he lay on his mildewed cot and tried to sleep, but the soldier next to him, a Brooklyn sergeant, wanted to talk. Chase had trouble following Spec's Yankee accent, which sounded like a gravel mixer. "Man, I got ninety-seven more days left in this jungle," Spec was saying. "The number's tattooed on my eyeballs."

Somewhere down the row of cots a soldier piped, "Try cleaning your glasses, Spec."

"Go screw yourself, Omaha," Spec told the black soldier.

"Speaking of screw," another soldier said, and the darkness was filled with laughter, "did ya'll see that Red Cross nurse that came through the base last week?"

"You're the guy that's been here too long," Spec shot back. "The dame was old enough to be your grandmother."

"Forget the nurse," Omaha said. "Did ya see the camp's new laundress that came on base today? Jeeesus Christ! She's built like the China Wall!"

A Navajo Code Talker, Blue Tail, who was two cots over from Chase, let out a low catcall that could have resembled a war whoop. "My laundry gets dirty just thinking about her!"

Several chuckles erupted in the darkness. Chase smiled. He had seen the young Filipino girl at headquarters during his processing and mentally screwed her half a dozen times himself.

As it turned out the laundress began to flirt with Chase, coyly watching him whenever their paths crossed on the minuscule base, touching his hand shyly when she took and delivered his laundry.

Lelani was petite with almond-shaped eyes and long, thick

black hair, and for a while Chase found himself intrigued by her, enjoying their casual companionship, for in some ways her Oriental attitude matched the fatalism of his own ancestors. And he was somewhat surprised that she had not attached herself to one of the officers, which offered her so much more prestige—for, everything taken into consideration, he knew she was just that, a camp follower.

But Lelani, of the swaying hips and straight back, wanted no one else. "All women—I betcha they have eyes for you, just you," she told him one afternoon when he had been in the Philippines a little over a month. He was off duty, and the two of them had ferried to the Luzon mainland and boarded a packed bus of World War I vintage bound for the mountain city of Baguio. Uncaring of the disinterested gazes of the other Filipinos on the bus, she had reached over and touched him on the thigh, letting her small, wash-reddened fingers rest near his crotch. "You, Chase, are a man."

Chase had laughed at her impish daring. "I should hope by now you know that."

Yes, Lelani had been good in bed, knowing all the tricks. And he was certain that after he left there would be other soldiers. But just as Baguio had reminded him much of Santa Fe with its invigorating mountain climate and resort hotels, Lelani, with her saffron-colored skin, had reminded him in a superficial way of Deborah, whose skin was the dusky hue of summer roses. All in all, it was a comparison that made him uneasy to dwell on.

On their return from Baguio Chase looked up the CBS Foreign Information Bureau in Manila, but all he learned from the one correspondent in the small office was that Deborah was on an assignment in Tokyo, covering the story of the new Japanese cabinet that had taken office and photographing its new premier, General Hideki Tojo. She was due back in Manila about the first of December.

Lying on his cot that night, he took out the picture of Deborah that Will had sent. He missed her more than he thought. She had a way of understanding him, of communicating with him without words, that no one else had. With reason, he told himself. They shared the same Navajo blood and many of the same memories. He told himself he would make another trip back to Manila when his next leave was due, about the fifteenth of December.

But his leave never came. For the Japanese chose the seventh of December, it was the eighth there in the Philippines, to surprise the world by bombing Pearl Harbor.

48

With the news of Japan's treacherous attack on Pearl Harbor, Nichols Field was immediately put on alert. On December 8, 1941, the air field was strafed by Japanese zero fighter planes, and Chase was transferred the same day with the 275th Materiel Squadron to the Bataan Peninsula for infantry combat.

The bark of the machine gun emplacements and the whoomph of bombs and anti-aircraft became part of an unbelievably bad dream for the American soldier. But the killing and dying was something Chase had lived with all his life, and the war's horrors could not touch him. What did was his worry for Deborah that ate away at him like a parasite. Was she still in Tokyo when war broke out in December—or was she in Manila where the nearby Nichols Air Base even now underwent daily bombings?

Any time Chase was in communication with Corregidor he asked Blue Tail what news there was of the American civilians trapped in Manila by the open outbreak of the war. When the chipmunklike Blue Tail learned that Chase was specifically interested in another Navajo, a female photographer, the Code Talker daily kept Chase apprised of the gossip flowing out of Manila. But always there was nothing about Deborah.

Chase spent the next four months on Bataan's front line with the walkie-talkie, coding and decoding vital messages out of Corregidor's rocky fortress, the last holdout of the Pacific fleet now that General MacArthur had withdrawn from Manila.

Because of his special status as a Code Talker, Chase sometimes enjoyed the luxury of an officer's pup tent during the times he was in communication with Corregidor. But more often he knew the miserableness of a foxhole.

"Man, how do you stand coming back to this dump?" Spec asked when Chase slid into the foxhole beside him. "Did ya ever realize if we had a few more of Hardheart's stripes we could be enjoying the good life of his cot and mosquito netting 'stead of this Prairie Dog Town?"

Hardheart, Colonel Rabinowitz, was disfigured by a purple, egg-sized birthmark on his left cheek, and Omaha swore the birthmark marked him as the meanest son-of-a-bitch in the army. The colonel had yet to eat Chase's ass out, so Chase could have cared less about the man's infamous reputation.

Chase drew on one of the few cigarettes left of the Red Cross boxes that had been salvaged. All about him phosphorus and occasionally fragment bombs exploded, lighting the night like the Fourth of July. At last he said, "If I get ready to walk out, Spec, I don't want to have to worry about Colonel Rabinowitz telling me I can't."

Spec laughed, his teeth a light in the temporary darkness. "Ohh, come on man." He swallowed another bite of his beef and stew C-rations and said, "I been thinking about walking outta here, too. Just haven't made up my mind where I wanna visit next."

But Chase was not joking. He stayed with the army only because he was drifting. There was nowhere special he wanted to go. It would be a good way to die—fighting—but he was not ready to die. At least not fighting in a white man's army.

Toward dawn Chase was roused from the foxhole and ordered to report to the colonel. The man looked like he had not slept since the siege of Bataan began. Worry showed in the eyes rimmed by crow's feet. For once Chase felt pity for an Anglo. Colonel Rabinowitz rubbed his forehead several times times as if trying to erase the worry. At last he looked up at Chase. "Strawhand, get a hold of Corregidor. Tell them the Nips have moved into the village of Pilar. Tell them we're retreating for the last time. I want their mortars ready to protect our flanks."

Blue Tail was a northern Navajo, and his Abathascan speech differed in the nasal intonation from that of Chase's, but Chase was able to make the message understood above the deafening sounds of shelling before the tent's equipment had to be loaded up and orders given to fall back.

From then on the retreat became a nightmare for the soldiers, but not the living horror it would be by May, three weeks later. There was little sleep, no food, and last-ditch efforts at fighting an enemy you could not see but could hear as their tanks mowed down the banyan and mango trees like ants plowing over grass blades.

There were simply no supplies left to feed the troops that had been separated from the main troops by the width of the Pacific Ocean. "We'll ultimately be starved into having to surrender," Colonel Rabinowitz told Chase when he relayed the last message there would be to Corregidor—*Proceeding into guerrilla warfare fighting.*

Chase looked at the man, wondering why the officer was bothering to explain it all to him, because he certainly felt

263

nothing of the colonel's patriotism. Then, seeing the weary eyes, the hands that twisted the fatigue cap, Chase knew the man was exorcising from his system what he felt to be a failure—the inevitable surrender of Bataan.

"But maybe we've accomplished our objective," Rabinowitz continued. "Maybe we've held out long enough to let our troops in Australia build up sufficiently to keep those damned Nips from taking it, too. With the largest harbor and ship facilities in the Orient, Australia is just what those penguins want."

You poor dumb animal, Chase thought. Do you think it matters to the Great White Father in Washington—or Bug-out Doug in Australia? What's one more, or a hundred more, or even a thousand more dead men? It's the system.

Before Chase signed off with Corregidor, he asked Blue Tail if there had been any word yet of Deborah DeBaca. He was hoping against the obvious that she had been able to get out with MacArthur and his troops.

A long pause, then, "Underground reports subject arrested as civilian in Manila. Nothing else is known."

Chase felt like a hand grenade had gone off in his gut. He saluted Rabinowitz, who understood nothing of the coded communication, and quit the tent. He was ready to fight now.

After that final communication with Corregidor, the order went out to abandon everything but the bare necessities. Explosions followed by leaps of fire meant that jeeps, transport trucks, and the large machine gun emplacements were being destroyed rather than left for the invading Japanese.

It seemed odd to Chase as the various units set out along the jungle trails to hear a soldier complain about the lack of shaving equipment or bedding. For Chase it meant freedom again. He carried his .30/.30 caliber rifle with bayonet, a bandolier of shells, and a .45 Colt automatic along with a water canteen, first-aid kit, and a mess kit with chlorine flakes. The other soldiers loaded themselves down with gas masks, digging tools, blankets, field glasses, and C-rations.

Chase moved easily, unhampered by the mosquitos. The insects did not seem to bother Omaha either, whose black skin camouflaged better with the jungle surroundings. "Just don't smile," Chase told him, "and they'll never see you."

While Rabinowitz consulted a grid map, Chase showed the other five men left in the platoon how to rub mud on their bodies to protect them from the insect bites and better camouflage their skin—something the army's field training had incredibly neglected in its effort to outfit the maximum amount of soldiers in the minimum amount of time.

"Where you go, Red man, I'm gonna go," Omaha said during one of the few rest periods allotted.

Chase sat with his back against a coconut tree, digging halfheartedly at the tin of Spam and wishing the coconuts were ripe. "Why?"

"'Cause you're a survivor," the black man said and swallowed another bite from his #2 can of fruit cocktail. "You don't let feelings mess up your instincts."

"Do you think the Japs—or anyone for that matter—really give a big shit about your black hide, Omaha? Or my red one?" Chase finished off the Spam in silence.

It was the last food the platoon was to have for many days as they were kept on the move constantly. The Japanese intensified their bombardments, but the heavy American mortars on Corregidor were silent for fear of hitting the dense concentration of United States troops which had been forced to retreat to the tip of the Bataan peninsula. Now Chase's troop was only a couple of miles from the sea and surrender. He could smell the salt in the air.

That night the flash of the batteries turned night into day with a barrage that lasted for two more nights straight. The third night toward dawn a large shell burst near and to the rear of Chase's column. Everyone scattered into the bushes, looking for a ditch. When Chase waded out, he could not find Omaha. Colonel Rabinowitz, looking worse with a gray, unshaven face and blood trickling down one sleeve, was bent over the black man. Omaha had been hit in the thigh with shrapnel. There was no corpsman with the diminishing platoon, and Chase had no sulfa powder left in his first-aid kit. His face was grim as he bandaged Omaha's leg.

Within minutes Rabinowitz had them on the trail again with the report that the enemy was within a mile. Chase and Spec supported Omaha between them. "Hey, men," Omaha wheezed, "don't be pigeons. I'm holding you back. Come on...drop me."

"We thought about it," Chase grinned. "But there's no special place we want to go right now, so we'll just stroll along with you."

"Listen, Omaha," Spec said, laboring under his load, "when we get back to the States—how about putting in a good word for me with those monkeys in Harlem?"

Then, within the space of seconds, there came the crushing sound of leaves and limbs and guns firing, and Japanese burst through the trees, surrounding the seven American soldiers.

Chase and Spec alternated with Rabinowitz in helping
265

Omaha walk. Four Japanese rode in a 1938 Mercury holding rifles on Chase and the other soldiers of his platoon who marched ahead of the car. There was a continuous column of Japanese troops moving south along the main road—long lines of tanks, cavalry, and infantrymen. Occasionally Chase glimpsed Bataan's west shoreline.

They had walked about fifteen miles, with other clumps of prisoners swelling the ranks to nearly a thousand, when Chase noticed a supply sergeant who had been at Corregidor lying face down with a gaping hole in the back of his head. Nearby, beneath the branches of a banyan tree, lay the nude body of a Filipino spread-eagled on his back. He had been bayoneted just beneath the rib cage, and fresh blood still poured from the open wound.

Chase looked away from the corpse. He could only hope Lelani escaped Corregidor before the Japanese took the island, for those Filipinos suspected of working for or helping the Americans would be the first to be executed.

From the little Bicol, the local Filipino dialect that Lelani had taught Chase, he learned that the military prisoners were destined for Cabanatuan, a large town near the center of Luzon, and the civilians were to be interned at the University of Santo Tomás in Manila.

By now most of the prisoners were terribly hungry, for it had been six or seven days since they had eaten. When Rabinowitz complained about the starvation to a Japanese lieutenant, saying, "It's against the International Law dealing with prisoners," the officer signaled to a guard who slammed his rifle butt against Rabinowitz's head.

After a day and a half of layover at the village of Mariveles, the Japanese began to get the prisoners lined up in columns of fours. Between Chase and Rabinowitz, they managed to get Omaha near the front of the column. To fall out of the columns would mean certain death.

The guards shouted at the men as though they were on a cattle drive headed for the slaughter pens. They beat the men with their rifle butts and jabbed them with their bayonets to get them in line in a hurry. They were giving orders in Japanese, and no one could understand them. Chase looked along the column at the men's faces. They were zombies.

"Tell me, Colonel Rabinowitz," Chase asked mockingly, "do you really think we will be treated in a decent and humane way—according to the International Law dealing with prisoners of war?"

The sun beating down was searing, and men began to fall by the wayside. At times Chase did not think he could continue to support the stumbling Omaha, but if Spec could, he knew he could. Except that his head had begun to ache; every time he moved, a hundred pounds of cement banged around inside it.

Occasionally a scream was heard as a soldier fell out of line and was either shot or bayoneted. One time Chase's sensitive nostrils flared at a particularly foul odor, and he looked down to discover he was walking on human flesh that belonged to corpses abandoned where they had fallen and been trampled by columns of trucks, tanks and cavalry.

After a while it was difficult for Chase to stand up. His head was dizzy with fever, and Rabinowitz took his place opposite Spec to support Omaha. When they halted about five that afternoon near Lubau, the colonel looked at Chase and told him he had malaria. "For someone used to the high, dry, arid places, this will be the worst on you."

"You don't look so good yourself, Colonel," Chase told him with a weak smile.

Across the road from where the columns had halted was a creek, little more than a trickle. Chase knew he would die if he did not bring his fever down, so without bothering to ask the guard he got up and filled his canteen. About that time some of the Filipino prisoners made a break for the nearby sugar cane fields, and the Japanese began firing into the fields. While they were kept busy gunning down the Filipinos, the creek was swamped with the prisoners, fighting for the water. The guards began shouting for them to get back into formation.

Chase gave some of his water to Omaha before pouring the rest into his hands and wetting his temples. Omaha was out of his head now with fever. Rabinowitz said, "We can't continue to carry him, or we'll also end up along the wayside."

Chase had known this, but Rabinowitz looked as if it cost him his soul to admit it. "Look, Colonel," Chase said, "if each one of us hangs onto the prisoner's belt in front, we might be able to keep up 'till we get where we're going."

It worked for the rest of the afternoon until halt was called for the evening. But next morning it was harder to get up and prepare for another long march. Some soldiers started to faint as they stood facing the hot sun again. Omaha was one of them and did not get up.

Chase began to laugh, and Rabinowitz's wiry brows arched over dust-caked eyes. "He's gone bananas with the fever, Colonel," Spec said.

"Oh, I'm not hysterical, Colonel. I was just remembering what an old shaman told me—that I'd go through the Long

Walk again, the one my people did a century before. Long Walk—hell, it's a death march. Wish I'd thought to ask him if I'd survive this."

The column moved out with the unconsious Omaha left behind. Rabinowitz's face resembled an Indian mask of carved wood, and Spec looked as if he were about to cry. Chase was too sick and weak from malaria to care at that point. But Rabinowitz made him hold onto his belt. When the prisoners were forced to halt, Chase would drop down on his haunches to rest, and Rabinowitz would haul Chase up by his belt when it was time to move out. "Get up! You dumb son-of-a-bitch! You stinking Indian! You going to die in the white man's army?"

Out of sheer anger Chase dug down inside himself for a last ounce of reserve and struggled to his feet. He wavered like a sapling in the wind.

In front of him a master sergeant staggered out of the column. The front guard turned around and fired. Then he ran over to the sergeant and jabbed his bayonet through his chest. Witnessing this, Chase made up his mind not to fall out of line.

But about noon of the next day he felt death near and just did not think he could go any further. He stumbled and let go of the belt before him. At the same moment he heard the dreaded flapping of the wings of an owl—death's messenger. In his delirium he held up his arms before his face to ward off the fearsome bird.

Suddenly the shadows of the wings lifted, and Chase thought he could see a *barrio* down the gravel road ahead. Deborah was standing near one of the palm-leafed huts holding out a package of cigarettes for him with teasing lips and laughing eyes. *I'll walk 'till I get there. After a cigarette I'll feel better.*

49

The Cabanatuan prison camp was built before the war near the foothills of Luzon's Sierra Madre mountains. It had been a United States agricultural experiment station, covering about one hundred acres. Army barracks built for a Filipino army division dotted the camp.

The barracks' roofs were made of cogon grass, and the walls were closed in with nipa. The floors had cracks between the bamboo slats to allow for air circulation. Several guard towers were stationed at intervals on the outside of the camp, and a high barbwire fence enclosed the prison compound.

This was the *barrio* that Chase could have sworn he saw on the Death March, although it had taken seven hours more to reach Cabanatuan. It had been seven hours of following a strange light and with his head buzzing. But he had made it.

Many times he wondered if the Death March had been worth it. For the first time in his life he was afraid. His own helplessness frightened him. He did not mind dying in combat like a warrior. But it was a depressing sight to see how the troops were. They had sore throats, bad colds, malaria, and dysentery. Not a single soldier was well. Chase's own weight of two hundred and five pounds fell to one hundred and thirty. With his six-foot-three frame, he looked like a cadaver used in medical classes.

Hair and beards were matted from sweat and dirt. Most skins were pale, but Chase's swarthy skin was a hue of gray. Everyone had puffy eyes. Spec could not wear his shoes because of the swelling in his feet and legs, caused by a lack of vitamin B known as beriberi. Many soldiers were simply too sick to get to formation for roll call each morning.

One of these was Rabinowitz. He had dysentery, and his stools were pure blood. And he could not make himself eat the things in his bowl of watered rice. Once Chase counted seventy-four items in his own bowl—mostly pebbles and worms. Since Chase was only seriously ill during the seizures of the malarial fever, each morning he would go look for Rabinowitz, who was housed in the separate officers' quarters, to be sure the colonel was not in the pile of men listed for burial.

The damp, foggy, or rainy days that kept the men wet from lack of shelter were the worst on Chase. Once when he lay too weak in his bay to move, Spec showed up with quinine, something that Chase had been unable to obtain. "How'd you get that?" he mumbled through the fog of his fever.

Spec smiled. "Through the black market." He took off his glasses and wiped the dirt off the lenses with his shirttail. "It's a trick you learn best on New York's streets. The stuff cost seven cigarettes."

"There's a Navajo word," Chase rasped. *"Ukehé.* It means thank you—and is almost never said. Except in return for very great favors. *Ukehé."*

"It comes hard, doesn't it, Red Man?" Spec asked. "Admitting that a white man might just be that—a man like yourself?" And he smiled again, showing the funny overlapping teeth. "But, God, I hope not. If I look like you right now, then I'll bypass the human race."

Chase grimaced and looked down at his long frame, seeing mostly bones, though there was a fresh scar, a two-inch purple welt just below his navel—engraved by a Japanese bayonet when he had not gotten into formation quickly enough. He knew his cheeks were sunken hollows and his eyes were deep sockets. Even his perspiration smelled different. That happened when the body underwent great changes.

But what was worse than the suffering of the body was the deterioration of the mind. Several men suggested that permission be obtained to use the books left in the Agricultural Station's library and hold classes. Rabinowitz volunteered to teach finance and Hebrew; an A&M student, fruit production; a private whose father had been a pastor, the Bible; and so on.

While Chase realized Navajo was practically impossible for someone to learn who was not actually living in a Navajo village and subject to the daily activities, he did have a working knowledge of Spanish. This and the little Bicol he knew he taught in exchange for banking and finance from Rabinowitz and law from a lieutenant who promised his students that when, not if, they were freed from the prison camp they would have no problem in taking their bar exams and getting a degree.

One evening when the lieutenant was going over the Code Napoleon and its merits versus the Justinian Code, the conversation somehow got off on International Law and the Japanese breach of this law, especially in the two camps of Cabanatuan and Santo Tomás.

"What I wouldn't give to be a civvie at Santo Tomás," a pimply-faced English private sighed. "It's been so long I can't remember what a round-eyed woman looks like!"

"You can bet, cobbers," an Australian officer said, "that whatever looks a woman had are gone after a month at the Santo Tomás resort!"

The last thing Chase was interested in was a round-eye. He had been burned once by one of the most beautiful of the round-eyes, and for all he cared their kind could rot in Santo Tomás. But the nagging knowledge that Deborah might be in Santo Tomás, if she was not already dead, was like a vise—ever tightening on his brain. Sometimes he thought he would go crazy with the thought. Only when he was in the depths of malaria's delirium was he free of anxiety. But the Australian's comment roused Chase from his lethargy.

He was going to escape—and take Deborah with him, if she was at Santo Tomás. How, he did not know.

With the advent of Christmas Deborah was more than ever on his mind. While the other soldiers sat and talked about their families back home, wondering how they were celebrating the holidays, it hit Chase hard that he had no family—unlesss he counted Deborah (and every member of the Tahtchini clan). It was the loneliest he could remember ever being.

It was about this same time, when he had learned as much as Rabinowitz could teach him about finance—and the passing of the New Year of 1943, which he did not even bother to celebrate with the others—that Chase began to realize he was being watched.

He felt this most acutely when he was on water detail. He hated burial detail, though it did not require as much work, so he had opted for the hauling of the water. He went to the large artesian wells for about three weeks before he began to notice, toward the middle of February, that one particular Filipino came more often than the others at this same time to fill the large jugs. Chase scrutinized the monkeylike man. The little eyes never wavered under Chase's penetrating regard. One day the small brown hand went up to the straw hat, removed it, and fanned the short, narrow face. More than once the fingers ran about the inside of the hat's band.

It could be his imagination that the man wanted to speak with him. It could be a trick. But since Chase had made up his mind to escape, he felt he had nothing to lose. The next time the monkey man went through the same routine—two days later—Chase moved nearer, setting down the water jugs he supported on a wooden yoke.

At the same time the man dropped his hat. Chase took the initiative and bent to pick it up. No gunfire erupted from the towers, but his back felt terribly broad at that moment and exposed. He began to hand the hat back to the little man when the man's eyes communicated with his. Chase looked inside the hat. In its crown was a folded, dirty piece of paper. Carefully Chase's large hand concealed the paper within his palm as he passed the hat back.

Chase waited an agonizing three hours until he found himself alone at the rear of a barrack. The note was from Lelani. *I can have parao for yu. Say to Hector wen yu nid it.*

Slowly Chase shredded the note, feeling a deep sense of humility. His mind ticked off the people who had befriended him, none of them of the *Dine'é:* first Will; then Spec—the Yankee; Omaha—the Negro; Rabinowitz—the Jew; Lelani—a

Filipino, and on and on. And then there were his own people, Blue Tail and steadfast Deborah.

Chase began to plan his escape. A small sailboat like a *parao* would get him off Luzon but where then, he did not know. And he knew little about sailing.

The Japanese constantly patrolled the islands, shelling them and requisitioning what food the Filipinos were able to grow, since the mountainous islands of Japan did not supply enough food—and especially little food at wartime when much of the Japanese labor had been diverted to military endeavors. So escape from Luzon Island appeared hopeless. Yet Chase was determined.

The first thing he did was to arrange to exchange places for the garden detail. After the next rain he calculated it would be easy to dig under the barbwire. The following day he returned the note to Hector with instructions. *At dawn after next rain*, he wrote in Bicol, which he figured was as badly spelled as Lelani's English, *leave clothing at well*. He'd worry about getting a sailboat later.

Taking someone with him could seriously handicap his escape, but nevertheless Chase decided to ask Spec and Rabinowitz, both of whom were on garden duty already. He went to them three days later as clouds billowed on the horizon. "I'm leaving tonight," he told Spec. "Do you want to go with me?"

Spec moved along the row of sweet potatoes, *camotes,* giving no indication he had heard. But a few minutes later he said, "Man, I got a sure thing here—a roof over my head and food to eat, if you can call it that. Out there—" he shrugged his bony shoulders, "it ain't so sure. I better take my chances here and hope for liberation."

When Chase asked Rabinowitz, who was on his knees weeding the rows, the colonel smiled wistfully. "Nothing I'd like better. But for every officer who escapes, the Nips execute another one. I can't do that to the men, Strawhand."

Chase was tempted to ask, "Do you think another officer would give you the same consideration?" but did not. He had learned that the possibility did exist.

"If anyone has a chance, you do," Rabinowitz said. "You almost look like a Filipino. You could mix with the natives, but I'd likely be spotted right off." The colonel looked around and deemed it safe to hold out his hand. "If you make it back—don't let your distrust stand in the way of making something of your life."

* * *

As Chase had hoped, the ground was soft enough following the evening rain to tunnel out. The guards were nearly asleep at their posts, and Chase half-crawled, half-wriggled until he had made it to the safety of the artesian wells. There on the stone ledge was clothing—a shirt of mosquito netting, ragged and patched white cotton trousers, and a floppy straw hat. Beneath the clothing was a bolo, a deadly-looking machete.

While Chase stripped in the shadows of mango trees, the little monkey man, Hector, suddenly materialized. "You will need a guide," he announced to Chase in almost perfect English.

Chase concealed his surprise. "I'm going to Santo Tomás for a woman."

Hector nodded his head sagely as if Chase's plan of action was acceptable and even expected. "We have contacts there who will help us."

After burying Chase's clothing, the two set out at a trot in the predawn darkness, keeping the rising sun to their left as they made their way deeper and deeper into the lowland forests. Chase figured there were ninety miles more or less of jungle between him and Manila. Seven days between him and Santo Tomás.

That first day was the easiest. Chase judged they made twenty miles that day. Although Hector looked like a monkey, he did not chatter like one, and it was only through the occasional words exchanged between the two that Chase learned the man was an educated Filipino guerrilla. Hector found pineapple to eat, though the fruit was still a little green. And once, when Chase almost stepped on a cobra, Hector's bolo neatly sliced away the head.

The second day the heat and the exertion began getting to him. They came across a farmer's *camote* patch, and Chase ate the *camotes* so quickly his stomach began cramping. "You are suffering from protein poisoning," Hector advised him. That same night, barking geckos, or lizards, warned the two men of an approaching crocodile while they slept.

Toward the fifth day, as they dropped down into the rice paddies that marked the outskirts of Manila, they came upon more and more people making their way in *carretas* filled with abaca, rice, tobacco, and bamboo mats. Once they stepped off a main trail and flattened themselves against an earthen embankment as a troop of Japanese cavalrymen passed by. At a whim the Japanese officer arrested the Filipinos moving ahead of Chase and Hector.

Later that day they came upon a lone man in a *carromata*, a pony-driven cart loaded with lumber. Chase and Hector followed the man for nearly three miles, then when the man left the road to kneel at one of the lazy creeks that wound through the steamy lowlands, Chase watched as Hector took the hilt of his bolo and struck the man across the head. "Let's go," he said, grabbing at the pony's reins.

With Hector pulling and Chase following behind the cart, they entered Manila's outskirts, which was mostly nipa and bamboo huts with oyster-shell windows, then progressed past the business district and warehouses. After they crossed over the Pasig bridge, which teamed with Chinese, Japanese, and Filipinos, they were in the older, walled part of the city, the Intramuros, where lay the famed shopping district. Anything one wanted could be found there, from precious ice cream or dental work to prostitution.

Chase had no eye for the shapely girls in their slit silk dresses nor the painting of the strawberry ice cream on a storefront plaque. He shoved his way behind the cart through the crowds until Santo Tomás came into view. The internment camp looked like what it was—a university campus with ancient brownstone buildings crawling with ivy, a university older than any in the United States, twenty-five years older than Harvard.

Undaunted by the fierce-looking guards with their .27 caliber rifles, the little monkey man lined up with other carts, apparently bringing the daily food supplies. When their turn came, Hector rattled off something to the head guard, and the Japanese soldier pointed a finger at two isolated buildings.

"What did you tell him?" Chase asked after they had trudged on through the gates.

"I told him I was delivering lumber for the new barracks they're building for the women."

"How did you know they were building new barracks?"

"They're not, but the guards don't know that."

Chase grunted, amazed at the man's temerity.

The men and women they occasionally passed seemed in somewhat better condition than the Cabanatuan prisoners, though they still had the zombie, glaze-eyed look and were pitifully thin. "Getting in is not difficult," Hector said. "Getting her out will be."

Hector stopped before the women's dormitories and lit the stub of a cigarette, took two puffs, and rubbed it out on the pavement with a bare sole. Chase watched him, waiting. Soon, from the nearest building, an old Filipino woman, who was almost bald, hobbled out, using a bamboo stick for a cane. She bent and picked up the flattened stub, saying, "You should not waste anything, old man."

Hector shrugged. "The day is too hot to smoke."

The woman, whose face was a mass of lines, peered out at him. "It will not always be so," she replied at last.

"We are looking for a woman," Hector said more softly. "An American called Deborah DeBaca."

The woman jerked her head toward one of the buildings. "She's there. You want her."

"Yes, get her," Hector said.

The four or five minutes that Chase waited seemed the longest in his life. Then Deborah, dressed in a loose cotton shirt and baggy pants, crossed the lawn toward him, moving in slow steps that lacked her former gracefulness.

When she was closer, Chase realized her hair was not rolled atop her head but had been wacked off. She was terribly emaciated, as shriveled as the old woman, but there was an iridescent quality about her skeletal form, like an Indian who has fasted for a religious revelation.

She looked suspicious and cautious of the two men. When Chase shoved the floppy straw hat back from his face and she was near enough to see, she halted as if frozen.

50

"It is good to see you, little sister."

Stunned, unable to move, Deborah's great eyes looked at Chase through a shimmering mist in disbelief.

"We must go!" Hector said, snapping the dreamlike quality of the moment for the two who had traveled halfway around the world to meet each other again. The Filipino took his hat off and flopped it over Deborah's head, and Chase's large hands encircled the wisp of her waist and set her atop the load of lumber.

It was a tense moment as the wagon moved toward a different gate than the one they had entered by and halted at the check-point, but Hector simply told the guard they were hauling off the lumber. When he even paused to ask the guard for a cigarette, perspiration broke out on Chase's forehead. He wanted to curse at the guerrilla's rash bravado. But the guard merely replied, "Move along, old man!"

Chase never dared look up at Deborah who sat perched on the lumber like a little boy. Once out of the main part of Manila, they threaded their way through the crowds that jostled for

275

room along the narrow streets that led down toward the spacious harbor. It was out along one of the longest piers in the world that Hector stopped before a *barrota*, a fishing boat, of about three tons with housing of thatched coconut palm leaves across its middle. Once again the little man talked to an old woman, this time a *tao* with a flat nose and broad lips. She nodded, pointing to the sailboat and talking.

"We're going to Mindanao," Hector said, as he helped Chase and a dazed Deborah aboard the sailboat, while the *tao* woman plodded back up the pier with the *carromata*. "A guerrilla there will see that you are well hidden until the next submarine out of Australia puts in—maybe a month, maybe more."

Chase and Deborah sat braced in the *barrota* as Hector maneuvered it through the honeycomb of Japanese tankers and destroyers in the bay and past the prewar ships, looking like rust-streaked skeletons, wrecked on the reefs off Luzon's coast. Out on the open sea now, the fresh salt wind hit the *barrota*'s three passengers as the craft swooped and dived over the waves of the Mindoro Strait.

Chase watched Deborah, the bridge of his hawklike nose furrowed with worry. Her face was ashen as if she might be seasick. But that was not what troubled him. She treated him as if he were a stranger. She kept her face averted from his gaze, looking instead out toward the islands the outrigger skirted as it sailed southward.

It was a perilous journey of eleven days. The wind and salt burnt their skin, and waves washed over them. They went without food and water for as much as three days one time, for Hector did not feel it safe to put in at some of the islands they passed for fear of Japanese patrol boats.

Deborah did not speak much. Once, the rig was caught on the edge of a typhoon that lashed at the *barrota* like it was a leaf in a dust devil. Deborah choked under the onslaught of wind and water, and Chase could see the fear on her face. But for the first time she smiled. "It's not exactly a pleasure cruise, is it?" she shouted at him.

Toward the end of the tenth day Chase was ready to order Hector to put in at one of the islands, it did not matter which one, and surrender. They were blistered, bleary-eyed, and hungry. Then on the eleventh day, when they were passing through the Bohol Strait into the Mindanao Sea, Hector informed them that part of their journey was nearing its end. "The guerrilla force operates in Mindanao under Colonel Herrera. He will see that you are kept hidden until the rescue sub arrives."

As they neared the shore the *barrota* tacked endlessly. The coral reef sucked and hissed around them. When they were within a half-mile of shore, Hector put them out. They were inside the reef where the water was quiet. Chase shook Hector's hand and thanked him. Another man, not a Navajo, had helped him.

Chase and Deborah watched with something akin to despair as Hector put out to sea again. When the craft was a speck bobbing on the waves, Chase turned to Deborah. He held out his hand. "Ready?"

She nodded, her eyes wide and serious. "It doesn't seem real, does it? We've come together on the other side of the earth to be marooned on an island—sort of like the Swiss Family Robinson story, isn't it?"

Her hand was small in his, trusting. He frowned, and she asked, "What is it?"

He shook his head. "Listen—a motorboat. Did your Swiss Family Robinson have Nippies for neighbors?" As they began to wade ashore, he tugged at her hand, hurrying her. The waves slapped against their thighs and impeded their progress. The rumble of the motorboat increased. The forested shoreline was still too far away! Chase shoved Deborah into the water. With the ocean salt and Deborah struggling, it was almost impossible for him to keep the two of them submerged beneath the knee-deep water.

When Deborah stopped fighting him, he was afraid she might be drowning. He shot to his feet, jerking her up with him and expecting any second the bullets to riddle the water about them. Even as he tugged her limp body ashore, he cast a heartsick look over his shoulder, knowing that their escape had failed.

No military launch but an outdated, warped-looking motorboat rode the waves not a hundred yards from Chase. A lone man sat in the boat, watching. "Hey," he shouted, "I been waiting for you. You late!"

The island of Mindanao lay only degrees from the equator, and Chase estimated that the temperature must have been at least a hundred and the weather as sultry as a humidor. But the man, clothed only in an abaca breechcloth, wore on his head a Japanese aviator's fur-lined helmet.

Deborah began choking and gasping, and Chase grunted in relief that both situations had worked out so well. He staggered ashore with her in his arms and dropped her on the white, warm sand. Behind closed lids he could hear Deborah next to him, breathing more normally, and the slap of oar paddles against the water; then the scraping on the sand

277

as the man dragged the boat up out of the water.

Chase opened his eyes and looked into a young brown face. The man could not have been more than twenty-five. "Where you been?"

"A storm," Chase managed and laid his head back down, then raised it again. He squinted at the man. "How did you know when to expect us?"

The man's gapped-tooth smile was enigmatic. "The bamboo telegraph, it tells everything."

"I should have known," Chase said, smiling for the first time.

"What? What?"

"An old trick of my people," Chase explained and laid his head down once more, closing his eyes. The year's stay at the Cabanatuan Resort had cost him more in strength than he had realized.

"We go now. A patrol boat comes soon—in two hours, maybe more, maybe less."

"Just leave me alone," Deborah moaned when Chase tried to stand her on her feet. "I want to sunbathe."

The man, Herrera, looked at Deborah as if she had lost her mind. "She been in Santo Tomás, yes?"

"She's always been a little crazy," Chase said and swung her over his shoulder like a sack of sugar.

He followed the man, who carried a bolo in one hand and a carbine in the other, into the primeval forest that grew darker the deeper in they went, so that the bright March sun faded into a twilight. In places moisture dripped from the flower-crowned trees. Herrera hacked away with his bolo at the encroaching tangle of trees, shrubs, and creeping vines. It was a never-never land.

Then the three came into a clearing where stood on stilts a large nipa hut made of East Indian palm leaves. When Chase and Deborah followed the man up the bamboo steps to the veranda, a duck waddled out from beneath the hut, quacking at their trespassing.

"No eat Cebu," Herrera said. "Him good duck. Make eggs." He spit a stream of red betelnut juice over the bamboo balustrade, and the duck went flapping back under the hut.

Inside the hut mats served as both couches and beds, and a kerosene tin with a hole punched in its side was the lamp. Toward the rear of the small room netting draped from the ceiling like a circus tent. The hut was otherwise empty except for a couple of small sacks filled with staples—tea leaves and rice—and a military boot with a hole in its sole which lay in one corner.

278

"American pilot," Herrera said, following Chase's gaze. "Him here last. Maybe month, maybe more before sub come for him."

Somehow the knowledge that other refugees had inhabited the hut not long before made the jungle hideaway seem less formidable. Still, as Chase and Deborah stood on the veranda and watched the mass of verdant trees swallow up Herrera, they became gradually uncomfortable in each other's presence, as uneasy as two cats.

"Are you hungry?" Deborah asked, for lack of something else to say or because there was so much to be said that could not be.

Chase shook his head. "Just tired, I guess."

Together they re-entered the sanctum of their hut. Chase stretched out on one mat and Deborah on the other, their heads at an angle to one another. Chase buried his face in his arms, and for a long while there was only the noise of the forest animals to fill the room.

He thought Deborah had drifted off to sleep, but she broke the silence, her voice coming lazily from the well of her arms. "Chase, you never ever told me what your secret name is, not in all the years we've known each other."

Chase chuckled. "By this time I don't guess the evil spirits can do any more to me if they know my secret name than they have already. It's Black Wolf."

He raised up on one elbow and looked at her scrawny, child-sized body, and his heart cramped for the one person who had been his friend for so long. Except for the porcupine haircut, Deborah looked much as she had that first time he had seen her at the boarding school. All eyes in a doll-like body. Alone and frightened but smiling anyway. "What's yours?"

Deborah turned her head toward him and grinned. "War Dance. All good Navajo girls have to have the word *war* somewhere in their name, you know."

"I know. I think my father's mother's secret name was War in the Face. Her face did look like a war hatchet had caught it."

They laughed together, and the tension was gone. From secret names their talk turned to the secret ceremonies of the Kachina Dancers a boy or girl went to when they reached puberty. It was like a floodgate had been opened, and all the trivial memories of the past poured forth with laughter, and exclamations, and questions.

Neither Greg Red Bird nor Christina Raffin was mentioned.

The marathon talk went on steadily for a week while Chase

and Deborah did nothing but intermittently rest and eat the eggs the duck supplied (Deborah called the female duck "Donald") and the occasional fruit—mostly mangos and coconuts—found close to the hut, for Hector had warned them about straying too far in case of running into a Japanese patrol.

The talking was like a cleansing of the mind, like a visit to the psychiatrist's couch where all the secret little fears and sins were confessed. Chase admitted to being afraid of closed-in places since his internment in Cabanatuan, and Deborah confessed to stealing another Indian girl's tortoiseshell comb at boarding school.

With the cleansing of the mind returned the normal desire for the cleansing of the body. Although they feared being spotted by a patrol boat, they nevertheless made their way back to the ocean at the end of the first week.

Their skins and scalps were encrusted with a year's accumulation of dirt that could not be easily scrubbed away, and the saltwater irritated their skin, already damaged by improper diet, especially Deborah's whose texture was finer. "Oh, Chase, it stings!" she wailed as he held her head between his knees and knuckle-scrubbed her scalp. She shoved him off her and scrambled to her feet in the water. "My hair's clean! I swear!"

Then she performed his ablutions with a scrap of cloth, scouring his body, which was clad only in tattered khaki pants. Chase lay lazily on the sand, half in, half out of the water, as he relaxed under the ministration of her caring hands. Her fingers softly traced the ropelike welt that scarred his belly. "Wouldn't it be easier," she said sadly, "if the only scars we had were the ones that showed?"

At the contact of her fingers, Chase's stomach muscles popped like an electric wire had fallen on them. "Don't!" he said.

Deborah looked at him with laughter in her eyes. "You're ticklish!" Her fingers began to play along his ribs, but when he swiftly rolled away, laughing now, and came to his feet, she jumped up also, alert for sign of retaliation.

With only a week of fruit and eggs in her stomach, her full cheeks already glowed with color, her eyes shone, and her tiny body was once more filling out. Her wet hair was plastered in a gamine style to her small head. Standing warily before Chase, with the wet cotton blouse and pants clinging to her breasts and molding her waist and hips, she had no idea of the tantalizing picture she presented.

The sudden desire that jangled Chase's senses surprised him . . . not only because it signified the return of his sex drive, but also because it dangerously signaled something else. The realization of what he was thinking flashed through his brain like a red alert light. "We better get back to the Waldorf," he snapped.

The moonlight that night dappled the hut's bamboo floor. It was a great tropical moon, the kind of moon, Chase thought, that could not be seen anywhere else on earth. He and Deborah lay in the hut's darkness and talked softly about more recent experiences, skirting the tales of horror each could tell.

"I feel so strange now," Deborah said with a small laugh, "like not knowing what to do with myself. For a year now I've had other people tell me what to do, when to eat, when to bathe. You know, Chase, maybe once every month or so we were allowed a shower. There were women there—mostly wives of foreign engineers who had operated the mines here before the outbreak of the war—some of those women lost so much weight they held their stomachs over their arms while they bathed! And after a while you could tell by looking at the legs who were the Caucasians and who were the Malayans, even though by that time we all had faded skin—the Anglo women couldn't shave and all had long hair on their legs."

Involuntarily Chase thought of Deborah's legs. Even though she wore the trousers, he knew they would be smooth.

"And after about three months, I stopped having my per—" She broke off, and Chase sensed her embarrassment. "How were things at Cabanatuan?" she asked softly. "We heard they were awful there."

Like Deborah, there were some things too terrible to talk about, and Chase picked the trivial. "About the same. Except we had no showers or baths. When the rains came, we'd run outside and stand. It seemed at the time that nothing could be more glorious than the rain. To beat the boredom we held races for the tics and leeches that crawled up the walls."

They talked that night until dawn, letting the small talk bridge the gap of time and pain and act like a balm to the sore. Both admired and wondered at the other's tenacity, the ability and will to survive under horrifying circumstances.

Chase told her how, when he arrived in the Philippines, he had tried to get in touch with her at the CBS Foreign Information office, but she had just left for Tokyo. And she related to Chase about Will's letter telling her that Chase was also stationed in the Philippines.

She did not tell him that it was only the hope that he might be alive and only miles away that kept her from taking her own life, as a few of the Red Cross nurses and engineers' wives had during that time. Somehow it seemed perfectly right and natural that he should have rescued her—just as he had taken care of her when she was a child. Only she was not a child anymore. And she was disturbingly aware of Chase as only a woman could be.

The large orange moon, the heavy scent of the tropical flowers, the lulling sound of the surf pounding against the beach—all the ingredients united into a bewitching potion too dangerous to taste. Deborah knew now the temptation of Eve—one drink and she was lost.

In her frantic effort to put Chase back into the perspective of her tribal brother, she said the forbidden word. "Christina—are you still in love with her?"

In the silence that followed Chase tried to analyze his thoughts. He had not let himself think about Christina Raffin much in over a year. He did not know how Deborah could know about his feelings for Christina, but he supposed it was obvious to her. Deborah had always possessed an uncanny insight when it came to his feelings and thoughts.

"I don't know," he answered, trying to be honest. "I suppose it's a love-hate feeling I have for her—something that I can't get out of my blood any more than I can the damned malaria I contracted."

He turned his head to look at her darkened form, streaked by shafts of moonlight. "And you—is that Navajo sculptor still in your wedding plans?"

"I suppose so," Deborah answered with equal carefulness.

51

It started out with trifling arguments. Three weeks of isolation—broken only by Herrera's occasional visits to deliver what supplies he could scrounge up—had taken their toll on Chase's and Deborah's nerves.

One morning, after one of Herrera's visits the day before, Chase stepped out onto the veranda, feeling really good about the day. Herrera had brought a razor, soap, two bottles of rice sake, and three Hershey's chocolate bars...and the news that the American Pacific Force had taken Guadalcanal in its drive to retake the Philippines.

But Chase's smile faded as his gaze fell on Deborah below, kneeling at the small fire with the duck flapping and quacking about her. Not only had Deborah tied her shirttail beneath her high breasts, revealing her small waist and flat stomach, but she also had whacked off her trousers high on her thighs. Standing on the platform, Chase could look down the cleavage of her melon-ripe breasts.

Sensing his presence, she looked up to meet his frown. "What's taking you so long?" he asked sourly.

Deborah looked back to the duck egg she fried in coconut oil. "I had trouble getting the fire going—the Japanese matches don't work very well." She looked up again. The usually tilted corners of her mouth for once pulled down in irritation. "Besides, you didn't cut enough kindling—which I might remind you, you promised to do yesterday!"

"You're beginning to sound like a nag—I feel sorry for Red Tail!"

"Red Bird!" Deborah shouted after Chase as he disappeared back into the hut. "And I think Christina's lucky she didn't get stuck here with you. You bore me, do you hear!"

Chase reappeared with the bolo and looked down at the scantily dressed child-woman. *I'd like to bore you;* then he wished he could wipe the thought from his mind like chalk from a blackboard. But he could not. The thought had taken root and now grew in the dark recesses of his brain like the poisonous mushroom, and it was fed by merely the sight of her—and the sound of her voice and the smell of her skin and hair. She pervaded the hut even when she was not in it. "I'm going for your damn precious kindling," he said and descended the steps two at a time. "And get some clothes on!" he snapped when he passed by, not looking at her.

"And you think you're Adolph Menjou in that breech-cloth?" she shrilled after him. When he continued on, Deborah picked up the cracked skillet and hurled it at him.

The skillet missed, but some of the hot grease popped on his back. Chase dropped the bolo and whirled. The fury in his black eyes glowed hotter than the coals in the fire. Deborah backed away. Chase went after her, diving for her legs as she turned to run.

Her breath exploded from her lungs as she hit the ground. "If you were a man, I'd slug you!" Chase said, straddling her.

"You're no more a man than—than that duck Herrera calls a male!"

Chase's fist jerked back...and halted. In that second all his keen senses prickled with the acute consciousness of the woman he rode like a stud a mare.

Deborah blinked back her tears. "Why can't we just be friends like we used to be?" she whispered, unaware still of the war that raged between Chase's conscience and the desire

283

that enflamed him. "Why do we have to be either enemies or..." Her voice faltered.

"Lovers?" Chase finished for her, his face cast in a steely mold. Wordlessly he staggered from her and picked up the bolo as he left the clearing.

That night they tried to pretend that nothing had happened. Deborah prepared brown rice with tea leaves, while Chase turned his attention to the shirt of mosquito netting he was fashioning. The flare of the burning copra cast a soft intimate light over the small room. Like a couple who had been married for years they talked of unimportant things— the approach of the monsoon season, Chase's sudden craving for fresh cow's milk, Deborah's desire for a mirror.

After dinner Chase broke out the sake. "Here's to rescue," he said, and the two touched their sake-filled, hollowed coconut shells together in a toast.

"What do you plan to do when you get back to the States?" Deborah asked after a couple of sips from the shell. The sake tasted terrible, she thought, but it was a treat, something special to break the monotony of their days and nights.

Chase laughed, and as always Deborah was startled by his laughter, maybe because it came so rarely in that harsh countenance. "You won't believe it," he said, taking another swallow. "I'm going to use the back pay I've got coming to me and open a bank. I learned a little bit about financing from a colonel at Cabanatuan."

Chase had surprised himself, because until the words were actually spoken he had not really given it that much serious thought. But now, on reflection, it seemed like a pretty good idea. He didn't know of any other Indian-managed banks. "And you?"

Deborah took another sip of the sake. It really wasn't so bad. "I still intend to have a painting career one day. My own one-woman exhibition." She shrugged and her lips turned upward in a small smile. "We can at least dream, can't we?" She lifted her shell and said, "Here's to our dreams—banking and painting," and gulped the last of the sake.

She knelt to refill her shell, and Chase noticed the way her cut-offs cupped her small, firmly rounded buttocks. He felt the hardening in his crotch. If rescue was much longer in coming, he told himself, he'd have to seek out one of the stocky Manobo women, though the idea of contributing his head to the headhunters' soup did not seem worth his body's demand for sexual release.

Sometime after midnight, when their bursts of conversation began to lengthen with interludes of drowsiness, they finished off the first bottle of sake and retired to their separate mats. But just as Chase was falling into a deep, pleasant sleep, the mosquitos began to attack. Chase suddenly realized that in his drunken stupor he had forgotten to draw the mosquito net closed.

Deborah was slapping at her arms and face, and Chase felt like he was being eaten alive by the swarm. His usual natural immunity seemed to have disappeared. When Deborah scrambled to her knees and headed for the door, Chase yanked her back. "It's worse outside!"

He dropped the abaca cloth over the doorway and pulled her back to her mat, cursing as he stumbled over one of the coconut shells. It seemed his feet would not move properly, and he could have sworn the mats were in a different place.

Grimly he eyed the one shroud of netting that hung from the thatched roof, then pulled Deborah inside along with the two mats.

"Just one snow—that's all I ask, just one good snow," Deborah mumbled, drowsy with the effects of the sake, as she stretched out on the mat alongside Chase.

Now that she had abbreviated her attire, Chase could feel her bare skin against his, and his hands slipped around her waist, touching skin as satiny and dusky as a summer rose. He waxed into heat, the desire igniting in him like a wildfire.

Deborah stirred and stiffened as Chase's urgent hands cupped her breasts, burning her skin through the thin cotton material. His thumb and forefinger captured one nipple, then slipped down the center of her small rib cage to the band of her cut-offs.

In the dark he could not see her stricken face as the realization of what he intended seeped through the intoxicated haze of her mind. "I thought I'd never make it through the day without touching you," Chase rasped, not fully aware it was his own passion-drugged voice he heard. His fingers snapped the waistband open and slid down the soft, flat stomach to entwine in the fine curly hair as his mouth closed savagely over her soft, protesting lips.

Deborah wrenched her mouth away and murmured something about incest. His fingers bit into her arms as she tried to twist free. "Chase, don't!" she begged. "You'll destroy us!" But it was too late. He was already past caring. All reasoning was lost in the lust that swept through him.

Deborah beat on him with clenched fists and cursed him. A fear engulfed her that went beyond the perimeter of physical terror. But when Chase yanked away the clothing that stood between them, she gave up her fight, knowing there was nothing she could do. She resigned herself to enduring the hard, thrusting ravishment of her body. In the absence of her fury, a small knot of pleasure that she tried to deny spawned in her belly. It expanded, its intensity convulsing her so that she whimpered with the strange torment and writhed beneath the driving force of Chase's violent passion. At last the knot gave way, releasing her from the unbearable pain of the sustained pleasure, and she pulled him to her.

Chase went out onto the veranda to cool the fire in his flesh. He could not believe what he had done. One hand rubbed at his eyes, oblivious to the few stings of the remaining mosquitos that had not departed with the swarm. He cast a troubled glance back at Deborah. She lay there, face down, unmoving.

He turned away, both ashamed and confused, for he could have sworn she enjoyed the act. Yet he could feel the hate pulsating within the room. He dropped down on his haunches, thinking, figuring. He sensed vaguely that something was lost, but he could not identify it. "Deborah," he began, "I don't—"

Instinct made him look around. Deborah had sprung to her feet, grabbing at the bolo in her ascent, and rushed at him. In that split second he was reminded of their ancestors whose fierce warrior blood ran in both their veins.

He dodged her first thrust and slid in under her arm and behind her, seizing her about her waist from the rear. She fought and struggled. Her arms and legs flailed the air until she was out of breath and her fury subsided. The bolo clattered on the floor. Chase was sure he heard a strangled sob, but there followed only the muted chatter of the forest's birds.

"Now listen to me, Deborah," he said, exasperated. "I'm sorry about what happened. I'd change it if I could. I can't. But I promise you it'll—"

"You bastard!"

She squirmed, and Chase dropped her, more from surprise than from her squirming. She whirled on him. Small of stature but filled with a regal dignity her anger could not alter, she stood facing him. Her eyes were bright brown stones. "If you had wanted me—for me—it might have been different. But to violate me out of sheer animal lust—when you've never gotten Christina Raffin out of your mind, her name still on your lips even—"

Deborah's anger was raging once more like a second volcanic eruption. She stopped and started again. "You don't need

286

to promise me anything, because if you so much as touch me, Chase Strawhand, I'll not rest until your bones are buried!"

52

The disappearance of Donald the next morning was as good an excuse as any for Chase and Deborah to escape the hut's confinement as they searched the area's undergrowth in ever-widening circles. Chase was always careful to keep Deborah in sight but made no effort to break her tight-lipped silence.

He was confused by her anger, for despite the fact he had forced himself on her, he was very aware of her active participation toward the last. And he did not think her anger had very much to do with the taboo of tribal incest. Chase's irritation grew with the passing of the morning. How could Deborah condemn him when she had enjoyed it? How could she bring up his involvement with Christina when she was engaged to Red Bird?

At last he convinced Deborah to give up the hunt, that Donald had probably followed the mosquito swarm the night before in hopes of another insect feast. Reluctantly they turned their footsteps toward the hut. The bleakness in Deborah's eyes worried Chase, but any effort he made to console her he knew would be rejected.

When they arrived at the hut Herrera stood in the clearing, shifting from one foot to the other as Donald pecked furiously at his toes. "Donald!" Deborah cried and ran to gather the duck in her arms.

"Where you been?" Herrera exclaimed. "I lookee everywhere! I told you no leave!" He thrust a pair of field glasses at Chase. "Lookee! Now we have trouble!"

Chase raised the binoculars and looked out to sea. In the gulf armed launches, light cruisers, and other transports, all bearing the flag with the red sun, lurked like sea serpents.

Herrera wiped at the sweat that rolled down out of the fur-lined helmet onto his brown face. "If they land, you must hide. I come back tomorrow. Maybe later, maybe before, and take you another place."

Both watched him leave, dreading being alone with each other again. Dismally Chase wondered how much longer the two of them could keep their sanity before they tore each other apart. He watched Deborah enter the hut, noting the scornful tilt of her chin, and knew that help had to come soon. He couldn't sleep in the same room with her without wanting her, without taking her.

But that night he found he did not have to worry about his raging lust, for chills and fever claimed his body, racking him and leaving him weak. It had been almost three months since his last bout with malaria, and he had hoped he had licked the disease with the quinine tablets Spec had gotten for him.

Deborah could hear Chase groan and toss on his mat. Even from the distance of inches that separated them she could feel the fever that flared off him like heat off a copra torch. Touching his scalding skin, she despaired.

She took the precious water she had boiled to desalt it and another patch from her trouser bottoms and bathed his forehead. He shook with the chills. There was no blanket, and she could only lie next to him, holding him close and cursing—him, Christina, Greg, the Japs, and everyone she could think of.

As soon as dawn came Deborah set out from the hut, leaving Chase in a restless, drenched-sweat sleep. She recalled that the bark of certain trees, particularly those with fragrant flowers like lilac blossoms, were used to make quinine. It was worth a try, she thought. She could not let Chase suffer even though she despised the bastard.

So many of the trees had fragrant flowers, but she settled on one old tree with a wrinkled bark. As she peeled away a section with the bolo, she heard distant voices—speaking in Japanese. They had come ashore during the night!

As quickly as she could run with the entrapping undergrowth, she returned to the hut. Donald hissed a welcome, but she ran past him without stopping to pat him. Chase was awake but looked much worse. Beneath the flush of the fever his usually swarthy skin was a pasty white. "We've visitors! The Japanese!"

Chase fell back on the mat. "Shit!" He opened his eyes and fixed Deborah with a cold glare. "Get out! Now!"

Deborah planted her hands on her hips. "No. I'm not leaving without you."

"I'm coming," Chase sighed. "But I'll hold you up. And there's things that need to be done here first."

"Then I'll do them," she said stubbornly. "But before that I'm hiding you. Let's go!"

"Get out of here, you dumb slut!" Chase roared.

Deborah did not flinch. "I'm not leaving unless you do. I don't give a damn about your hide, Chase Strawhand, but I need you to survive in this hellhole. So the Japanese might as well take me now."

288

Chase cursed her with every name he could think of as Deborah half-dragged, half-pulled him down the steps and out of the clearing into the tangled web of leaves and vines. Leaving him in the concealment of a bamboo thicket that bordered on the channel of a mangrove swamp, she hurried back to the hut and collected everything that pointed to recent human habitation—the bolo, fresh fruit, sacks of rice and tea leaves, clothing. Panting, she made several trips. On her last trip she scooped up dirt and threw it in a fine spray over the floor.

In the clearing she used brush to erase the footprints. She took one last look at the place. She hoped it looked as if it had been in disuse. Her teeth tugged at her bottom lip. It had been a place, a space out of time, that she would remember until she was a very old woman who knew all of life's secrets.

She turned to leave, and Donald, quacking, came from beneath the hut to follow her. "Oh, you silly duck!" she cried, gulping back the knot in her throat. She stooped and held it in her arms. "I can't take you, you'll give us away." She buried her head against its soft feathers. "Did I tell you what delicious eggs you make, Donald?"

Relinquishing the fat duck, she began to run toward the spot she had hidden Chase. Creeping vines and sharp branches tangled about her, scratching her face and arms, and she welcomed the pain. It took her mind off Donald, and the dinner he was going to make for some Japanese soldier. Roasted duck. She thought she would throw up. That would be something she would never eat again...if she ever had the chance to eat again. From behind her came the muffled crashing of leaves and grass underfoot. The patrol was making its rounds back toward the beach.

"Chase? Chase!" She recognized the alcove beneath the bamboo thicket and heard Chase's groaning. She pushed away the overhanging vines and knelt beside him. He was burning up with fever and delirious again. "Oh, Chase," she despaired. "Not now. Not now."

From the direction of the clearing she heard Donald's sudden indignant squawk followed by laughing shouts. "Oh, God, no!" she whimpered.

The noise increased in volume, and Deborah knew the soldiers were coming toward the hideout. And Chase was still groaning, talking about a march now. Deborah knelt beside him and covered his mouth with hers. She could taste the saltiness and the heat.

Her brain mocked her body. There they were, facing possible discovery and death, and already her insides were quivering with the excitement that only Chase could kindle in her.

At last Deborah raised her head, shaken and spent by the passion, a passion that Chase's lips did not echo. Apparently the soldiers had passed by unaware for in the distance now she could hear their shouts and laughter. Still, she stayed with Chase in the cave of leaves, not daring to venture out.

With a stone she ground parts of the bark she had chipped from the tree and mixed the powder with a little of the sake in the bottle's cap. The mixture seemed to quiet Chase, and toward evening she noticed that the fever was abating. He slept the entire night, though she did not, for fear of the soldiers' return.

With daylight she left Chase and returned to the clearing. From behind the trunk of a large mahogany tree she watched the hut, listening, waiting. When she thought it was safe, she moved into the clearing.

Suddenly a loud noise disturbed the trees and leaves behind her. Deborah spun around. Her heart hammered against her rib cage. She saw nothing. Then the leaves rustled again, and Donald waddled out of the undergrowth. "Donald!" She gathered up the quacking duck. "You weren't dinner for them!"

By the time she returned to the hideout with the news that all was safe, Chase was sitting up, drinking the sake. "That does it!" he said. He looked at her flushed face, her heaving breasts. "We're getting out of here! If we have to, we'll live with the Manobos."

Deborah raised a slanted brow. "What about Herrera?"

Furrows ridged Chase's brow. Weakly he rose to his feet. "We'll wait for his next visit. Then we move out." Reluctantly he accepted the support of Deborah's shoulder.

Those next few days were agony for Chase. Deborah's nearness was as bad as the malaria. She had only to bend over, exposing the shadow of her cleavage, and he would break out in a sweat. The fresh, delicate scent of her filled the room, as overpowering as the jungle flowers. It was worse now that he had had her and knew of the passionate responsive woman inside her.

She knelt to light the kerosene tin, and Chase began to shake. One more second and he would take her like a tom panther stalks and mounts an unwilling feline.

Fortunately Deborah rose, stretching and holding her arms up, hip thrust to one side. "Next time Herrera comes, let's see if he can't get us a wireless radio," she said with a yawn.

Diligently Chase turned his attention to the bolo he was sharpening. Sleeping was going to be hell.

But the next time Herrera showed his helmeted face was

to be the last. It was shortly before dawn, and Chase had come awake instantly. He listened and though he heard nothing, he knew something was outside. When Donald began to screech like a siren, Deborah jerked upright. Chase covered her mouth with his hand. They sat in the darkness, straining to hear, tense.

From below came, "Where are you? We go. Now. Time to go. Damn fucking duck! Hey, where are you?"

Chase began to laugh so hard his lungs seemed on the verge of collapsing. Tears of laughter streamed down Deborah's cheeks. They staggered to the veranda. Below Herrera was kicking at the duck, which flapped its wings viciously at the intruder. "Come," Herrera called up to them. "Hurry. We leave. No come back."

When Deborah learned that an American submarine was lying offshore in the high tide, waiting to take them on, she had a sudden moment of panic. Could she face civilization again, the pressures, and the questions...and giving up Chase, although she knew he had never really been hers?

But she had been able to be with him, to reach out and touch him, to share those magical and miserable moments of isolation. When they left Mindanao, her relationship with Chase would not be the same as when they had come to the island. He had come as her brother and would leave as her lover.

She looked at Chase to find his deep black eyes on her. Was he feeling the same...or was he anxious to return to battle with the Anglo, to battle for Christina Raffin? "Let's go, Deborah," he said gently. "We've nothing to take with us."

"Wait," she said and pulled away. She stooped beneath the hut where Donald had retreated. "Can we take Donald with us, Chase?" she asked, kneeling near the nesting duck.

Chase looked to Herrera. "Him need to lay eggs for others that come, missy."

"Of course," she said. Until the war was over there would be other refugees that Filipino guerrillas would hide there. She gave Donald one last affectionate pat and rose. "I'm ready."

Herrera's motorboat was beached not too far from where they first came ashore nearly three months before. Chase looked out, seeing nothing on the sea but the telltale light of a pink dawn about the horizon. "We hurry. We hurry." Herrera called above the slap of the waves on the beach. "If miss this trip, must wait until tomorrow night."

The three of them pushed the motorboat out into the water until the ocean bottom began its gentle slope with the coral reefs. Chase and Herrera held the boat steady while Deborah flip-flopped over its edge. After the other two climbed aboard, Herrera started up the noisy engine.

Slowly, slowly, as they left the island behind them, the submarine, the U.S.S. *Narwahl,* looking like the Loch Ness Monster, began to surface from the Mindanao Deep—the greatest depth of water known to man. Only the periscope, antenna, and air induction pipe showed above the water. Deborah caught her breath, as if in fear, and Chase swallowed, feeling the same emotion—something akin to patriotism as he looked at the symbol of his country's might.

The motorboat rocked violently as it came alongside the submarine. The bridge's hatch opened, and Commander Frank R. Latta emerged. Chase and Deborah blinked their eyes like owls as they looked at the red light of the sub's electric bulb. They had come back to civilization.

53

For Chase it was like the first year he had been taken from the reservation and been forced to learn a new language and new ideas. Now he was hearing words that had not been in the English language when he had left the States—words like carhop, amphibious invasion, and gremlins. There were new songs—"Don't Sit under the Apple Tree"—and "You'd Be So Nice to Come Home To"—and new movie idols—Lauren Bacall and a young singer, Frank Sinatra.

It would have been easier, he thought, if he and Deborah had been able to discuss this tidal wave of new information and compare their ideas, but they had been separated to different areas of the submarine.

Chase reported to Commander Latta, who, after congratulating him on his escape, ordered a complete medical examination from the sub's doctor. "If all's in order with you, son, the sub's galley is open to you night and day. Order whatever you want."

At the sub's hospital the doctor pronounced Chase in remarkable physical condition. Except for the malaria and three different kinds of intestinal parasite, it appeared he had suffered little deterioration. "And what of the young woman, sir?" Chase asked. "Deborah—how is she?"

"Miss DeBaca survived the ordeal admirably. I imagine it's been more of an emotional and mental shock, if anything."

Chase thought about requesting to speak with her, but then what would he say? Obviously she hated him.

For twenty-two days the *Narwahl* zigzagged a course for Australia, crossing the equator several times in its effort to elude the enemy. And when it finally did put into port at Darwin, Chase found that American press, along with half the press representatives of the Allied countries, were there to greet them. The two of them were heroes, especially Chase, who had survived the infamous Death March and escaped to tell about it.

Chase was bored by the attention showered on him. Since the questions were, for the most part, repetitious, he succeeded in concealing the fact he and Deborah were together when they were rescued. What Deborah related, he did not know, for she was interviewed in a separate quarter and at another time. With only one reporter did he relate some of the true horror of the Death March—a famed fellow New Mexican, the skinny, gray-haired Ernie Pyle, who seemed to have an empathy for the common soldier.

After the Darwin stopover Chase was separated from Deborah, each of them being returned to the States by different routes. For Chase it was the same at each stop—Honolulu, San Francisco, where the starlet Linda Darnell graciously bestowed a chaste kiss on his lips for the photographers, and all the layovers along the Southern Pacific and Atchinson, Topeka, and Santa Fe railroads—the crowd of reporters, the exploding flash of the photographers' cameras, the microphones pressed to his face.

At Santa Fe's depot Chase stood beneath the bright, white July sun and looked out over the horde of photographers and reporters, anxious for a story on one of New Mexico's sons. Cold ripples of self-doubt began to lap around his feet. What was he doing there? He no more belonged in a civilized place than his *Dine'é* ancestors had. At that moment he wanted only to hightail it to the emptiness of the hills.

"Private Strawhand," an aging male reporter asked, "Edward R. Murrow reports that you were involved in a project—the 'Code Talkers.' Can you tell us anything about it?"

"Private Strawhand has nothing to say, gentlemen," a familiar sultry voice broke in.

Chase turned to find Christina edging through the reporters toward him. There were shouts and wolf calls as the members of the press made way for the tall, chic blond dressed in a gray velveteen skirt with matching jacket thrown over the frothy apricot blouse. But Christina had eyes only for Chase. Her recurring dreams had not let her forget his in-

293

furiatingly lazy grin, the feline grace that belied his virility
nor the mocking eyes—blacker than the long nights she had
spent without him.

"Is Private Strawhand your fiancé, Miss Raffin?" asked
a woman reporter with a large-feathered hat. Her tongue
practically licked her lips in anticipation of a hot story.

Without taking her gaze from that of Chase's, Christina
said, smiling, "Just tell your readers that information is Top
Secret Classified Material. I'm sure the Pentagon will decide
what information to release."

"But, Miss Raffin, with—"

"Come on, Chase," she said, taking his arm. "I've taken
the liberty of making reservations for you at the Harvey
House. It's the best Santa Fe has to offer right now."

"You shouldn't of," Chase said, attempting to control the
conflicting emotions that bombarded him. "Will telegraphed
he rented my old place for me."

The photographers continued snapping their cameras long
after Chase and Christina had climbed into the 1938 Bentley
Sports Roadster. "Nice," he said, dropping his duffel bag in
the rear seat.

"It's difficult getting enough gas coupons for it," Christina
said and started the engine. A nervous tension seemed to lay
beneath the surface of the coolly composed, beautiful face.

"I'm sure you're able to manage," Chase said dryly.

Christina flashed him a feigned look of reproach. As she
whipped the car out onto the highway, she dug into her purse
and handed him a package of cigarettes, her own personalized
brand still. "Are you surprised to see me?"

Chase withdrew a cigarette, and she passed him her gold
plated lighter. "Nothing you do surprises me, Christina."

She looked at him, then looked away, concentrating on
the road ahead. After a lengthy silence, she asked, "Are you
still angry at me?"

Chase stretched out his long legs as far as he could in the
confines of the car. "Does your father know you're here?"

"No. He thinks I'm meeting with Phil's Campaign Committee for Governor."

"So Masters thinks he's ready for the big step? Have you
two set a wedding date?"

Christina's gaze flashed to Chase's chiseled countenance
and skittered back to the road. Ahead she could see the plaza.
"No," she said so softly that Chase was not sure he heard
her. "Chase, there hasn't been anybody to take your place."

"I bet that didn't keep you from looking, did it?"

Christina's eyes filled. "Don't. I know I was wrong."

Chase slouched further down in the seat. "Don't, also. I'm too tired to play your games right now, Christina."

She maneuvered the roadster out of the plaza, turning onto Castillos Street and halting before the old two-story Victorian home. She turned toward Chase. "I want you. But I don't think you know your own mind."

Chase wanted her, too. His nostrils flared with the subtle scent of her perfume. But he told himself that he wasn't ready to be her plaything. Too easily he could get caught in the web she spun. He got out, leaning his hands on the door. "So long, Christina."

She met his gaze steadily. "I won't wait for you to change your mind," she said and sped off, leaving him watching her...and wanting her.

A mousy old lady, who roomed on the first floor and who had turned up her nose at Chase when he lived there previously, stopped him at the stairs, asking for an autograph. Chase blinked in surprise; then, repressing his old mocking smile, said, "Certainly, Miss McCauley," and scrawled his name beneath his photo in the newspaper clipping she handed him.

Later that afternoon, as he sat reading the newspaper, trying to catch up and assimilate all the news that had occurred in his absence, Will came by. The old man took his hand affectionately. "It's great to have you back, Chase!" He stepped away and looked at the tall young man in uniform. "It looks like that stint in the service civilized you."

Chase grinned. "Uncle Sam succeeded where you failed."

He invited Will into the sparsely furnished room and offered him a cigarette, but the attorney shook his head. "May's threatening to poison my coffee if I don't give up smoking. I would have been at the depot, Chase, but I was in court with another IBA case."

"What's the Indian Bureau done this time?"

Will ran his hand through his thick, snowy hair. "The same old thing. They've issued an order to the superintendents in the field to prosecute any 'so-called religious ceremony.'"

Chase grimaced. "What's the reasoning behind that?"

Will rolled his eyes. "The religious ceremonies, they say, promote idleness, cause Indians to give away their property recklessly, contain danger to health, or promote indifference to family welfare. That means the destruction of a ten-thousand-year-old religion that contains the same moral code as Christianity!"

"The offense," Chase said, "is that the Indian religion stands in the way of the meddling Christian missionaries—

who you know represent a considerable political power. It's just a modern-day Spanish Inquisition, isn't it?"

"The Taos Pueblos have hired me to fight the order in court. They'd rather go to jail before they abandon their religion."

Chase was reminded of a sign he had seen in the San Francisco PX drugstore—*ONLY ANGLOS NEED APPLY*. "Why do you do it, Will? What do you get out of all this? You're certainly not making a name for yourself—nor a fortune."

Will scratched his head. "I haven't rightly figured that out yet, son," he said with a deprecating smile. "May claims I'm getting senile in my old age." He fixed an eye on Chase. "Your old job at AID is still open if you want to take on the IBA."

Chase looked thoughtful as he ground out his cigarette stub in the chipped ashtray. "Thanks, Will, but I plan to start a bank." He looked over at the attorney, expecting derision.

"Put me down for ten shares of stock."

Chase looked at Will, trying to hide the surprise and the gratitude. It was another one of those times when the Indian "thank you" would not be out of line, but Chase could not even manage that. "What if I lose your money?"

Will shrugged, reminding Chase of the Indian's fatalism. "Working for AID I'm not going to get rich anyway. Why not take the chance?"

Ten shares was one thousand dollars, and Chase estimated his back pay amounted to thirty-nine shares. With a goal of three hundred shares, that left him only two hundred and fifty-one shares to go.

Chase bought a piebald and set out to ride the reservations that encircled the Santa Fe–Taos–Albuquerque area. For the first time he was selling himself, his word, his integrity.

It was not easy.

All the rest of the summer and fall and into the new year of 1944 he rode back and forth over the mountains and up and down along the Rio Grande, pouring out a torrent of words after the initial Big Smoke in the tepees and frame houses and adobe homes. Firmly he shook hands with the more progressive Indians and even exchanged the formal *abrazo* with the growing number of Mexicans who were willing to invest their few hard-earned dollars in Chase's scheme. In the barely accessible trappers' camps even a few Anglos contributed toward the bank. A share here, two or three there—his goal was coming into sight.

He found out a lot about raising money. He found out also that he could not give up his goal for a bank if he wanted to. He did not want to, of course, but there was a yoke of responsibility that attached itself to him like a tic the minute someone had trusted him with his capital.

However, the strong protectiveness he felt toward his investors was not the first time he had experienced the feeling. He had first known that feeling as a senior at the Indian Boarding School when a little girl with frightened eyes had stood before him.

One afternoon he stopped by the AID office, ostensibly to keep Will abreast of the bank's progress. After a few moments he asked the old man, "Do you hear anything of Deborah?"

Will hooked his thumbs under his suspenders and fixed Chase with a penetrating look. "You haven't told me everything that happened between you two over there in Mindanao, son. And I know it's none of my business. But the one time I ran into Deborah she asked me not to mention her name to you."

Chase grunted and looked down at the linoleum floor. "I guess she has a right to feel that way." He looked back to Will. "I want her to be happy, Will. I'll stay out of her life."

When he turned to go, Will said, "Chase." Chase looked at him. "She's opened an art gallery over on Canyon Road—in partnership with another Navajo. Ma-Pi-We, I think his name is. You might wander by there sometime."

Ma-Pi-We—Navajo for Red Bird. Slowly Chase shook his head. "I don't think so, Will. It's easier this way."

By July Chase had reached his goal of three hundred shares, $30,000. The Mercantile Bank of Santa Fe became a chartered fact, and it opened its doors in a small square stucco building just behind the old Military Church off the plaza.

For a few days, weeks, the success was heady for Chase. The evening of the stockholders' first meeting he went by the Aid office for Will. After Chase had cranked his torpedo Ford, Will said, "You'll be able to afford a Rolls Royce Phantom when you're elected Chairman of the Board."

Chase tugged at the tie around his neck, unused to the wardrobe of a civilized man. "I ought to hang myself with this," he muttered. Then, "I'm not going to accept the nomination, Will."

Will's mouth fell open. "But this is what you wanted. This bank was your idea. Jumping jackrabbits, Chase, it's your bank!"

"No, it's the stockholders' bank—the Indians and Mexicans and even the Anglos who trusted me." Chase let out on the clutch, and the car shot out into the traffic. "Besides, the bank is not what I wanted."

"You want Christina Raffin," Will said.

297

Chase looked at him. "Yes. I guess that's it."

The small building was packed, mostly with Indians proud of the accomplishment, but a few men from the press were there to cover the story, also. As he looked around at the assembly, Chase felt a thrill of pride that was quickly tempered as he wondered what he would do next. Maybe start a hotel, he reflected wryly. Conrad Hilton, another New Mexican, was making a success of buying hotels.

Chase and Will made their way to the board room where a highly polished new table fenced by hardback chairs dominated the surroundings. When the stockholders saw Chase, they began sitting down. Taking his seat at the head of the table, Chase looked around. He recognized almost everyone. Friends.

As he called the meeting to order and began the Order of Business, a very old woman interrupted it when she was wheeled into the room by a giant, barrel-chested Mexican. There were gasps of recognition from two or three of the people there.

Chase leaned to Will and whispered, "Who is she?"

"Rosemary Rhodes," Will replied with something like a mixture of respect and awe.

54

Chase found it strange that a woman who owned the Santiago Silver Mines, was a stockholder in the Santa Fe Railroad, and practically controlled the largest bank in Santa Fe, the First National Bank, would have wanted to invest in his insignificant one, but there was no accounting for people, he thought. And she did seem somewhat eccentric—an extremely rich old woman wearing only one little ornament, the cheap tourist jewelry fashioned by the Navajo. But it was, of course, beautiful work.

He scrutinized the turquoise and silver bracelet on her veined and brown-spotted wrist more closely. He realized it was the work of the bracelet that intrigued him. Each bracelet was as individual in workmanship as was a painting. By merely looking at the design or the quality of the stones and types of turquoise used, one could determine almost within a hundred-mile radius where in the state the design was fashioned.

But that particular bracelet—Chase knew he had seen the handiwork somewhere before. It was very distinct, excellent craftsmanship. He should have remembered. He frowned, aggravated that he could not recall.

He continued with the business in hand, addressing the stockholders in Spanish, which seemed to be the language of common denominator. He wondered if the old woman understood the Spanish and glanced once or twice in her direction, always somewhat distracted to find the intense gaze of those greenish blue eyes on him even when someone else held the floor. In that seamed face the eyes were alive and ever-young. He found himself fascinated by her and had to force himself to keep to the business at hand.

When it came time to elect the Chairman of the Board and a Señor Romero put forth Chase's name, he stood and declined. As he expected, there was a murmur of surprise among the stockholders. "Gentlemen—and lady." He bowed slightly in deference to the old woman, and she inclined her head. "I thank you for the confidence you have shown in me. But I am not a financier. My knowledge of banking is rudimentary. The bank was my dream, so perhaps I am a dreamer. And what you need is a doer. I would like to suggest for nomination Wilbur Fairchild. As Director of AID, he has served the people of the reservations. He is someone I trust, though he is an Anglo." Chase grinned at Will, saying, "I think you would be wise to put your trust in Wilbur Fairchild."

The name of Blackwing, a minor San Idlefonso sub-chief, was also put forth, along with three other Mexicans, but the runoff was between Will and Blackwing, with Will winning by a close margin.

After the stockholders' meeting was finished and the stockholders adjourned for the party to be held in the foyer, Chase looked for the old woman. But he was detained by some of the investors, and by the time he escaped she had disappeared.

When he returned to the celebration going on in the foyer, three men, obviously all Indian, were waiting for him. All three wore business suits. The heavyset one introduced himself, saying in a gravelly voice, "I'm Peter Portales of the Nachanie clan of the Navajo. This is Harold Little Sheep and Gray Wind. We represent the Business Committee of the Indian Tribal Council, and we would like to make a proposition for you."

The Indian Tribal Council was the most powerful organization in the complex network of New Mexico's Indian tribes, and Chase was intrigued that these men should have an interest in him.

299

The man, Peter Portales, had a broad, flat nose that dominated a kindly, round face. But the eyes were shrewd and hard. "Could we adjourn to the board room?" he asked. "This is of a very confidential nature."

Chase nodded and indicated with his hand for the men to pass on in. He took his seat at the head of the long table, Will's seat now, he reminded himself. When the three men had seated themselves, he asked, "Yes?"

"To get to the point, Mr. Strawhand," the older, stoop-shouldered Gray Wind began, "the Indian Tribal Council would like to back you in the primary race for governor on the Republican ticket."

Chase stood up. "I'm not amused, gentlemen, by your idea of a joke. And I don't have time to waste. Good evening."

The three men sat unperturbed by Chase's anger. "Wait, hear us out," said Harold Little Sheep, the youngest of the three.

Chase leaned his hands on the table. "Don't you think, gentlemen, that it would be a little difficult to back an Indian for governor when the Indian race is not even allowed to vote?"

"Agreed, Mr. Strawhand," Harold said. "But the end of the Indian's disenfranchisement is near. On March thirtieth, to be exact, the State of New Mexico will give the Indian the right to vote."

Slowly Chase resumed his seat. He laced his hands before him, chewing on his thumbs, as he studied the three men. "Tell me, do you seriously think that an Indian stands a chance on God's green earth of becoming the governor of New Mexico? You don't appear to be that foolish—the proverbial Three Blind Men—so what is behind all this?"

"You're probably right, Mr. Strawhand," Peter said. "What we want to do is make a showing . . . give some evidence of the Indian's serious interest in politics. If we don't make an attempt, the Indian will be doomed forever to be controlled by the precinct's *jefe politico*—the political boss."

"Why me?"

"You've had some college education, you have initiative—your bank is evidence, you have charisma. Look how the press has glamorized your escape from Bataan—and how the Indians have readily gathered to claim you as their own. And then you've been instrumental in working for the Indians on AID.

"The old people will not change their ways. They will not come in out of the canyons to vote—or we would have chosen someone on the Business Council. But you are young—what

300

is it, thirty-eight? You appeal to our younger generation which is becoming, like yourself, more westernized."

Chase sat back. He was astonished, an emotion his Indian countenance did not manifest. He considered the idea. All logic and reasoning was against the scheme of actually running for office.

An Indian as governor—it was unheard of!

Still a gut feeling in Chase asked why not. The bank had been a whim, a successful whim. But representing his people, campaigning to ultimately represent all the people of the State of New Mexico, to be able to do something constructive for once—it was a temptation. A temptation whose seed had been planted in him some thirty-three years earlier by an Anglo who told him, "If you want to change things for the better, become a politician."

And then there was another reason he would not even admit to himself. The campaign would put him in the same political arena in which Christina Raffin moved. The campaign would pit him against her fiancé—if Chase won the primary.

"As I understand it, gentlemen, you want me to campaign for the office with the absolute knowledge that as a token candidate I will be kicked in the teeth, ridiculed, and ultimately defeated. Right?"

The three men looked at each other, then Chase. "Right," they echoed.

Chase appointed Will as his campaign manager, and the AID office was used as campaign headquarters. The two sat facing each other over cold coffee after working hours, mapping out their approach.

After long deliberation and several midnight discussions with the Three Blind Men, Chase had decided his platform would promise that the Indians' resources would be exported from the reservations along a guideline that did not rip them off, more fair representation, suggestions of a coalition of the people of color, and—what interested the Indians the most—a promise of protection of their sacred lands, such as Painted Mountain and Medicine Lake. Small concessions on the part of the Anglo the Tribal Council felt.

"What do you think it'll take to win the primary?" Will asked.

Chase swallowed a sip of the coffee and made a face at its bitterness. "Voting in a herd of sheep to begin with."

"It'd take more than one herd," the old man countered.

"How about the entire population of the Santa Fe cemeteries?"

The two men laughed, then sobered as they talked over the weeks of work that still lay ahead. "Here's how I see it, Chase. The Council has been leasing vast tracts of oil, coal, and helium-producing lands. Peter has said the Council would be willing to divert some of these incomes as proceeds toward your campaign. But better than some big promotional campaign would be to apply the same tactics you used to raise funds for your bank."

"You suggest we make it a grass-roots campaign—go from tepee to tepee and jacal to jacal?"

Will nodded. "Exactly. After all, everyone knows that Masters has the Democratic ticket and the office of governor in the bag. You or your opponent—García?—would merely be a token representative for the weaker Republican Party. But first you have to convince the precinct's *jefe político* that you and not García would make a worthwhile showing in the race."

Angrily Chase squeezed his empty paper cup into a ball. "I won't buy the *jefe* off, Will!"

Will smiled. "I didn't think you would."

Chase approached the *jefe político* of the precinct, who was also the *patrón* of the largest ranch in the precinct, an Hispanic. "I am interested in obtaining the votes of the residents of your precinct," Chase said blandly over the telephone. "Before I campaign among them, I wanted to talk with you. I hope to enlist your aid."

Señor Martinez invited Chase out to his hacienda. Custom demanded a polite exchange of amenities—talk of the weather, inspection of the rancho, and several glasses of wine before the slightest innuendo of business was broached. At last the aristocrat opened the subject. A smile appeared beneath his hooked nose. "I've been expecting you. My aid is not cheap."

"You would benefit in proportion to the benefits acceded the Indians."

"How? If they're allowed national sovereignty, mineral rights, liquor laws, water management? I doubt it, señor. As I said, my aid is not cheap. Five thousand dollars to be exact."

Chase returned Martinez's smile over the rim of his wineglass. "It would almost be worth the five thousand to find out what kind of man you are," Chase said.

Martinez toasted Chase's verbal sally. "And you, Señor Strawhand, may be my kind of man."

Ignoring the man's comment, Chase said, "Unfortunately, whatever you gain by supporting me will be indirectly." He rose to his feet. "I hope you will think on it, Señor Martinez."

"I will think on it."

With only two days left before the May primary elections, Chase made one last stop—it was on the winding, tree-shaded Canyon Road where fine old adobe homes rubbed elbows with art galleries and studios. He stood before the *Kachina Korner* that had *Studio of Indian Arts* printed in italics below the shop's name.

Because he missed Deborah's friendship more than he could have thought possible (and that gamine face with the ever-curved lips), did that give him any right to come back into her life—if only for even a moment? Yet Chase could not help himself. He knew she would always be a part of him.

A quaint little bell tinkled when he opened the heavy, hand-carved door. Paintings, sculptures, and jewelry showcases jostled for space with the racks of clothing of Indian design. A curtain rustled, and Deborah appeared, dressed in the traditional Navajo garb of flounced calico skirt and velveteen blouse with the ever-present silver and turquoise jewelry. Her hair had grown, swaying loosely below her shoulders. She was beautiful, he thought and wondered why he had never really noticed it before.

"I didn't expect to find you returned to the blanket," he said with a smile, feeling ridiculously somewhat like a schoolboy. Any moment he'd start rubbing the hardwood floor with the toe of his patent-leather shoes and stammer and blush furiously.

"Only for the day," Deborah said. Her smile held all of its old warmth. "I'm posing for a painting for Alfonso Htchapi."

"And are you still painting?"

"Yes, and Chase," she caught his hand in her enthusiasm, "I've been commissioned to paint historical backgrounds and pictures for the museum at Bandalier National Park. Greg helped arrange the commission."

In the awkward moment that followed, the late afternoon half-light made everything seem hazy, the usually sharp lines indefinable...a time suspended. Chase ached to reach out and touch the small, oval face that incredibly hid so much strength and will.

The moment passed, and Deborah, her face flushed with embarrassment, dropped her hand from Chase's. "I'm glad to see you so happy," he said.

"Word is out that you are very successful. First with the bank and now with your political campaign."

"Not yet. This may be a big fiasco."

"I don't think so, Chase. I think whatever you do you will be successful. I only hope..." She broke off and stepped away from him. Her hands moved nervously over a leather jacket she straightened on the rack.

Chase came up behind her. "What do you hope?"

She turned to face him, tilting her head back so she could look up into his face. "I hope that you will be able to help our people. That you will not let the *bilagaana* manipulate you for their own purposes."

"Are you going to marry Red Bird?" Chase asked huskily.

Deborah shook her head. "No," she whispered. "The war changed me, changed him, everything. We're just close friends."

Against his will and better judgment, Chase reached out and enfolded Deborah in his arms. There was the fresh scent of mountain air, of piñon, and sweet grass in her hair. His lips lowered to claim her soft trembling ones, and a rush of heat rocketed through him like the swift feverish attacks of his old malaria.

For a moment he could feel Deborah's hesitation, her wavering. Then she placed her hands against his chest. "No, Chase. All these years I think I've been in love with you. I've even let myself be used by you. Always hoping. But you still have Christina carved on your heart, don't you?"

She moved away from him as if anxious to put a distance between them. "We've outlived our childhood friendship, and there's nothing left in me to continue it. And what you want from me, I can't give you. Don't come back, Chase. There's nothing here for you."

55

Will raised his glass to Chase, and Peter, Harold, and Gray Wind joined in. They ate at one of the finest and newest restaurants in Santa Fe, The Pink Adobe, which was filled that night by people celebrating Germany's surrender the day before, on the second of May. "To the end of the war," Will said, "and to the Republican candidate for governor of New Mexico. Congratulations, Chase."

"Thank you, gentlemen." Chase took a drink of the champagne before continuing. "To have won the primary was difficult. But to win the race—it may well prove impossible."

Peter said, "We're having the campaign literature delivered to our promo man this week. The sooner—" He halted as the Railroad Commissioner, a distinguished man with salt-and-pepper hair, stopped by the table to congratulate Chase.

"It doesn't take much to make an Indian acceptable, does it?" Chase asked after the man left. "A year ago—hell, a month ago—an Anglo wouldn't be seen shaking hands with an Indian."

"It's the 'in' thing to do now," Will said.

That night the five men retired to the empty AID office to plan the last half of their campaign. "What you will have to be," Peter said, "is the Great Mediator of the problem of Sovereign Nations of the Indian reservations versus the State. This is the crux of the problems facing you. It'll be the *hot issue* of this campaign. You must be prepared to face Masters with solutions and answers."

Will went over to the state map tacked to the wall. Multicolored pins splotched the various counties. "There are three basic voting blocs." His gnarled finger pointed to the northern area of the state. "Here, and in Bernalillo County, are the Rio Grande Democrats—mostly Spanish surnames. Then there are the widely dispersed Republicans with no one concentration.

"Lastly are the Border Democrats, mostly Anglo and from the eastern and southern counties, known as Little Texas. The Anglos there are racially biased—especially the Texas cowboys and oilmen who run the Border counties." Will shoved a pin in Lea County. "Here's where we'll start."

Thus Chase began his grass-roots campaign with the Border counties. He explained what he proposed to do calmly and concisely to the Mexican peon, the Anglo roughneck, the Indian miner. When he at last visited one of the powerful oilmen in the county, he was told, "All I'm interested in is sending to Santa Fe the best damned governor that money can buy!"

If Chase won the office, he realized it would only be through voter apathy on the part of the Democrats. Hardly a triumph, but still it would be a beginning.

He had expected some word from Christina, at least a biting condemnation at his challenge of her fiancé, but neither saw nor heard anything of her until Will charged into the office one afternoon late in August. "Chase! Chase! You won't believe it! I've located a pocket of powerful Anglos that *can't* be bought—that will consider listening to you. I've arranged for you to debate Masters at the town's auditorium."

Skeptical, Chase narrowed his eyes. "Don't tell me— you've located another cemetery for a captive audience."

"I'm serious! It's the town northwest of here—Los Alamos, the one that's filled up so rapidly over the last year."

Chase smiled. "The town they say is supposed to be a home for pregnant WACS?"

Will threw up his hands, and Chase said, "I know, I know. The town has something to do with the atomic bombs dropped over Hiroshima and Nagasaki earlier this month."

"Will you do it?" the old man asked. "Will you debate Masters?"

"Set up an appointment," Chase said. "I'll be there to talk—if they want to hear my answers."

It was not that easy, for first Chase had to be cleared by a governmental war agency, known as the Manhattan Project, quartered in the long Arias de Quiros complex of buildings along the north side of Santa Fe's Palace Avenue. The erect army major refused to discuss with Chase anything about Los Alamos, though he did hint that the people were a high-grade cross-section of the nation.

"As newcomers to New Mexico they're uninformed, Mr. Strawhand, but interested. They're cordial, a bit curious about their Spanish-speaking associates—and notably without prejudice."

Chase thought he was prepared when he arrived at the small school auditorium. He was mildly surprised to see it was packed. At one end of the stage were two chairs draped with his campaign colors, black and beige. At the other end two chairs were draped in purple and gold, Masters's colors.

By all accounts he should have been nervous. He had never spoken before a large group of people. All his campaigning had always been a handshake here, a few words there. Maybe he was not nervous, he reasoned, because there was so little hope of winning.

Calmly he took his seat. Masters still had not shown up, and Chase wondered if at the last minute Masters had considered it beneath him to debate an Indian. However Chase's opponent did appear, fifteen minutes late and with an entourage that mounted the platform with him. Secretaries, ad men, and advisors. There was a smattering of applause for the Senator, and he nodded genuinely. Then Chase noticed in the front row the elegantly dressed, starkly beautiful woman.

Christina Raffin had come. Chase was curious why she had not taken a seat on the platform with Masters. Her presence would be a certain sign of her support, and thereby her father's support. Obviously just being there was enough, for people were nodding toward her, whispering. Wherever Christina went, stares were to be expected.

Masters opened the debate, keeping on safe ground until midway through his speech, then, "But if my worthy opponent, who represents the minorities of our state...and I might add, it's time they were recognized...were to be elected governor, it would be enacting legislation which presently gives the Indians immunity—as they pay no county, state, and city taxes.

"You must realize if the Indians become a part of state politics too soon, they will lose the services and protections accorded them by the specialized agencies and programs of the federal government. These programs assist in the support of Indian cultures and communities. It would be brutally inhumane to the Indian," Masters concluded.

Oh, clever, Chase thought. Not fighting the minorities openly, only expressing concern for their welfare.

It was his turn now. "I'm impressed, Senator Masters, by your concern. But I hope you realize that to continue the policies you mention will tend to deny to the individual Indian the right to opt for whatever life and role he seeks. What must be done, and what I hope to do, is to find a middle ground in which all three of New Mexico's cultural heritages—the Indian, the Hispanic, and the Anglo—can meet and work out our problems."

There was more, but as Chase thought about it later he felt his speech lacked Masters's expertise. Masters was a brilliant orator. His words drew the attention in soft-spoken tones one time, then compelling, urging, motivating his audience, his sheep, with gripping, reverberant oration the next.

Afterward Masters cordially shook Chase's hand before the audience. "You're wasting your time with these people," he told Chase quietly. "Our political machines may not be able to control their votes, but we can have their votes thrown out for the very good reason the Los Alamos people are residents of a federal reservation and subject only to federal jurisdiction. They know it and may not like it if we do it, but there's nothing they can do about it."

"Oh, but there is," Christina said, appearing suddenly backstage. She came to stand between the two men. "Some of the Los Alamos people are already threatening to petition Texas for admission."

Masters scoffed, and Christina shrugged her shoulders. "Agreed, nothing will come of it—except that before election time you can bet Governor McDonald will make certain that Los Alamos is made a separate county. He can't afford not

307

to, Phil. This is a highly paid group of people with scientific and technical backgrounds."

"I don't want to debate the issue here, Christina." He took her arm. "Let's go."

Christina looked to Chase. "I think," she told Masters without looking away from Chase, "that this gentleman and I have old times to discuss."

Masters's smooth façade erupted, as if he could not believe what he heard. Chase was not sure he had understood correctly either. Not what she said but what she meant. He wanted her just as badly as he ever had. But with reason he was leery. What was she after this time?

"Nothing," she told him when she slid into his new car, a 1939 Plymouth. She sat beside him but not touching him. "Just a ride home."

Her mere presence charged the car with electricity, and Chase felt if he were to touch her tiny lights would go off in the darkness. She smoked in the taut silence as Chase drove down the wretched, narrow road that connected Los Alamos in the Jemez Mountains with civilization.

Santa Fe came into sight before Christina finally spoke. "Chase, I want to talk about us." She stretched out a hand, and he felt her fingertips rest on his arm.

"Don't, Christina. Find yourself another stud."

"I don't want anyone else. I've tried to forget you. I told myself that you weren't capable of living in my world—and I wasn't capable of living in yours. That we'd be miserable together. But I'm miserable without you." She paused, waiting for him to say something. When he did not, she said, "Well, do I have to ask *you*? Okay, I'll crawl. Will you marry me, Chase?"

Chase stopped the Plymouth right in the middle of San Francisco Street and came around to Christina's side of the car. While traffic backed up and horns honked, he pulled her from the car and kissed her. His fingers bit into her arms, and his mouth bruised her soft lips. He half expected her to pull away, but she didn't. She clung to him, returning the fierceness of his kiss.

"Take me home," she said, when they returned to the privacy of his car, ignoring the shouts and laughter of the people on the streets. "I've something to tell my father that won't make him happy. And besides, I think it's time he met his prospective son-in-law."

It was a mansion, a sprawling Victorian house that lay inside the city, though at one time it was beyond the city's outskirts. Hired guards were posted at the iron-picket gates. When Chase drove down the long, tree-lined drive that circled before the veranda's steps, Christina asked, "Nervous?"

Chase shook his head. "Should I be? What can he take from me or do to me?" He smiled at Christina. "There must be some good in him to have produced a daughter like you."

Christina laughed, an unaffected joyous laugh. "Meet him first. I'm a late-in-life child. His first wife never had any children. And his second wife, my mother, had only me. So I'm special."

"I didn't know Raffin was married before."

"Not many people do. It's a secret I think he's ashamed of. She was Mexican. And in case you haven't heard, my father's terribly bigoted."

"Then why did he marry her?"

"It's all history. She was heiress to a reasonably large land grant. In any event, *she* left him. Interned herself in a convent where she died some years later." Christina leaned over and brushed his jaw with her lips.

"I guess that's one of the reasons why I'm so attracted to you. You obviously aren't after my inheritance, or I wouldn't have had to beg you to marry me." Her fingers slipped inside his shirt, and she murmured, "Of course, there were other reasons."

Chase grabbed her hand and moved it down over the swelling crotch. "See what you do to me? Come on, or I'll change my mind and haul you off to the bushes."

Chase had known that the Senator was very old, nearing eighty. But his age did not lessen the power that exuded from the man's dominating presence. "Daddy," Christina said, "I want you to meet Chase Strawhand. He's running against Phil, you know."

Chase put out his hand to the old man who sat in the winged-back chair with a crocheted blanket across his lap. The man ignored it, looking past him, to his daughter. "Where's Phil? Weren't you two going over the campaign notes later tonight?"

"Daddy! Stop being rude!" Christina put her hands on her hips. "You might as well know now I don't intent to see Phil again. At least not on a romantic basis."

Raffin fixed his ferret eyes on Chase. "And you intend to see this—this man of color?"

"Daddy!"

"Christina, I've spoiled you. You've always had what you wanted. But this time I won't permit it! I won't let you ruin your reputation, gallivanting around with this redskin!"

"I'm perfectly old enough—"

Chase turned to leave. He wanted to hit the old man. And it was not the man's age that kept him from doing it. It was the realization that hitting Christina's father would not change the old man's prejudice or the thousands like him.

"Wait, Chase, I'm going with you!" Christina said and left her father raving after her.

Chase sat behind the steering wheel and found his hands were gripping it as if he'd break it. Christina passed him a cigarette. "Daddy's a touchy old bastard. But he knows he can't manipulate me like he does everyone else."

Chase inhaled deeply on the cigarette and switched on the ignition. "I'm bushed, Christina. Go back inside. I'll see you tomorrow."

"No, I'm going with you."

Chase raked a brow. "To my attic room? The landlord would really get a charge out of that."

Christina smiled like a cat. "How about our summer hogan?"

They compromised and settled for a hotel off the plaza.

Christina could have cared less about the poorly hidden look the desk clerk gave them when Chase informed him there was to be no luggage. She had carried the night of the summer hogan with her for three years, and no man had been able to satisfy the passion that burned in her like Chase had.

Chase sprawled in the chair. "Take off your clothes."

Her breath sucked in. Excitement, fear, desire raged in her like an epidemic fever. Slowly she peeled away the protective layers of civilization. When she stood naked, her pale pink skin shimmering in the dark, Chase said, "Come here." His hands buried in the flesh of her buttocks as he drew her against him, his lips branding her firm belly with kisses of fire.

56

The two of them were seen everywhere together, and Chase had a suspicion that Christina purposely arranged for certain reporters and photographers to be at the scene when the two of them arrived. Christina's support, and thereby her father's, made the race of governor a closer one. The possibility that an Indian could be elected governor of the state took on more realistic proportions that interested even the national press.

Chase found in his morning's mail a request by CBS to do a radio spot on him. "It would help your image," Christina told him when he laughingly told her about it. And that was when he realized she was extremely serious about his winning the governorship.

Will did not seem to take Christina's backing as lightly as Chase did. He sat on the other side of Chase's desk, poring over a two-day old Scripps Howard column. RAFFIN HEIRESS BEATS WAR DRUM FOR INDIAN read the heading. Will slammed the folded newspaper against the desk. "I don't like what you're doing, Chase. It's the last thing I'd have suspected from you—a straightforward man."

Chase put aside the morning's mail. "All right, what is it that has you so up in arms?"

"You're using Christina." Will leaned forward, his gray-shadowed jaw jutting. "It's a form of revenge, isn't it? Marry the richest, prettiest Anglo woman in the state and become the state's most powerful man—show those damned palefaces! You're not doing it to better help the state—or even the Indian nation—which I might remind you is a minority."

"But their money and resources no longer are, damn it! And I intend to see that they're no longer stolen blind. Just as I intend to see that they are taken off welfare rolls and all the other damned programs that are crippling them—and the state."

Will rubbed his forehead. "Sorry, Chase. I guess the pressure of the last-minute details are getting to me."

"Myself included. I don't know if I can hold out for another month of this society bit. It's boring me to tears."

"What you need to do is get away on a weekend hunting trip." Will pulled a letter from his coat pocket and tossed it across the desk. "It's an invitation from the Elks Club in Albuquerque. They want you to speak at their next meeting. I think you ought to do it. Then take that weekend and go up into the Sandias on one of your big buffalo hunts—or whatever it is you Indians are supposed to do."

"It's scalping, Will," Chase said, smiling.

"I've got an idea you've got enough pubic pelts to tie to your lance for years to come."

"Wilbur Fairchild—a man of your age!" Chase said in mock disapproval, then chuckled. He shoved the letter back at Will. "Tell them I'll come."

That night he took Christina to the Santa Fe Opera House to see the last performance of the season, Strauss's *Salome*. When he told Christina about the Elk invitation and his planned weekend of hunting, her lower lip thrust out in a pout. "And what am I supposed to do that weekend?"

Already the lights were lowering. "You might try working up a sweat for me," he whispered. He laid his hand on her thigh, teasing her as she had so often teased him in public when they could not be fully observed.

"Chase, don't!" she hissed, as he stroked just above her knee, his hand sliding up the silken thigh to loose the snap of her garter belt. Yet her hand did not push his away, and her legs shifted for the fingers that jerked on the wiry curls. But her whimper was drowned out by the tenor's German voice soaring on stage.

Christina's eyes were shining, her lips parted, when intermission came and they joined the elite of New Mexico in the lobby. "How about champagne?" Chase asked.

She held his arm, her hand caressing the muscles bunched just beneath the tuxedo jacket—a tuxedo that was not rented this time, since his shares in the Mercantile Bank were paying handsome dividends by now. "I don't want to let you out of my sight," she whispered.

Every time Chase tried to break away toward the refreshment table, there were always more people that Christina was introducing him to—the District Attorney and his wife, an oilman up from the raw boomtown of Hobbs for the opera, and an old woman in a wheelchair that Chase remembered from the night of the bank's stockholders meeting. "The Grand Dame of New Mexico," Christina said. "Mrs. Rhodes, I'd like you to meet the future governor of New Mexico—if I have anything to do with it—Chase Strawhand."

Chase took the thin hand. "We've met before, at the Mercantile Bank, Mrs. Rhodes."

"Aye, it was," she said, her voice clear and sharp in spite of the press of the crowd and noise.

Chase felt as if she were measuring him, felt the power behind the wrinkled face. A power of the soul the old shaman would have called it. But there was nothing evil in it; rather a warm gentleness that surprised and intrigued him.

"You're a man who could carry the burden of authority well," she said. "If you're careful."

"That is a benediction," Christina said. "You've been approved, Chase."

But Chase felt it was more than that. There was something about the old woman. Her keen eyes fixed on him. "Perhaps Senator Raffin's daughter has also told you I'm a patron of the arts." She gestured to the big Mexican behind her. "Find Miguel and bring him."

"Miguel Montoya?" Christina asked. "He's here?"

Rosemary Rhodes nodded. "He has been scouting new talent in Paris. But he plans to set up a foundation here for New Mexico's promising artists."

A tall man, almost of Chase's height but much more slender, with frost streaking the collar-length hair that was the shade of burnt cork, joined the small group. His smile made each person there feel as if he alone were singled out as the recipient. "Nice to meet you, Mr. Strawhand," he said after the introductions were made. "I've seen your name quite often in the newspaper, of course, and I've heard Deborah mention you."

Chase's face never mirrored the tight knotting in his stomach when Deborah suddenly appeared at Miguel's side, saying, "Sorry to take so long." And the way she looked at him made the knot in Chase's stomach wrench like a tourniquet.

"I think you two know each other," Miguel said.

If Deborah was surprised, she covered it well as she put out her hand. "Chase, it's good to see you again."

The most natural thing for Chase to have done would have been to take the petite woman in his arms, but he constrained himself. "You look lovely, Deborah," he said and meant it. She was dressed in a single-strap white satin evening gown that dramatized her exotic dark coloring, and her long, heavy hair was swept up into a cluster of curls that adorned her small head like a queen's crown.

"You've known each other a long time?" Christina asked.

"A very long time," Chase said, his gaze holding Deborah's. "We escaped from the Philippines together."

Christina eyed the young woman, obviously an Indian with the rose-hued skin and almond eyes above high-planed cheeks, and wondered just what she meant to Chase. "Why couldn't you have been fat and ugly?" she asked with a smile.

"At that time I don't think Betty Grable would have interested Chase," Deborah said, laughing, but her eyes, wary as a doe that has scented danger, did not.

"I imagine you two would have a lot to discuss," Rosemary said as she watched the two closely.

"Have you got a moment?" Chase asked in Navajo.

"I'm sorry, Chase, but no—"

He ignored her and took her arm. "We'll join you in the boxes in just a minute," he told the others.

Miguel started to say something, but Rosemary put up a restraining hand. "You must tell Christina and myself about your plans for the artists' foundations."

To avoid a scene Deborah was forced to go along with Chase. He pulled her into a corner near the gentlemen's

313

restrooms where several of the passing men eyed her appreciatively. Deborah would not look at him but turned her head; her lips set in a firm line. Chase put his hand against the tiled wall on either side of her, preventing her escape. "I don't care what kind of spectacle I make, Deborah, but I want the truth."

"Chase, leave me alone! What happened is over."

"Is it? You haven't forgiven me. And if you hate me so, why did you save my life that last night on the island?"

She looked at him now, but he could read animal tracks easier than he could read her eyes. "I'm going to marry Miguel." She pushed aside his hand and stepped out of the enclosure of his body.

Chase slid in behind the steering wheel, glad that the Stillwell party was over. The doctor and his wife were pompous social climbers, and Chase could well imagine what it had cost the surgeon to welcome him into his house.

A countdown of twelve days before election, Chase thought grimly. Could he hold out?

He lit a cigarette and offered it to Christina who sat quietly on her side of the car. During the drive back to the Raffin mansion, the image of Deborah as she had been on Mindanao kept flashing through his brain. Her courage, her strength, her will to survive in the face of incredible odds. He wondered if he had been confusing power with strength all those years.

"All right, Chase, what is it?" Christina asked softly when they halted before the well-lit house. "I'm not going inside until you tell me what's bothering you."

If there was one thing about Christina that Chase admired, it was her directness. She did not waste time with polite chatter. "Christina, I may be making the biggest mistake of my life...but I'm going to play the rogue and break our engagement."

In the dim flare of the cigarettes Christina's face whitened, but Chase went on. "My idea of marriage—well, it's not the same as yours, Christina. I don't like the idea of being paraded as a house pet, something diverting and amusing for your friends."

"I don't feel that way!"

"I think that's how you've been brought up."

"Chase, I'll make any change necessary. I love you and want to keep you!"

He took her hand. "Christina, it's not all your fault. And it's not fair to you either. In my own way, though I might have thought it a love of sorts, I've used you also. I've used

314

you as the quickest road to acceptance and power. And, Christina, you deserve more than a parasitic husband."

Her arms came up around his neck. "I don't care, Chase! I want you!"

Gently Chase kissed her lips, then disengaged her arms. "Christina, I was wrong."

"You'll regret this! I'll see that you rue this day, Chase Strawhand!" She vaulted from the car and slammed the door. "By the time my father's finished with you, every *jefe político* in every precinct will blackball you. You'll never see the inside of the governor's office!"

Chase sat in the car and finished his cigarette. He was indeed seven kinds of a fool, he thought. Intelligence, logic, and self-interest stood side by side in his marriage to Christina. And now he stood to lose the race that he had come so close to winning.

He flicked the cigarette stub off into the darkness. Ah well, it was time he went back to the blanket. After the election was over—a little hunting, a little *tiswin*...the combination could work wonders at healing the bitterness of losing the race.

57

The two people sat facing each other over the long table of mahogany that could seat at least sixty guests. The butler who served them saw only a very old woman, an invalid, and an equally old man, though the man was some twenty years the woman's junior.

Yet these two people represented the pinnacle of power and influence wielded over the state of New Mexico. Between them they had seen the railroads usher in civilization, the gold era and oil boom enrich the state, the minor potentates who had briefly ruled the cattle kingdoms, and finally the influx of the world's most intelligent people to create the ultimate in natural power, the atomic bomb. And these two people had had a hand in it all.

"I think my father always loved you," Wayne Raffin said, his wheezy voice echoing in the enormous room of the Raffin mansion.

Rosemary sat looking at him, and a flicker of melancholy flared in her for the handsome man who had been Grant's son. Grant had loved his son, just as she had loved Stephanie. Where do we go wrong in loving? she wondered. Is it too much, not enough—or are we merely victims of fate's whimsy?

"Grant Raffin was like a Roman deity, Wayne. But he was not Lario. For me there was only Lario."

The old man hunched over his plate, squinting to better see his venerable opponent. "What was he like . . . this Indian whom you preferred over my father?"

"Lario was a simple man. A man capable of great tenderness and gentleness despite his savage Navajo blood." Rosemary stared down into her glass, not seeing the ruby wine but images of a time never to be repeated. "I used to think of him like the fierce dust devils—you remember the way the sand would get in your eyes so you couldn't be seeing anything else? Lario was like that, except he got in my heart and mind so there was nothing else."

"Not even your husband?" Wayne asked with a touch of spite.

Rosemary looked up sharply. A tight smile added to the creases in her face. "Stephen could see only a great dynasty controlled by his Anglo-bred children. 'Tis a great visionary he was, only I don't think he ever planned that the heir to one day rule the state of New Mexico would be an Indian." Her lips twisted wryly. "A fitting retribution."

Wayne shoved his plate from him. "What makes you think this Chase Strawhand is your grandson—Stephanie's child? And why are you just now bringing it to light?"

"Cody found Chase—and his records—in one of the Indian boarding schools thirty-five years ago. He immediately wrote me, but it seems that with his death the letter was never mailed but boxed in a crate with the rest of his personal effects and shipped back to his ranch. Last year the family who bought the ranch went through the old boxes and trunks stored in the attic and forwarded the letter they found to me."

The old man made an elaborate pretense of folding his napkin. "I see, but—"

"I hope you do—I hope you see that it's a fair chance I want Chase to have in the governor's race."

Wayne laughed shortly. "I hate to disappoint you, Rosemary, but the Indian doesn't stand a turkey's chance on Thanksgiving."

"I'd think 'tis glad you'd be if he broke off the marriage with your daughter," Rosemary said, unperturbed.

"Hell! He's made a laughing fool of her. An Indian rejecting a white girl—a senator's daughter! No, that damned redskin'll have to come crawling back, first."

"That he won't be doing."

Wayne shrugged his stooped shoulders. "Then he'll never see the swearing in."

Rosemary sighed. She took the folded piece of paper from her dress pocket. "What's that?" he asked.

"'Tis a copy of a letter I received nearly sixty years ago. The original is in my safekeeping. 'Tis from your father—asking that I keep you at my ranch. It was the summer after your scandal."

She watched a shudder pass over the old man as he read it. The parchment skin around his eyes and mouth changed like a chameleon's to a dull gray. He looked up, his hands shaking. His voice cracked. "So even then he knew about me?"

"He had heard the discreet rumors about your affair with that young man at the University, the one that was your best man, I believe. Your father thought if I kept you busy that summer you might forget your—what is it they call it these days—lover?"

The shoulders sagged. "Then it's blackmail?"

"'Tis justice," she said tiredly.

It was odd, she thought. So many times when she had writhed at the blows dealt her, life had twisted everything around, somehow tying up all the loose ends, making everything right with age. Lario's fatalism would have appreciated life's joke.

Chase repeated the last words with his hand on the Bible. He was now governor. The first Indian governor of the state of New Mexico! His dark eyes swept over the assembled crowd to pause on the old woman seated in the front row in the wheelchair.

His grandmother, Rosemary Rhodes!

He had found it hard to assimilate—if what she told him was true. And somehow, he knew it was. His joy should have been complete. But out there in the audience he did not find the one particular face he was looking for, the pair of laughing eyes. They had been like guiding lights in his mind—like the campfires of his youth, bright and warm.

He had sent her the invitation to the Inaugural Ball, but apparently she was not going to come. And Chase knew that the inaugural events could go to hell. He'd search out every house in Santa Fe, every shop, until he found her. He'd go back to the reservation if he had to.

But a peculiar kind of fear, foreign to him, seized hold. In all his masculine ego, he had never believed that Deborah might have married Miguel Montoya. Was it too late?

He stepped up the tempo of his acceptance speech, and when he finished, the reporters and people in the audience surged forward to congratulate him. He shook their hands, all the while his eyes searching.

His gaze crossed that enigmatic one of his grandmother. And something about the look she directed at him before she instructed the Mexican to roll her away told Chase she knew about Deborah. Why wouldn't she? Didn't the old woman know everything?

He edged his way through the people, shaking hands, politely thanking them for their support, as he tried to catch up with his grandmother. At the exit, he excused himself from the others and rushed to block the old woman's way. His hands grasped the arms of the wheelchair. "You know, don't you, Grandmother? Where is she?"

Rosemary smiled, pleased at her grandson's impassioned face. She had seen the same blazing look of love in Lario's eyes. Aye, she thought wistfully as she studied the man before her, the two looked very much alike now that there was the touch of humility in Chase's eyes. She had never liked the bitterness she had seen there.

"Deborah? You may find her at Cambria. Not too long ago I asked her to do a painting of the old Castle for me—I'm donating the painting to the Museum, you know."

Deborah tilted her head and looked from the ugly cottonwood tree and the Castle that stood starkly against the backdrop of the Pecos escarpment to the image on her canvas. Somehow she did not think she quite caught the Castle's grandeur. It was something you could not paint. It was like character. The house, the old lady—it had taken years to make the two the strong characters they were. She imagined the Castle—the old woman—had seen years of love and sorrow and joy and disappointment. Somehow the two seemed entwined with each other. Strength and beauty of spirit.

It was generous of the old woman to offer the place for her to paint. From what Miguel told her artists had been besieging the old woman for years to paint Cambria's Castle. Yet Deborah felt no triumph in having secured the honor. The sight of the occasional Navajo shepherd boy, the wrangler, the store's clerk—too often she saw the same dusky eyes, the bronzed skin to remind her of her own people . . . and of Chase.

She must shake him from her mind. For years he had

318

occupied her every thought. Now he was governor. He had his life to make...as she must make hers.

She shook her head, as if she were indeed shaking Chase from her mind, and returned her concentration to the old house. She blinked her eyes, not quite certain of what she saw.

It was a man striding through the tall grass toward her. The red flannel headband marked him as Navajo. But it was the arrogant way he walked, the powerful build, that caught her attention and finally held her spellbound. She knew then as he moved inexorably closer and she saw the wickedly handsome face that it was Chase. Her heart began to beat in time to some primeval drum.

Chase took the paintbrush from her motionless hands and put it on the easel. In spite of her longing to clasp him to her, to rain impassioned kisses on that uncompromising face, she stiffened. "Chase," she begged in a hoarse whisper as he drew her into his arms, "please, I can't...I won't be a stand-in for—"

"I've only three days before I have to return to Santa Fe to assume my duties," he told her, his lips kissing her eyelids. "But it should be enough time for the singers to perform the Navajo marriage ceremony and a judge the civil one."

Not quite believing that after all those years her secret childhood fantasy about this one man was coming to pass, Deborah abandoned herself to the fierceness of his kisses. "There's time enough later for the singers," she whispered and let him draw her down into the concealment of the tall, sweet grass.

The old woman sat in the wheelchair beneath the ravaged cottonwood and watched her grandson stride across the land that was his—to the woman that was his. She felt no embarrassment, as the very old often do, when the young couple came together in a passionate embrace. Tactfully her gaze moved away. For a brief second it rested on the nearby headstone that bore the name of Lario Santiago. Her beloved would have been proud of his grandson, she thought.

Then her gaze moved beyond to the red-tinted horizon, and a small smile belied the glistening eyes that watched what surely had to be a dust devil dancing on the rim of Cambria's far, far boundaries.

AUTHOR'S NOTE

In an effort to blend fact with fiction, I have at times deviated from the actual date of an event.

The most obvious case is the fictional recounting of Chase Strawhand's election in 1945. Tragically, though the Indians of New Mexico served in both World Wars, giving their lives for their country, they were not accorded the right to vote in that state until 1948.